Mel McGrath is an Essex girl, the author of the critically acclaimed and bestselling family memoir *Silvertown*. She won the John Llewellyn-Rhys/*Mail on Sunday* award for Best Writer Under 35 for her first book, *Motel Nirvana*. She has published three Arctic mysteries featuring the Inuit detective Edie Kiglatuk, under the name MJ McGrath, two of which, *White Heat* and *The Bone Seeker*, were longlisted for the CWA Gold Dagger.

She is the co-founder and one of the moving lights of the website Killer Women, which has rapidly established itself as a key forum for crime writing in the UK. This new standalone marks a change in direction.

GIVE
ME THE
CHILD

MEL
McGRATH

ONE PLACE. MANY STORIES

HQ
An imprint of HarperCollins*Publishers* Ltd
1 London Bridge Street
London SE1 9GF

This edition 2018

18 19 20 21 LSC 10 9 8 7 6 5 4 3 2
First published in Great Britain by
HQ, an imprint of HarperCollins*Publishers* Ltd 2018

Copyright © Mel McGrath 2018

Mel McGrath asserts the moral right to be
identified as the author of this work.
A catalogue record for this book is
available from the British Library.

ISBN: 978-0-00-830012-8

Printed and bound in the
United States of America by LSC Communications

This one's for my siblings.

PART ONE

Then

CHAPTER ONE

My first thought when the doorbell woke me was that someone had died. Most likely Michael Walsh. I turned onto my side, pulled at the outer corners of my eyes to rid them of the residue of sleep and blinked myself awake. It was impossible to tell if it was late or early, though the bedroom was as hot and muggy as it had been when Tom and I had gone to bed. Tom was no longer beside me. Now I was alone.

We'd started drinking not long after Freya had gone upstairs. The remains of a bottle of Pinot Grigio for me, a glass or two of red for Tom. (He always said white wine was for women.) Just before nine I called The Mandarin Hut. When the crispy duck arrived I laid out two trays in the living room, opened another bottle and called Tom in from the study. I hadn't pulled the curtains and through the pink light of the London night sky a cat's claw of moon appeared. The two of us ate, mostly in silence, in front of the TV. A ballroom dance show came on. Maybe it was just the booze but something about the tight-muscled men and the frou-frou'd women made me feel a little sad. The cosmic dance. The grand romantic gesture. At some point even the tight-muscled men and the frou-frou'd women would find themselves slumped together on a sofa with the remains of a takeaway and wine enough to sink their sorrows, wondering how they'd got there, wouldn't they?

Not that Tom and I really had anything to complain about except, maybe, a little malaise, a kind of falling away. After all, weren't we still able to laugh about stuff most of the time or, if we couldn't laugh, at least have sex and change the mood?

'Let's go upstairs and I'll show you my cha-cha,' I said, rising and holding out a hand.

Tom chuckled and pretended I was joking, then, wiping his palms along his thighs as if he were ridding them of something unpleasant, he said, 'It's just if I don't crack this bloody coding thing…'

I looked out at the moon for a moment. OK, so I knew how much making a success of *Labyrinth* meant to Tom, and I'd got used to him shutting himself away in the two or three hours either side of midnight. But this one time, with the men and women still twirling in our minds? Just this one time?

Stupidly, I said, 'Won't it wait till tomorrow?' and in an instant I saw Tom stiffen. He paused for a beat and, slapping his hands on his thighs in a gesture of busyness, he slugged down the last of his wine, rose from the sofa and went to the door. And so we left it there with the question still hanging.

I spent the rest of the evening flipping through the case notes of patients I was due to see that week. When I turned in for the night, the light was still burning in Tom's study. I murmured 'goodnight' and went upstairs to check on Freya. Our daughter was suspended somewhere between dreaming and deep sleep. All children look miraculous when they're asleep, even the frightening, otherworldly ones I encounter every day. Their bodies soften, their small fists unfurl and dreams play behind their eyelids. But Freya looked miraculous all the time to me. Because she was. A miracle made at the boundary where human desire meets science. I stood and watched her for a while, then, retrieving her beloved *Pippi Longstocking* book from the floor and straightening her duvet, I crept from the room and went to bed.

Sometime later I felt Tom's chest pressing against me and his breath on the nape of my neck. He was already aroused and for a minute I wondered what else he'd been doing on screen besides coding, then shrugged off the thought. A drowsy, half-hearted bout of lovemaking followed before we drifted into our respective oblivions. Next thing I knew the doorbell was ringing and I was alone.

Under the bathroom door a beam of light blazed. I threw off the sheet and swung from the bed.

'Tom?'

No response. My mind was scrambled with sleep and an anxious pulse was rising to the surface. I called out again.

There was a crumpling sound followed by some noisy vomiting but it was identifiably my husband. The knot in my throat loosened. I went over to the bathroom door, knocked and let myself in. Tom was hunched over the toilet and there was a violent smell in the room.

'Someone's at the door.'

Tom's head swung round.

I said, 'You think it might be about Michael?'

Tom's father, Michael Walsh, was a coronary waiting to happen, a lifelong *bon vivant* in the post-sixty-five-year-old death zone, who'd taken the recent demise of his appalling wife pretty badly.

Tom stood up, wiped his hand across his mouth and moved over to the sink. 'Nah, probably just some pisshead.' He turned on the tap and sucked at the water in his hand and, in an oddly casual tone, he added, 'Ignore it.'

As I retreated into the bedroom, the bell rang again. Whoever it was, they weren't about to go away. I went over to the window and eased open the curtain. The street was still and empty of people, and the first blank glimmer was in the sky. Directly below the house a patrol car was double parked, hazard lights still on but otherwise dark. For a second my mind filled with the terrible possibility that something had happened to Sally. Then I checked myself. More likely someone had reported a burglary or a prowler in the neighbourhood. Worst case it was Michael.

'It's the police,' I said.

Tom appeared and, lifting the sash, craned out of the window. 'I'll go, you stay here.'

I watched him throw on his robe over his boxers and noticed his hands were trembling. Was that from having been sick or was he, too, thinking about Michael now? I listened to his footsteps disappearing down the stairs and took my summer cover-up from its hook. A moment later, the front door swung open and there came the low murmur of three voices, Tom's and those of two women. I froze on the threshold of the landing and held my breath, waiting for Tom to call me down, and when, after a few minutes, he still hadn't, I felt myself relax a little. My parents were dead. If this was about Sally, Tom would have fetched me by now. It was bound to be Michael. Poor Michael.

I went out onto the landing and tiptoed over to Freya's room. Tom often said I was overprotective, and maybe I was, but I'd seen enough mayhem and weirdness at work to give me pause. I pushed open the door and peered in. A breeze stirred from the open window. The hamster Freya had brought back from school for the holidays was making the rounds on his wheel but in the aura cast by the *Frozen*-themed nightlight I could see my tender little girl's face closed in sleep. Freya had been too young to remember my parents and Michael had always been sweet to her in a way that his wife, who called her 'my little *brown* granddaughter', never was, but it was better this happened now, in the summer holidays, so she'd have time to recover before the pressures of school started up again. We'd tell her in the morning once we'd had time to formulate the right words.

At the top of the landing I paused, leaning over the bannister. A woman in police uniform stood in the glare of the security light. Thirties, with fierce glasses and a military bearing. Beside her was another woman in jeans and a shapeless sweater, her features hidden from me. The policewoman's face was brisk but unsmiling; the other woman was dishevelled, as though she had been called from her bed. Between them I glimpsed the auburn top of what I presumed was a child's head – a girl, judging from the amount of hair. I held back, unsure what to do, hoping they'd realise they were at the wrong door and go away. I could see the police officer's mouth moving without being able to hear what was being said. The conversation went on and after a few moments Tom stood to one side and the two women and the child stepped out of the shadows of the porch and into the light of the hallway.

The girl was about the same age as Freya, taller but small-boned, legs as spindly as a deer's and with skin so white it gave her the look of some deep sea creature. She was wearing a grey trackie too big for her frame which bagged at the knees from wear and made her seem malnourished and unkempt. From the way she held herself, stiffly and at a distance from the dishevelled woman, it was obvious they didn't know one another. A few ideas flipped through my mind. Had something happened in the street, a house fire perhaps, or a medical emergency, and a neighbour needed us to look after her for a few hours? Or was she a school friend of Freya's who had run away and for some reason given our address to the police? Either way, the situation obviously didn't have anything much to do with us. My heart went out to the kid but I can't say I wasn't relieved. Michael was safe, Sally was safe.

I moved down the stairs and into the hallway. The adults remained engrossed in their conversation but the girl looked up and stared. I tried to place the sharp features and the searching, amber eyes from among our neighbours or the children at Freya's school but nothing came. She showed no sign of recognising me. I could see she was tired – though not so much from too little sleep as from a lifetime of watchfulness. It was an expression familiar to me from the kids I worked with at the clinic. I'd probably had it too, at her age. An angry, cornered look. She was clasping what looked like a white rabbit's foot in her right hand. The cut end emerged from her fist, bound crudely with electrical wire which was attached to a key. It looked home-made and this lent it – and her – an air that was both outdated and macabre, as if she'd been beamed in from some other time and had found herself stranded here, in south London, in the second decade of the twenty-first century, in the middle of the night, with nothing but a rabbit's foot and a key to remind her of her origins.

'What's up?' I said, more out of curiosity than alarm. I smiled and waited for an answer.

The two women glanced awkwardly at Tom and from the way he was standing, stiffly with one hand slung on his hip in an attempt at relaxed cool, I understood they were waiting for him to respond and I instinctively knew that everything I'd been thinking was wrong. A dark firework burst inside my chest. The girl in the doorway was neither a neighbour's kid nor a friend of our daughter.

She was trouble.

I took a step back. 'Will someone tell me what's going on?'

When no one spoke I crouched to the girl's level and,

summoning as much friendliness as I could, said, 'What's your name? Why are you here?'

The girl's eyes flickered to Tom, then, giving a tiny, contemptuous shake of the head, as if by her presence all my questions had already been answered and I was being obstructive or just plain dumb, she said, '*I'm* Ruby Winter.'

I felt Tom's hands on my shoulder. They were no longer trembling so much as hot and spasmic.

'Cat, please go and make some tea. I'll come in a second.'

There was turmoil in his eyes. 'Please,' he repeated. And so, not knowing what else to do, I turned on my heels and made for the kitchen.

While the kettle wheezed into life, I sat at the table in a kind of stupor; too shocked to gather my thoughts, I stared at the clock as the red second hand stuttered towards the upright. *Tock, tock, tock.* There were voices in the hallway, then I heard the living room door shut. Time trudged on. I began to feel agitated. What was taking all this time? Why hadn't Tom come? Part of me felt I had left the room already but here I was still. Eventually, footsteps echoed in the hallway. The door moved and Tom appeared. I stood up and went over to the counter where, what now seemed like an age ago, I had laid out a tray with the teapot and some mugs.

'Sit down, darling, we need to talk.' *Darling.* When was the last time he'd called me that?

I heard myself saying, idiotically, 'But I made tea!'

'It'll wait.' He pulled up a chair directly opposite me.

When he spoke, his voice came to me like the distant

crackle of a broken radio in another room. 'I'm so sorry, Cat, but however I say this it's going to come as a terrible shock, so I'm just going to say what needs to be said, then we can talk. There's no way round this. The girl, Ruby Winter, she's my daughter.'

CHAPTER TWO

'We already have a daughter.'

Tom glanced at me then looked away. It was as though I was viewing him through an early morning fog. He seemed at once both real and spectral. Cold suddenly, I pulled my cover-up more tightly around my body. Words fizzed and flared without my being able to catch hold of them. Stupid thoughts flooded in: *This can't be happening because it's a Monday and Monday is clinic day.*

'No,' I said. 'No, don't do this to us.'

Tom reached out for my hand and I let him take it. His face was a strange mottled colour, barely recognisable.

'I'm so, *so* sorry, Caitlin. I don't know what to say. I swear I didn't know anything about her until a few minutes ago. This is as much of a shock to me as it is to you.'

Something rose up in me like a thundercloud, raw and fearsome. I yanked my hand away. This was the worst kind of dream, the one you can't wake up from, the one that turns out to be real.

'I doubt that,' I said.

Tom bit his lip.

I needed the facts, the data. 'How did this happen? *When?*'

'Not long before Freya was born.'

'When I was in *hospital*?' My mind zoomed back to the madness of my pregnancy, how helpless I had been, out of my mind and afraid. 'Jesus, don't tell me you had sex with someone in the *psych* ward?'

Tom shot me a wounded look. 'Of course not. Please, Cat, just don't say anything and I'll try to explain and then you can ask me whatever you want.'

It was quite some explanation. Strung out after one of his visits to the hospital to see me, my husband had gone to a nearby pub with the intention of having a quick drink before getting on the bus home. One turned into two, turned into plenty. A woman appeared, apparently from nowhere – *ha ha* – and sat next to him at the bar. They'd got chatting and what followed – the whole tired suburban cliché – happened in some shabby B&B around the back of Denmark Hill station. He left for home sometime after dawn and that was that. He'd never seen or heard from the woman again. A moment of madness, the result of overwhelming stress. It hadn't meant anything then and he begged me to believe how much he regretted it now. I couldn't know how much, he said. *More than anything.*

As Tom spoke I couldn't help thinking just how bloody old and worn and unoriginal the story sounded, a clapped-out tale of a faithless husband led on by some mysterious femme fatale. If you saw it on TV, you'd reach for the remote. This wasn't *us*. This wasn't who we were meant to be. So how was it that it was what we had become? I felt myself reaching for words that had already fled. Odd swoops of energy were tearing up my legs and escaping out into the room through my arms. I made to stand up, got halfway, and then sat down again, defeated by legs that no longer held any weight.

'What's her name?'

'Ruby.'

'I know that! I mean the *woman*. Your fuck buddy.' I twisted my head and glared at him but he averted his gaze.

For a moment there was silence, then Tom said, 'Her name is Lilly, Lilly Winter.'

I felt as if someone had opened my skull and unloaded a skip of building waste inside. Images of lilies crossed my mind. When had they become junk flowers, the carnations or chrysanthemums of their time, the sweet, cloying gesture you made when you'd run out of more meaningful ones? One thought morphed into another and I remembered what happened with the lilies that time just after Freya was born when we'd thought everything was back to normal and then discovered it wasn't. *Oh God, don't let this bring the madness back. Please, God, not that.* Then my thoughts were broken by the faint murmur of female voices in the living room and I was reminded of the policewoman and the time and the fact that there was still so much to know.

The girl's name was jammed inside my throat but I couldn't say it. 'Why is she here? What's the policewoman doing?'

Tom folded his arms. 'There was an accident. Ruby found her mother dead in bed sometime around midnight when she got up to have a pee. The police… I don't know, Lilly must have told Ruby my name and the police looked me up on some database. In any case, they got my address somehow.'

He went on: 'They think it was carbon monoxide poisoning – faulty boiler, no batteries in the carbon monoxide detector. The policewoman said you don't smell it, you don't hear it, you don't taste it. If the gas leak is big enough, it only takes thirty seconds to kill you. Ruby's mother was dead drunk, she wouldn't have known anything about it.' He stopped and rubbed a hand across his face as though trying to obliterate something, but I was relieved to see there were no tears. Whatever feelings were going through his heart right now, grief for Lilly Winter wasn't among them.

'Oh God, that's horrible,' I said.

'Ruby's room is in a separate corridor in the flat and she was sleeping with her window wide open, otherwise…' He frowned and sat with the thought a moment, then, getting up, went over to the kettle and refilled the pot. He brought the tea over then seated himself once more in the chair beside me.

'Drink this, you'll feel better.'

I pushed the mug away. I didn't want to feel better. Not now. Not at five thirty in the morning with my husband's love child in the room next door. I thought about Freya asleep upstairs, still oblivious to the existence of a half-sister, and wondered what we were about to do to her world.

Tom's head was in his hands now and he was rubbing at his temples with his thumbs.

'What were you *thinking*?'

He swung up so his face was angled towards me and let the air blow out of his lips. 'Evidently, I wasn't,' he said.

I let out a bitter laugh. Even when he wasn't trying to be funny Tom managed to be amusing. Maybe that's why we'd lasted as long as we had. The Tom I first met was a glossy, charming man who smelled brightly of the future. I wanted him and he wanted me. We were young and wanting one another seemed if not enough (we weren't that stupid), then at least the largest part of the deal. Not long after we'd married, life came along. The sex, at first wild, calmed into something more manageable. But it was all OK. We got on well, rarely fought and seemed to want the same things. The years slid by. We had our daughter and moved into a house and enjoyed trips to the seaside on the weekends. We were good parents. We respected one another's careers. When Tom left Adrenalyze to start his own company, I'd kept the joint account ticking over. He'd supported me as I'd worked long hours at the institute, cheering me from the sidelines when I'd been called as an expert witness in child psychosis. When I'd failed so publicly, so devastatingly, and all I'd worked for had come tumbling down, he'd stood by me. Over the years we somehow turned into the couple other couples pretend not to envy. Unflashy, boring, steady. The couple who never got the point of counselling sessions, 'check-ins' or 'date nights'. 'Never let light in on magic,' Tom used to say – another of his jokes. We liked it that the outlines of our marriage were blurry and out of focus. Because what is marriage, after all, but a kind of wilful blindness, an agreement to overlook the evidence, a leap of faith for which, in these days of Tinder hook-ups and casual sexting, it pays to be a little myopic?

Tom was going on about something, but I'd stopped listening. The room had begun to feel very claustrophobic. It was as if everything was speeding inwards, converging into a single laser-like beam of almost blinding intensity. *Everything has changed. From now on our lives will be different in ways neither of us can predict.* Eventually, when I realised he'd fallen silent, I said, simply, 'I'm so bloody angry I can hardly speak.'

Tom's chest heaved. 'I know, I know.' His voice carried on but the words were lost to me. Instead I began thinking about how things had been after Freya was born, when we'd tried and failed for another child. The doctor's best guess had been that our bodies were in some undefined way biologically incompatible. Tom hadn't wanted to go through IVF again or risk another episode of my prenatal psychosis, that wild paranoia which had overwhelmed me in the weeks preceding Freya, and he wouldn't entertain the idea of adopting. What had followed was a kind of mourning for a child I'd never have, years of hopeless and, for the most part, unspoken longing. Through it all I'd at least been comforted by the notion that neither of us was to blame.

'Biological incompatibility' had been my 'get out of jail free' card. But now, the arrival of my husband's other daughter was proof that the 'incompatibility' was actually something to do with *me*. *I* was the problem. And not just because of my hormones and my predilection for going crazy while pregnant, but because there was something fundamentally wrong with my reproductive system. *I* was the reason we'd had to resort to

IVF. And now here was the proof, in the shape of Ruby Winter. Concrete evidence of the failure of my fertility.

Tom had stopped speaking and was slumped in the chair picking at his fingers. He seemed angry and distracted.

I said, 'Why isn't she with a relative or something?'

He looked up and glared. 'I *am* a bloody relative,' then, gathering himself, he said, 'Sorry. There's a grandmother, apparently, Lilly Winter's mother, but they couldn't get hold of her. In any case, they said Ruby asked to be taken to her dad's.' He shot me a pleading look. 'Look, we'll sort all of this out and Ruby will go and live with her gran and maybe we'll see her at the weekends. The most important thing for now is that she's safe, isn't it?'

I glanced at the wall clock. It was nearly six in the morning and the little girl in our living room had just lost her mother. I pushed back my hair and forced myself to think straight. In a couple of hours' time I would be at the institute doing my best to work with a bunch of kids who needed help. How could I possibly live with myself if I didn't help the kid on my own doorstep?

I stood up and cleared my throat. 'We're not done talking about this, not even close. But for now I'm guessing there'll be paperwork and we'll need to show the girl to the spare room so she can get some sleep. You go back to the living room. I need a few minutes alone then I'll follow on with some fresh tea and a glass of juice for' – the words fell from my mouth like something bitter and unwanted – 'your daughter.'

* * *

While Tom went through the admin with the social worker, Ruby Winter followed me up the stairs in stunned silence, still clutching the rabbit's foot key, and my heart went out to her, this motherless, pale reed of a girl.

'You're safe here,' I said.

I switched on the bedside lamp and invited her to sit on the bed beside me. Those off-colour eyes scanned my face momentarily, as if she were trying to decide whether I could be trusted. She sat, reluctantly, keeping her distance and with hands jammed between her knees, her skinny frame making only the shallowest of impressions on the mattress. We were three feet from one another now, brought together first by drink and carelessness and then by the terrible fate of her mother. Yet despite all the shock and horror she must have been feeling and my sympathy for her situation, it was as though she possessed some kind of force field which made being close to her unsettling.

I pointed to the rabbit's foot keyring in her hand.

'Shall I keep that safe for you? We might need it later, when one of us goes to fetch your things.' The social worker had brought a bag of basic clothes and toiletries to tide Ruby over while the police did whatever they needed to do in the flat, but the policewoman had told us that they'd been working for several hours already and, given there were no suspicious circumstances, would probably be done by the morning.

Ruby Winter hesitated then handed me the keyring. The combination of fur and metal was warm from her hand.

'I'm sorry,' I said. 'I'm really terribly sorry about your mother.

It's going to take a while to sort everything out, but we will. For now it's best if you get some sleep.'

I pulled out a toothbrush and wash cloth and a pair of pyjamas from the bag the social worker had brought. 'Would you like me to come with you to the bathroom?'

Ruby shook her head.

While she was gone, I unpacked the few remaining bits and bobs then sat back on the bed, scooped up the rabbit's foot keyring and held it in the palm of my hand. It really was an odd thing, the claws dirty and the skin jagged and ratty at the cut end. It had been Lilly Winter's, I guessed. Who kept animal-part charms these days except maybe Wicca nuts or sinister middle-aged men living with their mothers? I dropped the keyring into my pocket and tried to separate the new arrival from the circumstances of her creation. It wasn't Ruby's fault that she'd been conceived in an act of betrayal. But it wasn't going to be easy to forget it either.

When she returned, dressed in her PJs, I took her wash things and put them on the chest of drawers and sat in the chair at the end of the bed as she slid under the duvet. 'Did your father tell you we have a daughter about your age? Her name's Freya. You'll meet her in the morning.'

I waited for a response that didn't come. In the dim light thrown by the beside lamp, with her tiny body and huge hair, the girl appeared otherworldly but also somehow not quite there, as though what I was looking at was a reflection of a girl rather than the girl herself.

'Your dad told me you have a grandmother.'

Ruby Winter looked up and gave a little smile, oddly empty of feeling, then looked away.

'She's a bitch,' she said flatly. Her voice was soft but with the sharpened edges of a south London accent.

'I'm sorry you feel that,' I said. I sensed she was testing me, hoping to catch me out. Perhaps I should have left then and allowed her to sleep but my curiosity overcame me.

'Did your mother ever tell you anything about your dad?'

Ruby gazed at her fingers and, in the same expressionless tone, she said, 'Only that he was a real shit.'

This was the kind of behaviour I dealt with on a daily basis at the clinic, but in the here and now, I felt oddly at a loss. 'I'm sure she didn't really say that. And, anyway, he isn't.'

Ruby looked at me then shrugged as if what she had said was of no consequence. 'I'm tired now.'

'Of course you are,' I said, feeling bad for having pushed her into a conversation she didn't want to have. I went to the door. 'Sleep now and we'll talk later.'

Back downstairs I made another pot of tea and some toast and took a tray out to the others. The policewoman was in the middle of saying that there would have to be a post-mortem on Lilly Winter and a report would be filed with the coroner, but it was unlikely that the coroner would call an inquest. The situation at the flat had been straightforward enough. An old boiler, no batteries in the carbon monoxide detector, Lilly passed out from drink.

'Presumably Ruby will go and live with her grandmother?' I voiced this as a question but I hoped it was also a statement.

The social worker briefly caught Tom's eye.

'That's the plan,' Tom said.

The policewoman's phone went. She answered it, listened briefly, then, turning to Tom, she said, 'I'm afraid we'll need to keep you a little longer to go over a few things – but we're done at the flat if...' She smiled at me. 'Perhaps you'd like to go and fetch Ruby's personal effects?' She told me the address and began giving me directions.

'That's OK, I know the Pemberton Estate.'

'Oh!' the policewoman replied, her voice full of amazement, as if neither of us had any business knowing anywhere like the Pemberton.

'It's where I grew up,' I said.

CHAPTER THREE

According to the police, Lilly Winter had taken over the lease on flat sixty-seven in the Ash Building, one of the red-brick hutches forming part of the original estate, from her mother, Megan Winter, who had moved into the flat from another council property near Streatham. Ruby was born at the flat while her grandmother was still the registered tenant so grandmother, mother and baby must have been living together at that point. The names didn't mean anything to me and it seemed unlikely that we'd ever coincided. I'd left the place twenty years ago and hadn't been back since the death of my mother. I didn't particularly want to go back now, but I was too curious about Lilly Winter to let the opportunity pass. So I left a message on my assistant Claire's mobile asking her to move my nine o'clock, then Tom and I had a brief discussion about what to tell Freya if she woke up while I was gone and I got in the car and headed south.

When I was growing up, in the nineties, working-class kids of all ethnic varieties lived on the Pemberton, which we called the Ends. The whole district was more than a bit scrappy and shitty. The main road south towards Croydon split the area in two and it was impossible to leave without running into a busy arterial road, as a result of which we rarely ventured far. The surrounding workers' cottages were occupied by first-generation immigrant Jamaicans who put up cheery curtains and planted their gardens with sunflowers. A handful of elderly whites and some Asian families lived among them and a few middle-class gentrifiers had taken over flats in the villas behind the cottages, though a lot of those were still squatted. But even as kids we could tell that, in some unspecified way, the area was on the move, which made the Ends feel as if it was about to be cut off by the tide. For years there were rumours that the whole estate was to be completely redeveloped and the residents moved elsewhere. At the time, we felt like anarchists, free to run wild without consequences. With hindsight, the instability left us feeling insecure. Those of us who grew up on the Ends did our best to ignore the sense that we had drawn the short straw. We lived for music, sex and a bit of weed. Destiny's Child, N.W.A., Public Enemy, R 'n' B, urban, whatever. Friday and Saturday nights you'd meet your homies around the ghetto blaster, roll some joints and have yourselves a party. There were gangs and the odd gang-related ruckus but you could steer your way around them. We felt free but at the cost of knowing we didn't matter, that kids like us were only of any consequence within the narrow confines of the Ends themselves.

At the traffic lights I made a right, skirting around the southern side of Grissold Park, then up along the wide, leafy road that ran along its western border, and turned again at the filter into a grid of half-gentrified Victorian terraced houses punctuated by shabby corner stores and fried chicken shops.

I slowed and tried to quell the fluttering in my chest. Memories. My manor. Approaching the rack of brutalist tower blocks fronted by older, lower tenements of red brick and what might once have been, but were no longer, cream tiles, I was a teenager again. Furious, mouthy and secretly determined to escape. The parties and the friendships and the 'what the fuck' Saturday night feeling had never been quite enough. There had been an itch in me to leave and I knew it would take everything I had to make it happen. Because the trouble with the Pemberton was that if you didn't get out fast, you didn't get out at all.

The late July sun was steadily beating down now and, despite the early hour, the estate was already sticky in the heat, the pavements speckled with clumps of dog shit – dark matter in an expanse of Milky Way. Some kids were mooching their way to school, kicking a football along the tea-coloured grass, their elder brothers and sisters hurrying them along, weapon dogs strung in tightly beside them.

I parked up and got out, conscious of being watched – someone is always watching in the Ends. It wouldn't do to be taken for a social worker or, worse still, a Fed. Two girls were standing at the foot of an external stairway smoking, one in wedge sandals too small for her feet, the other sporting a set of sprayed acrylics which she was tapping on the handrail. Tough kids, showing off their credentials. I headed over; they'd spread the word among whoever needed to know.

'Hey,' I said.

'All right?' the girl in the wedge sandals replied.

The girl with the acrylics looked me up and down then squinted and tipped her head. 'You slippin' here, man.'

'Nuh uh. This my manor.'

'I never seen you. Who your people?'

'Lilly Winter. Me and her got the same baby daddy.'

The girls exchanged glances. Then the girl with the wedge sandals said, 'You too late, innit. Feds bagged her up. Some accident, I dunno.'

'Yeah, I heard.'

'She not my crew.' The girl turned to her friend. 'The young'un, though, the gingernut?'

'Yeah,' said the friend. 'Facety bitch.'

'What I'm sayin'. Nobody give a shit if she gone the same way as her mother, and that's the truth, innit.'

* * *

Sixty-seven Ash Building was the second to last flat on the top floor of one of the older, red-brick blocks overshadowed by the towers, and distinguished only by its tattered, unloved exterior. You didn't have to step a foot inside to know the place was a dump. Close up, everything about number sixty-seven exuded neglect. It was the only dwelling on that floor which hadn't been customised with door gates, a window box or some cheerful paint. Where the number had once been attached to the door two rusted screws jutted from their holes. The letter box had fallen out and the hole in the door was duct-taped over. There was grime on the windows and the blue-painted windowsill was feathery with disrepair.

Ruby's key was an awkward fit and got stuck in the barrel. The door rattled in the jamb but remained firmly shut. I was thinking about giving it a good kick when I became aware of a woman in her early thirties who was peering around the door of number sixty-nine, dressed in a pink onesie.

'You want something?' The door opened wider.

'The little girl who lives here, Ruby Winter? I'm picking up some of her things but the key...' The woman's face softened. She said her name was Gloria. Eastern European accent. Something familiar about her that I couldn't put my finger on.

She came over and, waving me away, pressed her shoulder to the door. 'You got to push hard. Council said they sort it out, but they don't. Lilly always waking me up.' When the door gave, Gloria righted herself and stepped over the threshold. 'Terrible what happen. And that kid, Ruby, she got no mother.' When I hesitated, she beckoned me with her hand, saying, 'Come on then.'

I followed her in. The place was filthy, the smell of stale tobacco overpowering. Damp marks on the walls did a bad job of disguising the thin sheen of grease underneath, and dust and hair had accumulated into dark brown hummocks where the lino had lifted in the corners. Two doors led off the hallway. The first opened into a cramped, dark space which must have been Lilly's bedroom. Her body had been removed, but something in me resisted entering, afraid of what I might find. A mildewed shower was visible through the other door.

At the end of the hallway was a decent-sized living room, one side of which had been sectioned off and made into a galley kitchen. On the opposite side a door led off into a passageway, presumably to Ruby's bedroom. The walls were featureless, unless you counted the yellow tar blossoms clambering up the paintwork. A cheap grey pleather sofa sat on the far side, nearest to Ruby's room. On the other there was a TV stand, though it looked as if someone had been in and removed the TV, leaving the cables splayed over the floor. As I picked my way across old, stained carpet tiles littered with improvised ashtrays, the butts still in them, I found myself wondering whether Tom would have rescued Ruby from all this squalor and neglect if he'd known about her – and realised I wasn't sure. Strange how you could spend more than a decade of your life with someone, have a child together, and yet discover in the moment it takes for a policewoman to ring a doorbell that you hardly know them at all.

I turned my attention back to the flat. Gloria was standing at the entrance to the kitchen.

'Is same boiler as in my flat, combi. So is strange.'

'Strange?'

'Lilly is leaving window open a little bit. She put nail in the window frame, so no one can get in while she sleeping. But police tell me window was shut this one time.'

'Is that what's strange?'

'No, I mean, is hot at night. So why is boiler on?'

'The pilot light blew out, the police said.'

'Oh.'

The death-boiler sat on one side of a long, narrow window in the kitchen. The cover had been removed, presumably by the police, exposing the interior, and it looked like the mechanism had been disabled. Evidently, the carbon monoxide had snaked its way undetected through the living room and down the hallway into Lilly's room. The policewoman had said that the door leading into a small passageway which separated Ruby's bedroom from the rest of the flat had probably saved her life. I thought about what Gloria had said and realised there was an undeniable logic to it. I was no expert in boilers but it seemed unlikely to me that a dead pilot light would have led to a massive leakage of carbon monoxide unless the boiler had been firing and the flue had been blocked. If that was the case, the policewoman hadn't mentioned it. As Gloria said, it was hot, and everyone in the flat was asleep. No reason for the boiler to be on at all.

'I see what you mean,' I said. 'It *is* odd, isn't it?'

Gloria was standing at the window with her back to me, looking out across the view of tower blocks and tiled roofs. As she turned I realised where I'd seen her before.

'You work at St John's Primary. My daughter's there.' I'd seen Gloria after hours polishing the lino tiles.

I pulled Freya's picture from my wallet.

Gloria's eyes lit up. She seemed genuinely delighted. 'Oh yes, I know. Very sweet girl. She want to be Pippi Long Something.'

'Pippi Longstocking. Yes, she does!' I smiled. We stood looking at one another for a moment, while the fine thread of female connection wove its spidery web between us.

'You have any kids?' I said.

Gloria pressed her lips into a tight line and my instincts told me to change the subject rather than pursue it.

'Ruby, the girl who lived here? She's Freya's half-sister.'

'They look completely different,' Gloria said.

'I'm guessing Ruby looked more like her mother?' I said and Gloria nodded. 'I never met Lilly. The police say it's a miracle Ruby's alive. It was that door over there and maybe the direction of the draught which saved her.'

'Miracle,' Gloria said.

I returned to the kitchen and went back to inspecting the boiler. Gloria followed.

'Maybe the man make a mistake.'

I asked her what she meant.

'Repair man, come to look boiler. I don't know name or nothing. Maybe since two weeks? Lilly knock on my door to borrow twenty pounds to pay him.'

The breath caught in my throat. No one had mentioned a repairman. The policewoman had said only that the police inspection of the boiler revealed the pilot light had gone out – something which could have happened at any time – that there were no batteries in the carbon monoxide detector and that Lilly was dead drunk. According to police, it was a freak accident.

'Did you report that to the police?'

Gloria let out a raw, indignant yelp. 'Do I look like a person who talk to police?' She looked me up and down and raised a finger to her lips. 'Shh, immigrant like me or brown person like you is same. I don't say nothing to no one. Pemberton has ears like elephant.'

'All the same,' I said, sounding like a judgemental idiot.

Gloria shot me the disapproving look I deserved and began to head for the door. I fumbled around in my pocket for something to write on, found an old receipt and a pen and scribbled down my mobile number.

'You're right. I wouldn't have said anything either when I lived here. But listen, if you see the boiler man again, would you call me? Just as a favour? Or ask him to call me?' A pause while I thought this through. 'Best not say anything about Lilly. Just tell him I've got some work for him.'

Gloria hesitated for a moment, weighing this – me – up, and after a cursory inspection, folded the paper into her bra. Then she waved a hand in the air and was gone.

I waited until she'd left before going into Ruby's room. A mattress with no bedframe lay on the floor, beside it a cheap clothes rack almost empty of clothes. There were no drawers. Ruby's underwear was piled into an Asda bag in the corner. On a tiny plastic bedside table were some old bottles of nail varnish, a few pens, a nail file, a packet of tissues and a few loose batteries. A couple of damp and musty towels on the floor gave out a fusty, faintly fungal smell. I went about the place picking up the clothes and towels and indiscriminately jamming them into the Chinese laundry bags I'd brought from home, my heart full of contradictory feelings, resenting the girl and her mother for intruding into my life, and at the same time feeling desperately sorry for them.

CHAPTER FOUR

I left the laundry bags in the hallway back home at Dunster Road and went into the kitchen where Freya and Tom were sitting at the table having breakfast.

'Hi, Mum!' Freya leaped up and clasped her arms excitedly around my waist. I dropped a kiss on her head.

'Hey, sweet pea.' My eyes cut to Tom but he was looking away. 'Did Dad tell you, we've got a visitor?' Before I'd left we had agreed that the best way to break the news was to tell the truth and be positive about it.

Freya nodded. Something passed across her face I couldn't read. She gave me a cheesy, pleading look. 'Can you stay home today, Mum? Pleeease.'

I'd been dreading this question, because I knew I wouldn't be able to give her the answer she needed and deserved. Not with a new parent meeting at the clinic and the big grant application looming.

'I'm really sorry, darling. Dad'll be here and I'll try to come home as early as I can, OK?'

* * *

I was already horribly late for work as it was. I thought about taking the car but I knew Tom would want to take the girls out somewhere and he needed it more than I did. In any case, it was rush hour and probably quicker to do what I usually did and run. Plus, I could use the thinking time. So I pulled on my gear and set off, one leg following the other in a two-step so familiar now it was automatic. I'd been running for over a decade, since a therapist had suggested taking regular exercise might help ward off another episode of mental illness. It was good for the brain, she said. I knew that, though I didn't tell her so. Actually, I could have quoted her the studies: Dr Solomon Synder at Johns Hopkins, who discovered endorphins in the seventies; Henning Boecker at the University of Bonn, whose work on the opioid receptors defined the runner's high. All the same, I took her advice. For years now I'd used my running time between home and work as a bridge between my two selves: Cat Lupo, mother, wife, sister and mild wino, with a penchant for trashy TV and popping candy, and Dr Caitlin Lupo, specialist in child personality disorders, clinician, ex-expert witness and all-out serious person.

As my legs found their rhythm, I wondered how Cat and Caitlin had become so disconnected from each other. Who was this creature, this mother, wife, psych, who looked like me and sounded like me, but who had never once in a dozen years suspected her husband of cheating, let alone of having another child? Had I somehow wilfully closed my eyes to Tom's betrayal? Or was I just blind to his faults? I tried to think back to the late stages of my pregnancy and the stay in the psych ward. I had never apologised for my illness because I hadn't thought mental illness was something anyone needed to apologise for. In any case, how could I have spotted that things had become so difficult for Tom when I was myself so radically altered? Or perhaps they hadn't been as tricky as Tom was now making out. Maybe Tom simply made the most of an opportunity. And if he'd done that once, who was to say he hadn't done it a dozen times? For all I knew he'd been cheating on me for the whole twelve years of our marriage.

At the top of Dunster Road, I stopped for a second and glanced back at the house which had, for so long, been my unquestioned home. The safe haven which I'd worked and fought for and sweated over. For some time now, we'd needed to cast a questioning eye over the fabric of our marriage and accept it had threadbare patches. We were too wedded to the idea of being the couple who didn't 'do' state-of-the-nation discussions, of always being cooler than that. But what if our coolness was just dishonesty in disguise? What had only yesterday seemed like a marriage built of bricks and mortar now felt more like a tent, and a broken tent at that. I imagined Ruby Winter lying in the spare bed, an unwanted presence, like some sinister-shaped cell which might at any moment begin stealthily to consume the healthy cells around it. And then I felt bad for the thought, because what was Ruby, after all, but a little girl who had lost her mother?

I arrived at the entrance to the park. The sun was already

hot, and I'd forgotten my water bottle. As I headed towards the drinking fountain by the bandstand, I wondered how two intelligent, articulate people could have failed so completely to ask the hard questions. At first it was all mad, carefree sex. Then came our high-octane period when we were so focused on our careers that nothing could distract us. After that was the period of trying to get pregnant. Once Freya was born we'd both been distracted, me fragile and with a new baby and Tom putting in the hours at Adrenalyze. Was that when things had changed? Or was it when the Rees Spelling 'boy in the wood' case blew open and the tabloids went after me? Or did it happen later, once Tom had quit Adrenalyze to work on *Labyrinth* and the success he so longed for hadn't come overnight; when our finances had got tight, we'd had to give up the part-time childminder, and Tom had been sucked into becoming a househusband, a role he'd never wanted and often complained bitterly about? So many gathering clouds we'd chosen to ignore. Now the storm had finally arrived, would we be strong enough to weather it?

As I turned into the car park at the institute, I began to tell myself that somehow we were going to have to come back from this. If not for us, then for Freya. And that meant I was going to have to accept the new member of the family and find a way to learn to trust Tom again. Maybe not now, not today, not next week even, but soon. Because if I didn't, or I couldn't, the effects would ripple outwards to our daughter in ways none of us could predict. And we would all live to regret it.

I showered and changed into my usual work uniform

– navy skirt with a white blouse – then swiped my card through the reader at the research block and went down the corridor to my office. Claire wasn't at her desk, but she'd left a thermos of coffee for me. I sat down, poured the black oily brew into a mug, and woke up my screen. It was just after ten but the heat of the day was already distracting and I felt the lack of sleep, coupled with the events of the early morning, roll over me like some dense, tropical fog. As I turned to set the fan going, a tap came on the door and Claire's face popped round.

'Good, you're here. Leak fixed?'

There was a momentary pause while I recalled the lie I'd told and formulated a response. 'Thanks, yes, the emergency plumber came.'

Claire pulled up her hair and flapped her hand over the air current to cool her neck then stopped in her tracks. 'Are you OK? You look a bit knackered.'

'Just the heat.' I wasn't ready to talk about the arrival of Ruby Winter with Claire yet. Or with anyone.

'Did you see on the news about those stabbings? Quite near you, weren't they? One day the whole city's just going to, like, implode.' There had been a spate of gang-related knife crime over the summer. Yellow boards had appeared in unexpected places, along with mournful shrines to dead teens reconfigured as 'warriors' and 'the fallen'.

I said I'd seen the news though, of course, I hadn't.

'Your rescheduled nine o'clock is here. I said ten fifteen, but she's a bit early.' Claire's voice dropped to a whisper. 'You may wish to adopt the brace position. I think you're about to hit some bumpy air.'

I surprised myself by laughing. 'Give me a few minutes to review the file, then show her in.'

I took a few breaths to clear my head of the events of the past few hours, and turned my attention to what lay ahead. As director of the clinic, it fell to me to deliver the news that in our view, Emma Barrons' twelve-year-old son Joshua was a psychopath. Not that I would use that word. Here at the institute the official diagnosis was CU personality disorder. Callous and unemotional. Like that sounded any better.

Joshua Barrons had been referred to the clinic from an enlightened emergency shrink after he'd tried repeatedly to flush the family kitten down the toilet. A week before, a plumber had used an optical probe to locate a blockage in the drains at the Barrons' family home. Joshua liked the probe and wanted to see it again and maybe even get a chance to use it. He thought that flushing the kitten would be a good way to do this, and when his nanny tried to stop him, he set fire to her handbag. According to the nanny, who we'd already met, Joshua's behaviour, though extreme, was nothing new. His exasperated mother had taken to spending weeks at their country home, leaving Joshua in London so that she could avoid dealing with him. The boy's father, Christopher Barrons, was rarely at home and when he was, there were fights. Once or twice, the nanny reported, she'd heard the sounds of scuffling and Emma had appeared with scratches and bruising, though, so far as she knew, the father had never hit his son. There were no other children. There was no kitten now either. The nanny had dropped it off at a shelter on her way to the doctor's office. Hearing the story, the doctor had referred Joshua to a psychiatrist.

Over the years, Joshua had gone through many nannies and many diagnoses: ADHD, depression, defiance disorder... The list went on. He'd seen a psychologist and been prescribed, variously, methylphenidate, dexamfetamine, omega 3s and atomoxetine, been put on a low sugar, organic diet, and had psychotherapy. None of that had worked. The emergency shrink had done some initial tests and referred the boy to the clinic. In the report he was characterised as impulsive and immature with shallow affect, an impaired sense of empathy and a grandiose sense of himself. Left untreated, the psych thought the boy was a ticking time bomb.

Here at the clinic we specialised in kids like Joshua. During his initial assessment, we had run him through the usual preliminary tests – Hare's psychopathy checklist and Jonason and Webster's 'Dirty Dozen'. Until I'd had a chance to assess him more thoroughly and run some scans I couldn't be absolutely certain of a diagnosis, but there was little doubt in my mind. In my opinion, as well as that of the clinic's therapeutic head, Anja De Whytte, Joshua Barrons was a manipulative, amoral, callous, impulsive and attention-seeking child whose neuropathy showed all the signs of conforming to the classic Dark Triad: narcissism, Machiavellianism and psychopathy. He wasn't evil, but the way his brain worked could make him seem that way.

I was prepared for a tricky conversation. For the next hour or two I'd have to put thoughts of Tom and Ruby Winter out of my mind as much as I could and focus on my patient. Joshua Barrons and his family deserved that. It was my job to do whatever I could to help him. Plus, we needed him. There were children all over the country who displayed at least some of the traits of CU disorder but to find a kid whose personality was at the extreme edge was rare. Joshua had much to teach us. And we were keen to learn from him. His was exactly the kind of case most likely to win us the grant we needed to advance the clinic's work on kids with personality disorders of all kinds.

Joshua's mother was thin and brittle, with the anxious, hooded eyes of a starved cat. She took the seat I offered her, scoping out the featureless walls, the shelves stacked with neuroscience journals and research files.

I'd read about the Barrons family in the file. They were rich and local. Christopher Barrons had made a mint in the London property market in the eighties and nineties, buying up workers' cottages like those around the Pemberton, installing laminate flooring and selling them on to middle-class professionals, using the profits to accumulate an enormous portfolio of ex-local authority flats which he rented out at exorbitant rates to twenty-somethings unable to get on the property ladder themselves. A few years ago he'd been knighted, though not, presumably, for buying up publicly funded housing on the cheap and using it to subsidise his private empire, though these days, of course, anything was possible.

I introduced myself and went through a few preliminaries. Emma waited for me to finish. In an immaculately clipped voice, she said, 'My husband refuses to believe there's anything wrong with Joshua that one of the major public schools can't fix. He thinks if we get Joshua into Eton, our son will stop flushing kittens down the lavatory.'

I'd run into the 'my child's too well bred to be a psycho' argument before and knew it for what it was: embarrassment combined with a wafer-thin sense of superiority brought in as a defence against the situation in which a woman like Emma Barrons found herself. The Barrons were used to being able to buy themselves out of almost any situation. I didn't judge them for that; what parent doesn't do whatever it takes for their kids? But money wasn't the point here and that was what left Emma and Christopher Barrons at a loss.

I leaned forward and steepled my hands to give myself more professional authority.

'And what do you think?'

I felt her pull back. A pulse thumped in her throat at the suprasternal notch. She wasn't here to have her opinion canvassed. What she wanted was exactly what we couldn't offer her: a cure. A tiny frown appeared on her otherwise waxy face. 'I should have thought that was rather obvious. I'm here, aren't I?'

'You are, and I'm very glad about that, because we're going to help your son.'

The tiny frown returned. 'Forgive my scepticism, Dr Lupo, but Joshua has been diagnosed any number of times by a series of private psychiatrists and prescribed dozens of pills with names I can't pronounce, but he's still trying to flush kittens down toilets. I'm here because I'm afraid for my child and I don't know what else to do and because the emergency psychiatrist who looked at Joshua hinted that he would section him if I didn't agree to come.'

I sat back and settled in for the long haul. Emma Barrons had a point. Diagnosis of paediatric mental disorders was both complex and highly controversial. Cases of child psychopathy were missed or misdiagnosed all the time, in part because it was relatively rare and in part because psychiatrists were resistant to giving kids such a devastating label. Even the most experienced psychiatrists and neurologists often got it wrong, either because they couldn't see it or because they didn't want to.

As I began what I hoped was a reassuring speech about how different our approach was at the clinic, I found my mind once more wandering back to the situation at home. A bubble of anxiety burst at the back of my throat. By now Freya would have met her half-sister. What if they didn't get on? What if Freya blamed her father and turned against him? Against both of us? So many what ifs. Hurriedly, I put those thoughts back into the box labelled 'home life' and returned my attention to my patient's mother. My upbringing had made me good at compartmentalising. It was something Tom liked about me. The hallmark of survivors. He thought of himself as one too. 'You and me both have a ruthless streak,' he'd said to me once in the early days. At the time, I let it go. I let a lot of things go back then.

Emma Barrons waited for me to finish and said, 'I sometimes wonder if Joshua behaves this way because he hates me. On the rare occasions Christopher comes home, Joshua runs into his arms. *Runs.* And then it's all "Daddy this" and "Daddy that". That's why my husband can't see it. He thinks I haven't put in enough effort to find the right school for our son. He won't accept that Joshua is too disruptive to go to a normal school.'

I mentioned we could arrange to have Joshua home-schooled by a specialist tutor, at least while he was still in treatment. As I was speaking, Emma Barrons began twirling the index finger of her right hand around the left. She wasn't listening. I couldn't blame her. By the time the kids in our clinic had been referred to us, their parents had usually gone through years of anguish. Most often they were on the brink. Taking an e-cigarette from her ostrich bag and holding it briefly in mid-air, she said, 'Do you mind?' and, without waiting for an answer, drew the metal tube to her lips and sucked like an orphaned lamb at the teat.

'I suppose there's no point in asking how Joshua got this way?' she said.

'We don't know exactly. The only thing we're sure of is that there are certain genetic and neurological markers often associated with children with the disorder. Joshua has the low MAO-A variant gene. It's an epigenetic problem, an issue with the way a particular gene expresses itself, which can affect the production of serotonin in the brain and lead to flattened emotional responses and a tendency towards problems with impulse control. You might have noticed that Joshua doesn't have the same fear response as most other children. He may need to go to extremes in order to feel pleasurable emotions. In fact, to feel anything at all. But I can explain it in more detail to you as we go along.'

Emma paused just long enough for her nicotine fix then launched into a diatribe about her son's reckless behaviour. I checked the clock. I loved my work and I was motivated by a strong sense that we could help kids like Joshua, kids who we in the brain business call 'unsuccessful psychopaths' because they are unable to disguise their dangerousness, but knew from experience that it would be a slow and painful process, one which could derail at any time. I steered the conversation towards more productive territory and spent a few minutes outlining what the institute proposed for the boy's therapy programme. Most of our kids were in residential care but, since the Barrons lived nearby, I thought it might be better for Joshua if we tried him out as a day patient. We would spend the first few weeks attempting to unlock Joshua's deep motivators, the things that really drove him, and then use them to try to modify his behaviour. Eventually we hoped to alter the neural pathways in his still malleable brain.

'I do really want to emphasise that there is hope,' I said.

Emma Barrons shot me a baleful look. We finished up and Emma Barrons stood to go. At the door, she turned and, with an odd, damaged smile on her face, she said, 'I didn't really want a child, you know, but Christopher had an heir thing going on. I suppose Joshua is the price I paid for marrying money. Quite a high price, as it turned out.'

For a moment she just stood there in the doorway

working the rings on her hands. 'I suppose that shocks you, Dr Lupo?'

'Call me Caitlin. We're going to get to know one another quite well.'

'Caitlin, then.' One side of her mouth rose up in a half-smile. '*Do* I shock you?'

'Right now, Emma, absolutely nothing would shock me.'

CHAPTER FIVE

After Emma Barrons had gone I called Tom's mobile and left a message. He and Ruby were spending the morning with social services then with police liaison, so I knew he would be unlikely to pick up, but I wanted him to know that I was thinking about the family and to remind him that we needed to talk tonight after the girls had gone to bed. I knew he'd try to sidestep it if he could.

What a bastard Tom was. What a complete shit. To go behind my back would have been one thing, but to do it when I was *on* my back. After everything I'd been through to bring our daughter into the world. After all the moral and financial support I'd given him. After all the badly cooked meals I'd laboured over so he could spend more time on *Labyrinth*. After all the bloody perfunctory sex.

Oh, the moral high ground. It was a dangerous place to linger, I knew that; barren and lonely and with air so thin it's difficult to breathe. If I allowed myself to follow the angry road and turn righteous at the top, I might feel I'd won, for an instant, only to sense a moment later that all I had really done was run away.

For now the only way forward was to think myself into accepting what had happened. Tom had cheated on me, it was over and the woman was dead. All that remained was the girl, Ruby Winter. Once she went to live with her grandmother, our day-to-day lives would remain essentially unchanged. I figured that we'd see her some weekends, support her financially and perhaps include her in our holiday plans, but that was more or less it.

By the time I finished my notes from the meeting with Emma Barrons it was nearly one o'clock. I was meeting Anja for lunch to discuss the grant application we were putting together to expand the clinic. On my way out, I asked Claire to take messages, then, swiping myself out of the building, I walked through the car park and out into the street.

As I made my way along the slip road towards Holland Hill and the Wise Owl Cafe, which was where Anja and I usually had lunch when we had something to discuss other than our patients, I was struck by a sudden and wholly unexpected sense of loss. The feeling was so intense I felt nearly floored by it. For most of the girls I grew up with on the Pemberton Estate, weed, booze, coke, even crack, were no bar to pregnancy. A few were on their third child – or abortion – before my eggs had so much as asked a sperm for its phone number. I came late to the sex party but I assumed that, once I'd arrived, I'd be pretty much like anyone else. I'd find a time when starting a family seemed to make sense and I'd do it. It never occurred to me that my body would prevent me getting what I most wanted. That my flesh and blood would become the enemy.

Tom once told me that my reproductive system was like one of those multi-layered computer games where you need to know the cheats to be able to complete the game. By 'cheats' he meant two rounds of IVF, the last of which, by some scientific miracle, brought us Freya. And that, for Tom, was that. The arrival of Freya was game over. We'd won. Move on.

But you know what? Completing the game only made me want to start from the beginning and play it again. Despite the cost, despite the expense, despite all the medical advice and evidence suggesting that, had I got pregnant again, there would have been a significant chance of my ending up in the psych ward for a second time, I would have gone on. Because the heart wants what it wants. And the womb wants what *it* wants. And my womb and my heart both wanted more.

And this was what floored me now. The knowledge that, while Tom was putting his foot down and refusing to give space to the idea that we might have another child, he'd gone out and made one. Just like that. From that most simple, tried and tested formula: a few drinks plus one willing woman plus nine months equals one child. And then – who could have predicted it? – one day, more than a decade later, the child he denied me would show up on our doorstep. I could forgive the cheating; I could forgive the lie. But tell me, how the hell was I supposed to forgive the child?

By now I'd reached the Wise Owl. Anja had already arrived and was sitting at a table at the back near the air con, one hand leaving snail trails with an ice cube across the soft mound of her left arm, while the other pecked at her phone. I rearranged my features, sent the demons back under the bed and waved. Her eyes flicked up and registered me, smiled briefly, then went back to finishing up whatever she was doing on her phone.

Anja and I had one of those close professional relationships that rarely spilled over into our personal lives. We'd trained together and run parallel careers for a time, and we could perhaps have been proper friends if the Spelling case hadn't forced me to give up forensic work to focus on research. Anja had backed away from me a little after that. We never socialised outside the institute and I'd only ever met her husband, Marc, at institute parties. I knew he worked for a hedge fund and put in crazy hours, and that they usually went away to the Caribbean at Christmas, and that they didn't have kids, which Anja regretted, but that was about it. From time to time, I wished we were closer. But I completely got it that we weren't. For a while, close association with me would have been career suicide. Now, ironically I supposed, given the dive my career had taken back then, I was effectively Anja's boss.

I took the seat beside her, noticing that a bottle of sparkling water and two large iced glasses already sat on the table. Anja dropped her phone into a leather bag at her side and clasped her hands to signal her switch in focus.

'Now, I can't *wait* to hear how you got on,' she said with a smile, which faded as she met my eye. 'God, you look tired. Hardly surprising, I suppose.'

For a single shocking moment, I imagined that she'd found

out about Ruby Winter, but no, she'd be thinking I'd been up late finishing off the grant application.

'All those bloody forms,' I said and gave a hollow laugh.

The waitress appeared to take our food order. Anja waited until the waitress had gone, then, leaning towards me in a half-whisper, she said, 'You're not pregnant, are you?'

This was so unexpected, the timing so ironic, it floored me. 'Why ever would you ask that?'

She eyed the menu.

'Oh, yes.' I'd asked for a cheese toastie and double brownies with double ice cream. 'No, not pregnant, just fatigue munchies.'

'Sounds like a band,' Anja said, a little disappointed, then, changing the subject, 'So, this morning, the mother? Have you told her we need her son to be one of our guinea pigs?'

'Funnily enough, no.' I hadn't broached this with Emma yet. After the Spelling case I was terrified of putting my foot in it. There was nothing the news outlets loved better than a 'devil children' story and I wanted to be sure Emma could be trusted before I put our funding application at risk. 'I'm still thinking about how best to phrase it,' I said.

'How's about: "Your kid is a bloody nightmare but what's great is that he's also a funding opportunity"?'

'That should do it.'

The waitress was heading our way with the food. I unfolded a paper napkin and laid it on my lap, and by the time I looked up Anja was enthusiastically scooping tuna into her mouth. She was a woman of considerable appetites, which made her sexy in an obvious kind of way. I'd seen men follow her with their eyes without realising they were doing it. At last year's Christmas party, Tom gawped at her cleavage.

'Not my type,' he'd said in the cab home, pulling me into an exaggerated clinch. 'I'm-alike de dusky ladies.' Always the joker. Ha ha, Tom.

We dutifully addressed ourselves to the grant application while we ate, then, over coffee, chatted briefly about our other charges. There were currently five children in the unit, none as extreme as Joshua, but all deserving of our time and attention. Ayesha, the girl who'd come to us from the care system, having manoeuvred a boy into sexually assaulting one of the girls in the group home Ayesha didn't like, was getting ready to go back to mainstream school and had found a long-term specialist foster parent. Adam, our borderline CU patient, a seven-year-old with a habit of violent tantrums, had begun to come off the drugs prescribed by another psychiatrist and was making some early progress. We went on through the list and, as we were coming to an end, I reached into my bag for my credit card, meaning to pay the bill, when my hand slipped and knocked my glass of water, which swayed then tumbled, pouring its contents across the table. I sprang up, grabbed a handful of paper napkins and began wiping and dabbing. Anja's hand landed on my arm.

'Are you all right, Cat? You seem a bit distracted.'

Before I'd even registered the words I heard myself say, 'It seems Tom has a daughter I didn't know about.'

Anja froze, then, looking at me, wide-eyed, she said, 'Oh fuck.'

I almost went on to talk about the strange circumstances in

which Ruby had arrived. The death-boiler. The window that should have been open. But something stopped me. An obscure feeling of disloyalty crept in. Anja wasn't the right person to be telling this to. Confused, I said nothing.

'Sorry, I didn't mean...' Anja said, registering my discomfort.

'No, I know. It's fine. We'll be fine. I'm just trying to process it all.'

'Yes, yes, of course. It must have come as a shock.' She caught the waitress's eye and air-scribbled for the bill, which she then insisted on paying. ('Oh, for heaven's sakes,' batting away my twenty-pound note, 'it's the least I can do.') We wandered back to the institute along sticky asphalt, meticulously avoiding any further mention of my personal life.

Claire had gone to lunch. A bunch of cream roses sat on my desk. No note – none necessary. A first attempt at some kind of reconciliation. An intimate little in-joke. The phrase 'not quite white' had been a running gag between us for years. It began as our way of dealing with Tom's awful mother, who, when introduced to me for the first time, had taken her son to one side and said, 'She seems very nice, but she's not quite white, is she?' You had to laugh. And we did. From then on, 'not quite white' became our little joke. A wholemeal loaf morphed into 'not quite white bread', brownies were 'not quite whiteys', a fashionably drab paint job was a 'not quite white number'. Tom in particular relished the game, especially when it came to taking revenge on his mother, whom he loathed. When Freya came along he introduced her to his parents as 'your not quite white granddaughter'. Predictably, Geraldine was clueless.

Michael flushed purple and didn't say anything. Afterwards, Tom and I laughed like drains.

Neither of us was laughing now.

The roses went in the bin.

A little while later my office phone rang.

'Dr Lupo?' a vaguely familiar voice said. 'James White, the *Herald*.'

It was White who had first made the link between my expert evidence in the 'boy in the woods' case and the terrible events that followed.

'You've got a bloody nerve.'

'Please don't hang up. It was all such a long time ago. I wonder if anyone even remembers?'

'I remember. Every day.'

White gave a little cough. 'Well, I'm giving you an opportunity to put your views out there in a less personally charged situation, to be part of the conversation again, so to speak.'

'I don't want to be part of the conversation.'

I sensed White was after a comment on the spate of stabbings across the city and was trying to provoke me into a reaction. My rational self told me to put the phone down but I felt a sudden urge to knock White off his perch.

'Look, you must have seen some of the tabloid headlines. Monster kids, devil children. I bet you hate that.'

'Of course I hate it.'

'So you wouldn't say the children in your psychopath clinic are evil then?'

I took a breath. White had succeeded in provoking me. How

had he found out about the clinic? We'd gone to some length to keep its existence quiet. On the institute's website I was listed as the director of research into child personality disorders. No mention of psychopathy, or any clinic.

'I have no idea how you came about that information and I don't suppose you're going to tell me, but it would be *deeply* irresponsible of the *Herald* to print anything about the clinic. The work we do is highly sensitive. You start bandying about words like "evil" you are stigmatising vulnerable children and potentially putting them at risk from vigilante nutcases.'

'In that case, give me a quote and I won't mention it.'

I tried to think clearly but with everything going on that wasn't easy. And I really just wanted White off the phone. Finally, I said, 'How's about this? Some kids are genetically predisposed to respond to environmental stressors with violence, but it's vanishingly rare to come across a violent child who hasn't first witnessed violence in their environment. Kids pattern their behaviour from what they see around them.'

'So you're basically saying we get the kids we deserve?'

I thought about this for a moment. 'I don't think I'd put it like that, but I guess so, perhaps.'

I put down the phone and took some deep breaths. The brassy, citrusy smell of whatever Emma Barrons had loaded into her e-cigarette still lingered in the room. I knew what I'd just done would probably come back at me, but for now I was more worried about how White had come by his information. However I looked at it, the clinic was vulnerable. Which meant I was vulnerable. And there was nothing I could do about it.

CHAPTER SIX

On my run home I spotted a new yellow police board outside Jamal's. The place was one of those ratty not-actually-on-a-corner corner shops selling super-strength lager, haircuts and money transfer services that Londoners rely on to be open all hours. I often dived in there on my run back from work. Beside the board, on the wall separating Jamal's shop from the Caribbean takeaway next door, an impromptu shrine had appeared. Bunches of cheap flowers lay scattered around a central core of lit candles and someone had glued a photo of a young, heartbreakingly open-faced boy to a piece of card and nailed it to the wall. Beneath the photo the word 'warrior' was misspelled in red ink.

'What is happening to this city?' I said, while Jamal was ringing up my purchases. 'Since when did dead kids become warriors?'

'I blame designer trainers and computer games.' From his jovial tone I knew Jamal didn't quite mean this. He was aware of what Tom did for a living. They'd talked many times about playing *FIFA* together.

'I blame us,' I said.

* * *

Tom and I were twenty-five when we met. I'd just finished my PhD and was giving a paper on the use of psychological games to develop empathy in kids with antisocial personality disorder at a gaming conference in London. In the lunch break this lean, rangy games developer with chocolate curls and a dazzling smile appeared at my side. We talked about the paper for a while. Then, in a voice like a week on a beach, Tom said, 'Has anyone ever told you that the left side of your mouth turns upwards when you're thinking hard?'

I laughed. 'Not till now.'

'So, what are you thinking about?'

I laughed again. 'I'm going to assume you're being ironically suggestive.'

He met my eye then and our smiles faded. At that point in my life, I'd never been to a forest but there was something about his gaze that was redolent of the thick silence of trees at dusk. It had a specific stillness and a density which you only found in ancient woodland.

Tom winked at me. 'Well, whatever you *were* thinking about, I know what you're thinking about now.' Then, with perfect cool, he added, 'So, lunch?'

We went to an Italian place around the corner and ate whatever. I don't remember what we talked about because it didn't matter. I think we might have shared a tiramisu. But then again it could have been something else.

'How's about we go somewhere and play grown-up games?' he said, after we'd finished coffee.

'Do you ever stop?' I said. He'd been flirting with me throughout the meal.

He looked at me. 'Would you like me to?' Then, and as if it was the most natural thing in the world, his hand went to my waist. His touch was so light but so absolute it was like being webbed in spider silk. I heard myself laughing. The question was so cheesy but at the same time so hot that no was the only possible answer. I didn't want him to stop. Not then. And not for a long time after.

We went to the first hotel we could find and played grown-up games. Later, drinking room-service whisky, I asked Tom what he thought made a great gamer.

He propped himself up on one elbow and, running the fingers of his other hand along my belly, said, 'Perfect hand–eye coordination, precision, responsiveness and the ability to focus completely on the game to the exclusion of everything else.'

Basically, I thought, the exact same stuff that makes a man great at sex – and I decided there and then that I wanted Tom Walsh in my life.

* * *

Jamal handed me my change. I thanked him and went out of the shop. At the shrine I stopped a moment and read some of the messages, absent-mindedly pouring a sachet of popping candy down my throat and waiting for the miniature explosion.

I wasn't looking forward to going home. I wished I could sit Tom down and say, 'You know what? Let's just draw a line under this, make a fresh start.' But I wasn't big enough to allow that to be the end of it.

I broke back into a run. I wanted it to work between us but I wasn't about to be a martyr to my marriage. I had my pride. I also had Freya to think about. I didn't want her growing up thinking that the long-suffering wife was any kind of role to aspire to. At the same time, things were delicate. I needed to be strategic about this. Like many men of his class and upbringing, Tom couldn't deal with any kind of direct confrontation, especially not from a woman. I wanted to make life uncomfortable enough for Tom that he would never be tempted to stray again but I knew if I tried to box him in, he'd do whatever it took to game his way out and I'd lose the upper hand.

The girls were in the garden. Ruby, a thin, sallow-skinned, befreckled creature with an enormous shock of red hair in whose delicate blue frame I couldn't see anyone I had ever loved, was sitting beside my daughter and pulling at the grass, the two of them building something with Lego. A brief, fleeting moment of relief came over me then, followed by an odd sense that the girl with the orange hair wasn't real and any minute now she would vanish, leaving the three of us alone once more.

'Hey, girls!'

Freya jumped up and came running.

'I'm showing Ruby our magic castle, only she doesn't believe me,' she said, clasping me around the waist and burying her head in my belly.

At eleven, Freya still occupied a world of childish possibility. She was young for her age, emotionally, and I was happy with that. I knew what growing up too fast in the city was like and I didn't want that for my kid.

'Well, you can show it to me later.' I took my daughter's sweet, small, 'not quite white' hand and we walked up the garden to where Ruby was sitting.

'Hi, Ruby, how was your day?'

'Hello,' the girl said, regarding me with a level gaze. Her eyes were the colour of the late summer sun catching in a mirror. Amber beads with pupils trapped inside, like something very old which had never found a name. She reached for a brick and, pressing it into her hand, said, 'My mum died, so now I'm living here.'

'I'm very sorry about what happened to your mother.'

The girl nodded without looking up so I couldn't properly read her face. She didn't look as though she'd been crying but maybe it hadn't hit her yet. Or maybe it had but she didn't feel like crying. Or maybe she was all cried out? Ruby Winter was a mystery to us. Probably even to herself.

'You didn't return my call.' I felt Tom's presence and swung round. His hands were on his hips and there was a little tic playing on his jawline. I remembered then that he'd called me back and left a message.

'The day ran away from me.'

He eyed me questioningly as if waiting for me to thank him for the roses, which I was in no mood to do. It was Freya who lightened the atmosphere.

'Mum, Ruby likes pizza and ice cream. Isn't that cool?' Our daughter was sitting beside her half-sister now, idly picking at the grass.

'Well, good, that's our tea sorted, then.' It was a relief, suddenly, to be talking about the everyday. 'How was the bed in the spare room, Ruby? Did you sleep OK?'

'She likes my room better,' Freya said, handing her half-sister a frogged brick.

Pudge the cat wandered over. On any normal day, Freya would have held Pudge in the air and kissed his paws, but I saw Ruby pull up her hands like a drawbridge, a look of mild distaste on her face, and my daughter, ever in tune with other people's feelings, reached over, picked him up and gently deposited him over on the other side of the garden before returning to her spot.

'Ruby prefers Harry to Pudge, don't you?' Freya had been allowed to take the school hamster home to look after in the holidays.

'Sort of,' Ruby said.

Tom had sat down on the grass beside his daughter and was now rifling through the Lego bricks.

'We can fix up your room any way you want it,' he said casually. 'For when you come and visit.'

A thin smile broke out inside me. At least on that matter Tom and I were in accord. The girl would live with her grandmother. For the majority of the time Dunster Road would remain just us three.

'Good idea,' I said.

Later, after pizza and ice cream and when the girls had gone into the living room to play a dance game on the household Wii and Tom and I were clearing up, I said, 'Roses. *Really?*'

'Worth a try,' Tom said.

'I binned them.'

'Can't say I blame you.'

So he had decided to play nice, which meant I had to do the same or hate myself.

'Did you get to talk to Freya on her own today?' I went on, changing the subject.

Tom stopped what he was doing, went over to the counter where the open bottle of wine sat and poured himself a glass.

'Of course. She's super cool about having a new sister.'

'*Half*-sister.'

Tom shot me a little look of reproach. 'Yeah, whatever.'

Then, as if magicked, Freya appeared and the conversation ended before it had begun.

At eight thirty I hustled the two girls up to bed and sat with Freya a while. Just as Tom said, she was excited about the new arrival and full of girlish plans and if there was any hint of jealousy or foreboding, or even anxiety, she didn't show it. I loved her all the more for that – her generosity and innate decency.

By the time I got back downstairs, Tom was on the sofa playing on his games console. I joined him, poured myself a glass of wine and invited the cat onto my lap.

'Shall we talk?'

Tom stiffened then looked up with raised eyebrows as though I'd said something surprising.

'What, now?' He had this way of making it seem as if all conversation should only ever be about an exchange of essential information, that there was no such thing as simply *talking*. Because talking brought up the possibility of confrontation. And avoiding confrontation was the way Tom absolved himself from responsibility whilst seeming completely reasonable. *If you want to talk, of course we'll talk, but I wonder if this is really the right time? Wouldn't tomorrow be better?* If I pushed it, he'd usually run off, returning a few hours or even, on one or two occasions, a few days later, as if nothing had ever happened, knowing that I'd be too spent to want to start up again. A couple of times, when I had, he had lost it in the most spectacular way, one time pushing his hands through a window, another (we'd been in the car) driving straight into a wall.

I met his question with another. 'How has Ruby seemed today?'

'Calm. OK. In shock a bit, I guess. She could do without the social workers and all that administrative bullshit.'

'Maybe we could come to some arrangement with the grandmother for Ruby to stay with us every other weekend on a sort of experimental basis?'

Tom reached for his glass and took a long gulp. 'Maybe.' He sounded as though he was hiding something.

'But?'

'But I haven't spoken to her. When the police finally got through she said she was too upset to talk to me or Ruby. I'll call her later, find out what the funeral arrangements are. The social worker seemed to think it's important for Ruby to go.'

'How *were* your meetings with social services and the police?'

He shrugged. 'If I'm honest, most of it went straight over my head.' *If I'm honest.* I liked that.

'But there's no suggestion of anything weird, is there?'

'No, why would you think that? The woman had a drink problem and, from what the cops said, a rather chaotic life.' The way he said 'chaotic life' made it clear that he was expecting me to feel sorry for Lilly Winter, which I did, but that didn't make me any sorrier for Tom.

We fell silent, the dead woman in the room between us. Eventually, when I couldn't stand it anymore, I said, 'Did you really only sleep with Lilly Winter once?' My voice was breathy, and with no weight to it, like sea foam breaking on pebbles.

Tom twisted around to look at me.

'*Yes.* Jesus, Cat, you want the truth. I regretted it then I forgot about it. It was just a really stupid mistake. And I'm sorry, really.' He reached out but I pulled back. As a conciliatory gesture, he picked up the bottle of Malbec on the coffee table and waved it in the air. He was quite pissed, I realised then.

'A glass of this? Or there's some chilled "not quite white" in the fridge.'

'That was funny before you fucked that woman.'

Tom cocked his head and grinned. 'Nah, that was *actually* funny.'

I snorted and gave ground and immediately the tension between us eased.

'Was it really tricky? Back then, I mean.'

'Bloody awful. ' His knee started beating under the table. 'Not just tricky, actually *scary*, like I'd lost you just at the moment when you were about to give birth to our daughter. You were so paranoid you wouldn't even be in the same room as me.'

'What did I think you were going to do to me?' I didn't remember much about my mental state back then and now I felt trapped between my anger at Tom and the fear of expressing it. The look that came into his eyes from time to time when he was afraid of what he saw as my *instability*.

He went quiet for a moment, his fingers rubbing the wine glass. I could tell he was working out his next move.

'That's not the point. Anyway, we've never talked about whether you cheated on *me*. I know you wanted to, with that lawyer guy on the Spelling case. Dominic. You were hot for him.'

I dismissed this with a wave, but Tom was more right than he knew. I'd been far from the perfect wife. I stood up.

'I'm going to check on Freya.'

* * *

Our daughter was sitting in bed watching the hamster turning aimlessly on its wheel. It was far too late for her to be awake.

'What's up, sweet pea?'

She crossed her arms over her delicate little chest. 'Auntie Sally's *your* sister. Now I've got one too.' Her tone had a hint of reproach. Jealousy? Resentment of my failure to provide a sister? A kind of possessiveness? It was always hard to tell with Freya.

'Yes, darling.' I bent down and we kissed each other. She

snuggled into her duvet and I stroked her head until she fell asleep, but as I crept back through the hall past the spare room, darkened now, where Ruby Winter slept, I remembered her words, *I live here now*, and a feeling of disquiet trailed me like a shadow.

Sometime in the middle of the night I woke to the sound of murmuring voices. Tom was beside me, dead to the world. Creeping out of bed, I found the two girls sitting at the bottom of the bed in Freya's room, playing with the hamster.

'What are you two doing?'

'Ruby wants Harry in her room,' Freya said, by way of explanation.

'I see. Well, we can talk about that in the morning. For now, I think it's best if the hamster stays here and we all go back to our beds and get some sleep.' I put the animal back inside his cage and, as I held out a hand for Ruby, the girl slid by without a word and went onto the landing. I kissed Freya then followed Ruby to the spare room and waited for her to get back into bed. As the light went out, she was lying stiffly with the duvet tucked under her armpits and her arms uncovered, hands working into little blue-white fists on the counterpane.

CHAPTER SEVEN

I woke early, with Ruby Winter on my mind. There had been some hint of slyness about the way she'd been with Freya last night that I didn't like. Although she was a few months younger than Freya she already knew things, sad, troubling things that had yet to darken Freya's horizons. I was familiar with what knowing too much too soon could do to a kid's spirit because I'd been one of those kids who'd had to grow up too fast. Unless you were very careful or just plain lucky, a background like that could make you cynical, angry and preternaturally old. I sensed that with Ruby the damage had already been done. You might be able to apply a few sticking plasters but you could never erase the scar. I didn't want that happening to my girl.

I got up and padded out to the landing in my nightdress. Pudge the cat let out a greeting, but otherwise everything was quiet. Tom had decamped to the sofa bed in his study in the early hours, disturbed by my restlessness. The girls' bedroom doors were closed and the house was still thick with sleep. I went back into the bedroom, pulled on my running gear then slipped downstairs to make breakfast.

The coffee wasn't yet brewed when Tom appeared, looking maddeningly sexy. He'd flung on some cargo shorts and a T-shirt and was leaning on the kitchen worktop, the lean lines of his body visible beneath the fabric. I knew he wouldn't want to continue last night's conversation. Not really. If I allowed it, a few days would pass and I would bring the topic up again and we'd start afresh, as though the earlier discussion had never happened.

'Did you get some sleep?' I said.

Tom grunted.

'Sorry about my fidgetiness.'

I watched him flex his shoulders and stretch out his arms, then I bit my lip and looked away, my anger rising at what he'd done and at myself for wanting him in spite of it.

He yawned and pulled the Weetabix towards him. 'It's all a bit of a head fuck,' he said, with some understatement. I checked the clock. There really wasn't enough time to have a proper discussion. It would have to wait. I told Tom that I had to go into the institute but I'd ask for a couple of personal days and we'd carve out a few hours to talk then.

'You'll let me know how your chat with the grandmother goes, won't you?' I had forgotten her name. I guessed my old therapist would have found some kind of meaning in that.

'Of course. I want to sort this out as much as you do.'

There came the sound of feet on the stairs and our daughter appeared, followed, moments later, by Ruby Winter. On any normal day Freya would have come over and given me a kiss but today she waited for Ruby to choose a seat then pulled out the chair beside her.

'Morning, girls.'

'Can we have pancakes?'

I looked at Tom who shrugged a 'why not?'

They were getting the pancake batter together when the phone rang. I picked up. It was Shelly Frick, our neighbour. When we were alone together Tom always referred to the couple as the Pricks. Shelly Frick was one of those uptight, insecure women who spends her life competing with other women but only ever looks to men for validation. When I'd been in hospital she'd fussed about Tom as if he were a toddler, then, when I was back home again, crowed about how well she'd 'looked after' him. One night not long afterwards she came round to supper and expressed surprise when I flipped on a playlist that I wasn't more into hip-hop. Because, *what*? I'm *brown*? In other words, she was a basic bitch. Nicholas we saw less often but whenever we did he was braying about the amazing deal he'd just pulled off on the derivatives markets, which made Tom want to poke out his eyes. Not our kind of people. But Charlie Frick was a sweetheart, Freya was very fond of him, and we figured it was good for her to have a younger kid to play with.

Shelly said she'd called to warn us that the builder was about to start hollowing out their basement and also to remind us about Charlie Frick's seventh birthday party at the weekend.

'I wanted you to know that you're *all* welcome. Including the new arrival, obviously.' There was a moment's pause which Shelly was clearly hoping I'd fill with some gossipy titbit and when I said nothing, she added, rather desperately, 'My goodness, what *amazing* hair she has, doesn't she? Just like a tiger.'

I muttered something about seeing her on Saturday and hung up, waiting until the girls were absorbed in their pancake making at the stove before ushering Tom over to the table.

'Did you say something to Shelly?' I felt unsettled that Tom had told her anything before we'd had a chance to talk through an official story. Was it unreasonable to expect to at least have control of who knew what and in what manner?

'She came over,' Tom said flatly, as if it were of no consequence.

'I wished you'd discussed it with me first,' I said.

Tom's eyebrows rose. 'You didn't return my call.'

'I was *busy* at work.'

'Oh yeah,' he hissed. 'Your *work*.'

At that moment I happened to glance over at the oven and saw Ruby whisper something in Freya's ear, before my daughter nodded and, turning to us, said, 'Will you help us toss the pancake, Dad?'

With an expression of enormous relief on his face, Tom got up and went towards the oven.

'Of course I will, darling.'

* * *

The heat in the office later that morning brought on an instant headache. Or, perhaps it wasn't the heat so much as the stress – or just tiredness from two disturbed nights in a row. Whatever the cause, it left me feeling out of sorts as I sat down to my morning's work. I'd been in the office an hour or two when my mobile started up the 'Hallelujah Chorus', which signalled a call from my little sister. I'd left a message last night asking Sal to get back to me urgently. It was now nearly twelve hours later but in Sallyland this was what was known as an emergency response.

'Hey, Cat, sorry, late night. What's up? I'm in a cab.' She sounded her usual upbeat, flirtatious self. Since starting in fashion PR six or seven years ago, Sal had stopped *going* anywhere. Instead, she nipped and popped and Ubered her way around the most stylish parts of the capital, looking fresh and straight out of the box. Living with our lush of a mother and the great disappearing act that was our father had left her fragile, but she made a spectacular show of hiding it and for that I loved her. Of all the responses among friends and family about the news of Ruby's arrival, Sally's was the one I dreaded least. She might say something flaky and funny but she wouldn't judge and I could at least rely on her not to be horribly earnest.

I recounted how it had happened, at least in Tom's version, then described how Ruby had arrived in the middle of the night after her mother's death. When I'd finished, Sal gave a low whistle.

'God, Cat, I bet you're raging at Tom. Except you don't do rage. Smouldering, then. I bet you're *smouldering* at him.'

'I could bloody murder the bastard, but I'm not going to let the kids see that.'

Sal absorbed this for a moment. Then she said, 'A whole girl, though. Is she cute?'

I laughed. 'Since you ask, she's, well, quirky. *Loads* of red hair. Nothing at all like Tom.'

There was a pause while Sal thought this through. 'And sooo… ?'

'This isn't really the time to start asking for DNA tests. Tom's on the birth certificate and he seems a hundred per cent sure.' I *had* wondered why, if Tom was listed as Ruby's father on the birth certificate, the authorities hadn't been in contact with him about child support, but I didn't really know anything about the rules. Maybe Lilly Winter had wanted to go it alone?

Sally piped up: 'How is darling Freya?'

'She seems fine. Well, fine-ish. A bit in awe. Her half-sister's big on street smarts. There's something slightly odd about her.'

'Poor girl, though. To find your own mum like that.'

For an instant I saw Freya walking into a room where I lay, dead, and felt winded, so tried to put it out of my mind.

'She doesn't seem upset, particularly.'

'Were you upset when Mum died? I mean, really?'

'That was different. We were older and…' I tailed off. Sal had a good point even though it was painful to concede it. After Heather died all I felt was relief.

'Once things have settled down a bit Ruby's going to live with her grandmother so that will take the pressure off us.'

'That's probably a good thing. I'll bet Tom's creeping around like a whipped dog, isn't he?'

'Yes and no. He sent roses to work like that was going to

make everything just fine. We haven't really talked about it, not properly.'

'You *were* a bit of a nightmare. At the hospital, I mean.'

'I was *ill*. And apparently no one wants to let me forget it.'

There was a pause. 'You won't leave, will you?'

'Do you think I shouldn't?' Even as I asked the question, I realised that I wasn't so sure what my answer would be. There was Freya to think about and, besides, Tom wasn't the only one with a spotty record. Tom's infidelity was all out in the open and undeniable. But Tom knew nothing about mine.

'It's just, well, for the last four years Tom's been the stay-at-home dad and...' Her voice tailed off but I knew exactly where she was heading. The D word. Which led to the C word. If divorce led to a battle in the courts over our child, would someone like me, with my history, get custody? The thought had occurred to me too, but the possibility of losing Freya was too awful to think about for long.

Just then Claire appeared and stuck a Post-it note on the computer: *An audience with MacIntyre at 2 p.m.* I gave her a thumbs-up and waited until she had closed the office door then finished up the call with my sister and rang off.

The remainder of the morning was busier than I'd anticipated. Ayesha had attacked a therapist and there was no time to think much about the situation at home. By one thirty I was back in my office, which was now wonderfully cool, with an air conditioner humming in one corner. As I was angling my chair to take advantage of the air, Claire popped her head around the door.

'You're a genius,' I said, meaning the air con.

'The old lady I had to trample to get it didn't think so.'

I waved the Post-it note. 'Did the Master of the Neuroverse say what he wanted to see me about?'

'Nope.' Claire checked her watch. 'But you've just got time for a sandwich before you find out. Shall I get you the usual?'

* * *

As was befitting for the director of a high-profile pubic institution, Sir Gus MacIntyre was half gatekeeper, half cheerleader. Staff called him, variously, the Master of the Neuroverse or simply Emperor Gus, though never to his face. His bald dome and jaunty bow tie were a regular feature on the late night and Sunday morning current affairs shows and it was his media appearances, almost more than his undoubted brilliance as director, which had kept him in the public eye long enough for him to have made it onto the Queen's Honours list and secured his place in the Establishment. He could have easily sat back on his heels in the comfort of his club but a restlessness, or maybe some chink in the armour of his ego, necessitated a continued starring role in the constant drama of busyness and hustle. His family had been big in the Colonial Service and it was a running joke that he ruled the Institute of Neuroscience as if it were an empire over which the sun never set. I liked him well enough and, as long as I continued to produce major grant-attracting, cutting-edge research, I was confident the feeling would be reciprocated.

When I landed in his office fresh from a quick do-over in the ladies', MacIntyre was on the phone and looked up only to wave me into a chair with an exaggerated swing, as though directing traffic in Kolkata, before returning to his conversation. He made no effort to cut short the call but the moment he put the phone down it was as if it had never happened and his attention was immediately all on me.

'Ah, Caitlin,' he said. 'All well?' His tone suggested a subtext. I outlined the latest at the clinic, but MacIntyre was only half listening.

'We are, of course, primarily a research institute,' he said finally, as if I needed reminding.

'Is that what you wanted to see me about?'

'Ah, yes, well, not quite.' MacIntyre pulled up something on his screen and peered at it for a moment.

'Are you familiar with James White at the *Herald*? Apparently you told him "We get the kids we deserve".' He looked up, adjusted his glasses, and went on, wearily: 'That's a little incendiary, wouldn't you say?'

I felt affronted. 'At no point did I say that.'

MacIntyre swung the screen around and there it was, in bold, stomach-turning letters on a subheading, attributed to me.

'Since the *other matter*, I thought we both agreed that you'd keep a low profile with the press?' MacIntyre said.

The 'other matter' had begun on a cold January night fifteen years ago when a disturbed twelve-year-old named Rees Spelling had taken his sleeping brother Kai from his cot and left him under an upturned dustbin on a patch of woodland not far from his flat. The mother, who had been out scoring heroin at the time, finally realised the baby was gone, seven hours later, and questioned Rees, who denied all knowledge of his whereabouts. By then Kai was probably already dead but it took the police dogs till the following afternoon to find him. CCTV footage recovered later showed Rees carrying the baby through a nearby alleyway.

My own dealings with Rees Spelling came a few months later. He was being kept at a secure unit in a secret location a couple of months before going to trial. The CPS had decided to charge the boy with murder and try him as an adult. I'd been called in by his defence solicitor, Dominic Harding, to decide whether or not the boy had legal capacity. Had Rees understood that by leaving his brother out in the open and covering him so that he would probably not be found, Kai would likely die? Dominic also wanted to know if, in my opinion, Rees Spelling was an ongoing danger.

I was young then, newly qualified as a forensic psych and full of the certainties of youth. I interviewed Rees three or four times. The kid had the kind of childhood nightmares are made from. His brother, Kai, had been a colicky baby and his mother had told her elder son on many occasions that Kai was 'doing my head in'. She'd taken to spending more and more time away, leaving Rees to look after his little brother. When Rees took Kai into the woods to die he knew that what he was doing would probably end his brother's life but he did it in some mistaken belief that this would please his mother. I considered it unlikely that Rees posed any danger to the public in the future and I didn't want to see the kid locked away in a young offenders' institution, too many of which are hatcheries for career criminals. He was disturbed and needed psychological help. I said this in court and on the basis of my assessment Rees Spelling was detained in a secure psychiatric unit for a few years, then, at the age of eighteen, quietly released. Not long afterwards he abducted eighteen-month-old Kylie Drinkwater from outside a branch of Asda and abandoned her in remote woodland. A dog walker found the body weeks later.

'White caught me at a bad moment, it won't happen again,' I said now. I didn't want MacIntyre to know that White had found out about the clinic until I was sure of the source of the leak.

MacIntyre listened then smiled and shifted in his seat. 'Let's try not to have any more bad moments then, eh?'

* * *

When I arrived home later that afternoon, Tom was shut in his study, a 'do not disturb' sign over the door. I called up the stairs and the cat appeared but there was no reply from either of the girls so I left my bag on the hook in the hallway and went into the kitchen. Through the window I saw two coltish figures on the trampoline, their laughter skipping across the patio and down the steps to the French windows.

How could I resent Freya for liking the sibling I've never been able to give her?

I found some lemonade in the fridge, poured three glasses

and walked out onto the patio. Ruby was leaning up against the trampoline frame now, taking in the sun. Her hair had been bundled into an inefficient ponytail from which long auburn trails escaped like fireworks. She was barefoot and wearing what looked to be a newly purchased T-shirt and shorts. On the ground beside her lay a bright pair of trainers. They'd been shopping. I was glad of that; the stuff I'd fetched from the flat was old and tatty. I watched her for a moment. She seemed oddly at ease, as if, after some long journey, she had finally arrived at her destination. Behind her, oblivious to me, Freya carried on performing flips and rolls.

'Hey, I brought lemonade.'

Freya gave a little whoop and, steadying herself to a stand-still, waved, clambered from her perch and ran over. I put the glasses down on the grass and opened my arms. She grasped me around the waist. I planted a kiss on her brown hair. She was sporting a new, unfamiliar hairstyle, which made her look more vulnerable and, I thought, younger, but the moment I laid a hand on the plait, she pulled away. 'Don't muzz it up, Mum. Ruby helped me plait it. She says it looks fuzzy wuzzy when it's loose.'

'Well, I think it looks brilliant both ways,' I said, alarmed that the words 'fuzzy wuzzy' might have some racial over-tone.

Freya picked up a glass of lemonade and handed it to Ruby. Changing the subject, I said, 'Did you have a nice time today?'

'We went to the park and the lido. Then some boring people

came to talk to Ruby, so I went next door and played with Charlie. After that it was OK, though. Dad took us to the shops and for ice cream.'

In the twenty-four hours since Ruby's arrival the dynamic of the household had shifted. A new routine had emerged, and I wasn't part of it. I wasn't surprised but I wished I felt less left out.

Freya pointed to the dark patch on my running shirt and said, 'Mum, you need a shower.'

'I do. Have you two thought about what you'd like for tea?'

Freya shrugged but it was Ruby who answered.

'Chicken McNuggets.'

Tom was keen to go to McDonald's but I resisted. I'd spent the best part of five years flipping burgers there while trying to get an education and support myself and Sal, which left me loathing everything about the place. We settled on a regular favourite, Hoopoes, not only because the chicken was great, but also because there was an enclosed garden at the back that the owners had made into a little playground where the girls could muck about when they got bored inside.

Tom drove. The girls tumbled out and went off hand in hand so Freya could show Ruby the play area while Tom and I grabbed a table. I waited until they were out of earshot.

'Doesn't Ruby seem a bit *odd* to you?'

Tom frowned, not pleased by the question. 'Odd how?'

'It's like her mother's death hasn't really impacted on her.'

'It probably hasn't yet. You of all people should know that.'

Our usual waiter, Eddie, came over with menus, took our drinks order and offered to go and call the kids. Tom thanked him and said he'd do it. I sensed, as I always did with Tom, that I was going to have to drag him into having a conversation he didn't want to have, but I was absolutely determined so, as he got up, I held out a staying hand.

'Did you speak to the grandmother today?'

Tom looked away. 'You want to know the truth? I had a bit of a thing with the social worker. You know the type: interfering, self-righteous. So I didn't get round to it.'

I sensed this was a lie. Just then Eddie returned with drinks and Tom took the opportunity of the distraction to go and get the girls and I couldn't pursue it. Once we were all settled around the table Eddie came over again.

'Our usual, please, Eddie,' I said. There was an awkward pause.

'And what would *you* like, Ruby?' Tom said pointedly.

It took me a moment to realise what I'd done, then I reached over and, tapping Ruby on the arm, I said, 'Ruby, of course you must have whatever you want.'

The girl stared at me with those implacable amber eyes and I thought I detected hatred there or maybe contempt. 'Chicken McNuggets. From McDonald's.'

A pained silence spread around the table. Sensing he'd got in the middle of something, Eddie sidled off. Tom threw down a tenner for the drinks, stood up from the table and said, 'Come on then, we're going to Mickey D's.'

As we got into the car, I noticed the sly smile on Ruby's face. The moment she spotted me looking, the smile vanished.

Back home, Tom waited until the girls had gone out into the garden, then he said, 'Would it really have *killed* us to do what Ruby wanted? And did you need to be so rude to her?'

I went to the fridge and poured a large glass of Pinot Grigio. Tom had been moody all evening, for reasons I suspected had something to do with his earlier lie.

'I'm really, *really* sorry about what I said. It was an honest mistake.'

Tom sighed and helped himself to a glass of Rioja.

* * *

Ruby Winter was sitting on the picnic rug in the garden sucking on a long straw. In the fading sun she was like some exotic plant raised in the dark, spindly and unnaturally white. I sat down next to her.

'I grew up on the Pemberton Estate, did your dad tell you?' I said.

Ruby stared at me in disbelief. 'That must have been, like, a million years ago?'

'Yeah,' I said, smiling. 'I left before you were born.'

Ruby shrugged and went back to her straw.

I started again, summoning a brighter tone. 'How's about we go shopping at the weekend, just us girls? We can go to McDonald's afterwards if you like.'

'Maybe.'

'Listen, I'm really sorry about what happened in the restaurant. I'm just so used to it being the three of us, I wasn't thinking.'

Ruby was listening but she didn't say anything.

'We're glad you're here, safe, with us,' I went on, but even as I said it I knew that, for me at least, it was a lie.

CHAPTER EIGHT

When I arrived home from work the following evening, Tom told me he'd got through to the grandmother, and that Ruby would be speaking to her later. Finally, some progress – and while I was sad for Ruby, I was also quite looking forward to her moving out. We'd support her and see her regularly but she would no longer be part of our household. Freya would gain a sister and I'd be able to develop a relationship with her without having my nose rubbed daily in Tom's infidelity. Seemed like a good compromise.

I poured myself a glass of wine in the kitchen then carried it into the living room where Freya was watching one of her *Pippi Longstocking* DVDs. My daughter had always been a thoughtful, interior child whose courage often failed her. For years, Pippi had been her invisible sister and her alter ego, the stroppy, crusading kid in whose fearless footsteps Freya desperately wished to tread.

I took her delicate hand with its ballet-pink nail beds in mine and she turned to look at me.

'You know that Ruby's arrival makes no difference at all to how much your father and I love you, don't you?'

She nodded.

'How would you feel about Ruby going to live with her grandmother? We'll still see her a lot, of course.'

Freya shrugged and twisted her body so that she was no longer directly facing me. She'd always been careful with her opinions, eager to please, and worried about offending.

Tom appeared then and, spotting my glass, just as quickly disappeared into the kitchen to fetch one for himself. When after a while he hadn't come back I got up and padded after him. The kitchen was empty. I figured he must be hiding in his study. The study door was pulled to but the light was on and I could hear the low repetitive rhythm of Ruby's voice coming from inside. Through the gap in the door, I saw her perched on Tom's desk with the phone in one hand. She seemed to be talking into the handset. There was no sign of Tom himself, though. I hadn't heard him going up the stairs, and was about to slip back into the kitchen on the assumption that he'd gone into the garden when something stopped me and I held my breath for a moment. What I thought I heard was repeated. I stood there listening for a few minutes longer. Ruby was on the phone but she wasn't talking. She was repeating the word 'blah' over and over again. '*Blah, blah, blah, blah.*' This went on until, pushing the door open, I walked into the room. The instant she saw me she threw down the phone. Her face was flushed.

'Did you get cut off?'

Ruby bit her lip and slid from the desk. 'She hung up.'

'You know what? She probably didn't realise you were still speaking. Why don't we call her back?'

'No, I'm going to my room.'

I watched her go up the stairs then returned to the kitchen to find Tom sitting at the table with a wine glass to his lips flipping through the pages of a gaming mag.

'What happened to you?'

He frowned and said defensively, 'I was in the garden.'

I told him about Ruby's strange behaviour in the study.

'This is all so weird. She won't speak to her own grandmother and she's barely mentioned her mother.'

'The poor kid's in shock.'

'Well, OK, but there's other weird stuff too. Aren't you bothered about the boiler man coming a week before the accident? Or the window in the bedroom being shut even though Ruby's mother almost always kept it open?' I'd mentioned this to Tom the day Ruby arrived but, just as he'd done then, he dismissed me with a wave of his hand.

'I've talked to the police. They checked the boiler. It was old. The pilot light went out. End of.' He seemed rattled and angry and I thought I knew why.

'How was the chat with Ruby's grandmother?'

'Meg. Her name's Meg,' he said irritably. I'd touched on a nerve.

'Is there a problem?'

Tom threw down his magazine. His face was a sudden hailstorm, then, just as quickly, it readjusted itself and, in a flat tone, he said, 'Look, we're going to need to have a rethink.

Meg Winter lives in a tiny one-bed flat on that arse-end of an estate. She has emphysema and she's basically a bitch. She's not prepared to take on Ruby.'

'Is this about money? Because if it is…' I was willing to pay.

'Maybe. Social services think there's some past history with drugs, so I'm not sure they'd let Meg have Ruby anyway.'

It took a moment for what he'd said to register. A feeling of panic rose up. 'Any other relatives?'

'An uncle. He's in prison. No one else.'

'Jesus, Tom. We can't do this. We don't know anything about her.' I heard myself listing all the reasons why it would be impossible for Ruby Winter to come and live with us. Tom let me finish, but I could see he wasn't listening.

When I ran out of steam, he said, 'Actually, we do know something about Ruby: she's my daughter. You think I want this any more than you do? But what choice do we have, really? We can't put her into care. She's family. We'll talk about getting some help tomorrow.'

'Help?'

Tom slid the magazine away. '*Obviously* we're going to need someone in the house. I can't look after two kids and work.'

'We can't afford "help".' Tom had borrowed money from his father to put into his business. For the last three or four years I'd been paying all the household expenses. The mortgage was huge and Tom had remained very attached to his expensive wine and skiing holidays. And now, what, another mouth to feed? The services of a childminder?

'Oh, but we *could* afford to pay a sick old junkie to take the problem away? What we *really* can't afford is for me not to be able to work. I'm nearly there, Cat.' He pinched his fingers. 'Just a whisker away.'

The anger on Tom's face had been replaced by a weary resignation. 'I know, it's a fucking nightmare.'

The door swung open and Freya's face appeared. She looked anxiously from one of us to the other.

'Will you come up and read me a story?'

I nodded a yes. 'You go up, I'll be there in five minutes.'

Tom waited until Freya had gone then muttered, 'You know, this has hit me too. But you might make a better job of trying to like Ruby.'

Then pushing his wine glass away, he sprang up and walked out of the door. Moments later, I heard the front door slam, then the sound of the car engine.

I slugged back the last of the wine, put both glasses in the dishwasher then climbed the stairs. Originally, I hadn't been minded to sympathise with Lilly Winter, but the visit to the Pemberton had changed things, made me regard her with more compassion, as a woman trapped inside a world from which she could not escape, a single mother who had been forced to borrow twenty pounds to pay a cowboy tradesman to fix the boiler that, as it turned out, would kill her. The visit had also made me glad all over again to have escaped. What it didn't do is make me any happier about living with her daughter.

From the upstairs landing, I could hear Freya brushing her teeth. Ruby was sitting on the bed in her pyjamas, holding a pen in her fist like a weapon. She looked up as I entered and the patched-on smile appeared on her face but her eyes were big with tears. I went to comfort her. As I approached I saw a series of crude squiggles on her arm. She had picked up a paper clip and, with her right hand, was pressing the cut end of the wire in under the fingernail of her left index finger. Blood had begun to bead out over the top of the nail. I reached towards her and grabbed her right wrist.

'Please, Ruby,' I said, extracting the paper clip from her hands. She was crying now, but when I cupped a hand around her head in an effort to comfort her, she stiffened. I felt terrible for wishing that she was somewhere, anywhere else but at Dunster Road. But still I did wish it.

'You know what happened to your mum wasn't your fault, don't you?'

Ruby turned her face to me.

'Your neighbour Gloria told me a man came to fix the boiler. Do you remember him? You won't get into trouble, but if you do know anything about him, you need to tell me.'

Ruby looked up and for an instant I thought I saw a pulse of alarm cross her face. There was a chill silence.

'Ruby?'

'I don't know what you're talking about. I never saw any boiler man.' The tears had all but dried up. She turned her back to me. 'I want to go to sleep now.'

I got up and pulled open the door to find Tom on the landing. Evidently I'd surprised him because he took a step back and angled his body away. His jaw had a peculiar set to it. I couldn't work out whether he was angry or afraid.

'I thought you'd gone out,' I said.

'Apparently I'm back.' He spread his arms. There was something hostile in the gesture. I followed him into our bedroom and shut the door.

'You of all people should know better than to bring up the accident,' he hissed, jabbing a finger at me. He'd obviously overheard. 'You think you know better than the police?'

'It's just weird, that's all.'

Tom was standing on the side of the bed nearest the window now, as if he couldn't bring himself to be near me. There was a cruel set to his mouth as he said, every word loaded with meaning, 'You know, I'm really beginning to think this is all making you a bit *paranoid*.' He turned on his heels and, with his hand on the door and his back to me, he said, 'I'll sleep downstairs tonight.'

I watched him disappear then moved across the landing to my daughter's room. She was sitting up in bed listening to something on her MP3 player. I lowered myself onto the bed beside her and she flipped off her headphones.

'How's about at the weekend you and Ruby and I go and do something you both want to do, OK? Then I thought maybe we could have lunch with Sally. She's so looking forward to meeting Ruby. And seeing you, obviously.'

Freya shrugged and mumbled something incoherent. I was taken aback. She loved her glamorous, fly-by-night auntie and the feeling was reciprocated. Why was she being so low-key? Maybe she'd heard Tom and me fighting?

'How does that sound?' I pressed.

She was frowning now, her mouth set in a little moue. Suddenly, as if out of the blue, she said, 'I want to swap rooms.'

The remark caught me off guard and I didn't have a ready reply.

'Ruby lived in a horrid place and her mum was drunk all the time and you could have rescued her but you didn't.'

I reeled back, genuinely shocked. No wonder my daughter's allegiances had shifted if Ruby had been drip-feeding her misinformation about what Tom and I did or didn't do. On the other hand, we only had ourselves to blame. I realised then that at no point during the last few days had I sat Freya down and talked through what had happened. Not in any detail. And, given Tom's preference for avoiding difficult conversations, I doubted he had either. Hardly surprising that Ruby had become Freya's chief source of information. She'd had no one else to turn to.

I sat with her on the bed and told her about the circumstances of Ruby's conception, about Tom and Lilly not really knowing one another and Tom having no idea of Ruby's existence till this week. I tried to reassure her that if we'd known about Ruby, we would have intervened.

'It's very kind of you to want to swap rooms, sweet pea, but it's not your job to try to make it up to Ruby for having a difficult time.'

Freya took a deep breath and gave me a long, hard, accusatory look.

'Well, whose job is it then?' she said.

* * *

The following two days were dominated by work. Joshua Barrons' scans had to be completed, there were the final amendments to the grant application to make, research data to analyse. When I got home Tom would be in his study working on *Labyrinth*, and the two girls would be playing in the garden, with the sawing and banging of the basement extension next door providing background accompaniment. Tom took to sleeping on the sofa bed in his study and we spoke only about domestic practicalities. But if everything appeared relatively smooth on the surface, the dynamics of the household, those intangible flows of energy that give a family shape and movement, had fundamentally changed. Without anyone making a conscious decision, there had been a shift. Ruby Winter had become part of the fabric of the place. She was here to stay.

Even as I adjusted to the fact, I didn't like it any better. Not least because a series of small, unexplained events gave me cause to wonder if the bond between my daughter and my stepdaughter was a relationship of equals. On Thursday evening, a small silver locket Sal had given Freya and to which she had long been terribly attached turned up in Ruby's room. Both girls insisted they had no idea how it had got there but it was clear in my mind that Freya had either given it to Ruby or Ruby had taken it. After that, a bottle of perfume on my dressing table disappeared. The girls denied all knowledge, but I noticed after it had gone a faint remnant of freesias and musk on the landing. Then, on Friday evening, when I was in the kitchen clearing up, something more significant happened. Freya came thundering downstairs yelling that the hamster had disappeared. The door to the cage was open and she'd searched her bedroom but Harry wasn't there.

For the next hour all four of us scoured the house and, finding nothing, eventually had to resign ourselves to the likely possibility that Harry had escaped and been devoured by the cat. Freya was inconsolable, convinced it was her fault, full of self-recrimination and bewilderment, since she was also sure she hadn't left the cage open. When she'd finally cried herself into a daze, I helped her to bed and sat stroking her hair, reassuring her that Harry hadn't suffered and that we would explain what had happened to the school then go to the pet shop and get another hamster which she and Ruby could share.

While all this was going on, I noticed, Ruby Winter kept her own counsel but there was something about her withdrawal that felt strategic. She denied all knowledge of the hamster's whereabouts but I wasn't sure I believed her. While I'd taken on board the social worker's entreaties to expect the unexpected in Ruby, and I knew from my own experience of child psychology that numbness along with denial and a simple inability to process the events are some of the ways kids – and adults – cope following a parent's death, it still felt ominous to me that here we were nearly five days after Lilly Winter's demise and the only reaction Ruby had shown to that momentous event had been to act out, steal things and cut herself with a paper clip. I worried that we'd allowed a deeply disturbed girl into our house and given her unsupervised access to our daughter. In what world was this a good idea? The more I thought about it the more I became convinced that if Ruby was to stay with us, we'd need to get her some therapeutic help. The sooner the better.

Tom had other ideas.

'How would you feel if your mother had just died? All she needs is stability.' We were sitting on the sofa on Friday night, long after the girls had gone to bed. We'd both had a few glasses of wine. Since Ruby's arrival Tom and I had been drinking far too much. It wasn't helping, I knew.

I mentioned the paper clip incident. 'What if Freya copies her?'

'Why would she?'

'You see the way our daughter looks at Ruby, like she's some sort of red-haired goddess.' As I said this, I noticed the resentment in my voice. 'Look, I'm not denying the awfulness of Ruby's situation or saying I don't want her to be part of the family, but neither do I want our daughter being drawn into a fucked-up situation. You know how eager to please she is.'

Tom drummed his fingers on his wine glass in an effort to quieten his irritation. 'I'm not putting my daughter into care, Cat, and I'm not getting her any therapy so perhaps you'd just stop fucking going on about it and let us get on with our lives.'

He picked up his phone to indicate that the conversation was over and left the room. Ten minutes later, I heard the front door close and that was the end of that.

CHAPTER NINE

The weekend arrived. While Tom was at the park practising for his five-a-side league, I drove the two girls to a shopping centre in West London. I hadn't intended to go retail crazy or to let the girls do so either, but in Claire's Accessories Ruby proved unstoppable, loading her basket with whatever came to hand, and the sight of this thin spindle of a girl snatching at gewgaws as if they were tiny life rafts in an uncertain sea brought back such poignant memories of my own childhood spent rooting for swag in Brixton's charity shops that I shelled out for whatever Ruby decided she wanted.

We bundled our haul into a couple of carrier bags and made it to McDonald's in time to meet Sally, who was already sitting at a table waiting for us, with an obvious whisker burn on her chin and a hungry gleam in her eyes. She winked at me to say, *We'll talk about this later*, then stood and embraced both girls and I was struck by how willingly Ruby allowed herself to be hugged. She even smiled with her eyes when Sally asked her what she'd bought, pulling a few things from the bags to show them off, and

I was surprised to find myself envying them, just a little, for the ease with which their relationship had begun.

After a while, Freya and Ruby went off to order. The moment they were out of hearing range, Sal said, 'She's *adorable*, poor mite. All that *hair*.'

'I do worry about Freya, though.'

'Why? Freya looks amazed by her,' Sally said.

'Exactly.'

Sally frowned her disapproval then moved towards me and, slinging an arm around my neck, dropped a kiss on my cheek. 'Don't be such an Anxious Annie.'

The shopping trip really seemed to have helped Ruby turn a corner. All through lunch, she chattered and cooed happily, laughing and sucking up Sally's tips on everything from how to apply nail polish to how to keep red hair in good condition. Lunch was followed by an uncomplicated afternoon back home and, by the end of the day, I really thought that maybe Tom and Sal were right and everything *would* settle down and I would find a way to forgive Tom and that the arrival of Ruby might actually mark a turning point in our marriage. Maybe I *should* stop being such an Anxious Annie.

The good feeling lasted through Sunday. It was hot, of course. I made scrambled eggs and Freya showed Ruby how to decorate the toast with stencils. Then Tom went to his match and the girls played outside until it was time to get dressed up and head next door to Charlie Frick's party. While they were away, I busied myself with some housework. It was while I was vacuuming Freya's room that I found my perfume bottle under the bed. I'd assumed Ruby had been responsible for the bottle's disappearance but it now seemed my daughter wasn't the innocent she was making herself out to be. This was new and unsettling. A Freya I didn't recognise.

Around five, the girls returned, hot, tired and triumphant from the party, dropped goodie bags at the door and zoomed into the garden to claim the final few hours of sunshine. When I went out with iced lemonade an hour or so later they were performing cartwheels in their underpants and T-shirts. Ruby was wearing two friendship bracelets on her bony wrist and an orange T-shirt she had selected from the rack in H&M, which, in combination with her hair, lent her a biblical look, like a pillar of fire.

I called them to me and, handing over the lemonade, asked once again about the perfume. Ruby turned towards Freya and, with her back partly to me, I saw her flash her sister a conspiratorial look.

'Maybe Pudge moved it,' Freya said. I thought I saw something dark I'd never seen before scuttle across her face.

'Don't lie to me, Freya!' I said. I was suddenly afraid I was losing her.

It was then I noticed the bruise on her right arm, in the tender stretch of skin just above the crook of the elbow.

'How did you get that?'

'She fell off the trampoline.' Ruby Winter's face tilted towards mine. Perhaps it was just the effects of the heat, mixed with my own confusion, but when our eyes met I found my head filling with visions of imps, goblins and sinister spirits. Ruby Winter was lying. I knew it and she knew I knew it.

'I don't believe you,' I said.

Ruby's head swung round to look at Freya then back again to me. Then she raised her chin and a little smile came on her lips and, with a dismissive gesture of the head, she said, 'I don't give a fuck what you think.'

Freya took in a big breath and looked away.

At that moment, Tom strode out through the back door. He'd returned in an upbeat mood, his team having won their match, and immediately challenged Ruby to a game on the Wii. Freya and I sat on the sofa reading. I decided to not to confront the girls about their behaviour because I wasn't convinced that Tom would back me. I'd wait until I got them on their own again. Maybe there was some innocent explanation for the bruises on Freya's arm, but I wasn't prepared to take the chance. Tom and I hadn't returned to our fraught discussions about his daughter but I was decided. I would not allow Ruby Winter to continue living with us unless we got her some professional help.

Tom and Ruby were finishing their game when the doorbell rang. Shelly Frick was standing in the porch with her fingers pressed together, her head cocked, and with an alarmingly immaculate expression of concern on her face. Though that could also have been the Botox.

'Is something wrong?'

'Probably not, but...' Shelly continued to witter for a while then finally managed to spit out what she'd actually come to say. The iPad Charlie Frick had been given for his birthday by his grandparents had gone missing. 'It's in a blue plastic case with a sort of handle. This is a bit awkward, but Charlie says he saw your girls with it.' Shelly withdrew a small piece of paper from her pocket and held it out. 'And I found this.'

It was a note addressed to Charlie written in alternating red and blue pens.

Dear Charlie,

We are sorry your birthday had an unhappy ending.

The red handwriting was Freya's. The blue was unfamiliar but I guessed it belonged to Ruby.

I took the note, apologised and promised to look round the house.

'I'm sure it's all a misunderstanding,' I said, unconvincingly.

The girls were sitting where I'd left them, Freya buried in her book and Ruby at the Wii with Tom.

I relayed what Shelly had told me. The girls exchanged glances. Neither of them said anything. I went on, addressing myself this time to Freya, who was the easier target. 'Maybe you thought you were just borrowing it?'

Freya looked at her lap.

'Ruby?'

The girl sighed and rolled her eyes. 'We don't know anything about the iPad. One of the boys was crying because he didn't like his party bag so we just, like, wrote a note to be nice to Charlie.'

I said, 'I'm sorry, Ruby, but I don't believe you.'

Tom shot me a disapproving look. 'For heaven's sake, Cat, stop going on and on. You heard them. They don't know anything.'

I didn't believe that either. They all knew something but whether it was the same something or a set of different some-things I had no idea. All I knew was that, whatever *they* each knew, no one was telling *me*.

CHAPTER TEN

The events of that evening left me watchful and troubled but they seemed to have the opposite effect on Tom. By the time I turned in he'd been asleep in our bed for a couple of hours. Trying not to wake him, I crept under the sheets. My thigh brushed against something. Imagining a balled-up tissue, a sock or maybe some underwear, I reached down only to find my hand clamped around something soft and covered in fur with sharp points. Horrified, I threw off the sheet and scooted from the bed.

'Jesus, what is it?' Tom's voice was still heavy with sleep.

The edginess in my voice caught me by surprise. 'There's something on the mattress.'

'A husband?' Tom said drily.

I turned on the bedside lamp and saw a tiny leg with a foot attached. The sharp points I'd felt were hamster claws.

'Oh, God, it's Harry.'

'Jesus Christ! What's it doing there? Pudge must have got him. Go back to sleep, we'll deal with it in the morning.' But something told me this wasn't the cat's doing. And I knew too that when the morning came we wouldn't deal with it, not really, because to deal with it would mean confronting Ruby and Tom would not allow it.

It was then I started to wonder if there wasn't more to Tom's protectiveness than paternal concern.

* * *

Another unpleasant discovery on my run into work on Monday: a stabbing on Holland Hill. It had happened overnight. Two teenagers caught in some terrible and pointless turf war. I thought about James White saying that we get the kids we deserve. And then I forgot about it in the hectic rush of budget meetings, scans, research papers and clinical work. One notable thing: I had no further contact with the Master of the Neuroverse, so it looked as though the business with James White had died down.

In the afternoon, Emma Barrons came by on her way to pick up her son from the clinic. She seemed jittery and on her jawline I noticed a cut but Emma dismissed it as nothing. A little accident in the shower.

'Did Joshua tell you he'd seen you in the park? He was with his nanny.'

'No, he didn't.' I *had* seen Joshua and his nanny near the lake on my run. The nanny had been wearing a striking pair of red shoes, but I didn't think either of them had recognised me. Even if they had, it would have been crossing professional boundaries to have acknowledged them or to have mentioned anything to Emma Barrons.

'How do you think he's getting on?' I said.

We chatted for a while about Joshua and, as Emma was leaving, I brought up the cut again and suggested that if it happened another time she ring one of the domestic violence helplines.

'I can give you some numbers if you like,' I said.

She flapped a hand as if trying to hold back tears, then, taking a hold of herself, she said, 'Oh, I wouldn't dream of wasting their time. Not for a silly slip in the shower.'

* * *

When I got back that evening the house was empty. Tom had taken the girls to one of the summer blockbusters. I poured myself a Diet Coke from the fridge and as soon as I went into the living room I knew something had changed. It took me a while to work out what was different and the moment I did it seemed so obvious I was astonished it hadn't jumped out at me the second I'd walked in the room.

On the table in the bay window with all the other family pictures sat a framed photograph of a thin-faced woman with red hair and a face so white it was as if she were peeled down to the skull. It was Lilly Winter. I felt an overwhelming need to leave the room. Returning to the kitchen, I noticed, as I poured away the Coke I no longer wanted, that my hand was trembling. What was a picture of my husband's dead lover doing on the table with the family photographs? Surely even Tom couldn't have been *that* insensitive? More likely, I thought, it was Ruby's doing. Either way, it seemed my home was no longer my own and that it had been taken over by a ghost – and the ghost's troubled daughter.

An opened bottle of Pinot Grigio stood in the fridge. I took it and went out through the French doors into the garden. Despite the late hour there was still heat in the sun and the air was noisy with next door's diggers. I sat on the bench under the leylandii tree at the back of our patch where I always went to think. For years Tom and I had been promising to take the tree down – it was sprawling and unattractive and it cast a shade on the rest of the garden – but for some reason we'd never got round to it and, over the years, it had become the place I went to when I needed to think clearly. I had named it the 'ideas tree' and was attached to its quiet company. I sat for a long time under its branches now, trying to empty my mind of the image of my husband's lover, but it was firmly lodged in my brain, only one among hundreds of thousands stacked like old newspapers in a vast library, but every bit as indelible. I idly flicked through the catalogue, by date order, from mine and Tom's first few dates, our weekends away, holidays, Christmases with friends and family, mental images of Tom in our first flat, bursting from the Ritzy cinema in a spray of laughter at the film we'd just seen, Tom buying oranges in the market, Tom playing computer games, Tom looking out at the view from Waterloo Bridge, Tom crouched over my hospital bed with a newborn Freya in his arms. But no matter how many images I had stored away or how vital the memories they conjured, none would now erase the ghost of Lilly Winter.

One picture stayed at the front of my mind. It must have been taken nearly fifteen years ago. Tom and I had only recently moved into the flat in Brixton. Our neighbour there, Paul Fellowes, was an art director for a free sheet called *London Style*. Shortly after we moved in, we invited him for a drink and a couple of days later he knocked on the door and he said he'd like to feature us in a photo essay. The idea was to take a picture of ten couples who were in some way emblematic of the capital. Paul was going to call the essay 'Ten Defining Twenty-First-Century Couples'. And he wanted us, a science geek and a gaming geek, to feature as Couple Number One.

I didn't want to do it, but Tom managed to twist my arm. Paul showed up a week later with a lanky kid who styled us in borrowed gear that made both of us look way hipper than we were, and before we knew it our picture was stacked in piles outside every Tube station above the legend 'Couple Number One'.

What followed was completely unexpected. Invitations began to arrive, slowly at first then almost daily, to gallery openings for artists we didn't know, book launches for writers we'd never heard of, celebrations of obscurely distilled boutique vodkas we were never going to drink, and birthday celebrations of people we only knew from seeing their names in the papers. It was bullshit but by the time we realised that, we were already along for the ride. Besides, it was bullshit with benefits. Games developers began calling Tom, wanting to work with him. At the time he was working at a small start-up with only one moderately successful game under its belt but only a couple of weeks after the piece in *London Style* came out, he got an approach from Adrenalyze, the coolest gamers in the capital. The job was perfect, the pay was amazing and they wanted him to start as soon as he could. My husband was in geek heaven.

But then, only months later, a dog walker came upon the body of Kylie Drinkwater in an East Anglian wood, Rees Spelling was arrested, and the press descended on the flat in Brixton like some malevolent blizzard, keen to pick over my part as an expert witness in the first trial. My chief persecutor throughout that terrible time was James White. His coverage was outrageous, incendiary and not entirely wrong but the effects were monumental. I was accused of being misguided, unprofessional, in cahoots with criminals, almost everything short of actually murdering Kylie. For months I was forced to shuttle by cab between work and home to avoid reporters. I didn't go out, I barely saw friends or family; I became virtually a prisoner, safe only in my home or at the institute. A few weeks after Spelling was tried and convicted for Kylie's murder the media lost interest but by then Tom and I had become Couple Number One in a whole new context. No more invitations and freebies. No parties or boutique vodka. People we'd considered friends drifted away, extended family members stopped calling, neighbours no longer waved hello on the stairwell. Even Paul Fellowes went out of his way to avoid us.

Tom took our fall from the number one spot badly. Even though it was all hot air, and we both knew that, Tom had loved the ride. His career suffered too. Adrenalyze held back from letting him go but they soon found a way to sideline him.

The publicity was too much for the institute. I was forced to give up clinical and court work and move into the less public realm of research.

But I wasn't so bothered about our status or even my career. What *I* couldn't get over was knowing that in an indirect way I was responsible for the death of Kylie Drinkwater. If I hadn't misjudged the threat Rees Spelling posed, he might not have been released back into the community and left free to kill.

Once the worst was over Tom and I stopped talking about the case. It was all too painful. But even though he would never admit it, I'm pretty sure my husband never quite forgave me. I never quite forgave myself.

A voice propelled me back into the present. Shelly was standing at the garden fence with a forced smile on her face. 'Oh, Caitlin, I'm so glad I've caught you. I don't, um, suppose you found Charlie's iPad?'

I relayed what the girls had told me, even though I didn't really believe it. It was evident from Shelly's reaction she didn't believe it either. Pointing to a gap in the fence panel where it had come loose from its vertical and, adopting an icy tone, she said, 'Well, anyway, I was hoping you might get that fixed since it's on your side.'

After she'd gone, I finished up my wine and went back into the house, picked up the photograph and, holding it picture side down, took it upstairs and left it on Ruby's bedside table.

Sometime later Tom and the girls returned. When the kids

had gone to bed, I cleared away the evening meal and Tom went into his study. Neither of us said anything about the photograph. Intending to check over the grant application for the final time before submitting it, I took another bottle of wine and a bar of chocolate into the living room, put the wine down on the table and settled myself on the sofa. It was then I saw it. The picture of Lilly Winter was once more sitting among the family photographs by the window. I got up and knocked on Tom's study door.

'Did Ruby bring that picture of her mother back down?'

Tom lifted his head from the screen and, looking steadily at me, said, 'No, I did.'

I felt something inside crack. 'What makes you think I need your dead lover looking at me every time I enter my own living room?'

Tom sucked his teeth in a manner that was both high-handed and patronising. 'Really, Cat, there's no need to get so worked up. It wasn't my idea. The social worker said it was important for Ruby to keep her mother's memory alive.'

'Can't she do that in her own room?'

Tom shot me the kind of pained look you might give an errant child. 'If you absolutely insist. I thought you were better than this, I really did.'

* * *

Sleep eluded me again that night. The gnawing, rotten heat didn't help, but the real problem was Lilly Winter. Over and over again, I'd be about to drop off when a mental image of Tom and Lilly sprang into my mind fully formed. *A dingy B&B.* I could see the ugly desk with its pleather chair, the strapped luggage rack and the tiny silent TV and, in the midst of it all, of course, Tom and Lilly naked, their limbs tangled together, sheeny in the muggy aftermath of sex. I kept telling myself, *She's dead, she's gone*, but Lilly Winter was very far from gone. She was there in my living room on the family photo table, she was there among the rubble of my husband's memories, and she was there in the girl sleeping across the hallway.

I thought about Ruby then. Was she responsible for washing up on our doorstep? No. Was it even her fault that I didn't like her? Of course not. Her origins would always have made that hard. The truth was, I resented her both for who she was and for where she came from. And yes, I knew how poorly that reflected on me but you know what? Deep down, knowing that didn't make me like Ruby Winter any more.

* * *

I must have worn myself to sleep eventually because I woke with the fading fragments of a dream still playing in my mind. Lilly and I were in the locker room of the local municipal pool getting dressed after a swim. I had left my purse in one of the lockers and wanted to retrieve it but Lilly had the key and she was in the shower.

A light was on in the bathroom. Evidently, Tom was having trouble sleeping too. I checked my watch and saw it was early.

Then my eyes fell on the date. The second of August. Our wedding anniversary and also, by some creepy coincidence, the day of the Lilly Winter's funeral.

CHAPTER ELEVEN

I was downstairs in the kitchen making breakfast when Freya appeared.

'Is Ruby awake?'

'She wants a lie-in,' Freya said, placing four juice glasses on the table before taking a seat and helping herself to Shredded Wheat. I moved behind her and began idly stroking her hair. This was the first morning since Ruby's arrival that I'd had my daughter to myself. I hadn't fully absorbed quite how much I'd missed her company. She'd grown quieter in the last couple of days and I was worried that the funeral might be too much for her. But there was also an anxious ticking at the back of my mind, a faint suggestion that Ruby had something to do with her subdued mood. I was tempted to ask but I wasn't convinced she'd tell me. I took the seat beside her and we ate our cereal in silence for a bit. While she busied herself, I checked her face for signs of fragility but saw only the remains of the night's sleep.

Eventually, Freya put down her spoon. 'Mum, you're not going to die for ages, are you?'

So she *was* feeling anxious. I laid a reassuring hand on her head. 'Of course not, darling. Look, there's *really*, honestly, no need for you to come today. I can stay behind with you and we can have a lovely day together if you like. Your father and Ruby will understand.' I wanted her to say yes but I wasn't surprised when she shook her head.

'Ruby says anyone can die any time.'

My mind buzzed.

'Well, that's factually true, but it's so unlikely to happen to any of us any time soon that you don't have to think about it.'

'It happened to Ruby's mum,' Freya said, sounding unconvinced.

'That was just a terrible accident. A freak event. Freak events are freakish because they hardly ever happen.' I thought about the plumber fixing Lilly Winter's boiler. *Was* it a terrible accident, a freak event? Or something else?

In any case, my words were of little comfort to Freya. In a shrill voice she said, 'But hardly ever isn't never.'

I rested my hand on my daughter's head once again and she leaned in to it and allowed me to comfort her for a moment, but we both knew I'd lost the argument.

Freya had gone back upstairs to get dressed by the time Ruby Winter appeared. Instead of the purple dress Ruby had picked out at the shop (which she had insisted upon, despite my considering it far too old and sophisticated to be suitable) she was wearing a navy pinafore of Freya's that we'd bought for our daughter's birthday. The dress hung off her and I thought about saying something then decided that, in the circumstances, it hardly mattered.

As she launched herself like a wild thing on the cereal, I sat down beside her. Despite her thinness she looked strangely invulnerable, like a thread of spider silk, and I was moved to reach out a hand and touch her just to see if she was real. As my fingers neared, she whisked her hand away. It was a calculated rejection.

I turned and stood, swallowing away any hostile feelings once my back was to her so as not to give her the satisfaction of having got to me. After pouring myself another cup of coffee, I resumed my seat.

'I'm wondering if it might help to go through again what to expect today?' Tom and I had both taken Ruby through the likely programme of events. We'd talked about the hearse arriving, the service, the coffin progressing along its rollered conveyor towards its final destination, the curtains discreetly whining closed.

She had finished her cereal and was twirling the spoon around in the milk.

I tried again. 'Is there anything you'd like to know?'

Her eyes widened and a kind of brightness came over her face as if a light had been turned on inside her head. 'Will there be ice cream afterwards?'

'If you want it.'

She moved back on her chair and turned towards me. 'I bet you're happy about Lilly Winter dying. If I was you, I would be.'

* * *

Later, in the shower, I thought about myself at Ruby Winter's age. Dad had gone back to Jamaica and more or less disappeared from our lives and our mother, Heather, had embarked on what Sally and I later referred to as the Slow Stoli Suicide Slide, though by then, strictly speaking, Stoli had given way to the kind of cheap, supermarket vodka that comes in two-litre bottles. I hadn't thought about Heather in years, at least not in any sustained way. A shrink once told me that living in the present meant giving up all hope of a better past. And that's what I'd tried hard to do. Since Ruby Winter's arrival, though, the dark places I thought I had escaped had come boomeranging back as if they had been out there in the air all this while, tracking their elliptical orbit back to me. Alcohol, abandonment, life in the Ends. Even the drive to the South London Crematorium, which I was dreading, would only be a replay of an earlier event.

Twelve years had passed since the coffin containing my mother's body had been rolled into the furnace. The grief I felt at my mother's funeral was less about the body lying in the coffin than the final extinguishing of the distant but still vivid hope that Sal and I would ever have a loving mother. Sal and I had returned only once since, to scatter her ashes in the rose garden. Then we'd brushed her dust from our hands and walked away. I wanted life for Freya to be different from mine and Sally's. I wanted for her to be able to live fully in the present with no reason to have to look back.

* * *

Arriving at the crematorium, we left the car park and walked slowly across hot tarmac. The girls ran on ahead, attracted by a graceless water feature to one side of the main building, while Tom and I headed towards a small knot of mourners gathered in the shade of a drought-browned sycamore to await the hearse. Two stragglers from the previous funeral lingered by the entrance, in the hands of one a photo of a boy not much older than Freya who I recognised from one of the newer shrines near the park. I guessed from the raw shock on the family's faces that it had been a sudden and violent death. South London had seen too many of those recently: kids killed by kids. People said a few days' rain would put a stop to it, at least for a while, but the rain hadn't come.

A tiny gnarled woman with a hard, edgy, heavy smoker's mien and short, faded red hair was standing nearest to the entrance of the chapel. From the way people approached then retreated around her, I guessed this was Meg Winter. We still hadn't spoken and I had a feeling Tom would prefer it to stay that way. He'd never told me what exactly had been said between them and he'd made it clear he didn't want to be asked.

I waited until my husband was engaged in conversation with one of the mourners before I approached her, then introduced myself and offered the customary condolences. She seemed more overwhelmed than sad.

'Is Ruby your only grandchild?' I asked. There were no other children present.

Her eyes darted about. 'One's enough.' I turned to see what she was looking at and caught Tom's eye. Meg turned her gaze back to me. 'Why have you come? There's nothing for you here.' There was no aggression in her tone, only a wariness I didn't understand.

'I hope you're not offended,' I said. People are apt to blurt all kinds of things at funerals, I thought. At Tom's mother's funeral I heard someone whisper, as I walked up the aisle to give a reading, 'Fingers crossed we're not going to get a *rap* song.' Later, a woman with what looked like an overbaked meringue on her head approached me over the Waitrose platters and said, 'You must be so pleased the mayor's here.' For a while that became our family catchphrase. Whenever Tom and I were doing something we didn't want to do, scraping ground-in food off Freya's high chair or clearing the garden of fox shit, one of us would pipe up, 'I'm so pleased the mayor's here.'

Whatever was going through her mind, my response seemed to have calmed her a little. She shrugged her shoulders and in that gesture I saw my chance.

'Ruby seems to be getting on so well with our daughter Freya.'

Something flitted across Meg's leathery face. Maybe she was just a bitch, like Tom said, and maybe Ruby did hate her, but we were at her daughter's funeral and I decided that now was hardly the time to rush to judgement. Besides, I had cooked up a plan in the middle of the night and I needed Meg to pull it off.

'Are there any other family members here?' It was usual at these things to be able to detect a genetic thread in the crowd, but, so far, apart from Meg, I hadn't spotted anyone who even vaguely resembled Ruby or her mother.

Meg shook her head decisively. 'Me and Lilly never kept up with family.'

'Oh, well, we're glad to have Ruby – and you – in ours. You must come and see us,' I went on, as sincerely as I could. From across the small collection of heads, I saw Tom's eye flick towards me as he tried to extricate himself from a conversation with a young woman. 'We'd love to have you over for a meal.' I scrolled through my mental calendar as if the idea had only just occurred to me. 'Say, tomorrow?'

Meg Winter looked a little taken aback. 'I could, I suppose.'

'We'll see you at seven then.' I pulled out a notebook from my pocket, scribbled down the address and handed it to her.

At that moment, the hearse appeared and a cheap coffin containing the corpse of Lilly Winter slid along rollers into the waiting hands of the bearers and into a sombre, wood-panelled room smelling of floor polish and formaldehyde.

We walked into the chapel as a family, Freya holding on to my hand while Ruby took her father's. A rent-a-vicar gave a passable eulogy during which I learned nothing new about my once-rival other than her age – thirty-two – and the fact that, like me, she'd grown up on the Pemberton, had done moderately well in her studies and worked, variously, as a beautician and a hairdresser. I was sure I hadn't known her, the seven-year difference in our ages being sufficient to keep us apart, but our paths must have crossed every so often without either of us having registered the other. I was hardly in a position to mourn the dead woman but I was nonetheless struck by an abstract sense of loss. My thoughts went to that night all those years ago when Lilly Winter and my husband had – unwittingly? – created the reason we were here today. Had she ever longed for Tom to return? Or regretted what she had done?

Ruby reacted to the perfunctory rundown of her mother's life with indifference. Once or twice she swung her legs back and forth under the pew and gazed with rapt attention at her shoes. Other times she stared ahead, her face expressionless, eyes unfocused, and I recalled what the social worker had told us, that she would likely be numb for a while or, conversely, that her feelings would be as intense and fragmentary as comets and she would be blindsided as they shot past. The social worker had produced a pocketful of metaphors. Roller coasters, thunderclouds, stormy seas.

Afterwards, when everyone was processing outside to look at the flowers, a ritual that had always seemed oddly beside the point, or milled around, holding their faces to the sun to remind themselves that they were, as yet, among the living, I was surprised by the almost complete absence of grief. A young woman had died in horrible circumstances, leaving a child behind, and no one seemed anguished by this or even much surprised. To be so little mourned seemed itself a cause for mourning but I couldn't bring myself to do it. Instead, I wondered what impact Lilly Winter's death might have, and where it had left us.

Ruby and Freya were at the fountain with Tom, demonstrating some water trick they'd come up with, and, as I swung my head back to catch one last scent of the bunches of lilies now lying baking in the sun, I spotted Gloria, standing on her own in a leopard-print dress. I went over.

'Nice family,' she said, meaning mine.

I did my best to smile.

'You husband look nothing like Ruby.' Gloria leaned in and, tapping her finger on my chest, said, 'I tell you one thing, Lilly have a lot of men.'

The heating engineer sprung to mind along with the compelling idea that he and Lilly Winter might have been closer than Gloria supposed. I asked Gloria if she had heard from him. She took a beat before she shook her head and I got the feeling she knew something she wasn't about to tell me. Instead, she gave me a searching look and, placing her hand on the crook of my arm, added, 'How are you find the girl? Pleasant?'

My eyes flitted momentarily to the fountain. Freya and Ruby were no longer in view but I supposed they couldn't have gone far. Tom was over by the sycamore talking to someone. I wondered whether sharing my disquiet about Ruby might encourage Gloria to say whatever was on her mind, but we were only acquaintances and there was no reason for her to trust me. In the end I plumped for something equivocal and diplomatic. 'I think she's struggling to know how to react to the new situation. We all are really.'

A crimp appeared at the corner of Gloria's eyes and she withdrew her hand.

'Are you trying to tell me something about Ruby?'

Gloria raised herself up a little. Her eyes flitted about as if she were afraid of being heard and she tilted her head towards me, saying in a low voice, 'I don't know about this girl.'

My throat had tightened into a knot and it took a cough to clear it.

I could see Gloria pause in her thoughts as if questioning herself then she leaned back, withdrawing. A small, uncertain smile played on her face.

'Well, I go now, it was nice talking.'

She hurried away. As I turned back to the crowd, my eye caught the quiver of air above the furnace chimney. I looked around for the girls but couldn't see them anywhere. At the far end of the chapel a path turned along an ivy-spattered red-brick wall. Where the path gave out onto an open area two figures were seated on the grass bent over a memorial slab so preoccupied with some joke they didn't hear me approaching. As I got closer I understood what they were laughing about. Someone had scratched out two of the letters in the name on the slab and carved a horizontal to run through a double 'L' so the name, formerly Pearl Shill, now read Pear Shitt. The scratch marks looked new, the lines still raw and un-weathered. It didn't take a genius to work out who'd done it. For a moment or two I tussled with myself, then decided not to make a fuss. What kind of person gives a kid grief at her mother's funeral?

We drove home in silence. The parking space outside our house had been filled with a skip for the building works next door. Tom continued on a little way then backed in between two parked cars and the girls clattered off down the street towards number forty-two. I waited behind, knowing Tom and

I had air to clear and wanting to do it before we went inside the house. The electronic key *pluk-pluked* and Tom swung his head around to look at me.

'You just couldn't leave the Meg thing alone, could you?' He slammed the car keys into his pocket and gave me a look to shrink a giant, then stormed off down the street. I went after him and grabbed his arm and held him back.

'We have to talk.' I told him about the memorial slab. 'This isn't about me, Tom. I worry about Ruby being around Freya. If she's going to stay with us, we have to get her some help. Otherwise her grandmother is going to have to take her, at least for some of the time.'

Tom strode off without answering, leaving me to follow on with my tail between my legs like some chastened puppy.

Freya and Ruby were waiting by the front door. Tom unlocked the door and ushered them in. I was bringing up the rear, when I saw Tom freeze at something over my shoulder. An instant later the front gate squealed and I swung about and found myself face to face with a wiry man in his forties, with heavy, dark-blond eyebrows and weak blue, vaguely Scandinavian eyes. I hadn't seen him in nearly a decade but I would have recognised James White anywhere.

Addressing himself to me, White said, 'I thought you should know there's been another stabbing. Victim twelve years old, fifteen-year-old kid being questioned by police.'

My eyes bladed over to Tom who was standing with his hand on the door, blocking the entryway. Behind him in the hallway the two girls had stopped talking and were staring at the visitor.

No one moved for a second or two then Tom eye-rolled and went inside, slamming the door.

Turning back to White, I said, 'Please leave.' I wasn't going to give White the satisfaction of knowing that his article had got me into trouble.

White held out a staying hand. 'Look, I know you're treating Christopher Barrons' son.'

I felt my breath go walkabout. First the clinic, now this. How had he found out about Joshua Barrons? It was a sackable offence to leak details of patients. I was sure no one at the clinic would have been so indiscreet. Which left Emma Barrons herself. But what possible benefit could she have seen in exposing her boy to the attentions of the press and public? All I could think of was that she and her husband were engaged in the worst kind of destructive power play. I didn't want any part in it.

'I have nothing to say to you,' I said and, turning on my heels, strode up the path. I keyed the door open and slammed it behind me, leaning back against it, my hands in tight fists at my hips, trying to compose myself. Tom's voice was coming from the kitchen, telling the children to go upstairs. A moment later, he appeared in the hallway with a face like a hailstorm.

'I sent him packing.'

'Good.' Tom took a breath and collected himself. He seemed almost unnaturally calm now. 'You know, you keep going on about Ruby getting help but maybe it's you who needs the help. You really don't seem very stable right now, Caitlin, and we both know where that can lead.'

He looked at me and in his eyes I thought I saw something of the old Tom, the old us, then in a flat voice he mumbled, 'I've got work to do.' He turned his back to me and headed towards his study. I called his name before he got to the door and he twisted his head.

'Happy anniversary,' I said.

He gave me a weary look and disappeared.

* * *

'Are you OK? You sound weird,' Sally said, when I related the events of the day on the phone later, leaving out the incident with White.

'Yes, no. I'm fine. I'm just finding all this quite difficult to deal with.'

A sigh. 'Look, I know you're really protective of Freya.' Her voice softened. 'I get that. But maybe you're projecting, just a bit?'

'*Projecting?*'

'I'm just wondering maybe if you're somehow playing out some old shit here. You told me Ruby's mother was a drinker so I'm just thinking, maybe this is stirring up old feelings. I really did need saving back then, Cat, and you saved me and that was amazing. But Ruby's not Heather. And Freya's not me. I'm just saying, maybe you should cut Freya a little slack and trust her to make up her own mind about her sister. And be a bit easier on yourself while you're at it. You're under a lot of pressure right now and no one wants you to...' She tailed off.

I laughed. A mean, contemptuous laugh. 'Thank you so much for your fucking amazing psychological insights, Dr Sally. I might even take them seriously if you were actually qualified to give them.'

'Ouch.'

I apologised. Anger can turn anyone into a bitch.

'That's OK,' said my sister.

There was a pause during which an idea dropped into my head.

'Shit, Tom *called* you, didn't he? That's why you're calling me.'

My sister let the air out between her lips. 'He's just concerned about you, Cat. We both are.'

I could hear Sal's voice carrying on as I cut the call. Then I sat back, winded by the realisation that, for the first time in my life, I could no longer confide in the only person whose loyalty I had, up to that point, never questioned.

Later, in our bed, watching Tom's chest rise and fall in the dimness of our room, I wondered what was left of us. I remembered turning to Tom one time, not long after we'd got together. It was a Sunday morning and Tom had just brought up coffee – in those days we always had it in bed – and we were having one of those generalised metaphysical lovers' discussions which are really just analogues for questions they dare not ask directly. I remember saying, 'Do you think every relationship has a predetermined amount of love? Or, like, a fixed amount of trust? And once you've used up all the love or the trust then that's it? But there's no way to know in advance how much there was to start with until it's gone?'

Tom laughed – he found my worrywart self charming back then – and, taking my face in his hands, he said, 'Cat, I think we should have a baby, don't you?'

And, of course, I said yes.

The reality of trying to get pregnant took us both by surprise. The tests and investigations, the endless prodding around, the hollowing news that we would be unlikely to conceive naturally. Then, at the clinic appointments which followed, the porn-filled cubicles, the countless injections, and the awful cycle of raised and dashed hopes. Infertility isn't cool. It doesn't feature on the pages of *London Style*. No one will take pictures of your eggs being harvested or invite you to parties to talk about the mood swings and the lack of sex and the fact that your body is being factory farmed. The diary pages don't want to know about the relentless bloody monitoring of hormones and the crippling, gut twist of waiting, the agonising want and longing which leaves you feeling flattened.

Tom reacted to it all with anger, which was initially directed at the world, then at me. Though he only ever expressed it once, in the middle of a fight, I knew that at some level he thought all the soul searching, all the anguish and expense, all the embarrassment of the procedures and all the humiliation of our failure to succeed in this most elemental, animal thing could be laid at my door. I was a disappointment to him. I had taken the broad horizon of our future and obscured the view. I had failed 'us'. Over the years I've thought a lot about why he stayed with me and I've come to the conclusion that he knew he loved me as much as he would ever love anyone and he wanted a child, and because his loyalty made him the hero in his own story, the knight errant who had stood by his infertile, basket-case queen. And as bruised as I was from the fight to have Freya, and as grateful as I was to him for not simply shrugging off his armour and striding from the battleground, I wasn't in any position then to draw a distinction between heroics and common or garden decency.

I got up and cracked open Freya's door and there she was, still as a summer pool, and in the quiet rustle of her breath I sensed goodness and hope and everything that was right in the world. Then I slid back to bed and tried to quiet my mind.

CHAPTER TWELVE

The following morning, I left for work without seeing Ruby Winter. It was too early to be busy and most of the shops had yet to open up. Outside Jamal's store, a new shrine to a new 'warrior' had appeared overnight, perhaps the stabbing White had been talking about. A handful of teenagers, black, mixed race and pallid-faced, clustered around the shrine, smoking, and as they watched me running by, their expressions moony with whatever they'd taken to get them through the night, I was struck by the weight of their weariness. No wonder the kids were off their faces. How terrible to be young and poor in a city that kept telling you, in a hundred different ways, that you weren't wanted, that you were dispensable and the city would not protect you.

A few years ago, just before Freya was due to start school, Tom and I had talked about moving out to the suburbs to be near his parents, but in the end I'd resisted the idea. Freya expressed no enthusiasm for leaving and I told myself that a mixed-heritage kid stood a better chance of being treated the same as a white kid in a school where she was hardly a minority.

I saw little enough of my daughter as it was without adding a long commute to my day. Besides, I had a passion for the capital which I hoped Freya would one day share. Back then I thought you could be anything here. London was a fantastic web of brimming life, a daily carnival, a riot of opportunity. And for kids like Freya it probably still was, which was why, in spite of all the hassles, the expense, and the knowledge that we were living in a place where children were killing other children and adults were doing little or nothing to stop it happening, I still wanted my daughter to grow up a Londoner.

I continued my run, arrived at the institute, showered and went to my office. The first hour of my working day was spent checking the patient files from the previous week, then looking at Joshua Barrons' scans and preparing my notes. Our patient wasn't making the progress we'd hoped. A tough case, made worse by what was going on at home. You expose a kid to violence often enough it becomes the kid's first response. It gets hardwired into the brain. Particularly in a genetically vulnerable child like Joshua.

I finished my notes, packed up my stuff and made my way along the quiet, cucumber-green corridors of the institute's research unit, through the access door and out into the more frenzied atmosphere of the clinical areas. Anja and I had decided to call Emma and Joshua back in together. The purpose of the meeting was ostensibly to give them the opportunity to meet a few of the clinicians so they could give Emma a more comprehensive sense of why Joshua would be valuable to our research. But I had another unspoken agenda too. Joshua's disorder was an incredibly rare collision between genes, their expression and the particularity of experience. In seminars I sometimes likened the condition to a dark asteroid speeding through time and space towards earth on an unstoppable trajectory. You couldn't halt the asteroid but by blasting the rock with an opposing force greater than itself you might just alter its trajectory. For a CU child that force was love, or, perhaps more accurately, the root of love: empathy. Its opposite was violence. I didn't think anyone was being violent to Joshua but my hunch told me that he was a witness to his mother's beatings. I'd seen the bruises on Emma's body and listened to her unlikely explanations. I did believe her that no one was hurting Joshua but in the last few days I'd noticed that the boy had started acting out certain things he'd witnessed. If this went on, not only would it make Joshua's condition much harder to treat but I would eventually be obligated to inform social services, who would most likely put the boy into care and beyond the reach of my help. Within weeks, he'd be in some secure behavioural unit in another part of the country. Not that these places didn't do good work. But for a kid with a psychopathic profile like Joshua they could be a deadly training ground.

The door to Anja's office was open and she was staring at her computer screen. I knocked and walked in.

'Oh, Caitlin,' she said, 'you always look so fresh. Come in, come in.' She waved a hand in front of her face. 'I never thought I'd complain about the heat, but really, this is too much. Someone needs to tell the big controller in the sky to turn it down a notch.' There was a jug of iced water on her desk. She gestured for me to sit and poured some into a glass.

'A little bird told me you managed to wangle an air con unit for that lovely office of yours.'

'That was Claire. She's wonderful.'

Anja raised herself up in her chair, stuck out her bottom lip and blew away her fringe. 'I wish I had a Claire, I wish I had your office! Instead, I'm stuck here in this madhouse. Which reminds me: Ayesha; what are we going to do?'

Last week the girl had turned up with a series of small cuts on her leg that her therapist thought were probably self-inflicted. Most kids on the CU spectrum were more likely to be a danger to themselves than to others. We discussed what to do about Ayesha then turned our attentions to Adam. The boy was a harder case to crack. A vengeful kid, he played crude and alarming power games with the therapists. His care assistant had reported that he'd offered her a piece of brownie into which he'd pressed several dead spiders. We discussed his therapy and were about to move on to Joshua when Anja's phone rang. It was Claire calling to say that Emma Barrons had got caught in traffic and would be ten minutes late. Anja suggested we have coffee and wait it out.

'Do you have any biscuits?'

'Of course.'

'What kind?'

Anja grabbed a tin she kept on a shelf behind her desk and peered in.

'Hobnobs, some very melty choc digestives and a couple of curranty things.'

We drank our coffee and ate the biscuits and talked inconsequentially for a bit, until Anja said, cautiously, 'I've been meaning to ask you how yesterday went. I imagine it must have been tricky.'

I'd taken a personal day to go to the crematorium but so far as I could recall I hadn't told anyone the reason. Reading my expression, Anja said, 'It didn't take a brain scientist to work out why you were off.'

I gave a mechanical laugh. 'No, well, I'm glad it's over.'

Anja smiled and, observing some hesitancy in me, decided not to pursue the topic.

It occurred to me then that I should warn Anja about my encounter with James White. I was still pretty sure Emma Barrons was the source of the leak. The woman seemed to possess a giant internal self-destruct button and I thought we should be cautious around her. I was about to open my mouth to speak when there came a knock on the door and one of the clinic administrators popped her head around to say the visitors had arrived. She'd taken Joshua off to play with one of the clinicians but if we were ready, she would show Emma Barrons in.

The change in Emma was alarming. Purple crescents bloomed under her eyes and, as she sat and untied her silk scarf, thin bloodied fingernail tracks were clearly visible around her neck. Anja clocked them too.

'Are you OK?' I said. Through the window in the office

I could see Joshua digging through the soft mounds in the sandpit with a toy earthmover.

Emma sighed. 'Joshua went for his nanny again. I had to separate them. These are what I got for my trouble.'

Anja and I exchanged glances. I didn't know if Emma was telling the truth but even if she was, the latest injuries didn't explain the bruise she'd been sporting at the last meeting. One way or another something was very wrong in the Barrons household.

'I think it's time for a family meeting. You, Joshua and your husband,' I said.

Anja added, 'We really need both of you on board.'

Emma Barrons turned her head to the ceiling and gave a little snort. 'Christopher never gets "on board",' she air-quoted. 'Not at the same time as anyone else anyway. He's strictly the private jet type.'

'We're concerned about you. About *all* of you,' I said.

Emma Barrons' jaw trembled and for a moment her eyes seemed to expand and she blinked away whatever she was feeling. As she opened her mouth to speak, she looked very alone. 'The last time I allowed my son to reduce me to tears he must have been about four or five. We were out and about and Joshua was being Joshua. I was very distracted and I stepped out onto Holland Hill just as a bus was coming along. Joshua was behind me. He saw me step into the path of that bus but he didn't shout or try to get my attention or do anything to stop me. I would probably have been killed if a bystander hadn't rushed forward and pushed me out of the way. Joshua told me later that he was curious to see if the bus was going to roll me flat, *like in a cartoon.*'

I decided to steer the conversation into safer terrain.

'We spoke about the amygdala, remember? It's this tear-shaped bit, the part of the brain where the emotions are processed.' I had pulled up Joshua's scans and was pointing to the spot on the screen.

Emma Barrons touched the corner of her eye.

'In children with Joshua's disorder there tends to be slightly less grey matter – that's the processing stuff – and the neural connections within the amygdala are less pronounced. We don't know what came first, the behaviour or the neural pattern. What we do know is that if you show Joshua a picture of a scary situation, his heart rate doesn't rise in the way it might in a neurotypical child. The popular press likes to say that' – my tongue moved onto the back of my teeth to articulate the 's' in 'psychopath' but I managed to stop myself in time – 'people with Joshua's condition have a problem with empathy, but it's more complicated than that. Kids like Joshua understand other people's emotions but they pay much less attention to them. We call it impaired affective empathy. It really means that their own feelings trump everyone else's.'

Emma Barrons inspected her rings minutely, as if they were the spoils of war, while I went on. 'Now we know a bit more about how Joshua's brain works, we're hopeful that we can modify some of his more challenging behaviour.' I went on to outline some of the latest research suggesting that the condition was in all probability the result of a complex interplay between the epigenetic effects of the MAO-A gene variant and environmental triggers, among which, in Joshua's case, as in all the cases of violent CU kids we'd studied, there was likely to have been some exposure to violence, but the correlates were so complex and individuated and the research was in such early stages that coming to any conclusion was like trying to pick out a single star in the Milky Way without the benefit of a telescope. We were in unknown territory with only the sketchiest of maps. It was always so difficult to find a balance between how little we really knew and the confidence we had in being able to make a difference. Somewhere in the middle of that sat faith of a scientific kind, but this kind of faith was the hardest sell. People looked to science for answers and we had so few. 'What we do know is that once violence starts it can often escalate.'

Anja had begun to rub her hands across her temples, then, conscious of transmitting her anxiety, stopped herself. But it was too late. Emma Barrons' face contorted into a frightened wince. 'What you're really saying is that one day my son is going to kill someone.'

* * *

I got home early, just as the builders next door were finishing up. Tom was in his study. Time was he'd have come out to greet me but today, when I knocked on his door, a weirdly formal voice I barely recognised responded with, 'I'm working.'

Afraid that he would find a way to duck out of it or, worse still, cancel, I hadn't told Tom about Meg Winter's impending visit and, given her coolness at the funeral, I wondered if she would show up. What, other than curiosity, could be in it for her? I wanted to find out why Meg didn't want Ruby to come and live with her and I wanted to try to change her mind. If that proved impossible, I hoped to be able to change my own.

It was just after seven when the doorbell rang. Meg stood on the front step, scrawny and ill-looking. As she stepped inside, Tom burst from his study, with a look on his face somewhere between a wounded bull and Penguin from *Batman*, and, in spite of myself, I let out a little gulp of laughter and had to swallow it back.

'Meg has come for supper,' I said.

Tom swallowed hard and forced a smile. 'So I see.'

* * *

I guess I should have predicted that the evening would be a disaster. Tom and Ruby sulked comprehensively and Meg appeared to be interested only in the size of the house and, by extension, our bank account. If she was at all interested in how her granddaughter had settled in or how she had reacted to her mother's death, then she didn't show it. Other than to enquire how long we'd been in the house and where we'd bought a few of the things in it, she failed to ask a single question and did her best to avoid answering any of mine.

After we'd eaten, I sent the girls upstairs to play in the hope that Tom, Meg and I could have an adult discussion about Ruby's future, but each time I made an attempt to address the issue, Meg grew evasive and Tom changed the subject. It became very clear to me in a way it hadn't been before that Meg blamed her granddaughter for Lilly's death and the only way she was going to have anything to do with Ruby was if the law obliged her to do so. I didn't know enough about family law to know if that would be possible, but I knew it wouldn't be what Tom wanted. By eight thirty both Tom and Meg were looking for an excuse for her to leave. As we stood and said our awkward goodbyes, I got the distinct impression that unless we really pushed it, we were unlikely to see Meg Winter again.

Once Meg had gone, I expected there to be a row but Tom only said he was very tired and was going to bed. When I followed him up a while later he was either already asleep or doing a very good job of pretending. I lay in bed until it became clear I wasn't going to be able to drift off, then tiptoed out and went downstairs to the kitchen. A huge, low harvest moon, as vivid as blood, drew me out into the garden. The air was still and mild and, from somewhere nearby, a fox was screaming. I breathed its musk, then, in amber moonlight, walked up the garden path past the trampoline and the paddling pool and the still-broken fence, until I found myself under the ideas tree. After a while, when no ideas came and a cloud passed across the moon, I looked back at the house, my eyes resting on the spare room window, and I thought about the girl inside and all the moments of disquiet, the hamster claw and the iPad and the bottle of perfume under Freya's bed and the paper clip and the bruising on Freya's arm. With a thudding heart I made my way slowly back down the path. In the kitchen I put on the kettle and made myself a cup of chamomile tea. As I climbed the stairs I saw Ruby Winter standing in the half-light from the window, as if summoned by my thoughts, her lips curled upwards in a bright, tight little smile.

'Can't you sleep?'

She shook her head.

'In that case, I think we should have a little chat.'

The girl moved towards her room. I followed, closing the door behind me. Ruby got back into bed and I took this as my cue to sit down beside her.

'This must all be very bewildering, Ruby. I don't want to make it any more difficult. But there are some house rules and, since you're going to be living with us, at least for now, we need you to stick to them.' I raised my hand and stuck a thumb in the air. 'Number one is no stealing, number two is no lying and number three – the most important rule – is not to hurt or bully Freya.' I tried and failed to catch her eye before going on. 'I don't know if I believe you about the locket or the iPad and I'm not convinced you didn't have something to do with Harry going missing. That thing at the crematorium with the headstone? I understand it must have been a terrible day, but I expect you not to do anything like that ever again. As for those marks on Freya…' I could feel the anger rising and forced myself to push it away. 'What I'm trying to say is, if you're feeling angry or confused or upset in any way, you can talk to me or your father. We won't judge you and we'll try to do what we can to help you feel better.'

I reached out my hand, palm up, in anticipation of a high-five. 'Deal?'

Ruby Winter looked at my hand for a moment, then she turned her back to me and pulled the sheet over her head.

CHAPTER THIRTEEN

At breakfast the next morning it was as if Meg Winter had never come. Tom bustled about making eggs while Freya poured orange juice. Ruby was still upstairs. I grabbed a piece of toast, packed my rucksack and, after kissing my daughter goodbye, I went out.

The atmosphere had noticeably thickened overnight. Traffic poured by as usual but the buses seemed empty. There were plenty of people on the streets but it was oddly quiet and no one made eye contact. The tension was palpable, as if some unstable compound had been released into the city's air supply and all it would take would be one dropped match to hit flashpoint.

Not far from Jamal's shop I passed yet another fresh yellow board sitting beside a makeshift shrine. The incident had taken place overnight and the police were appealing for witnesses they were unlikely to get. There had been so many over the past few months, they were losing their power to shock. People thronged by, no longer stopping long enough to read the text, which, they probably figured, would only tell them what they already knew: that the capital wasn't a good place to be in right now if you were young and especially if you were young and black.

The moment I got into the office I switched on my laptop and checked the *Herald's* website. The incident on Holland Hill had made a paragraph low down. Fifteen-year-old kid. No one arrested. Motive for the attack unknown.

Claire popped her head around the door. 'Diary?'

'Yup.' I picked up my phone to bring up the calendar but for some reason the screen froze. I shook it then banged it hard on the desk. Claire cocked her head and gave me a quizzical look. 'You OK, Caitlin?'

'Yes, sorry. Bloody devices!'

Claire smiled briefly then pointed first to my shirt then to the mug on the desk. 'You're buttoned up wrongly and you haven't touched your coffee.'

I looked down at myself. 'Oh God. It's the heat. Driving everyone a bit mad.'

Mid-morning, I walked over to the clinic to meet with Emma and Joshua Barrons. Today Joshua was charming, running around the clinic with a lightsabre and making everyone laugh. Emma was wearing shades.

Anja, Emma and I watched him for a while then Emma said, 'On days like this, it's nice to pretend there's nothing wrong with my son. But there'll be a price to pay for his good mood. There always is.'

The boy approached us.

'Hello, Joshua', I said. 'Are you a Jedi?'

'Just for today.'

'Oh? And what would you like to be tomorrow?'

'A Tube driver.' Joshua swooshed the lightsabre around his head.

'And why's that?'

A beat. 'Because when people jump in front of the train their heads explode and it's cool.' With that, he was off. Behind her glasses, his mother met my eyes.

* * *

The last time Emma had come she'd seemed so vulnerable and damaged but now, while she was in a better frame of mind, the shades notwithstanding, I thought it might be an opportune time to tackle the leak to James White.

'Shall we go into Anja's office for a moment?' I let Anja take the lead then waved Emma in front of me and took up the rear. I waited until everyone was settled, then began.

'As you know, Emma, what we're doing here – with Joshua and the other children – is experimental and sensitive. Your husband has a high profile and so we all need to be particularly careful about who we tell, especially with so much coverage in the media about teen gangs and violence at the moment – the press are on the lookout for anything to fuel the hysteria. It could be very damaging to Joshua if word got out about his diagnosis.'

Emma gave me a strange look, somewhere between puzzlement and irritation. 'I'm well aware of that,' she said flatly.

'Another thing.' I searched for the right words. 'If there is some difficulty at home, perhaps we might think about admitting Joshua to the residential programme after all?' The situation was incredibly delicate. If Emma Barrons disclosed that she was being hit by her husband, we would be duty-bound to report it. We didn't want Joshua to witness domestic abuse but neither were we keen for social services to step in. The boy might well end up in the care system beyond our reach.

Emma stiffened and, pushing her shades further up her nose, said, in a glassy voice, 'I don't know what you mean by *difficulty*. In any case, his father would never agree.'

I was about to go on when I saw Anja narrow her eyes. Enough. We didn't want to push Emma Barrons so far that she took her son out of the programme.

We found Joshua standing at the side of the sandpit repeatedly smashing the clinic's toy truck collection into the walls. His clinical therapist was standing nearby trying to calm him. The charmer of an hour ago had flipped. Emma called out to him and, at the sound of his mother's voice, Joshua immediately stopped what he was doing and wheeled about. His face was as placid as a summer pond; he spread his arms to indicate the shambles around him and, without taking his eyes off his mother, in a voice full of recrimination, he said, 'Look at this, see? This is what happens when you leave me here alone.'

* * *

'Lunch?' Anja said afterwards.

'"Fraid not.' I had chores to do.

Anja gave me a sympathy grimace. 'Everything OK at home?'

'Why is everyone asking me that this morning?'

Anja's brow lifted. 'It's just, well, you seem a little distracted.'

* * *

Outside in the tiny park beside the institute, office workers lounged on dusty grass. As I passed McDonald's on the corner I noticed that a group of kids had begun to gather, chatting and smoking spliffs, fingers working the keypads of their phones. At the zebra crossing I stopped. Freya came to mind. I did my chores. The lunch hour was nearly over by the time I got back. At the institute car park, I stopped for a moment to adjust my sunglasses and didn't notice a man rapidly approach to my right until he was almost on top of me.

James White stepped deftly into my path and, reaching out an arm as if to open the door, he managed to swing his body in front of me so there was no way around him. He was close enough that I could feel his breath on my neck.

'There's been another stabbing.'

'I know. I saw the yellow board this morning and I read the piece in the *Herald*. What's that got to do with me?'

'He's one of yours.'

Immediately I thought of Joshua. But I'd already seen him this morning and anyway, the report had said the dead boy had been fifteen.

White went on: 'Name's LeShaun Toley. He lives on the Pemberton Estate. *Lived*. Isn't that where you grew up?'

I took a step back and waited for what I was pretty sure was about to come next. There was no point in denying this or asking White where he'd got his information. It was his business to know stuff and he wasn't likely to tell me anyway. A colleague slid by us, sent me a greeting and disappeared through the revolving doors. White waited until we were alone again, his eyes slicing from one side of the car park to the other, then, lowering his voice, he said, 'Listen, my editor's giving me hell for sitting on the Barrons story.'

'And?'

He held up his hands, palms towards me, in a gesture of surrender, but I knew it was anything but.

'What do you *want*? As you bloody well know, the kids I work with have personality disorders. Stabbings are not my area of expertise. Now, please, just let me get back to my work.'

White persisted. 'You're working on predictive models.'

It seemed unlikely that White had guessed this. Only a dozen people knew about it in any detail, all of them employees of the institute. My research was highly confidential. I hadn't published it yet so there was nothing in the public domain. Evidently there was a mole.

'Whoever is passing you information doesn't know what they're talking about. I work on correlations, not predictions. Anyone who says they can predict human behaviour is lying. Now, please.'

White's jaw tightened and he looked up, sombre now. He wasn't going to stop until he got what he wanted.

'Look, I don't want to break the Barrons story but my editor's a hungry bitch and it's my job to keep her fed.'

'Are you trying to *blackmail* me?'

'Of course not! Just a little friendly persuasion. People are looking for answers. I think maybe you have them. All I'm asking for is background. Unattributed, strictly off the record.'

'I give you what you want, you'll go away?'

White thumped a palm across his chest where his heart should have been. He was setting this up to be a favour, but I knew very well I had no choice. If he leaked the fact that Joshua Barrons was at the clinic, I could well lose my job.

'Not here, though, and not now. And only if you guarantee to leave the Barrons family out of it.'

We agreed a time and a place to meet later that day, then I swiped through security and went back into the building. I found Anja hunched over the screen in her office. A large box of sushi lay unopened on her desk.

I related my encounter with White. 'I don't think this came from Emma Barrons. "Predictive models", White said. Suggests an insider to me.'

Anja thought about this. 'Lucas?'

'I can't see how.' My postgrad research assistant had always been super loyal. More likely the leak had sprung from one of the few dissenters at the institute who felt threatened by the work we were doing. Going to the media was high risk, though. If whoever it was got caught, they'd be in deep shit.

'Can't we just ignore him?' Anja opened the box of sushi and pushed it towards me. I hadn't eaten but I didn't have any appetite.

'He's not going away until he gets what he wants.'

'Which is?'

'A quote about why the kids out there are killing each other, preferably one with enough scientific backing to make him look authoritative.'

'He's an arsehole.'

'I'll tell him that when I meet him.'

'Wait, you're *meeting* him?'

'He's threatening to expose the fact that Joshua Barrons is a patient here if I don't.'

Anja picked up her chopsticks and began mixing a glob of wasabi into a puddle of soy sauce. 'It does sound like you don't have much choice.'

Noting the swerve in her pronoun switch, I thanked her for her advice and went back to my office feeling troubled. Claire had returned from lunch and wanted me to look at a minor research grant application which needed my sign-off by the end of the day to meet its deadline. The paper began with a long and complex meta-survey of early experiments in the use of softbots in neurological disorders and, like so much of the cutting-edge research in the field, it questioned the need for psychiatry. In the author's view, future mental health would be left to psychologists and neurologists. Interesting if not particularly enlightening. It took me till 2.30 p.m. to finish reading and another half hour to write up my report. The remainder of the afternoon was taken up with meetings. In between, I texted Tom to say I'd be back an hour later than usual and received a terse reminder that he was taking the girls to the cycle track and they'd probably eat at McDonald's afterwards.

White was waiting for me at a corner table in the public bar at The Wheatsheaf, looking worryingly eager. The place was one of those very rare survivors from the seventies: dark, with a head-swimming carpet permeated by the sticky odour of a long-departed past. I chose it because no one from the institute would ever think to go there and because my former life had left me with an allergy to swankier places. A few old geezers propped up the bar. Otherwise we were alone. I hated White. I knew he was only doing his job, but I still hated him – for what he'd done to me but mostly for what he'd done to Kylie Drinkwater, turning a murdered baby into a cheap headline. But I knew he wasn't going to leave me alone until he'd got something from me. At least this way I got to set the agenda. I steeled myself and went over to him.

A pint of lager sat on the table. 'Can I get you one?'

'No thanks.'

He smiled. 'Straight down to business then. You've seen what's happening on the streets. Something's going to kick off. When it does, our readers will want to know who to blame. I just want to know what the science would say.'

'Science doesn't deal in blame.'

White had his pad out but at this he leaned back in his seat and rubbed a hand through his hair. 'That's no good to me,' he said irritably.

I wasn't about to let White unsettle me. 'I didn't realise I was here to be good to you.'

He leaned in. 'You're here because you're too scared not to be.'

'You're wrong,' I said. 'I'm here because if I hadn't shown up, you'd write what you usually write, that the streets are being taken over by evil monsters hardly worthy of the label "human".'

'So put me right.'

'Off the record and no names, mine or any other.' I was careful not to substantiate what he thought he knew about Joshua Barrons.

'Agreed.'

'You mess with me this time, White, I'll find a way to fuck you so hard you won't be able to sit down for months. As you found out when you were rooting through the muck, I'm a product of the Pemberton. I might look harmless but I'm not.'

White laughed but I noticed his leg twitch. 'Just give me something I can use.'

Where to begin? At the bottom of the pyramid of violence were the kids whose levels of cortisol had been raised by bad home situations, things they witnessed, and life on the streets. Most were stuck in permanent flight or fight mode. Trigger reactions. Others, the leaders, were tougher; their senses numbed by the daily bath in their own stress hormones. They were trying to feel something, anything. And in the midst of it all there would most likely be a sprinkling of kids whose amygdalae just didn't work the way they should: fearless, reckless, unstable but often alarmingly charming, charismatic kids, who didn't know how to give a shit about anything or anyone other than themselves. And sometimes not even that. They were the ones who were truly dangerous, the ones to watch.

White sat back, making encouraging noises.

'When you say dangerous, what you really mean is evil, isn't it?' he said, once I'd finished.

I shook my head. 'Evil is just a gap in the research.'

* * *

Everyone but the cat was out when I got home. I fed him, pulled a bottle of Riesling from the fridge, grabbed a glass and went out into the garden with the mountain of post which had accumulated on the hall table while Tom and I had been dealing with bigger things. I was feeling shaky after the meeting with White. I didn't trust him but, as Anja pointed out, what choice did I have? Next door's builders had gone home for the day and there was a blackbird singing in the ideas tree. The chair on the far side of the garden table looked temptingly shady. I sat, poured myself a glass of Riesling and opened a bunch of what turned out to be marketing letters and junk mail before reaching an envelope stuffed with bank statements. I leafed through, scanning the numbers without focusing on any in particular until my eyes lighted on the words *Invalid payee*. What did that mean? Flipping over to the next page, I saw a debit from June of the same amount. Also for May. As I flicked back through the months my heart kept pace. *Thud, thud, thud.* Why had neither of us noticed a sum this large leaving the account? It looked like we'd fallen victim to identity theft. As I thumbed back to the June payment, my eyes flicked up to the account information at the top of page and stopped there. It took me a moment to decipher the figures.

That explained it. The papers in front of me didn't relate to our joint account but to Tom's personal one. The envelope had been addressed to Tom and in my distracted state I'd opened it. We'd never been the kind of couple to share an email address or open each other's mail. There was a joint account for household expenses, otherwise we held on to our individual accounts. At the time – as now – this seemed like the more modern, defining, twenty-first-century couple thing to do. Fighting over money being the most dismal of the domestic arts, we'd always avoided it. When Tom had told me that he'd saved a sum when he'd been working at Adrenalyze, then borrowed a bit from his father to fund more work on *Labyrinth*, I had no reason to disbelieve him. But the figures here didn't fit. I paid the mortgage. We both paid into the joint account but the regular sums of money leaving Tom's account were in addition to that payment. As I went back over the sheets it was as if I was thumbing a flipbook of my past which was shifting before my eyes. A deadening realisation hit me.

On the fifteenth of every month, for at least six months, maybe longer, my husband had been making regular payments to Lilly Winter. The last of these had been returned marked 'invalid payee' because it had gone out the day before Lilly

Winter died and only reached its destination after her account had been frozen.

Tom must have lied to me when he said he knew nothing about Ruby Winter. The longer I thought about it the more it seemed to make sense. Hadn't Tom himself told me that he was named on Ruby's birth certificate? That was how the police had tracked him down. At the time some small part of me had registered this as odd but with everything going on, it had slipped my mind. It was suddenly very clear. Tom had known about Ruby Winter for a long time, perhaps all her life, and he'd been paying her mother for the girl's upkeep and perhaps also to keep her quiet. No wonder my husband hadn't wanted another child with me. He'd been too busy supporting someone else's.

I raced to Tom's study. In all our years together, I'd never looked at Tom's phone, gone through his drawers or worked my way through his browsing history, not so much because I trusted him, though I did, but because I'd never wanted to be *that* woman: the suspicious, jealous, snooping, controlling wife. But this was different. Now I had cause. His desktop responded to my password guesses by locking me out. He had a laptop too but it wasn't anywhere visible. I went to the filing cabinet and found it oddly empty then flipped through a random selection of the books on his shelves in the event that he'd left letters or hard copies of emails between the pages. A boarding pass stub fluttered from a biography of Steve Jobs, a remnant of a trip to a gaming convention in LA, but that was it. Next, I searched through his desk drawers, and coming upon a small key that looked as if it might open a cupboard underneath the shelves, I went over and tried it out. My hunch was right. Inside was an accordion file containing tax returns and tucked among the file leaves was a letter outlining a loan Tom had taken out on the house back in January. Not a huge loan, but enough to fund his payments to Lilly Winter. The agreement had been signed by the two of us. Except, of course, it hadn't. I had to take my hat off to Tom, though. He'd got my signature down pat. Must have taken a lot of practice.

I ran my hand down to the back of the drawer, wondering what other horrors might be lurking there, and behind the file I discovered something else, something wholly unexpected. A bright blue plastic rectangle with a built-in grip matching Shelly's description of her son's missing iPad. Only Tom could have put it there. The probability of one of the girls finding the key, locating the cupboard and stashing Charlie Frick's iPad inside was vanishingly small. But why? And why had he lied about it? Was he trying to protect his daughter from being found out? What else was he lying about in order to keep Ruby Winter off the hook? I picked up the device and switched it on, but the battery was dead, so I took it to the kitchen and plugged it into my iPhone charger.

At seven thirty, when neither Tom nor the girls had made an appearance, I texted Tom then speed-dialled Sally and left a message. I thought about calling Anja or Claire then decided against it and instead grabbed another bottle of Riesling. For a while I sat on the sofa with half an eye on news coverage of the latest stabbing and wondered why there was no one, apart from Sally, I could confide in. It hadn't always been like that. Back in the day my dance card was full.

One time, after my recovery from psychosis, when Tom and Freya and I had finally settled into a family routine, I called Judy, my best friend from way back, and suggested a gang of us from the old days get together.

'I hate to have to tell you this, Cat,' Judy said, 'but we already do.' There was a pause. 'After your *episode*, we just didn't think it was appropriate to have you around our babies.'

A few stood by me: Tricia, Sarah, gay Tim and straight Tim, Lyla, Sam. Then Kylie Drinkwater happened and Sam, Tricia and straight Tim stopped calling. And after months when I couldn't bring myself to speak to anyone Sarah and Lyla fell away. Eventually, even gay Tim faded out. Hands up. It was no one's fault but my own.

There came the unmistakable clatter of my daughter's laughter and, hastily rising from the sofa, I took my glass and the now empty bottle, went into the kitchen and hid Charlie Frick's iPad under a pile of heat mats. Then I threw the empty bottle in the recycling and went out into the hallway and walked straight into Ruby Winter. For an instant the girl froze, before taking a sidestep and heading towards the stairs.

Freya stood by the open front door.

'Hi, Mum,' Freya said, moving forward into my opened arms and allowing herself to be squeezed. Then she pulled away and, in a disapproving tone, said, 'Have you been drinking?'

'A bit.'

Tom appeared looking sweaty and a little breathless. He pulled the deadbolts and fixed the chain on the front door. By now Ruby had gone upstairs and Freya had disappeared into the kitchen, both far away enough not to be within earshot. With the Riesling swilling round in my belly, in as calm a voice as I could muster, I said, 'I've seen your accounts.'

Tom froze, his hand still on door. The theme tune from some cartoon started up from the living room. Tom's gaze shifted across my shoulder as if he was weighing up the possibility of getting past me so he could escape into the sanctuary of his study.

'What accounts?'

I held the statements out to him. He took them, his mouth slack.

'I'm guessing you forged my signature to get that loan on the house, on *our* house, to pay off your lover.' Tom held up a staying hand but I was on a roll now and prepared to take this wherever it needed to go. 'How long have you known about Ruby? You met her before she came here, didn't you? Did you two go out on fun dad and daughter trips? Was that why she was so keen to come here? Oh, and by the way, if you cared as much about your daughter as you say you do when you're depriving her of getting any therapy, maybe you can explain why you let her grow up in a pigsty with a drunk?'

I could see Tom heating up. Any moment now, I thought, he's going to start shouting and then he's going to storm out. But, to my surprise, he didn't. Instead, he gave a scornful shake of his head and said in a tone more sorrowful than angry, 'What, you'd rather I hadn't done the right thing and provided for my daughter?'

'With our *house*?'

Tom's hands were clutching his head. 'Christ, I made one mistake, one fucking mistake. What did you want me to do? Come clean and jeopardise our marriage, our life here, everything?'

'How long?'

A moaning sound escaped his lips. He shook his head. 'I don't know. A few years.'

Our voices were raised above a whisper now. Tom held up his hands, hoping to lower the temperature, and moved closer. When he spoke his voice trembled and there was an ugly, pleading tone to it.

'I didn't lie to you, Cat. Ruby coming here, that was as much of a shock to me as it was to you. How could I have known she was going to get dumped on us? I thought she'd be sent to live with her grandmother.' His eyes were huge and shining as if he was about to burst into tears. 'I'm so close I can smell the money. The instant *Labyrinth* is launched you won't have to worry about the house, I promise. We'll buy a dozen houses.'

I held my ground. 'You should have told me.'

Tom collected himself. His jaw ticked. He reached out a hand and tried to touch my face but I didn't let him.

'Caitlin, darling, I thought it might make you ill again. You have no idea what it's like living with that pressure.'

A kind of hollow sickness rose up from my belly. Tom was calm now. We were on familiar territory. The lies, the cheating, the loan on the house, this was all my fault. I was the nutjob, the maniac. It was me, Crazy Cat.

Tom moved towards me. When he spoke his voice was soft and there was a hint of slyness in his tone. 'You've been drinking! I can smell it. So that's why you're acting a bit mental. You're on the bloody *sauce*.'

His eyes cut to the kitchen door. I swung round and saw our daughter standing in the doorjamb, with her hands cupped over her mouth and an unbearable sheen of fear in her eyes. I rushed towards her, saying, 'It's OK, my love, everything's all right,' but she slipped past me and ran instead towards her father.

'Why do you have to be so horrible to Dad? Why can't you be normal?'

There was nothing to be said to that. I knew I had been defeated and, as I turned, fighting back tears, there, on the stairs, like a buzzard keeping beady watch over dying remains, sat Ruby Winter.

* * *

For the rest of the evening each of us kept our own company; me in the living room, the girls in their bedrooms and Tom in his study. At ten or thereabouts, I heard my husband pad up to the bathroom then come back down and shut himself in his study again. I waited until he had settled, then crept along the hallway to Freya's room. In the rumble of city light filtering in behind the curtains, I could just see the cascade of my daughter's hair on the pillow. I went over to the window, reached up inside the curtains and let in a little air. In the bed Freya stirred.

'Mum?' Her voice was as drowsy as a drunken bee.

'Yes, darling, it's only me.' I sat down at the end of the bed, felt for Freya's feet and curled my hands around them over the sheet.

'Are you still drunk?'

'A little probably. I'm sorry.' I felt ashamed and humbled by the knowledge that I'd brought this on myself. Ruby hadn't turned Freya against me, I'd done it all on my own. In my wariness and suspicion of the newcomer, I'd managed to alienate everyone else.

Freya turned on her side to face me and in the gloom I could just make out the shine in her eyes.

'Will you and Dad make up?'

'We'll try, sweet pea,' I said, though it felt like a false assurance. Right now it seemed Tom and I were beyond any kind of reconciliation.

Back downstairs, I took a long drink of water and fell into a fitful sleep on the sofa. In the quiet blank light of predawn I woke, my tongue like a lizard. I went into the kitchen and pulled Charlie's iPad from under the heat mats. While waiting for it to boot up I made a cup of chamomile tea and thought about the odd letter the girls had written. *Sorry your birthday had an unhappy ending.* I'd never believed Ruby's explanation. The message seemed to have come out of the same morbid box of tricks as the defaced gravestone, the pinch bruises on Freya's arm and the dead hamster.

The iPad screen flared into life. A screen saver of Charlie's face emerged from the blue light. His mouth with smeared with what looked like cake. Most likely the image had been taken on his birthday. Here and there the picture seemed blurred. I blinked and leaned in closer and saw the scratch marks. In a childish script someone had etched: *I hope you die.*

CHAPTER FOURTEEN

Two days passed in which none of us spoke about the row or the iPad or anything else much. The girls spent the Thursday and Friday evenings in their rooms or in the garden. I slept in our bedroom and Tom shacked up in his study. We didn't even eat together. By the time I got back from work, Tom had already taken the girls out to Hoopoes or McDonald's, leaving me to eat cheese on toast alone, reading my work papers. By Saturday morning, I figured if anything was to change then I would have to do the running. I waited till I heard Tom in the kitchen then made my way in to join him, but before I had a chance to say anything he brushed past me and headed back into the study. Not long afterwards Ruby appeared, looking even whiter and more ghostly than before, like some kind of daylight vampire. We'd barely spoken since the events of Wednesday evening.

'I had a bit too much to drink the other day,' I said.

The girl shrugged before remarking, pointedly, 'I'm used to it.'

I decided this was best ignored. 'I'm making bacon and eggs,' I said.

The bacon buckled as it hit the pan. I cracked in the eggs. Moments later, Ruby got up, went to the cupboard where the cereals were kept and took out the cornflakes. She poured herself a bowl, sprinkled on a great deal of sugar and began eating. She looked vulnerable and lost and for a fleeting moment I felt for her.

I said, 'I found Charlie's iPad. Did you write something on it?'

Ruby helped herself to more cereal. For a moment neither of us said anything, then Ruby put down her spoon and, taking a sip of orange juice, in a neutral tone, said, 'My mum was a lot like you: drunk and a bit mental.'

I felt my hands grip the cooker then a stinging flare where my fingers had touched the pan. Wheeling round to face my stepdaughter, I said, 'I know what you're trying to do, Ruby, but you won't succeed.'

'Oh, really?' There was a clatter then a cool spray of milk from the cornflake bowl Ruby had just thrown settled across my front and she was out of the door.

I was at the cold tap holding my burnt fingers in the stream when Tom appeared, hands on hips and a brittle expression of concern which somehow didn't ring true.

'What's going on? Ruby just told me you'd been incredibly rude to her.'

I shook my hands free of water and relayed what I'd found on the iPad.

'Does that give you licence to threaten my daughter?'

I should have felt the noose tighten then, but it all seemed too far-fetched, too *crazy*.

'Sit down,' I said.

Tom pulled out a chair and sprawled into it, his arm curled around the back rest in an attitude of blokeish confidence while I remained standing, clutching the worktop as if it were a life raft. I was vulnerable and I knew it but Tom had just drawn a line and, in order to protect my daughter, I was going to have to cross it.

'I need you to listen to me. I deal in difficult, dangerous kids every single day and I'm telling you it is not safe for Ruby to be around Freya right now. Your daughter is hardly safe around herself. She's morbid and obsessional. I've seen kids who've lost a parent change this way, sometimes overnight. It's as if death has set up camp in her. Let me pull some strings, get her into a residential facility. One of the good ones. We'll visit at weekends and Ruby will get a chance to work through some of her stuff away from Freya.'

Tom was sitting perfectly upright now, shaking his head condescendingly.

'How's the view from up there on the moral high ground?' I said. As soon as I said it I knew it was a bad move.

He gave a 'more in sorrow than in anger' sigh. 'Why do you hate Ruby so much? Is it because she's rubbing your nose in the fact that you couldn't have another child? Why can't you see, the stuff you're talking about, the shit that needs "working through", that's not Ruby's, Cat, it's *yours*.'

Me again. Defective, infertile, Craaaazy Cat. My cock-ups. My paranoia. The full fifteen rounds. But this was no longer about defending myself. It was about protecting my daughter.

'I'll say it again, Tom, so that we're both really clear. I am not prepared to allow Freya to continue living with Ruby Winter. Not at the moment.'

When Tom's face twisted round there was some ugly, unfamiliar script written there. 'You fucking know I hate it when you issue me with ultimatums. You really think if it comes to you versus me, you'll win? Honestly? The father who for the last four years has been Freya's main carer, the man who's been doing the right thing by Ruby, or some pisshead fruitcake who can't get over the fact that her husband fucked someone else?'

I took a breath, let go of the counter and felt my legs carry me towards the door. Whatever I might have said would have been too little and too late. A wide, deep, irreparable chasm had opened up in the landscape of our marriage and Tom and I were teetering on its edge.

* * *

That afternoon, when Tom took the girls to the lido, I thought it best to stay behind at home. The girls would sense the tension and Ruby might try to exploit it. Instead, I spent the hours googling psych facilities and papers on morbid obsessional behaviour in kids and formulating a plan.

At four, earlier than expected, the girls and Tom returned with the news that his father had fallen on the stairs and was in hospital. Michael Walsh's injuries weren't life threatening but Tom needed to go to the hospital straight away.

Tom and I were in the kitchen. The girls were watching *Finding Nemo* in the living room.

'I'd take Ruby but the last thing I want to subject my daughter to right now is the sight of an old man she's never met lying in a hospital covered in tubes.'

'No, no, of course not. You go. I'll look after Ruby.'

His voice took on an odd tone. 'Couldn't you call Sally?'

'Why would I do that?'

'I honestly don't think you're very stable right now.'

'Are you *serious*?' I could hardly believe what I was hearing.

Tom's brows raised. 'Yes I am. I'm bloody *deadly* serious.'

* * *

I speed-dialled Sally's number on speakerphone so Tom could hear and left a message. It was ridiculous but it seemed to placate him. While he went upstairs to pack an overnight bag, I checked on the girls. Freya had loved *Finding Nemo* when she was younger (which small child didn't?) but hadn't mentioned it for years. The fact that she'd gone back to it was a bad sign, I thought. It meant she was feeling insecure. She was fond of Michael, though, so maybe that was it.

'You OK, girls?'

Freya looked up and nodded. 'Mum, can I have a glass of milk, please?'

'Of course, darling. You know Grandad's going to be fine, don't you? Would you like one too, Ruby?'

Ruby didn't answer.

I fetched the milk then sat back at the kitchen table and got on with some paperwork, close enough so that if something happened I'd be in the next room. Tom came down moments later, said goodbye to the girls and left. A little while later when I went into the living room again the two girls were sitting on the sofa together and Freya was making gulping motions with her lips.

'What are you doing?'

Freya said, 'Practising holding my breath.'

I thought this was strange but decided it was better not to say anything in front of Ruby, but then the girl leaned towards Freya and whispered something into her ear and there was something about that which just set me off.

'What's the big secret?' My eyes shot from one girl to the other and, as I turned my head away from Ruby, I saw her flash Freya a warning look. My heart began ticking. 'Did something happen at the lido?'

In my peripheral vision I saw Ruby shake her head as if feeding Freya the answer.

'Mum, you are being *so* weird.'

The rest of the evening Ruby remained close to her sister. My first chance to speak to my daughter alone was just after she'd gone to bed, but when I brought up the topic of the pool Freya just frowned and gave a little head shake and I couldn't get any more out of her.

Around nine my mobile sounded the 'Hallelujah Chorus'.

Sal said, 'So now I'm freaked out. What's going on?'

I told her about Tom's accounts and the loan on the house,

about the hamster, the bruises on Freya's arm and the iPad and the incident in the crematorium, how I'd just found Freya practising holding her breath and how weird and sly Ruby had been when I'd asked if anything had happened in the lido. I told her I was worried that Freya was being bullied. Then I told her about the row I'd had with Tom. And the fact that he'd raised the issue of custody.

'That's bad,' Sal said.

'It's got to the point where I don't really want to leave Ruby and Freya together unsupervised...'

Sal made a tutting sound. 'No, I meant the C word. You don't really have any proof that Ruby did all that stuff, do you? If she really did do it, don't you think one of you would have caught her in the act? Wouldn't Freya have said something? Look, sweetheart, perhaps you just need a break? All those kids at the clinic, no wonder it gets to you. Don't take this the wrong way but maybe, you know, *think* about going to see someone? I'm worried all this has got too much for you.'

My head buzzed. In a calm voice I said, 'Maybe you're right, I'll get an early night and I'll probably feel better in the morning. You won't tell Tom any of this if he calls you again, will you?'

'God, no. Shit, no, Cat, you're my *sister*. Anyway, he won't.'

* * *

After the call my mind began to turn over too fast, like a car in the wrong gear. I felt trapped. If I took Freya away, Tom would use my mental illness to fight me to get custody of her. He'd seen me drunk in front of the girls and for all I knew he'd filmed me on his phone. And I couldn't rely on either of the girls to give voice to my suspicions about Ruby – Freya wasn't talking, and Ruby was too clever to give herself away. It would be my word against Tom's. But I had to protect Freya. An idea began to form. It was completely against the rules, but I thought it might work. I called Sal back.

'You know, Sal, I thought about what you said. Perhaps you're right and I'm overreacting. Can you come over and be with Freya tomorrow, just for the day? I was thinking maybe if Ruby and I spent some quality stepmum–stepdaughter time together, we could resolve some of this. I mean, I might feel reassured.'

'Oh.' Sal readjusted her ideas. 'Well, yeah, that might be cool.'

'Good, that's a plan then?' I named a time. 'And Sal?'

'I know. Mum's the word.'

* * *

Predictably, Ruby Winter didn't want to come with me. I had the feeling she understood my suspicions and was wary. Her instincts and watchful nature smelled a rat. *It'll be boring, I don't like science*, and, mostly, *I want to stay here with Freya*. But I pressed upon her how exciting it would be to try out the special movie goggles we had at the institute and Freya helped me out by saying that she'd used them and they were 'cool'. Eventually, the idea of being able to watch whatever she wanted seemed to win her over and, after a few shrugs and a bit of sulking, Ruby agreed to accompany me.

Lucas was setting up when we arrived at the lab, his eyes already glommed onto a screen. On Sundays the imaging machines were made available for research grads so I was taking the spot he needed for his own work. I'd done him a few favours and this was calling in the debt. Lucas was smart, hard-working, fun to be around and – here was the important part – deeply, unquestioningly loyal. If I asked him to do something, even something as unorthodox as what I had in mind, he would do it and keep it to himself. If either of us were caught, the consequences would be unpredictable but almost certainly serious.

I put a double macchiato on the desk beside him. His eyes smiled.

'Two sugars?'

'Of course.'

Introductions were made and I left Lucas showing Ruby the movie goggles in the annexe while I swiped through to the scanning room. The scanner sat angular and grey in the centre of the space like some vast, hibernating monster. However familiar it had become, there was something about the machine I always found intimidating. It was as if it were the repository of all kinds of as yet undiscovered secrets, the keeper of the iconography of the soul. I checked the settings and moved back into the annexe. Ruby and Lucas were playing *Angry Birds* on Lucas's laptop.

'Ruby was telling me about the pictures of monkeys with wires in their heads outside Brixton Tube,' he said, catching my eye and grimacing.

I squeezed Ruby's shoulder, more for Lucas's benefit than for my stepdaughter's. 'I'm sorry, that must have been upsetting.' I reached for the phone in my pocket and pressed record. Today was all about catching Ruby off guard and allowing her to reveal herself.

'I thought it was cool,' she said.

'Well, there aren't any monkeys here,' I said. 'Do you still want to do this?'

'Is there a choice?'

'We could sit here for a while and talk instead. You could tell me how you're feeling about stuff.'

'I'd rather go in the machine.'

As I took her through the procedure, she looked bored. I reassured her that it wouldn't hurt at all and if she wanted to stop at any time, we would.

I watched the scan in progress on the screen in the annexe. Grey-scale shapes pulsed and morphed on the screen and I marked them against what I knew was happening in the video. I'd need to go back and study them carefully before being able to reach any conclusions.

We were done in under an hour. In that time Ruby hadn't moved or made a sound. I saved the scans to my personal Dropbox then deleted them from the mainframe.

* * *

Lucas gave us a lift back to Brixton (Tom had taken the car) and we went to McDonald's. After that I took Ruby, protesting mildly, to an early evening show at the Ritzy, keen to keep her separated from Freya for as long as I could. We got back to the house just after nine. Sal was watching something on Netflix. A half-drunk bottle of Sauvignon Blanc sat on the table beside her. Freya had already gone to bed. Tired from staring at a screen for several hours, Ruby quickly followed suit. I fetched a glass from the kitchen and came and sat beside my sister.

'How did your bonding day go? What did you do?'

'Nothing terribly exciting.' I told her about the day. 'Freya showed Ruby her scanner pictures and Ruby wanted some of her own so I let her have a go,' I said, not entirely untruthfully.

'Oh. When's Tom back?'

My eyes went automatically to my watch. 'Late, probably after midnight.

'So,' I went on casually, 'did you get anything out of Freya? Did she talk about the lido? Or anything else?' I figured my daughter might confide in her aunt and tell her something she wouldn't tell me.

Sal scrolled back through the day. 'Nope, *nada.*'

'Nothing about the hamster? Or what happened to Charlie Frick's iPad?'

Sal's frown turned to a disapproving scowl. 'Cat, you're not still going on about that, are you?' She topped up my glass. 'Here, take a chill pill.'

CHAPTER FIFTEEN

Monday morning at work. I'd been the only one awake by the time I left the house. Around midnight I'd been woken by the sound of the front door and I guessed Tom had taken himself off to the study to sleep. I left him a note on the kitchen table – our only communication since he'd sent me a text with his ETA on Sunday morning – to say I hoped Michael was OK and to request that he kept Freya away from the lido or the pool. *I think she might have a cold coming on.*

At five I had a meeting with Simeon Turner to go through Ruby Winter's scans. Simeon and I had trained together. He'd gone on to work at one of the private clinics specialising in adolescent mental health. I'd told him I had a patient I could use a second opinion on. I didn't tell him the patient was my stepdaughter or that I'd forged her father's signature on the permission forms.

Around eleven, Sal called.

'Is everything OK? I would have called before but I've had all this fallout from a client about what happened last night. It's all over the news, that dead kid. Someone on Twitter suggested it started with a dispute over my client's branded trainers, so they're crapping themselves.'

I swung my chair over to my laptop and clicked on the *Herald*'s website. The pictures took a moment to gain definition then the whole thing crashed. I mentioned I hadn't seen the news that morning and Sal told me what she knew. LeShaun Toley, the unarmed fifteen-year-old boy James White had mentioned, hadn't been stabbed after all. News had got out that the cops had mistaken his Zippo lighter for a gun and shot him. My heart hollowed for the dead kid and his family.

'That's horrible.'

'Yeah, it's fucked up,' Sal said. She started talking about her client again. I tuned out and clicked back on the link and this time the homepage loaded. Kids killing kids, cops killing kids – the atmosphere in the city was as tight as a wet drum. My eyes scrolled down to a familiar name at the bottom of the page. Clicking the link brought me to an analysis of the violence with James White's byline. At the bottom of the piece I was shocked to see a mugshot of me taken at a conference last year. My heart sank.

'Sal? I have to go.'

I put down the phone and looked more closely at the piece. There was no mention of the Barrons family so that was good. White had used the information I'd given him, but instead of keeping it in the background as he'd promised, he'd named me and described my occupation as 'an expert in psychopathic children'. He'd also quoted me saying, *Evil is just a gap in the research.* I knew MacIntyre would tap in the nuclear code if he got wind of this. I keyed White's number and got through to his voicemail.

'I'm coming after you with my lawyers.'

My next call was to Anja. I didn't want her to find out from someone else and I was hoping she'd have my back and some good advice, but when I dropped the bomb, instead of offering support, she said simply, 'What were you *thinking*? It's the number one rule: *never* speak to journalists.' Then, rapidly changing the subject: 'But I'm glad you called. Emma Barrons is here. Can you come over right now?'

Emma was sitting on the sofa in Anja's office with a face like a rotten mango. I tried not to look, but it was impossible. The bruising was catastrophic. My immediate thought was Joshua, but even Joshua would have had a hell of a job inflicting that kind of damage on an adult.

'Have you been to the police?'

'Emma doesn't want to press charges,' said Anja. They'd obviously been talking about it a while before I'd arrived.

'But you know the cops can bring a prosecution without you?'

'Not if I don't tell them.' Emma frowned. 'Really, it doesn't matter about me but I think my husband's going to try to stop you treating Joshua.'

'On what grounds?'

'That there's nothing wrong with his son.'

As I was taking this in, Anja turned to me and said, 'What's the legal position?'

I considered this for a moment. We'd had patients whose

parents hadn't wanted them treated before, but we'd been able to argue that the kids were a suicide risk.

'We could section Joshua,' I said. 'That way his father would probably have to go through the courts to stop us treating him. We'd run the risk of CAMHs scooping him up, though. He might well end up in the secure system.'

'Christopher has access to some pretty heavy-hitting lawyers,' Emma said, before adding, 'he likes a fight.'

'Let me talk to him.'

Emma's eyes narrowed then the faint trace of a smile appeared on her face. I switched to speakerphone and dialled the number she gave me. A man's voice answered, gruff with sleep. When Emma nodded to confirm that it was her husband I introduced myself.

'You know the police can prosecute you for what you've done to your wife,' I said.

The gruffness disappeared and was replaced by a smooth, glassy tone. 'I tape all my calls, Miss Lupo. This one is going to be short since I have no idea what you're talking about.'

Emma's eyes flared. I held up a reassuring hand.

'I'm about to tell you. Your son has a mental disorder which means that there's a possibility he could seriously hurt someone. If he does, he will likely mirror what he's seen at home. You or your wife could be at risk as well as anyone else he associates with. He might even hurt himself. We're trying to ensure that doesn't happen.'

Barrons gave a contemptuous snort. 'The only danger Joshua's in is from a bunch of clucking cunts who are doing their best to turn him queer. Now, if you'll excuse me, I only got back from New York yesterday and I'm trying to sleep off my jet lag.'

And with that he was gone.

'That's mild, believe me,' Emma said. 'He obviously doesn't consider you much of a threat.'

'Well, he's wrong about that,' I said, thinking about the next step. 'Where is Joshua now?'

'With the nanny.' I thought how incongruous Emma looked, tricked out like a princess, with that terrible mashed face. I asked her if there was somewhere she could go tonight where her husband wouldn't be likely to find her.

'He's going away again tomorrow.' Emma fiddled with her rings. It was obvious she had no one to turn to.

'Hold on a moment,' I said. I dialled Sal's number, spoke briefly to her, then called a cab and made sure Emma Barrons got in it.

'Don't go back there till he's gone.'

I returned to my office. There was a knock on the door and Claire appeared with some coffee. MacIntyre wanted to see me at four. He'd read the piece in the *Herald* and wasn't happy.

I checked the clock on the screen. I had two hours to prepare myself for the meeting. I'd signed a contract giving over the copyright on my research to the institute which meant I could be legitimately locked out of my own work. I didn't think it would come to that but it paid to be safe. I told Claire to take messages if anyone called, swiped myself in through the authorised personnel door in the research department and moved down the silent corridor towards the administrative suite, then got to work making sure all my files and their supporting images were fully encrypted and backed up on a memory stick. Just in case. When my phone bleeped a reminder, I downloaded the last of the files onto the final stick, logged off and headed to MacIntyre's office, rehearsing my lines. The director's PA, Anita, flashed me a sympathetic smile, before showing me straight through.

MacIntyre, who was on the phone, nodded a greeting and gestured to the chair on the side of the desk nearest the door. I sat with my hands in my lap trying to steady my nerves. For what seemed like a long while MacIntyre carried on his conversation but the moment the phone went down, his face darkened. As he took a breath, and leaned forward on his elbows, steepling his hands, I thought I may as well get in first. The blood was singing in my temples.

'I'm assuming this is about the piece in the *Herald*?' I explained that White had somehow found out we were treating Joshua Barrons at the clinic. I had suspected Barrons' mother, Emma, of being the leak but I had no proof and now I wasn't so sure. I told MacIntyre that White had used the information to effectively blackmail me into giving him some general background on youth violence and that he'd promised to keep my name and the Barrons family out of the paper. He had only kept half his promise but it was at least preferable that he'd named me rather than giving away the identity of Joshua Barrons. There were too many outlets who'd jump at the chance of a story about a 'devil child'.

MacIntyre leaned back in his chair and interlaced his immaculately manicured fingers.

'What I'm still at a loss to explain is why you felt it necessary to verbally abuse Christopher Barrons on the telephone? You know, I presume, that he serves on the committee of the Halperin Trust?'

Shit.

'I didn't know that,' I said.

I knew Halperin all right. The fund was a major grant giver, funding some of the cutting-edge research into Parkinson's and Alzheimer's. My heart felt as if it had been unzipped and opened out. The only way to have screwed up more than I already had would have been to have punched Barrons in the balls then robbed him of all his money.

'Barrons is a wife beater,' I said lamely.

McIntyre looked at me unblinkingly. 'Even if that were true, why would it be the business of the institute?'

'Because we're trying to treat his son and Barrons is making it impossible. He refuses to accept there's anything wrong with the kid. How are we supposed to try to steer Joshua away from violence when he's witnessing his father beating his mother?'

I saw MacIntyre's complexion redden.

'I wonder if you are listening? Your actions have put the institute's work at risk.'

I readjusted my position. I had rehearsed for a wrist slapping over the *Herald* but I hadn't prepared for this. 'You must know that wasn't my intention,' I said. 'But Joshua Barrons *is* the institute's work. Part of it, anyway.'

MacIntyre flipped idly through some papers; his eyes had shrunk to two tiny unfathomable holes. 'That won't do, I'm afraid.' He looked up. 'There seems to be something of a question mark over your mental health.'

'There's no question mark,' I said, a little desperately. 'Just a bit of stress at home.' Who had MacIntyre been talking to? Not Tom surely. Anja then? 'My research—'

MacIntyre lifted a hand to cut me off, a matador readying himself to deliver the coup de grâce.

'I've taken your tremendous research record into account, Caitlin, as well as what have come to my attention as some personal issues. But you will appreciate the situation you've put me in. You can't simply call up our major funders with completely unsubstantiated accusations. I feel I have no choice but to suspend you pending further inquiries.'

'Inquiries?'

MacIntyre held up a staying finger. His eyebrows rose a little and he glanced at his watch as if to emphasise the point. 'I suggest you go home and take some rest and, in due course, perhaps you can sort out the distractions in your personal life. We'll be in touch. Now, if you'll excuse me…' He made a vague gesture towards the door.

CHAPTER SIXTEEN

Outside, the streets were almost empty of people and traffic and the shopkeepers were closing early and pulling down their grilles. Not far from the Wise Owl Cafe I came across a pile of free sheets dumped on the street, the front page dominated by a picture of the body of fifteen-year-old LeShaun Toley lying sprawled on the pavement, his blood bright in the morning sunshine. The police were in lockdown, their spokesperson saying they were continuing with their investigations into the shooting and insinuating without actually coming out with it that LeShaun had been a gang member and had threatened several police officers. LeShaun's mother was denying her son had any involvement in gangs and demanding more clarity from the Metropolitan Police. An earlier demonstration had been broken up and the mayor and community leaders were appealing for calm.

The stabbings had been almost daily front-page news in the *Herald* but this development felt different. It was the first time police had been involved in the killing and they were doing their best to minimise the kid's death and blame it on gangs. By talking to White I'd got myself mixed up in what was fast becoming a major political scandal. I'd allowed my heart to rule my head. Maybe MacIntyre was right. Once again I'd stepped over a line and just kept going. How could I have been so stupid?

Hurrying up Holland Hill, I noticed that Grissold Park had been shut and the gate locked. I texted Simeon and cancelled our meeting to review Ruby Winter's scans, and he texted back that he wouldn't have been able to get to me anyway: some of the roads were closing and the Tube lines were disrupted. The young crowd who had taken to hanging out at the bus shelter outside Jamal's shop had vanished, but the candles around the nearby 'shrine' had been relit, and someone had graffitied the words *Feds = murderers* onto the yellow board. Jamal himself was standing beside his shopfront nailing planks across the window.

I gave him a limp wave, which he returned with a grimace. He stopped what he was doing, stood up, his face sombre, and greeted me with a solemn, '*As-Salaam-Alaikum.*'

'Looks like you're preparing for a hurricane,' I said.

'Maybe,' Jamal replied. 'But this shop is all I have.' He flicked his head towards Brixton. 'This time people very angry.' Jamal turned his attentions back to me. 'You too. Your face. Very angry.'

In the years we'd known one another Jamal had never said anything so personal. Was it really that obvious?

* * *

As I turned into Dunster Road I made myself slow down and

take some belly breaths. By the time I reached home I was a lot calmer, at least on the outside. The girls were in the garden, Ruby playing on the trampoline while Freya sat under the ideas tree, absorbed in a book. I'd been uneasy leaving them with Tom this time, after the conversation about the lido. Something had happened in the water. Neither of the girls was about to reveal what but my instincts told me that Freya and Ruby's relationship had shifted as a result of that event. Ruby's interest in Freya, which had initially been a mildly envious curiosity, had in recent days grown darker and I felt sure that whatever small harm had so far come to Freya since Ruby's arrival was likely to increase as the newcomer grew in confidence. I'd seen the momentary look of fear on Freya's face when I'd caught her practising her breathing, as if she were too afraid either to stop or to tell. I knew from the experience of the last few days that giving voice to my fears to Tom or Sal would only arouse their suspicions about my mental state still further, but something concrete had to be done to protect my daughter.

In a way, I saw now, MacIntyre had done me a favour. It would have been impossible to carry on working while I felt Freya wasn't safe. This way I'd be at home for a while and able to keep an eye on the girls. I'd be able to get a second opinion on Ruby's scans from Simeon and find a family solicitor to talk through my options. It might be that Simeon's report would force Tom's hand and persuade him to enrol his daughter in some kind of therapeutic programme. I had enough savings to survive for a few months. For now I could focus on protecting Freya and buy enough time to come up with some plans to secure our future together. Whether that future would include Tom and Ruby I didn't yet know.

Freya spotted me at the French windows and came running. 'You're early! Guess what? We went to the park but they closed it, so our friend came to play here for a bit.' She flung her bendy arms around my waist.

'Oh,' I said. 'Which friend?'

'The one we met in the park.'

Ruby had stopped trampolining now and was standing on the grass, watching us.

'Hello, Ruby,' I said. 'Did you have a good day?'

When she didn't answer I turned to Freya. 'What did you play?' I asked, but my daughter just shrugged and looked away.

Tom appeared at the French windows. 'You're back. Did the institute close early?' He sounded frosty, but I'd come to expect that.

'I called you.'

He grunted to indicate he hadn't got the message.

I lowered my voice so the girls couldn't hear. 'How's your father?'

Michael Walsh was the last person on my mind but I didn't want to antagonise Tom by sounding unconcerned. Tom told me that the old man had sprained an ankle and bruised his arm badly. He had arranged for a carer to go in until Michael was more mobile.

'A word in my study?' Tom said, turning. I followed him. He so rarely initiated the kind of conversation I sensed was about to come that I felt winded and apprehensive.

'Who was that kid the girls were playing with today?' I asked.

Tom had sat on the love seat we'd inherited from his mother while I remained hovering by the door. Tom lifted a palm to stop me. 'Hang on, it's my turn to ask the questions. You took my daughter into work?'

'Yes.' I'd already rehearsed an answer for this. 'I was thinking about what you said and decided I should spend a bit more time with her. I thought it would be good for her to see what I do all day.'

But Tom wasn't about to let me off that easily. 'You put her in a scanner.'

I had a ready-prepared answer for this too. 'Well, no, I mean, not really. I let her lie on the scanner bed so she could see how it felt. Then Lucas came in and asked me to check something, so I let Ruby watch a movie with the goggles we've got in there.'

My gaze fell to the photo on Tom's wall of the three of us on Freya's third birthday in front of the butterfly house in the park. Three grinning faces and one double cone Mr Whippy with three flakes. I wanted to cry out, *What happened to us*? But it was already too late.

'You should have called and asked me.'

'You're right, I'm sorry. It's just with Michael being ill I thought you'd be rather preoccupied.'

Tom's eyes narrowed and I sensed he was trying to catch me out. 'And that message you left, about Freya not being well. She's feeling absolutely fine. So what was all that about the pool?'

'It was something Sal said…'

I hadn't practised this part and he knew I was lying. 'Cat,

really, are you listening to yourself?' He leaned in, a faintly menacing expression on his face. 'Because you're beginning to sound a bit mad, and I know you're drinking too much. Didn't the psych say that was the one thing you absolutely mustn't do?'

Suddenly, I heard myself say, 'Why did you hide Charlie's iPad? Was it because of what Ruby scratched on the screen?' I'd kept my discovery to myself until now, knowing that the worst thing I could do would be to bring it up mid-row, when Tom could throw it back at me and the whole thing would become about my invading his privacy. And now I was doing the exact thing I'd promised myself I wouldn't. I'd been manoeuvred into showing my hand too early. Damn Tom. Damn me. What was I *thinking*?

Tom looked up. His nostrils flared and there was something in his eyes that frightened me. He stood up from the love seat, went over to his desk, picked up the tin retro-robot sitting beside his laptop, wound it and set it back down. The robot made its faltering way across the desk. The movement seemed to calm him, because when he spoke again he was like a different person, cool and reasonable.

'First, you had absolutely no right to go snooping in my drawers. Since I evidently can't trust you, I'll be keeping the study locked from now on. If you must know, I hid the iPad because I knew you'd make up some ridiculous theory about it. So what if Ruby did take it? Kids pinch stuff all the time. Particularly when they've just gone through the kind of thing Ruby's gone through. I've dealt with it. She knows not to do that again.'

I opened my mouth to say something but Tom held up a silencing hand.

'Hear me out, Cat. Honestly, I think your work is getting too much for you. You seem to think that every kid except your own is some kind of psycho. Ruby is an ordinary kid who's had a tough time and deserves a stable, loving home which, as I'm sure even *you* can see, she's never going to get while you're living in this house.'

I looked at him and felt curiously detached. 'What exactly are you saying?'

'Isn't it obvious? You need to move out for a bit while you get some help. Then we'll see.' And with that Tom swept up the robot and dropped it into the desk drawer as if to say, *That's the end of the matter.*

* * *

The girls had gone to their rooms, sensing a row brewing. I went out to the ideas tree to calm down and think through my options. Tom had skilfully turned my own arguments against me and I hadn't even seen it coming. *I* was now the person deemed unfit to remain in the house. How could I have allowed that to happen? Everything seemed so tangled and confusing it was hard to think straight. Was it conceivable that Tom was right? What if my instincts about Ruby really were as hopelessly off as Tom seemed to think? It wouldn't be the first time. Kylie Drinkwater was dead because I had fatally misjudged Rees Spelling. Had my terror of making the same mistake driven me to view everyone who came close to my child as a potential threat? Was Ruby Winter merely a victim of my overprotectiveness and anxiety? People who knew me seemed to think I was losing it. I didn't feel crazy but wasn't that the first sign of madness? Who should I believe? Myself or everyone around me?

I took a few deep breaths. In the distance came the whump of helicopters. My head continued to spin. I thought of leaving. Just picking Freya up and going. The sounds grew louder. *Whump, whump, whump.* My pulse quickened. A wave of panic rose in me. I looked up through the branches of the tree and saw the spinning blades, felt something lurch and had a desperate need suddenly to be inside in the safety of the house. Rising, I ducked under the umbrella of branches and emerged in the open air of the garden. Directly above, the helicopter stirred the soupy summer air. My throat thickened. Was that the smell of burning? An inner voice told me to get closer to the house. I began to hurry down the garden, my pace accelerating until I reached the French windows. There I stood for a moment, leaning on the bricks, catching my breath, my hands trembling too much to pull open the door, until finally the helicopter moved away and the roar of the blades dimmed to a distant hum.

Back inside the house I poured myself a glass of wine. I wanted to go upstairs and see my daughter but I didn't trust myself not to alarm her. Instead, I went into the living room and switched on the BBC News Channel for the top-of-the-hour bulletin. It seemed the local news had gone national. While I'd been sitting in MacIntyre's office, a crowd had gathered in front of Brixton police station wanting answers about LeShaun Toley's death and demanding to speak to a senior officer. An officer had eventually appeared but radically misjudged the mood, claiming Toley's death had been referred to the Independent Police Complaints Commission and he had nothing more to say about it. Toley's family, who were outside the station, were unimpressed. Two days ago, they'd had to learn of their family member's death from bystanders and reports on Twitter. Since then no one from the police had spoken to them directly. The voiceover reported that the crowd had been particularly incensed by the police officer's suggestion that they go home. The police had responded by sending out officers in riot gear to move people away from the station. Jamal must have caught wind of this when I passed. Since then all hell had broken loose. The crowd had started pushing the phalanx of police back. The police had responded with a baton charge. People were setting fire to bins.

This wasn't going away any time soon. Already the buses had stopped running, the trains weren't stopping at Brixton and most of the local through roads had closed. South London was in lockdown. Terrified of losing control, the Met had drafted in officers from other forces to help police the situation. If ever there was a moment not to walk out on your husband and take your child from the only home she'd ever known, this was it. For the time being, at least, I was trapped.

My phone began trilling the 'Hallelujah Chorus'. I took the call.

'Cat! Are you rioting down there?' It was, of course, Sal.

'Not personally, no.'

'Everything's fine then?'

'Depends what you mean by fine.' I told my sister about White and Barrons and being put on indefinite leave by MacIntyre. I told her that Tom had brought up the possibility of my leaving. As I spoke, I was looking out of the window onto the street. The sound of sirens and helicopters was pretty constant now and the smell of burning had grown stronger.

'About leaving...' Sal went on. Her tone suggested she was about to advise me to do it. 'I just wonder, well, I mean, you haven't exactly been *yourself* and what with your history and now this thing with the institute... I'm just trying to be realistic.'

I felt my chest tighten. 'Whose side are you on, exactly, Sal?'

There was a pause and when Sal spoke again she sounded flustered. 'Oh, I just mean, you're not working now so you could, I don't know, take some time out, sit on a beach for a while.'

'And leave my kid with two people I don't trust?'

She sighed. 'All I'm saying is, maybe Tom's got a point.'

* * *

After the call ended I sat on the bed rubbing my forehead with my hands. I felt as if I was travelling down a rocky path into the dark. A memory surfaced. Guatemala, before Freya came along. Tom had wanted to climb an active volcano. I didn't, really, but I went along with it because Tom was always so persuasive. The volcano turned out to be harder and higher than we'd anticipated; we ascended into cloud forest then beyond the treeline onto rock and scree. Tom insisted on going all the way to the top. He kept saying we were Couple Number One. Invincible us. We'd gone up without a guide and I began to worry that we wouldn't have time to get down before the light failed. But on we went. Arriving at the summit at last, we were greeted by a smouldering crater and an awful stink of sulphur.

On the way down, with the sun setting, I tried not to get spooked by the loose stones and the encroaching darkness. Pretty soon, though, I fell behind. Up ahead, I could just see Tom. I called out, but he didn't turn so I shouted and this time he did turn and, in response to my frantic gestures, gave a single wave, turned back and carried on.

By the time I reached the path leading off the volcano, I was broken. It was dark, the kind of dark that makes all but the bravest soul quake, and I'd fallen and hurt my ankle and I was disorientated and afraid. I'd lost sight of Tom what seemed like hours ago and was beginning to feel hopeless when, through what was dark, jungly overgrowth, I spotted a light. *Thank God.* A family was sitting around a table under a kerosene lamp eating and drinking and there was Tom holding court in his terrible Spanish. He smiled and saluted me with his glass.

'I knew you'd feel such a failure if I came to rescue you.'

He was sort of right. But that was also completely beside the point.

* * *

I went upstairs to reassure Freya about the rioting and found her deep inside a book.

'Is it going to be OK? Out there, I mean.'

'Yes, of course. The trouble won't come up this far, but even if it does, we'll be safe inside the house.'

'Will we? Be safe, I mean.'

My breath caught in my chest. 'Is this about Ruby?'

Freya looked uncomfortably away and shook her head. 'No, it's about you and Dad.'

* * *

I didn't say goodnight to Ruby. I was angry with her for what she was doing to Freya and with myself for not being able to stop it. Best avoid her. When I went back downstairs the light was still on in Tom's study but I felt too rattled to talk to him. Instead I sat in the living room with the rest of the Riesling, zoning in and out of the chaotic scenes in the news. The spring had finally sprung. Violence was sweeping across the city. In Brixton, police cars had been set on fire and barricades set up in the streets from where youths were throwing missiles into lines of riot police. In parts of Hackney and Islington, banks and big-name retail outlets were having their windows smashed and their contents looted and set alight. It seemed that, even with the arrival of reinforcements from other forces, the police were hopelessly outnumbered.

I reached for the remote and the screen dissolved into static. Nothing about this was likely to end well. I stood to go to the kitchen for another bottle of wine and, as I did, my eye fell on the table in the bay window and the portrait of Lilly Winter. I went over and picked it up. For a while, I just stared at it as Lilly Winter stared back at me, familiarising myself with the set of the jawline, the shape of the eyes and the angle of the nose. The woman in the picture was a version of myself, the one who hadn't escaped the Pemberton Estate, and I thought of her lying in bed, as drunk as I was now, slipping into death as softly as into a warm bath.

Picking up the bottle of wine, I went to the kitchen and poured the remainder down the drain and, needing the cool of the night, wandered out into the garden. Through the branches of the ideas tree a crescent moon was hanging huge and ripe in the sky. The air was full of the slur of sirens and the thrum of helicopters, but I was no longer afraid. I sat under the ideas tree and tried to find a place in my head that wasn't already ablaze. I'd allowed myself to be manipulated, first by James White and then by my husband. I'd been guilty of bad errors of judgement both at work and at home. I'd stepped across boundaries and failed to trust my daughter. What I'd done to Ruby was unethical, futile and quite possibly illegal. It would take more than scans of the girl's brain to persuade Tom to get his daughter into treatment. He'd be more likely to dig in his heels just to prove a point. Ruby Winter had become a pawn in a game between the two of us. We'd both raised the stakes. And now there was no choice but to play it to the bitter end.

I went back inside and climbed the stairs. The window on the landing gave out onto a view of Holland Hill, the park just visible between the rooftops, London's sprawl beyond it and, in the distance, the flickering lights of Canary Wharf. From here a corona of yellow lights blazed on the horizon and I could hear the blare of fire engines. Somewhere on the other side of the park, orange lights danced then paled into smoke. Above it all, a blank sky in which the tiny trails of aeroplanes and satellites scattered. A sudden movement drew my gaze away from the window and Pudge the cat came tiptoeing towards me. I bent down and ruffled his ears. The wine bloomed hot on my skin. I felt exhausted and wired.

Remembering a foil of Zopiclone left over from a previous bout of insomnia, I went to the bathroom and, ignoring the warning not to mix the pills with alcohol, took them anyway, then stripped off and got into the shower in the en suite, suddenly needing to wash all the bad thoughts from my head. As I turned the taps, there was a loud belch. No water. I tried again and got the same result. The boiler in Lilly Winter's flat flashed before my mind. Faulty plumbing, an engineer who didn't do his job, a woman dead. I made a mental note to call out a plumber in the morning, then, padding across the hallway to the family bathroom and without turning on the light so as not to wake Freya, I hung up my nightclothes and stepped into the shower there. The window at the back let in enough city light to just about see and it was calming this way. I stood under the flow of water waiting for the pills to do their job and still my mind. A few minutes later, I brushed myself down with the back of my hand, drew back the shower curtain and stepped out into the deep gloom. As my eyes accustomed themselves, I noticed a shadow at the entrance to the room.

And then the shadow moved. Instinctively, I covered myself with my hands and peered hard.

'Freya?'

Nothing.

'Is that you, Ruby?'

The outline of the hair gave her away.

'You startled me.'

Ruby Winter did not move. Her eyes were tiny glass baubles. Once again she looked unreal somehow, more like a malevolent sprite than a girl. I pulled the towel from the rack and wrapped it tightly around my body. I thought about the sleeping pills I'd taken and how the GABA receptors in my brain would soon be making clear thought almost impossible. I didn't want to be in the dark anymore. Reaching out, I pulled the cord beside the mirror. A thin blue light spread across the room.

My pulse rattled in my forehead and in a faraway voice I heard myself say, 'What do you want?'

Ruby Winter's eyes narrowed and I felt the tug of her gaze.

'I know what you've done, Ruby. I know about all the things that went missing from my drawers; I know about the iPad and the hamster and the vandalism at the cemetery.' I felt a surge of excitement, as if something was finally being revealed and, when no reply came, I went on, almost breathless now. 'I know you pushed Freya under the water at the lido. I know that's what you did. It's why she was practising holding her breath, wasn't it? Because you hurt her.'

Ruby shook her head. She was looking at me through narrowed, assessing eyes,

'Why are you lying to me?'

'Freya needs to improve her swimming because one day someone *might* hold her down then she *might* drown.'

I felt something in me slacken, as if I was on the edge of some terrible danger but unable to see beyond the first moment.

'I don't want you around my daughter anymore,' I said. 'I don't want you around Freya.'

Ruby smiled. 'That's not up to you, is it?'

'What do you mean?'

'Well, I decide who I want around, not you.'

'Ruby, this isn't a joke.' I felt a rush of something, a dark energy careening towards the centre and emptying everything in its path.

'I want Freya here with me.'

'Ruby, you're a child. You don't get to decide who you do or don't want around.'

She held the smile long after all traces of it had vanished from her eyes. 'Oh no?'

'No.'

Her hands went to her hips and she cocked her head. 'Well, I didn't want Lilly Winter around and look what happened to *her*.'

I went to speak but the words stuck in my throat. I thought about the damp towels on the floor in Ruby Winter's bedroom, the batteries scattered on the floor, the open windows in her bedroom. And I thought about the window in Lilly Winter's bedroom which was always kept open except on the night she died. I thought about the look Ruby had given me when I had asked her about the heating engineer and the word used by the girl with the acrylic nails came back to me. *Facety.*

'You don't know what you're talking about,' I said.

The girl blinked at me, an expression of absolute malevolence on her face. Something in my head burst outwards as though I had been vapourised. I felt my legs come unstuck from under me. Without thinking, I rushed forwards, drawn by some inescapable force, my arms grabbing for the girl in the doorway. As my fingers curled around her pyjamas, she ducked and turned and my hand scrabbled momentarily in the air until it landed in a fog of hair. Ruby wheeled forwards, her hands snapping up to her head in an attempt to beat me off, and started swinging wildly from side to side. I took hold and pulled. With my hands clasped around the girl's shoulders, I began to shake her. It was madness. I knew it. But I couldn't stop. I wanted to go on and on until there was nothing of her left. Then a shocking, strangled scream arced across the room. For an instant the sound hung in the air.

What have I done?

A door swung open and Freya appeared, her face still busy with sleep. She looked at me, then at Ruby Winter. There was a sharp catch of breath followed by a terrible keening. Shocked, I let go of Ruby and stood back. A light went on in the hallway, followed by the sound of thundering footsteps, and for a moment we three froze. Freya and I were both in the doorway to the bathroom now; I had my hands on Freya's arm, trying to still her. A little further back, head bowed, rubbing at the spot where I had pulled her hair, stood Ruby. A pulse tap-danced crazily across my mind. I had no idea what I was doing but I knew what I had done. It was so out of character, so beyond my own frame of reference, it was as if someone else had been sitting in my driving seat.

Tom rushed up. I shrank back and, as I did, I felt Freya disengage herself from me and move away. I had no feelings of self-pity. I was violent and terrible, someone my own daughter no longer wanted to acknowledge.

Glaring at me, Tom said, 'What the *fuck*?' I watched him slacken and collect himself. He was smart enough to know that if he lost it now, neither of us would win.

I raised my palms in a gesture of surrender, stricken by my own failure. I'd lost, I'd been routed. I was down and out.

'Go to your rooms, girls,' he said. The two girls went, immediately and without comment. Tom waited until they were out of sight then said, 'In my study!'

I quickly pulled my pyjamas and robe back on whilst Tom glowered at me, then made my way to his study. He followed after me. I sat on the pulled-out sofa bed. Despite the heat, I was cold and my hands were shaking. Tom stood with his back against the study door. The cords in his neck looked taut enough to snap and his lower arms were sheeny, the muscles flexed. Around the groin area of his boxers I noticed a dark patch of sweat and, not for the first time, I felt a little afraid of him.

'God, I know how bad that looked. It was *unforgivable*. I had no right…' I was thinking wildly now, seeing where this was going and prepared to do anything to divert it. 'It was just, Ruby, well, she said – she *hinted* – that she'd had something to do with her mother's death. She said she didn't want Lilly around. She seemed to suggest the heating engineer had something to do with it. She said she could do the same to Freya.'

I knew precisely how saying this would make me sound. Eleven-year-old girls didn't plot the deaths of their mothers. They didn't threaten to kill their half-sisters. Except that I knew better. Because I worked every day with kids who did. All the time. Kids like Ayesha, Joshua and Adam.

Tom's expression was wintery and without softness as he stepped closer. He sucked his teeth and, slowly shaking his head, he said, 'I don't think you even know what you're saying. First, these ridiculous stories and now you physically attack an eleven-year-old child.' His jaw flexed, the electric impulses of his thoughts leaving trails across his face. I knew that whatever I did or said now would be like trying to ascend an escalator that was descending faster than you could climb it.

'Really, I'm not angry, I'm *concerned*.' His voice was uncompromising and mechanical and, in that moment, I suddenly realised that I had to get away from him. I had to get away before he tried to have me sectioned. I shot up from the sofa bed, but he'd anticipated me and before I could reach the door he'd slipped through and closed it behind him.

I shouted, pushing at the door with my shoulder, a dark plume rising up in my throat, but it was hopeless. Tom's combined weight and strength were too much for me. I heard the key turn in the lock.

'You'll thank me for this, Caitlin.' His voice grew fainter

as he retreated into the kitchen. Moments later, I heard him mumbling into the phone. 'Yes, yes. No. I did. Immediately, *yes.*'

I banged on the door and shouted as loudly as I knew how for Freya.

But Freya didn't come.

PART TWO

Now

CHAPTER SEVENTEEN

I know there is a little time. Not much, but some. The psychiatric crisis team will have to wait for a police escort. On a normal day this takes a while. But tonight, at this moment, not far from this house, this study, this locked door, city kids are setting buildings on fire and overturning patrol cars and throwing petrol bombs while, somewhere out there, LeShaun Toley's family are keeping vigil, wanting answers. The police have a job on their hands trying to keep some semblance of order. One woman who may or may not be having a breakdown is hardly going to be a priority.

Eventually, though, they will come. An escort will be drummed up from somewhere and the crisis team will arrive, they will look at my history and they will listen to Tom and the likelihood is they will ask me for a voluntary section. If I refuse, they will section me themselves. When you have been through what I have been through, been given the diagnosis I've been given, you are never safe. In small, subtle, but profound ways your life is no longer your own. A single episode of psychosis, even one with such an obvious, simple cause as an overspill of pregnancy hormones, is enough to mark you. You will never again escape the well-meaning surveillance of family and friends. *Is Caitlin OK? Don't you think she was a bit 'up and down'? Maybe she needs to go back on the drugs?* If someone says you are ill and you say you are not, they will always believe the other person. They will want to make you 'well' again even when you are not ill. They will always, *always* be on guard for the next time.

If I'm locked up or drugged, who will protect my daughter?

An idea evolves into a plan. To the side of Tom's study is a small exterior passageway leading into the garden. Estate agents usually call it a side return. A window looks out over it. Years ago, when we first moved in, it was a requirement of our insurance policy that we fit locks to the ground-floor windows. They can only be opened a few inches at the top of the sash but they are held fast by locking bolts which unscrew from the inside. I am wearing pyjamas and a robe with slippers on my feet. I have no phone, no money, and no ID, but if I can unscrew the bolts without Tom hearing, I can open the window and escape into the garden.

What if escaping only confirms my 'insanity' and provokes a police search? What am I escaping to? How long will I be able to remain free? If only there was enough time to think all of this through. But there isn't. There is only time enough to get out.

In the desk drawer is a couple of hundred quid in rolled-up twenties. This will help. Very softly, so as not to alert Tom, I pull back the curtains, unscrew the locking bolt on either side of the frame, pull the sash up then lower myself out of the open window and onto the side return. There is no access to the front from here, but I can sneak through the broken fencing at the back of the garden into the Fricks' house and from there I will find a way out through the temporary access created by the builders. And so here I am, a woman running away from the house on which she alone pays the mortgage in order to protect her daughter from another of the occupants. Of course they'll think I'm mad.

The moon lends a little of its borrowed light. Sticking close to the fence, I work my way along the side of the garden towards the ideas tree. From here I can see Tom, pacing up and down the length of the table, talking into the phone. If he looks up and out at this part of the garden right now, it will appear black and still. I will be invisible to him. I am working the loosened fencing now, feeling for the unevenness between the boards with my hands. Swinging the panel aside, I creep through. With a little chirrup, Pudge comes running. I freeze and hold my breath, praying the movement won't set off the security lights, but the garden continues to be lit only by the pink dust of the London skyline, the now-distant lights of police helicopters and the neon moon. All that remains is to slip under the tarpaulin, around the scaffolding and through the Fricks' tiny front garden and I'm out onto Dunster Road.

Relief.

At Holland Hill, I run into a stinking fog. Like the old pea-soupers, I imagine, but more toxic still. A violent blend of burning rubbish, disintegrating buildings and lit tyres. A long line of police vans bowls by in a northerly direction, heading for Brixton, many of them painted in the livery of distant forces. Out here the noise is tremendous: a sinister symphony of sirens, shop and car alarms. Throughout the city the usual plans and routines will be breaking down. Who knows where this will end? And when? And how? I stand with my hand veiled across my nose and mouth, adjusting to the acrid air. Anybody with any sense will be at home, staying out of trouble. This is not the hour to be out.

But I am. Out. And with nowhere to go. In other circumstances, I might make my way to Sal's place, but the bus shelters are empty and on the arrivals boards a red LED message blinks: *Await Announcements*. I could walk it in an hour and a half. But I'd have to get through the barricades at Brixton. And besides, I am not so sure I trust Sal right now. Anja lives not far away. But I definitely don't trust Anja. As for friends, well, there are none. At least not nearby. Not people I can count on.

Except. Except. There may just be one.

Sticking to the inside edge of the pavement, partly obscured by the shadow from the buildings, I edge around the back of the park, reaching the brow of the hill where it intersects with the South Circular. Here the light is a different colour from the blue-white of the street lamps. Up over the brow of the hill half a dozen burning tyres block the road. The only way to get through this night is not to be surprised by anything. Up ahead, it's as if a shockwave has rolled over the familiar parade of shabby shops, blowing out their windows and shooting a miscellany of cheap goods out into the streets. A knot of people, their faces obscured by bandanas and hoodies, are busy transferring the loot into shopping trolleys and rucksacks. There is nothing worth taking but, in an act of desperation and rebellion, or maybe just for the thrill, kids are taking it anyway. Broken glass is everywhere, so much that, in the yellow light from the burning tyres, the road looks like a path of gold shouldered by banks of blackening cloud. Several police vans stream by, ignoring the looters, on their way to bigger, more dangerous incidents to the south. As I edge my way around the scene, past a cluster of overturned dustbins, my adrenaline reserves run out and I'm conscious, for the first time, of the effects of the sleeping pills on my brain. I'm slow and a little spacey. The inhibitory circuits have the upper hand. I won't be making good decisions. Already I feel unreliable.

A group of youngsters register my presence, and, deciding I am of no consequence, return to their phones.

What's one madwoman in a city gone nuts?

I walk on. Or stumble. Or float. I am no longer in touch with the motions of my body. Still, despite the drugs and the craziness and the unreliability, there does seem to be method in my madness. Sometimes the body knows more than the mind can tell it. Sometimes only the body knows the truth.

Turning east, I head into the grid of streets leading to the Pemberton Estate. In the pink and orange light, the place is like something infected that people have abandoned for fear of contagion. The stairwells are empty, the walkways are empty, few lights are on in the flats. A kid's sock and yesterday's fast food wrappers lie abandoned in parched grass by the car park. It's then that the scent hits me. In the playground in the middle of the estate people have left bouquets of flowers, and also candles, toys, football scarves and photos of the dead boy. No police. They wouldn't dare.

I'm making my way to Ash Building when a shadow by the bins calls out.

'Hey, you want a smartphone? Pay as you go.'

I stop, turn, peer into the gloom as a young woman steps out of the shadow. The girl in the wedges. She doesn't recognise me.

I say, 'What you got?'

The phone is brand new, still in its packaging. Riot booty. Never mind, I need it. I volunteer a number, the girl gives a yelp of mock outrage and we see-saw our way to a deal.

'You knew LeShaun Toley?' I ask her as I'm counting out the money.

She shoots me a blank look. Not sure if it's real or fake.

'The dead kid.'

The same blank look. She doesn't want to talk about it. In any case, this whole thing has gone way beyond LeShaun now. It's seeped down into the cracks that people living on the Pemberton Estate have to negotiate daily, ruptures in the fabric of society which people living other lives closer to the park have, for the most part, chosen to ignore.

'This,' she says. She looks up at the police helicopter blading over. 'This is what you get.'

'Here.' She hesitates a moment then takes the extra twenty.

Moments later I am pressing my ear to the door of Lilly Winter's old flat. The peculiar silence of an empty home. Evidently, the place has yet to be assigned a new tenant, which means that the keys probably haven't been changed. I'll wake Gloria if I have to but I'd rather not have to explain myself. No one around. The window? I grasp at the frame from underneath, willing the hinge to give. Five minutes later, my fingertips reddened and sore, I give up. It is the darkest hour of the night now, the hour before dawn, and I'm cold, but wired too, no longer doing battle with my inhibitory circuits. The central executive in my brain has bypassed the drugs and moved beyond them. My mind toggles between its task-positive and task-negative networks. Daydreaming. Thought fragments begin to surface like bubbles of air on the skin of a dark pool. Finally, I can think. I ring on Gloria's doorbell.

A light goes on somewhere at the back of Gloria's flat then flips off. I press the bell again, this time in sharp staccato bursts that are impossible to ignore. The light returns and there are heavy footsteps in the hallway, followed by Gloria's voice, still thick with sleep, saying, 'Go away now!'

'It's Caitlin Lupo. We met.'

Silence, followed by the sound of a sliding bolt, the door cracking open on its chain.

Gloria sucks her teeth. 'I remember. You sleepwalking, lady? Go home.'

'My daughter's in trouble.'

The eyebrows rise, the lips a thin line. She doesn't want to deal with me but mention of my daughter has set off something. She checks about, sees nothing. The chain rattles and the door swings open and there's Gloria in a red and orange onesie.

'Can I come in?'

The flat is spotless and awash with gewgaws – little pieces of embroidery, family photos and reminders of home. I'm shown into a tiny living room and instructed to sit while Gloria disappears into the kitchen to make tea, reappearing moments later.

'You want to say why you do this middle-of-night scandal?'

'I'm trying to protect my daughter.'

'Why protect?'

She hands me a small glass etched with vine leaves. Weak black tea swirling in the cup, a tiny slice of lemon.

'At the funeral you told me there was something strange about Ruby Winter.'

Gloria's eyes flare. She sits back and crosses her arms over her chest. 'You come here in pyjamas in middle of night for this? Why are you bothering me? You know this girl.'

'But what do *you* know, Gloria?'

Her eyes cut about. She looks at me, blinks twice, and then really *looks* at me. Gloria shrugs then she criss-crosses her palms in the air. 'Ruby and Lilly, fighting, fighting. Always fighting.' This is what I have come for. Gloria is an ally, a witness, someone who can attest to Ruby Winter's unpredictability, her potential dangerousness. Gloria goes on: 'Maybe this sound bananas, but the mother die and the girl…' She tails off but her meaning is clear.

'I'm beginning to think that way too.' I tell her about the wet towels, the batteries.

Gloria is silent for a moment, not knowing what to say.

I take a sip of tea. Gloria refills the glass. I reach for it again but clumsily, almost knocking it over. A brief return of the drug fugue. Gloria is stroking her chin now, thinking. I blink and shake my head to rid myself of the fog.

'I want to take another look at the boiler. Can you let me in?'

Gloria thinks about this, though not for long. She's already decided to co-operate. 'First put on some clothes. I have a few things. Maybe they look better on you, but probably not.'

She disappears into her bedroom. While I'm waiting, I take out my new phone and plug the charger into the wall then I punch Sal's number into Gloria's landline.

Sal answers after the second ring. Evidently, she is already awake and has been expecting to hear from me. So they know I have escaped and Tom has called Sal hoping that's where I've gone. *No chance.*

The words tumble out with barely a breath between. 'Thank God. We're out of our *minds* with worry, Tom is going *spare*. I was going to go over there and mind the girls while he went looking for you but the cab was stopped at the bridge, the roads are all jammed up, no one's going *anywhere*.'

I wait for some dead air. 'Listen, Sal, I'm OK. But I want you to promise me something. I want you to pack a bag and, as soon they open the bridges, I want you to go over to Dunster Road and stay for a few days. Keep an eye on Freya. Just until I get back.'

There's a pause while this sinks in, then Sal starts up again, only this time her voice has an edge to it. 'Cat, you're scaring me. Where are you? What the hell's going on?'

'I'm fine. *Really.* But I need you to look after my daughter and make sure she's safe.'

'Freya's not safe? Why? Cat, you're not making sense.'

'Please, Sal, just do it.'

* * *

Lilly Winter's flat is as it was when I came to pick up Ruby's things: filthy and smelling of cigarettes. It'll take a lot to make this fit for new tenants. The boiler cover comes away in my hands, revealing the mess of valves and soldered piping. A concertina flue leaves the top of the unit and a U-bend connects to the outside vent. I take a kitchen knife from the drawer and unscrew the inner cover over the pilot light. No obvious signs of tampering. Next the flue. By hoisting myself up onto the kitchen counter and unscrewing the flue from the wall, I get a view through the tubing all the way back down into the machine. No blockage.

Gloria's face appears around the door.

'Didn't you tell me Lilly Winter usually slept with the window open?'

'Yes. One of her boyfriend fix screw so window only open a little way.' Gloria draws a line in the air between the middle finger and thumb of her right hand. 'For secure. From then, Lilly have the window open little bit all the time.'

'But on the night she died the window was closed.'

'Yes, also no. I went by after church, is open. Loud, loud music. But police say the window closed when they find her.'

'Did you tell the police it had been open earlier in the evening?'

Gloria's face darkens. 'What are you? Bad in head? People open windows, close windows. Anyway, I told you, police business is not my business. What kind trouble you in, anyway, lady?'

'I'm just trying to protect my daughter.'

'From who? The girl?'

Not answering is its own answer.

'You know, I have daughter too, her name Elmira,' Gloria goes on. 'My ex take her to Albania. It was four years ago. I have been to find but he doesn't let me see, or even talk. He is fierce man.'

'You miss her.' Not a question.

'Each second,' Gloria says, poking out the seconds with her finger. 'I tell you something. The afternoon that boiler man was here, it was hot like Kosovo summer. This man is standing on the walkway smoking, red like pepper. I fetch him cool drink. So we talk a little. He is Albanian from Tirana, not Kosovar like me. His name Ani.'

It's not much but it's more than I've had so far. And there may be more still. I reach out and grasp her arm in my hand. 'Thank you. Do you have a number for him? An address?'

Gloria stiffens and pulls away. 'We should go now.'

I follow her out. At the doorway, she makes a right turn and moves towards her front door, then, turning to me, says suddenly, 'Sunday. I will see. Call me at the end of today. For now, I am sleeping one hour more, because a crazy woman is knocking in the middle of the night and looking like shit in my clothes. Is all too much.'

CHAPTER EIGHTEEN

Perhaps by now the police are looking for me, an unhinged woman with a history of mental illness who has attacked a little girl. Perhaps they think I am dangerous. Perhaps I am.

Eleven years ago, thickly pregnant, my mind tumbled through a surreal world of my own invention. Because that's what psychosis feels like. I became a pioneer of a country only I could ever map. But then, not long afterwards, I gave birth and I came back from that country and I re-entered the world.

I came back.

Now I sit in a bus shelter and wait out the night and make my plans. Dawn comes dressed in dove grey. The cafe opposite opens up. I go over and get a cup of tea then wait till seven thirty to call my assistant Claire's mobile. She sounds surprised but pleased to hear my voice.

'Did you get caught up in the riots? I just walked through Brixton. It looked like a plane had fallen out of the sky. No bodies, thank God, but wreckage everywhere.' Sirens are increasingly drowning out her voice. 'I'll just go somewhere quieter!' There is a pause, the city's new theme tune has faded out, and Claire is speaking again, her voice coarse and half whispered.

'Is this about Joshua Barrons? I wasn't sure whether or not to tell you, but I thought you might have heard anyway.'

'About Joshua?'

'Yes. Anja discharged him. Though to be fair, I think MacIntyre pressured her. A ploy to keep the father sweet. In any case, Anja seems to have got her reward for caving in. MacIntyre has made her acting head of the clinic.'

Shit. All that time. All that persuasion. All that work. And now this. Rees Spelling comes to mind.

'Have you spoken to Emma?'

'A couple of times. She says Joshua's got worse. She wants him back in treatment. You couldn't call her, could you? I think she needs all the support she can get.' There's a pause. 'This isn't why you called, though, is it?'

I now have a hundred and forty pounds in my pocket, scarcely enough to buy me a bed for the night in a hotel in London.

'No, I called about me.'

'Oh?' Claire's voice brightens. 'Are you coming back?'

'Not yet. Listen, this might sound off-key but I need somewhere to hang out. And maybe stay for a night or two?' On the streets I'm vulnerable and not only because of the riots. The police may well be looking for me.

The words hang momentarily in the air then Claire makes a small coughing sound. 'Oh my God. *Of course.*' She rattles off an address in one of the shabbier streets running from the

South Circular. There's a bike shed. At the back on the left a short end of pipe. A Ziploc bag containing Claire's spare key is stuffed inside.

'Can I borrow a few clothes? Joggers and a T-shirt will do.' I'm still dressed in Gloria's cast-offs, sparkly leggings and a top that's far too big for me.

'Help yourself. There should be some clean stuff in my bedroom. Nothing in the fridge, though, sorry.'

'Thank you. For saying yes and for not asking why. And, Claire? Please don't mention any of this to anyone. Not to the police. Not even to Tom if he calls you.'

* * *

The key to Claire's flat is where she said it would be. The lock to the front door of the communal parts is sticky and takes a moment of fiddling around, but the pins give after a few tries and, in moments, I find myself inside a narrow passageway smelling of dust and cheap carpet. Two floors up is a tiny, spartan one-bedder but it's neat and clean, much like Claire herself. This is how young people survive in the city now. They live in tiny hutches with ludicrous rents in dodgy, distant neighbourhoods on maxed-out credit cards. The only thing they own in greater quantity than their parents, other than debt, is technology.

In Claire's bedroom there are a pair of black leggings and a grey T-shirt. I peel off Gloria's cast-offs and shower away the night then go into the kitchen and empty the small carrier bag of provisions I bought from a shopkeeper who'd been up all night guarding his shop. A cup of tea and a bowl of cereal later, overwhelmed by tiredness, I slide onto the sofa and feel myself very quickly vanishing into sleep. I wake with Freya on my mind and tap in Sal's number on the new phone.

'Cat?' Sal sounds anxious and uncharacteristically chilly. 'Where are you? Whose phone is this?'

'Can I speak to Freya?'

Ignoring the question, Sal says, 'Look, I'm at Dunster Road. I managed to persuade a minicab to take me. Cost a *fortune*.' She sounds anxious. 'Tom's told the girls that you've gone to hospital to get better.'

'Is Freya there?'

A pause follows. When my sister speaks again her voice is soft and with a quiet, unfamiliar authority. 'I don't know all the details about what went on last night, but the police have been round and you can't come back.'

'*What?* Dunster Road is my *home*. I pay the bloody mortgage.'

'It's called a DV something.'

'Domestic *violence*?'

'Yeah, a DV Protection Notice. You need to go down to Brixton police station so they can serve you in person. If you don't, they'll issue a warrant for your arrest. In any case, you have to keep away from the house and the family right now. Tom is taking the girls to his father's place for a few days to get them out of London. They're upstairs packing. Please, Cat, go down to the station and get yourself booked.'

'I'm not crazy, Sal.'

She sighs. 'You'll get a chance to explain. There'll be a hearing apparently.' Then in a hiss, 'But Jesus, Cat, I mean, assault a little *girl*?'

'You mean *Ruby*?'

'There's more than one?' Sal says. She's being sarcastic.

'Listen, Sal, Ruby said something and I lost it and I shouldn't have reacted the way I did but it was a grab and a push. And that was it.'

In the background I can hear my daughter's voice and Sal whispering, 'Go back upstairs, I'm on the phone.' My daughter's voice fades and there is the sound of a door swinging shut, then the hard whoosh of Sally's voice. 'You just don't get it do you, Caitlin? Ruby's got bruises. One of her fingernails is bloody.'

'The fingernail thing, that was self-inflicted. She did it with a paper clip. About a week ago. I talked to Tom about it. Ask him, he'll tell you.'

There's a harrumphing sound on the other end. Sal isn't going to ask Tom because she doesn't believe me. 'Look, all I know is what Ruby told the police. Besides, Cat, Tom saw you hit her.'

'Tom said *what*?' I'm conscious of my thumb scraping the fabric of the sofa. 'Is that what he told you?' I'm up now and pacing around the room, dizzy with outrage.

Sal says, 'I'll *tell* you exactly what Tom told me. He told me you threatened to *kill* him. You said it to me too. A couple of weeks ago. You said, "I could murder him."'

I laugh in spite of myself. 'This is absolutely insane. Tom's manipulating you; he's playing both of us. He wanted me out of the house; well, now he's got me out of the house. But I'm not going down that bloody easily, Sal. If Tom Walsh wants a mad woman, he'll get one. Let him try to take my daughter from me and he'll find out just how crazed I can be.'

An hour later, I'm picking my way through police cordons, broken glass and smoking buildings along Brixton High Street in the direction of the police station. The riots have calmed but it's edgy and at the station itself there's a manic overload of young people and their parents. Now that the DV thing has been flung at me, I no longer have a game plan. Until I do, I'm vulnerable. For the time being I need to play by Tom's rules, double bluff him, make him think he's got me.

I tell the desk what I've come for and am added to a long queue. While I'm waiting to be served and processed, Gloria calls with news. She's located someone who knows someone who might know Ani. He hangs out in the evenings at an Albanian cafe in Forest Hill but there's no point in going there tonight. With the police so much in evidence and the rioting likely to blow up again, the Albanians will be lying low. She will take me tomorrow, when she comes off shift at the old people's home, say at six o'clock?

The queue at the police station moves at glacial speed. Looks like half the kids in London have piled in. I could pick a copper, a woman perhaps, take her to one side, say that, for reasons I don't fully understand yet, my husband is trying to protect one daughter at the expense of another. I could mention Tom's attempts to gaslight me so he can get custody of our child. But she'd say I sound mad and she'd be right.

It takes four hours to be served with a DV Protection Notice.

The constable dealing with my case is a man by the name of Sergeant Neil Forrester, about my age, with pocketed, reddened eyes and the manner of a man dragged from his bed. Most likely been up all night. He flips through the documents and double-takes when he gets to my name.

'Oh, *Dr*, is it?'

I bite my lip and say nothing.

The conditions of my DVPN are that I do not enter Dunster Road and have no contact with any associated person. If I breach, the police have the power to arrest me without a warrant. Before too long there will be a summons to Camberwell Green Magistrates' Court for a hearing. I will be given a minimum of two days' notice.

'What's your temporary address?'

I give him Claire's.

'Can I go back and get some stuff from home? I left without any clothes or my bag.'

Forrester peers over his glasses. 'You probably should have thought of that before.'

Forrester drones on through the conditions. I am entitled to be represented by a lawyer at the hearing. I am also entitled to call witnesses. If I do not attend, the hearing will go ahead without me anyway. If the magistrate sees fit to convert the notice into an order, then there will be further conditions imposed upon me.

'Might they affect my chances of getting custody of my child?'

Forrester blinks as if to suggest that he's not a man without sympathy but it's more than his job's worth to offer advice.

'Get a lawyer.'

* * *

Back at Claire's flat, despondent and bone weary, I crash out on the sofa again. When I wake, my back is sore and my eyes hurt. Two mugs of strong coffee later I'm smoking a cigarette (the first in ten years) out of the window and thinking about Ani. Just say Ani deliberately sabotaged the boiler. Barring the very faint possibility that Ani is some random psychopath, the only logical reason for him to screw with the machine would be to get back at Lilly Winter. Maybe they were lovers or drinking pals or scored drugs together. Perhaps Lilly owed him money or he found out that she was getting a regular sum from Tom and hustled her for a cut. Maybe she cheated on him or rejected him. But whatever it was, if Ani did mess around with the boiler, Lilly must have trusted him enough to ask him to fix it and Ani must have been pretty confident Lilly wouldn't check on him.

If that were the case, why hadn't Lilly died on the night of his visit? This wasn't a slow, barely noticeable leak. It was a catastrophic gas escape. And why hadn't the police found any evidence of sabotage? Ruby told the police that she was alone with her mother all day. She and Lilly had watched TV and turned in around the same time. There was no one else in the flat.

If Ani had inadvertently broken the boiler, why had it taken so long for the fault to manifest? And if it was just a freak accident, as the police had said, why was Lilly Winter's window closed, when it was her habit to leave it open? To anyone who didn't know Ruby Winter the damp towels and batteries in her room would hardly have aroused suspicion. She was eleven years old. When Ruby had told the police she'd never met the boiler man, they would have had no reason to doubt her. But supposing she was lying?

I open a can of baked beans and switch on the early evening news. There's to be an independent inquiry into LeShaun Toley's death but, everyone knows, what's happening in the streets has gone beyond all that. It's a terrible mess. Just after eight, I scribble a note to Claire and go out. The light is foxed and patchy. Even the trees look tarnished. On the streets everywhere there is evidence of last night's rioting. The park railings flutter with police tape, the public bins are full of the hastily discarded and partially burnt packaging of looted goods and a tarry smell is blowing in from more distant southern suburbs. Some of the shops are boarded up. Others are still ragged with broken glass and the pavements are crunchy. All that glass and debris would be a danger to passers-by if there were any, but the streets are empty of almost everyone, including police. This little sector of the south-eastern inner suburbs appears all but abandoned.

At Dunster Road, light slices from the edges of the neighbours' curtains and here and there I can see the blue flicker of a TV. Number forty-two lies in darkness. Above the bay window the burglar alarm box blinks red. The security light clicks on in the porch. The spare set of keys has been removed from its usual place under the potted bay tree in the front garden. Tom may well have changed the alarm code too but there's a manual override key in the cloakroom. No way to get in from the front, other than to force the living room window, which is too risky. I will have to go back the way I came via the open side return next door. The Fricks have a motion-sensitive light at the front but theirs is larger and more sensitive than ours. Tom must have threatened to smash it a dozen times when, after a gust of wind or a cat jumping onto the wall, we woke to a blinding glare. And they are in. The dim glow of a light leaks from under the blinds in the bay window. It's too faint to be coming from the front of the house. The Fricks must be at the back, most likely, at this time of the evening, in the kitchen having dinner. I can knock on their door and make up some story about having my bag stolen with the keys inside it and Tom being away but nothing gets past Shelly. She'll know about the police visit and there's every possibility Tom will have told them to be wary of me.

The act of stepping inside the front gate sets off the security light. A hard white dazzle spreads across the front garden and, as I move along the side wall, I'm struck by the thought that anyone finding me here sneaking through my neighbours' house under cover of darkness would assume I'd lost it. What if I *have* lost it? Wouldn't I be the last to know?

I'm edging along the garden fence towards the loose panelling at the end of the Fricks' garden when my eye is drawn to a movement in one of the upstairs rooms. An instant later Charlie Frick appears at the window of his unlit bedroom. We squint at one another in the thin light from the kitchen. I freeze and hold my breath, anticipating that at any moment Charlie might call out and blow my cover. If that happens, I doubt I'll have time to make it to the end of the garden and slide through the panelling before one of the adult Fricks switches on the garden floodlight and I am exposed. Still Charlie gazes out from the window, his face pressed against the glass. What is he thinking? I try a smile. Does he know it's me? Seconds tick by. The little boy raises his right arm and waves. I wave back. Then, without warning, Charlie turns and is gone. To tell his parents? My instinct tells me no. But I can't be sure.

The fence panel gives with a soft *whump* and I am in my own back garden. I am hoping to find Tom's study window open but no such luck. Tom has closed and locked it. In the shed is an old pair of long-handled iron pruning shears Tom's father gave him after Michael downsized from the grand old vicarage Tom grew up in to the practical three-bedroom estate cube where he now lives. Once I've found the right angle, the lock of the box sash gives readily. After pushing the base upwards, I slide through the gap and onto the floorboards. Immediately, the alarm begins to chirp. I hurry into the hall and switch on the small table lamp then open the alarm cover and plug in Freya's birthday. But Tom has taken care of this too. Of course! He's a techie. It's too late to reach the manual override. Summoning Ruby's birth date, I tap in six digits. Silence falls. In this dark game Tom and I have begun to play, the trick, it seems, is to try to stay a step ahead.

I skip upstairs and cross the hall into my daughter's bedroom. On the little bookshelf by the bed is Freya's pile of *Pippi*

Longstocking books. I take one and slide it into my bag and am in my bedroom putting together a few clothes when there's a rattle and an instant later the whoosh of the front door. The blood is singing in my temples. A single set of footsteps travels along the tiles, pausing at the stairs.

Eventually, a nervous-sounding male voice says, 'Hello?'

Nicholas Frick is standing halfway up the stairs peering into the darkness of the landing. His features soften when he sees me but there's confusion scribbled across his face.

'Oh, you're here! Tom asked us to feed the cat.'

'*Sorry*, yes, I got held up at work, joining the others later. I should have called you.'

Frick's eyes dart about and his jaw twitches. He swings his head back in the direction of the hallway, as if wishing he could just wind back time. He knows. Tom has told him. Now he's trying to decide what to do. An instant later the question seems to answer itself as he takes a breath and with a nervous smile says, 'Oh well, then. I guess I'm surplus to requirements, so I'll be off. Will you, uh, be needing the cat fed tomorrow?'

'Yes, please.'

I watch him make his way rapidly down the stairs towards the front door. On a sudden impulse, I hurry after and stop him in the hallway.

'If you speak to Tom, I'd be so glad if you didn't mention you saw me.' I assume a fake smiley face and try to make it look real. 'I told him I'd leave directly from work but I remembered I'd left my bag here so I had to dash back. He'll be cross with me for leaving it this late. I was going to say the traffic was bad.'

Frick's eyebrows go up as he considers the request. Thought processes cross his face. A man like Frick *does* know how it is to be late home. The manufactured excuses. The little white lies. His lips smile at one corner. I'm reminding him of himself.

He winks and taps the side of his nose. 'Not a word.'

CHAPTER NINETEEN

You have trust issues, the therapist announced after my illness. Well, let's lay that out and look at it. Because, the way I see it, being alive now, in this time, in this world, when you might, on any morning, wake up to a financial crash or to rioting or to the realisation that the person you married is not who you thought they were, or that *you* are not the person you thought you were, you'd have to be nuts *not* to have trust issues.

Trust nothing, my PhD supervisor once told me, *except the evidence.*

I'm holding his advice close while waiting for the bus to Claire's flat. I'm jittery. Anyone seen roaming around this late with a large backpack is going to be a target tonight, either for a gang or for the cops. I'm now also technically in breach of the DVPN. It's still possible that Nicholas Frick will give me away. If the police find out I've been back to the house, or even to Dunster Road, they'll be within their rights to arrest me. So I'm intent on disappearing, at least until tomorrow when I can meet Ani the boiler man.

Somewhere not far away the rioting has started up again. Police helicopters are out and the air is abuzz with the sound of sirens. A bus appears at some distance further up Holland Hill and lumbers its way through a series of diversions, the driver stop-starting at unfamiliar junctions and traffic lights. The city's thoroughfares have short-circuited. This happens in the brain. Everything freezes, then, slowly and gradually, alternate neural paths emerge. Before long the city will route around the damage. New routes will open up and the traffic will begin to flow along them.

For now, though, it's a long journey. By the time I get back, Claire has retired to her room. On top of the sofa bed lies a crumpled sheet and a pillow with a note to say there's some cold pasta salad and a bottle of Pinot Grigio in the fridge. I'm tired and edgy, too fatigued to eat but most definitely in the mood for wine. How good it would be to drink enough not to have to think. How good and yet how dangerous. I pour a glass and take the bottle over to the sofa. The alcohol will allow me to surf the crest of my fatigue and barely notice it, at least for a while.

For tonight I am safe, but cosy and comforting though Claire's flat seems now, before too long it will become a trap. Charlie Frick will tell Shelly he saw me or Nicholas Frick will tell Tom. My husband will report my breach to the police. Claire won't give me away, but neither can I expect her to lie if the police question her, and I wouldn't want to get her into trouble. One way or another it won't take the police or Tom very long to figure out where I am and when they do, they'll arrest me for breaching my DVPN conditions. Tonight, I can sleep. Tomorrow, I will have to find a way to disappear.

* * *

I am woken by the aroma of toast. It's early. Through the curtainless windows the first iron-grey light of dawn is in the sky. Claire is at the kitchen sink. She's already dressed and has made coffee. As I sit up, she turns and looks over.

'You're awake.' She brings over a mug of coffee. 'I was hoping we'd get to talk.'

'I'm in a bit of trouble.'

'I guessed that much,' Claire says quietly, turning back to the kitchen.

'It's nothing for you to worry about, I promise.'

She brings over a plate of buttered toast. 'I'll worry anyway. Can we talk about it when I get back? Some of the research department's windows got smashed in the rioting last night. They want me to go in and make sure nothing's been taken then call maintenance to board over the broken panes.'

She sits, pressing her palms together, with an anxious expression on her face, weighing up whatever she's wanting to say next. 'I think I should tell you something. Joshua Barrons' patient file has been deleted.'

'*What?*'

'I know. I went into the relevant folders and they've all gone. His case notes, reports, images, genetic profile, everything. It's like he never existed.'

I lean back against the sofa and try to take this in. 'Are you sure?'

'I asked Lucas to double-check, just in case I'd got something wrong, but he couldn't find anything either.'

Deleting patient files goes against every institute research and ethical protocol but it's obvious why MacIntyre has done it. Both Anja and MacIntyre know that Joshua Barrons is a time bomb. While he was a patient at the clinic it was our responsibility to locate and defuse the detonator. Now he's no longer in treatment they're going to make damned sure whatever he might end up doing doesn't come back to the institute.

No one but me knows the files still exist. I know because I have them. The scans, assessments, research, all copied and stored away for such a time as when I'll need them.

I say, 'At some point this will all backfire. You know that, don't you? Maybe not now or next week, but eventually. MacIntyre will sacrifice Anja the moment he hears the drumbeat. But he'll go down too. The truth will all come out eventually.'

Claire leans in and gives me a hug, then picks up her rucksack and makes to leave. At the door she says, 'Oh, and by the way, there's still nothing in the fridge, except the stuff you bought. I'm a domestic shambles. But I can go shopping at lunchtime. Risotto for dinner?'

I set my face to a cheerful blank. I won't be here for dinner. Or for the talk. From now on, I need to be on my own. I have to hope Claire will understand.

Once she's gone I take a shower, get dressed in a pair of my own jeans and a bland T-shirt and make more coffee. As I'm drinking it, I cut up all my credit and debit cards with the exception of the one that gives me access to my secret stash. Because we women always have a secret stash. When it comes to money we've learned to be practical and think ahead. Thousands of years of history have taught us that we have to.

That done, I call the offices of Hunt, Baylor, Strachan and leave my new number on Dominic Harding's voicemail.

Dominic always felt bad about the way the Spelling case turned out because it was he who had hired me as an expert witness. But I didn't see it that way. He and I both had stakes in the game. Dominic was a young, ambitious solicitor who wanted to win the case. I was a young, ambitious forensic psych who wanted to make a point. We were united by our mutual outrage at the Crown Prosecution's desire to try Rees Spelling as an adult. The kid was twelve when he left his brother out in the woods. He couldn't write, he couldn't read and he was naive about the consequences of actions. In the months prior to the incident, he had been driven to the point of madness by his mother's continual bleat that his brother was 'doing her head in' and, if the crying didn't stop, she would kill herself. Rees was in an impossible position. He chose to leave his brother in the woods in a desperate bid to keep his mother alive. I told the court what I considered to be true: that, when Rees Spelling left his brother in the woods, he was suffering from a temporary psychosis brought on by his circumstances at home. In my professional opinion, what he'd done, while terrible, was a one-off. On that basis, I suggested he receive psychiatric care. I considered him not to be a significant risk to others.

What I hadn't spotted was that there was some core delusion remaining in Rees Spelling that would compel him to repeat the crime. Which he did, leaving Kylie Drinkwater to die of exposure not far from the spot where, six years earlier, Spelling had left his brother. It was Dominic who called me with the news. When the story broke in the press the following day, Rees Spelling was portrayed as a cold-blooded, psychopathic killer. It was James White – then a young and ambitious cub reporter – who first connected the two victims to my fatal misjudgement of the perpetrator. His suggestion that my desire to keep high-profile young offenders out of adult courts had clouded my professional judgement probably wasn't so far from the truth. And even though the series of grabby op-ed pieces he wrote broke my career and were the first nails in the coffin of my marriage, I knew I only had myself to blame. For a short while, the shock sent me into the consoling arms of Dominic Harding. Tom never knew. I walked away before it got out of control and for a long time afterwards Dominic and I avoided one another lest it all start up again. Years later, when there was no chance of our becoming anything else, Dominic and I decided to be friends, two souls bound together by guilt and grief and, perhaps, by the faintest memory of love.

Before leaving, I write Claire a thank you note and fold

away the bedding. Then I take the first bus going east. It has cooled down overnight and there has been some rain. The sky is a muddy grey wash stirred only by the echoes of helicopter blades. Perhaps the violence will calm now.

A roadblock at the South Circular sends the bus on a diversion into unfamiliar terrain. We're heading north. Somewhere near Hoxton the bus rattles by a cheap chain hotel. I get out at the next stop and walk back. The Travel Inn appears to be almost entirely empty. No real surprise. Business travellers will be avoiding London, lovers will have other things on their minds. The receptionist is a wiry young man in an ill-fitting suit with seams rubbed to a polyester shine, by the name of Khalid. He's used to business travellers and couples having affairs and doesn't quite know where to place me.

'You paying by card or cash?'

'Cash.'

'I'll need your credit card for extras.'

'There won't be any extras.'

'All the same.' Khalid's voice wobbles and he looks away. He's sticking to the script.

I hand over my secret account card. 'Please don't charge it. I'll pay cash for any extras.'

He tips his chin. 'No problem. I'll put a note on the account.'

In the mirrored tiles lining the lift I am startled to see a face I hardly recognise. My hair is an unkempt semi-fro and there is something wild in my eyes. I'm sensing the swell in my brain where the safe, calm waters of sanity give out to a muddled chop – I'm sailing close enough to madness to feel its salty spray on my face. I do actually look mad. But I'm not. At least I'm pretty sure I'm not. What I think I am is very, *very* angry.

Following Khalid's directions, I head through quiet corridors smelling of warmed plastic to room number 367 on the third floor, a small box filled with modular furniture whose cheapness is thinly disguised with cheery, formulaic prints of city views which, in the circumstances, seem rather ironic. Tower Bridge at sunset is not somewhere you'd want to be right now. I unpack my rucksack and sit on the bed. In the space of twenty-four hours I have lost my husband, my daughter and my job, the soil in which I was once rooted. In their place is a large hollow.

I call Sal from the hotel phone and ask her where she is.

'Dunster Road.' There's a tremor of impatience in her voice. 'You told me to stay with Freya, so that's what I'm doing. Good timing, as it turns out. Tom needs help with the girls so he can look after his dad. The atmosphere is horrific.' She sighs. 'I really don't know what to think. You're my sister and I love you but you've become someone I don't recognise. Tom thinks you're having another episode. Maybe he's right. I mean, what the *hell* were you thinking going back to Dunster Road when the DV notice specifically says you're not allowed to?'

So Frick reported me. Nick Frick, the bloody prick. All it would take to turn myself in to the machinery of madness right now is for me to say, 'You're right, I'm not myself,' and my sister would pop or whiz or zoom over and within an hour or two we'd be walking into the emergency department at King's

Hospital and I would be closing the door on getting custody of my daughter.

'Can I speak with Freya?'

Sal's voice is wobbly and full of anguish. 'God, I hate doing this. Tom made me to promise not to contact you. It's one of the conditions of the notice.'

When did either of us ever take any account of the *conditions of the notice*?

About six months after I took Sal away from Heather to live with me in a tiny rented room in a shared house, a woman with a soft voice called and introduced herself as Fionella. She explained that she was a social worker. Fionella wanted me to come in and discuss Sally's future. My little sister was fourteen, a minor. I knew that if I gave her up to Fionella, she'd be forced to return to our mother or be taken into care. So, on the day I was due in the office, I packed our things and Sal and I left the shared house and moved to another. We did that four times until social services eventually lost interest in us.

'Please,' I say, 'let me talk to my daughter.'

'Oh, all right. But only for a bit. Tom's not here but he'll go bananas if he finds out I'm doing this so you'll have to be super quick and ask Freya not to say anything to her father.'

A wait, then the tense, bright music of my daughter's voice: 'Mum, are you going to be ill for long?'

'No, my love. I am going to be well very soon. I need to ask you something, though. Are you on your own now? Do you have some paper and a pen to hand?'

Freya answers a yes. I follow the sound of her footsteps as she walks across the room.

'Good. OK, so take this down.' I give her the number of the new pay-as-you-go phone and ask her to keep it to herself. 'If anything happens, anything you don't like, I want you to call me and I promise I will come for you. Got that?'

'Got it.'

* * *

It rains all day, murky rivulets cascading down the window. In the late afternoon, I turn on the TV news. The city is calmer. People do not riot in the rain. Pretty soon, the recriminations will begin. People like James White will write hand-wringing 'analyses'. Pundits and politicians will weigh in. Before long everyone will be working their angles.

At four, I call Dominic Harding's mobile number and leave another message. By six I am standing outside Forest Hill station in the outer south-eastern suburbs of the city to meet with Gloria and, we hope, Ani. The sun is out again, but it's cooler now, more like the English summer Dad used to call 'Blink of an Eye'. Everything not Jamaican had been fleeting and a little unreal to Dad. It's been a long time since I thought about the shadow he left when he disappeared. Maybe I'll take Freya to Jamaica one day, I think, to find her roots. Then reality hits with a terrible thud. I may never be able to take Freya anywhere again.

'Caitlin! What are you doing in this neck?' A bloke in his

mid-thirties is standing on the pavement squinting into the sun. Six foot, male-pattern baldness, glasses, an air of genial surprise. For a moment I can't place him then I realise I'm looking at one of Tom's football buddies and an old colleague from the Adrenalyze days. Phil somebody? Yeah, definitely Phil.

For a minute or two we swap notes about the riots. Already they've taken on the character of old war stories. Evidently he doesn't know about me and Tom. Why should he?

'How is Tombo? Haven't seen the old bugger in a while.'

'Oh?'

Phil pats his left leg. 'Been playing up.'

'Ah.'

'He must be getting ready to launch that game soon. *Labyrinth*, is it? Sounds bloody amazing. I hope Adrenalyze will kick themselves for giving him the boot.'

'The *boot*?' The story Tom tells, he left the company of his own accord to develop *Labyrinth*. He lived off savings for a while then borrowed a bit of cash from his dad. Except now I know that's not true because at least some of that money was going to Lilly Winter.

Sensing he's put a foot wrong, Phil rocks awkwardly on his heels, searching for something appropriate to say. 'Yeah, well, you know, I mean, all that stuff about his expenses, I never believed it. But Tom wasn't really a corporate type, was he?' A light comes into his eyes. He's amused. 'Well, better get on. Good to see you, though, Cat.'

'Good to see you too, Phil.'

As I'm watching his back disappear down the hill, I'm

wondering what else I'll discover about my husband that I didn't know. From the corner of my eye I spot Gloria heading up the hill from the crossroads, panting a little from the effort but managing a wave. I wave back.

Gloria watches Phil leave. 'Why you have lover boy? Perhaps you are more stupider than I thought.'

'A friend of my husband's.'

Gloria gives me a penetrating look then decides to believe me. As we set off along the pavement towards the Albanian cafe where the man who knows a man who might know Ani works, Gloria talks about her daughter, Elmira. Losing a child is like having someone suddenly unplug you from the world, she says. The body remains but it's only really a shell.

'You know?'

'Yes. That's exactly how it feels.'

Gloria stops in her tracks, turns and looks at me carefully. 'What you want from Ani?'

'I need to know if he met Ruby Winter.'

I decide against repeating what Ruby told me in the bathroom about not wanting her mother around, not least because I think it sounds crackers – and Gloria is one of the few remaining people who doesn't think I'm losing my mind.

'I can't really explain it now.'

* * *

The pavement narrows in front of a parade of convenience stores and a corner off-licence whose owner had cleared the display shelves and braced the shop window with boards. Gloria leads me down a side road past a shoe repair outlet to a scruffy cafe going by the unlikely name of Dionysius. Inside, a sallow man with thick, custardy skin and hair like an oil slick quits polishing glasses and comes round the bar with his head cocked and an obsequious look of enquiry on his face. What can he do for us?

As Gloria launches into her explanation in Albanian, the sallow guy's face quickly loses its mask. He goes back around the bar and resumes his task. He hears Gloria out then waves casually towards a bead curtain at the back as if to say, *Help yourself.* Who knows what Gloria has told him but I know she wants to help me and I have a feeling that she'll lie if she has to.

We move through the curtains into a dank, windowless room packed with mismatching tables and chairs on which a dozen men are playing cards and dominoes. There's a pervasive smell of men, tar and drink. The men are quiet, their eyes on the visitors. Gloria says her piece. I pick up the names Ani and Caitlin and a word that sounds very much like 'English' but the rest is unintelligible. Murmurings follow. A good-natured argument starts up. A big fuss for such a simple question. Do they know Ani or not? Eventually, the owner turns and gestures towards me while addressing himself to Gloria and when I ask Gloria to translate she blushes.

'He want to know if you are proper English because...' She cuts off, shifts her weight and looks at the floor.

The cafe owner points to my kinked hair.

To me Gloria whispers, 'Please ignore this. I tell them you

work for landlord with lots of rental flats. I say you hear Ani is good worker. Cash under counter, all that. But is possible Ani has no papers for UK. They don't want no bad risk. Understand?'

'So that's a no?'

'Yes, is no.'

We've hit a blind alley. Outside, the grey sky is beginning to darken. I offer to buy Gloria a drink and something to eat. We duck into a nearby cafe. As we're pulling up chairs, a group of men and women tramp past armed with an assortment of dustpans and brooms. A new kind of community activist, one of the more unexpected by-products of the riots: friends, neighbours and business owners literally sweeping the fragments of the city back together. It's good to see. A small crumb of comfort.

Gloria rests her head on her hands for a while, the steam from her coffee rising like a thought bubble. Eventually, she says, 'Caitlin, I am going back to that place. Not now, later, on my own. Maybe this way I will find Ani.'

'Thank you.'

The corners of her mouth quiver. 'I know what is to miss daughter.'

* * *

Back at the Travel Inn, I turn in early, but the room gives out directly onto a bus stop and at regular intervals the night buses rumble and sway past. I have not slept properly for what seems like weeks now. All night, I drift on a dark swell, the madness creeping around me like fog. The boundary between sanity and insanity, riches and debt, life and death, is paper-thin. No one knows this better than someone who has been on both sides. I am spooked by the riots and I am frightened for my daughter. I am afraid of what Tom will do and of what Ruby will do. I am scared of myself.

Morning arrives and with it the chirp of the phone. It's early. The cheap curtains are topped by a halo of ashy light. Only three people know my number now: Claire, Dominic and Freya. Reaching out an arm, I pluck the mobile from the table and peer at the screen: 7.43 a.m. A number I recognise. It's Claire. She's picked up three messages on the office voicemail from Sal.

'What does she want?' My voice is edged with alarm.

'She just says please call her urgently and not to worry.' There's a pause. 'Caitlin, I got your note. You don't have to tell me anything but are you OK?'

'Yes, I think so.'

'Because if you're not…'

* * *

Moments later I am dialling Sal's number from the hotel phone. My sister answers, sounding anxious.

'Listen, we're at the hospital in Tonbridge. Freya's fine, but there's been an incident.'

A tightness grips my temples. An *incident*? 'What happened? Let me speak to her.'

In a frosty tone, Sally says, 'Calm down. Freya's OK. Everyone's OK.'

I've switched to speakerphone and I'm up and throwing on my clothes. Something is happening in my brain at the deeper, primitive regions to which I have no conscious access.

'Put Freya on.' My voice is a growl, more animal than human.

'I can't, she's sleeping.' My sister's tone is aggrieved and sour now. 'There's no need to be so *aggressive*. I shouldn't even be calling you.'

'I'm sorry, Sal. Please, just tell me what happened.' I'm sliding my feet into my trainers. Whatever bleary mood I'd been in last night has evaporated.

According to Sal, Freya woke in the night feeling breathless with a bad headache and somehow managed to fall out of bed and was then sick. 'There's some bruising and what's likely to be a mild concussion. But that's all. They've tested for meningitis and it's negative. It's nothing, really, probably just a bug.'

'I'm on my way.'

'You can't come.' Sal is silent for a moment, torn between her loyalty to me and her agreement with my husband.

'Look, I know I'm putting you in an awkward position, Sal, but I'm coming, whatever Tom or the police say. I'm coming, OK? Freya is my daughter. I need to know if Ruby was with Freya when she fell out of bed?'

'Nuh uh, Ruby slept in the spare room with Tom. Why?'

'Just tell me the best time to come when Tom's not likely to be there.'

'Can you get here in the next couple of hours? Tom left Ruby at home with her grandad but she had some kind of meltdown, so Tom's gone home to deal with it. I'm with Freya.'

* * *

At the reception desk on the ground floor Khalid calls a taxi. When I tell him where I want to go his face creases and he says, 'Isn't that miles away?'

'Yes, and I need to get there quickly.'

'I know a guy who drives like a maniac.'

'Perfect.'

CHAPTER TWENTY

The rain and the heavy police presence have brought the rioting to an end overnight but the route out of London is knotted with diversions and roadblocks. Forty-five minutes into the journey the residential streets give way to industrial parks. Somewhere out near Sidcup, that the driver – named Harpeet and who does indeed drive like a maniac – takes it upon himself to engage me in conversation, but I'm not in a chatting mood. He soon gives up and switches his attention to talk radio. We speed through suburbs in various states of disarray. The radio show is dominated by the riots. A local business owner calls in. His stock has been stolen and he's got no insurance. He doesn't know how he's going to survive. Next a copper, speaking on condition of anonymity, who's been on duty twenty-seven hours straight and wonders why the parents aren't out on the streets looking for their kids. Then a court clerk who was working till 3 a.m. and is about to start again.

We are beyond the industrial zone now, motoring through commuter belt towns unaffected by the chaos in the city, the kind of places where, in better times, Tom and I had briefly considered relocating after the Spelling case. Tom thought we'd get on better there. For him, the world of garden gates and village fêtes has a familiar, comforting feel. But there was nothing comforting here for me then and there's nothing comforting now. I belong to London. Everywhere else makes me nervous. Harpeet reacts to the change in mood by making frequent checks in the rear-view mirror as if expecting me to have come to some harm.

'My daughter's in hospital,' I say by way of explanation.

The driver nods and says nothing. A few minutes later he turns up the radio.

* * *

The West Kent Hospital Paediatric A&E sits behind a set of double doors at the end of the minor injuries department but it may as well be a planet away. There's an unmistakably curdled atmosphere in paediatric wards, a distinctive brew of youthful resilience and parental terror. In this one, the administrator, a plump woman with a severe ponytail and a monobrow, is leaning against the registration counter. Her colleague is a small-boned, impish man with dancing lips. I move up to the counter and ask to see Freya Walsh.

'And you are?' This is the plump woman.

'Her aunt. On her mother's side.' The woman eyes me carefully then checks her screen. At that moment the phone rings and the man picks up. The ponytailed woman seems to lose confidence. She hasn't heard about an aunt. Or, worse, perhaps, she's been told the girl's crazy mother might try to make an entrance. Either way, there's a look of indecision on her face I don't much like. A distraction is called for.

'By the way, as I came in, I saw some creep fiddling with himself on the other side of the double doors. You might want to investigate.'

Magic. The woman bristles and, straightening her uniform, careens off down the corridor. Her colleague, distracted by his phone conversation, waves in the vague direction of a set of double doors and mimes a left turn. Beyond the doors, a grey corridor smelling faintly of antiseptic and shit shrinks to the vanishing point. A nurse with Heidi hair hurries by and, at the mention of Freya's name, floats an arm towards yet another set of double doors and into a ward of eight beds screened by curtains. It's not far off ten now and the doctors are just finishing their rounds. From behind one screen comes low chatter, from behind another there's guttural sobbing. The usual hospital symphony of anguish, nervous bonhomie and fear. In the third cubicle along, Freya lies alone and asleep, a *Pippi Longstocking* storybook beside her. Seeing her there makes me want to cry but crying is not useful so I hold back, reminding myself of my doctoral supervisor's maxim. *Only ever trust the evidence.*

My daughter's nose works in her sleep, picking up my smell, the animal bond. Should I wake her? I'm not sure. What I'd most like to do is scoop her up and sweep her away from here and from Tom and Ruby, but the DVPN limits my options considerably. The simple fact of being here puts me in breach. Any attempt to take

Freya with me could be construed as kidnap. To stand a chance of getting away with it we would have to go straight to the nearest airport and get on the first plane. I have to admit there's a certain renegade appeal to that. Apart from Sal, what's keeping me here? We could carve out a new life together somewhere. Jamaica maybe. Swap the grey, burnt streets for coffee plantations and disappear into the warm, coconutty air. No more Tom or Ruby. No more MacIntyre. Freya's memories of home would start to fade the moment we stepped off the plane. But sooner or later, the first brilliant flare of adventure would dim. Then how would I explain to my daughter the decision to take her away from everything she knows?

A clipboard of medical notes hangs over the end of the bed. The symptoms are as Sal relayed them to me: heart palpitations, dizziness, nausea, headache and vomiting. Blood tests have revealed no obvious source of infection. Blood carbon monoxide at 1.5%. Normal for a city kid. They've tested the glucose in the blood for diabetes but that's normal too. On the summary page I see the words *panic attacks?* They're holding her overnight for obs and a psych referral. So far as I can tell from the notes, the referral hasn't yet happened.

Freya's breathing grows shallower and her eyes begin to flutter as her mind swims back up to the surface. A single eyelid opens.

'Mum!' She wriggles herself into a seated position, yawning and pressing her fists into her eyes, looking about. A shadow passes across her face. 'Where's Dad?'

'He's gone back to your grandfather's but your Aunt Sal's here.

Would you like me to fetch her?' I spotted my sister as I came in, slumped across two chairs in a waiting area, an expensive-looking cashmere thrown over her head.

Freya looks at her hands for a moment as if she's thinking this through. She bites her bottom lip and her eyes are shimmery.

'Things have got a bit complicated.'

'I know. Dad says we can't live with you anymore because you're not well.'

I lay my hand on her head. 'It's only temporary, sweet pea. Only for now.' Stroking her face with the back of my finger. Her eyes close again. 'Can you tell me something? It might be a difficult thing, but can you tell me if I promise you no one's going to get into trouble?'

She frowns then gives the smallest of nods, which is enough.

'Can you tell me what happened at the lido?'

Freya opens her eyes. I've surprised her. This isn't what she had in mind.

I repeat that no one will get into trouble. Freya hesitates then opens her mouth. The gesture is a stone thrown into a dark pool, its first ripples carving wet channels in the soft down of Freya's face. But still she can't bear to say it.

'It's OK, my darling, all you have to do is whisper it to me.' I lean towards her, turning my head so my ear is right beside her open mouth. We're so close now it's almost as if we can read one another's minds.

'Ruby said telltales end up like her mum.'

'Oh, sweet pea.'

She hesitates a moment then in a flash reaches out and slings her arms around my neck and in a voice hoarse with emotion she whispers, 'Ruby killed Harry. She got a hammer from the shed and she hit him.' She is trembling now. 'She left him in your bed. She said it was your fault for not letting her have him.' Freya slumps, the breath catching in her chest.

Keep on, my darling girl, keep on, we are so close to the truth.

'I thought having a sister would be more fun than this.'

My hands find the soft hair on my daughter's arms. 'What happened at the lido?' A long sob follows. 'Tell me, sweet pea.'

The sound of a nurse in the cubicle next door. The muffled cry of a sick child. I wait, my finger poised over my mouth. Footsteps fade out into the corridor. Sitting on the bed beside her, I take one of her hands in mine. The other cups her face. She's sobbing now, her face in her hands. 'I don't want Ruby to get into trouble.'

I'm suddenly conscious of the time. I don't want to push my daughter. I'm intensely aware of her fragility. On the other hand, Tom could be back any minute. 'Please, my love, please. I'll make sure Ruby gets help.'

Thoughts criss-cross Freya's face, then she rearranges herself, opens her mouth and speaks.

* * *

Afterwards, in the waiting room with Sally.

'She's sleeping now.'

Sally says, 'Poor Freya. I'm so sorry to have doubted you, Cat. Tom was drip-feeding me with this bullshit about you being unwell and I was stupid and fell for it. He just seemed so *plausible*.'

I laugh in spite of myself. 'Yes, Tom has always been very good at being *plausible*. Years ago, when we first got together, he told me a story about his childhood. I sensed he was testing me and I was newly in love and I wanted to pass the test. I've thought a lot about that story over the last couple of weeks. It was about this kid in his village he biked around with after school. The kid had a stammer and some of the other local boys teased him about it. Tom was happy for the kid to hang around with him because the boy was pathetically grateful. One day, though, the kid stepped over the line. He told Tom that he was his best friend. Tom was OK being around this boy but the last thing he wanted was for this boy to make any claims on him. So, the same evening, he crept round to the boy's front garden where he kept his bike locked and loosened the wheel nuts. The next day, he challenged the kid to a bike race. As the boy was racing downhill, he turned a corner and his front wheel came off. Kid was in hospital for a month. The boy's parents asked Tom if he knew what happened, he said he had no idea. He went to visit the boy in hospital. Even then his sympathy was *plausible*.'

'That's creepy.'

I pull some coins from my pocket. 'You want a coffee?'

'Is that what they call it?'

I fetch her a cup. She puts it to her lips, makes a face and drinks it anyway.

'You heard of that book, Dale something, *How to Win Friends and Influence People*?'

'Rings a bell,' Sal says. In Sallyland, this usually means no.

'It's this sort of self-help bible for manipulators. Tom had a copy when I first met him. He was embarrassed about it so he got rid of it, though not before I had a flick through. It basically says the best way to get ahead is by being whatever people want you to be.'

'Is that good or bad?'

'It means everything just becomes a performance. Maybe the reason he's so brilliant at performing Tom Walsh is that he doesn't even realise it's an act.'

A nurse swings by, offers a brief smile then hurries on.

'I'm trapped, Sal. If Freya comes with me now, the police will issue a warrant for my arrest. I can't let her go back home, not after what she's just told me.'

'She could stay with me. Would Tom allow that?'

'Hmm. With Michael not well and the hearing coming up he's got a lot on his plate. If you don't say anything about Ruby, and he thinks it's only for a little while, then yes, maybe. He might be glad if you took Freya for a few days.'

'She should really tell her dad what she just told you,' Sal says.

'She'd feel she was betraying him. And even if she did tell him, I'm not sure he'd do anything about it. Tom is refusing to get Ruby into any kind of therapy.'

'But why?'

'I wish I knew.' And this is the hard truth. Why *is* Tom protecting Ruby Winter? Guilt? Bloody-mindedness? Or – the idea flashes across my mind like a burst of gunfire – does Ruby have a secret that Tom doesn't want her to tell?

CHAPTER TWENTY-ONE

I'm on the train back to London from Tonbridge when Dominic returns my call.

'Hello, you. How's tricks?' The old, familiar voice.

'Getting by. Listen, Dom, you got any time today?'

'For you, of course.'

He checks the calendar on his phone and suggests a time. 'Better tell me what this about.'

'I need you to help me pull a rabbit out of a hat.'

'Ah, magician's assistant, is it? Then I'm your man.'

The train trundles on. At Sevenoaks, a passenger alights from the carriage leaving a copy of the *Herald* behind. The paper is full of the riots: youths in balaclavas or bandanas hurling bricks at shop windows, the police, and each other. One image in particular catches my eye – a group of younger kids who appear to be watching the looting and violence. A little way off, standing on his own, is a face I think I recognise. I peer in closer. The broad nose, the thick dark hair, the penetrating stare are unmistakable. In a flash, my fingers are dancing over the phone.

'Dr Lupo, I'm so glad you called. Can you meet me in the park?'

'Now?' I glance out of the window at the familiar red terraces of south-east London.

'As soon as you can.'

* * *

The Bandstand Cafe in Grissold Park is nearly empty. Evidently, the message hasn't got around that the park has reopened. Either that, or people are playing safe. Emma Barrons sits at a corner table where the light is dimmest, at an angle, as though she were riding side-saddle, turning the rings on her fingers.

Her voice is muddled with booze. 'You saw the picture?'

'Yes.'

'I've left Joshua with his father and the nanny. They're fucking, of course – my husband and the nanny, that is. So far as I know, neither of them has yet resorted to having sex with my son.'

A waitress comes over and, as we're ordering coffee, Emma absent-mindedly pushes up the sleeves of her blouse to reveal livid bruises splashed along both arms. She notices me clocking them and waits for the waitress to leave before murmuring, 'These were Joshua, not his father.'

Since his discharge from the clinic, Emma explains, Joshua's behaviour has gradually deteriorated and there is some new hectic charge about him, for which Emma blames the riots. 'I took him back to the consultant he was seeing before he came to you. Without his father knowing, of course. Defiance disorder and a prescription for Ritalin. I told her we'd been there, done that. And then she talked about therapy.'

'All the research shows that would be the worst possible thing for a kid like Joshua,' I say. 'He'd see it as useful training in manipulation techniques.'

Emma laughs bitterly and removes an e-cigarette from her bag. A trail of vanilla vapour rises on the thermal.

'It was a relief to see Joshua's picture in the paper this morning. We didn't know he'd gone; he got out of his bed in the middle of the night and must have got back into it in the early hours of the morning because that's where the nanny found him. But she told me his bed sheets smelled smoky. I was worried that he'd tried to set fire to his bed. He's always setting fire to things. Now at least I know what caused the smell.'

Emma Barrons takes a deep inhale. 'When we first met you told me about a "warrior" gene. Do you remember?'

'Of course. Back then we were speculating, but the genetic marker showed up in later tests on Joshua. Low activity variant MAO-A.'

'If his problem is genetic, then I suppose there's no cure?'

'It's more complicated than that. But that's why it's so hopeful. Research in behavioural genomics does point to a correlation between the low activity variant MAO-A gene and violent behaviour, but lots of people who have the genetic marker don't go on to be violent. We're beginning to understand that violence is more often than not a learned behaviour. While it's true that

Joshua may well be genetically predisposed to being violent, he's more likely to be violent if he sees it at home.'

The waitress returns with the coffee and casts an eye over Emma's arms before moving away.

'That's why it's so important that we keep Joshua away from any violence.'

Emma Barrons gives me a pointed look. 'You know, I suppose, that your colleague said there was nothing more they could do for Joshua.'

When I tell her about her husband's involvement in Halperin she first raises an eyebrow then shuts her eyes and, shaking her head, says, 'Christopher's not with Joshua most of the time, he doesn't understand. One day my son is really going to hurt someone.'

* * *

From the park I set off in the direction of the institute. The streets have been reopened in all but the worst affected areas now and sweeper trucks plough up and down the major thoroughfares. But glass on the pavement still crunches underfoot and the boarded-up shops, broken bus shelters, fluttering police tape and the spicy tang of burnt-out bins are testament to the events of the past three nights. Thank God for the rain, and for the cooler weather.

I call Anja's mobile from the Wise Owl Cafe.

'It's Caitlin. Can we talk?'

Anja arrives a few minutes later, spots me at our usual table and strides over. In the cafe lights, her hair is the colour of ripe oats.

'Caitlin! What a surprise. What can I do for you?' Her voice is calm and a little officious, but she shifts her weight between her feet as if there are tiny, sharp stones inside her shoes.

'Please, sit down.' I tell her what Emma Barrons has just told me.

She listens, hands steepled on the table, pretending to give weight to what I'm saying. I don't mention the records. When the waitress appears Anja waves her away, a signal to me that she's not staying long.

'You're making a mistake discharging Joshua,' I say finally.

Anja crosses one leg over the other and cocks her head. 'I'm afraid it's you who are mistaken, Caitlin. The clinic couldn't possibly have discharged Joshua Barrons. He was never officially a patient.'

* * *

I'm nearly back at the Travel Inn when my phone rings. It's Gloria. While I was at the hospital she went back to the Dionysius cafe as she said she would. Without me around the men seemed more willing to talk. She got chatting to a man who claims to know a man who knows Ani. He's promised to make a couple of calls and see what can be arranged but she's hopeful that, if we can't speak to Ani himself, we might at least be able to speak to someone who can get a message to him. Less encouraging news is she's heard the council is intending to replace the boiler and do some general renovations in Lilly Winter's flat next week. Another family needs the space. If there is any physical evidence of what exactly happened the night Lilly Winter died, we have only a few days left to find it.

* * *

I make it to Dominic's office in the city with half an hour to spare and spend it forcing down a cheese sandwich in a nearby cafe. He meets me at the reception desk of Hunt, Baylor, Strachan. The offices are in one of those huge cityscape-defining towers of glass which have sprung up in London since the nineties and which – on a weekday at least – lend the Square Mile a darkly glamorous air. Between Monday and Friday the foyer is a stew of psychopathic traits, Dark Triad operators and emptying souls. On a Sunday it's a zombie town, populated by sleepless functionaries who've given up their lives for something they once thought they wanted.

But there are exceptions.

'Cat. How wonderful to see you. It's been far too long.' Dominic hugs me in close. His smell is the unaltered aroma of events long ago. In an instant, the neurotransmitters of scent memory, norepinephrine and acetylcholine, rustle up in my mind Dominic's younger self, the two of us in a museum some-where. And then, in the blink of an eye, the memory is gone. A security guard makes up a pass and Dominic chaperones me through the barriers and into the lift.

I have a recurring dream about lifts. Some people dream

about being stuck in a broken one, others about lifts that plummet. In my dream, I'm in a huge, unstoppable lift which bursts from its building and, shaking like a rocket, heads into the sky.

We get out at the eighteenth floor and go through a set of glass double doors into a swanky reception area decorated with the obligatory ginger flowers in a large, high-status vase. I follow Dominic down a broad corridor and into a room decked out in a tasteful Scandi style with a sofa, an armchair, a desk and an expensive coffee machine in the corner.

'Coffee? Something stronger?' He motions me to the sofa.

'Just water.'

He fills a glass from a funky-looking water filter, puts it on the coffee table and sits back in the armchair beside the sofa. He's in expensive casual, a linen shirt, jeans, but unshaven.

'Sorry not to get back to you before. Hellish litigation case. Now, what's the problem?'

'I seem to have rolled over the stone of my marriage and found all kinds of dark, biting things living underneath.'

As I relay the story, he sits back, thumbs tucked under his chin, hands set into fists over his mouth in that way that he always does when he's thinking.

'I'm not going mad, am I?'

'Of course not.' Dominic scratches his cheek. 'What's Tom's game?'

'If I knew that, I might be able to anticipate his next move, but I don't. My best guess is that he's protecting Ruby.'

'From what?'

'I don't know that either, not for sure.' I have my suspicions, but I'm not ready to voice them yet.

Dominic sits back and folds his arms and a look of concentration comes over him. 'The DV Protection Order is brand new and it's tough. Legally, the magistrate has the power to order a custodial sentence and take Freya away. Obviously, we won't let that happen.' He flashes me a wan, only half-convincing smile. Scratching his cheek now. 'The order is designed to give protection to victims of domestic violence even when there's only he said/she said evidence. So both sides are allowed to admit hearsay. We can take advantage of that to show extreme provocation. If we can corroborate your suspicion that your stepdaughter had been violent towards your daughter, it would really help. You say your daughter confided in you?'

'Yeah. Freya told me Ruby hit her and held her underwater in the pool until she thought she was going to pass out. She threatened her too. Ruby said if Freya told anyone what Ruby had done, she'd end up like Ruby's mother.'

'Would Freya give evidence?'

'Against her father and her half-sister? What if we don't win the case and she has to go back and live with them? How can I ask her to do that?'

Dominic takes a breath and thinks again. 'Did anyone else witness Ruby bullying your daughter?'

'She's too clever for that.'

'Was anyone else there when Freya told you all this?'

'No.' A mistake, I realise now. I should have called Sal in from the waiting room. But it was all so delicately balanced. I wasn't sure Freya was going to disclose anything at all.

Dominic is leaning against his fists again, thinking. 'For mitigating circumstances, we need evidence to suggest that you had a reasonable expectation Ruby would carry out her threat against Freya and that she presents a real danger to your daughter. You work with disordered kids all the time, Caitlin. Isn't there something in your field you can call on, I don't know, some kind of research?'

There is. I take a breath, and tell him about the scans.

'But I haven't even had the chance to look at them properly and, as you know, I'm really wary of using anything involving my area of expertise.'

He grimaces. 'The Spelling case.'

'Exactly. Won't the other side use that to try to undermine me?'

'Maybe. But at least this time you'd be giving concrete evidence and courts like certainty.'

'Whatever is on those scans, Dom, it's not going to "prove" anything. Neuroimaging just doesn't work like that.'

Dominic fixes me with a steady look. 'No one in court is going to know that except you.'

'That's hardly ethical. Besides, even if the court doesn't question the evidence, they could very easily question how I came by it.'

Dominic raises his eyebrows. 'That might be a risk you'll have to take if want to protect your daughter.'

'It's *all* I want.'

'Then isn't it a little too late for professional scruples?' He reaches over and takes my hand. 'It's your life and your daughter's life we're talking about.'

'There is something else. About Ruby, I mean. But right now I don't have any hard evidence.'

'Then go and get it.'

CHAPTER TWENTY-TWO

At the top of Forest Hill you can see all the way across the soft silver rope of the river to the dazzle of Canary Wharf. It's a glorious view, even now, with the city in a state of chaos, and in other circumstances I'd stop and take it in. But there's no time for that now when there are so much more important things to do.

Trust nothing except the evidence.

The front door of the Dionysius cafe is locked, but there is a light on at the back and after a few minutes' knocking the sallow manager comes bustling to the door, waving his arms. He gives no sign of recognising me.

'We are closed. Private function.'

'I need to talk to Ani.'

He takes a closer look and, registering my face, regards me levelly.

'Go away, lady.'

He is about to turn his back on me when a small man in alligator shoes with a belly like a beach ball comes out from behind the bead curtain at the back. The manager's body language suggests subservience and a hint of hostility. The two men exchange a few words in Albanian. Whatever is said, the manager opens the door.

'You wait.' He gestures towards a small table with a single chair sitting by the cash till and taps his watch. I do as instructed and take a seat. From here I have a view to the back of the room where a dozen men are drinking what looks like moonshine and playing a game of dominoes. From time to time, one of the men at the large table raises a glass in my direction and says something in his language. Whatever it is cracks up the rest of the table. Before long, though, the men tire of their little game and forget me. Time passes. I've been at the table for an hour when a flat-faced woman in a headscarf bustles out with a tray on which sits a teapot, a fancy glass, a bowl of sugar cubes and a plate of tiny, dry-looking pastries. I nod a thank you.

'Ani?'

She presses her lips together and shakes her head to indicate this has nothing to do with her then rattles off back behind the bead curtain. I pour a glass of tea. It's strong and bitter. I add sugar and sip. No appetite for pastries. When, after another wait, there is still no sign of Ani, I rise from the table and make my way through the bead curtain to the room beyond. The manager is sitting with the elderly proprietor. The woman is nowhere to be seen.

'You want talk Ani, you waiting now,' the manager says simply, his eyes directing me back to the table on the other side of the bead curtain. The men at the large table have grown steadily rowdier. One among them, a pit bull in his early thirties, stands and lurches through the bead curtain, belting out a song. He's savagely drunk, barely able to hold his balance. Whatever he's singing seems to amuse the proprietor and his sidekick. There is a sense of expectation. A male tang of adrenaline and sweat drifts over. Behind my eyes a pulse begins to tick. The pit bull takes a step towards me. The eyes fixed on me are glossy and hard. He's enjoying himself.

'My friend says maybe you work *imigrim*,' the manager says.

Fear grips my throat. I think about the woman and hope she is somewhere close by. 'No, I am a friend of Ani's. I've got some work for him.'

The pit bull tuts and shakes his head. His eyes narrow. This is starting to feel dangerous. I stand to leave and, as I turn, the pit bull moves his feet a few inches nearer. Instinctively I back away but he suddenly lurches towards me. My heart drums. The pit bull can feel my hesitation. To be seen to be afraid now would be a big mistake. What to do? He is too far gone and having too much fun to be reasoned with and if I make any sudden movement to leave, he will reach out and grab me. My only chance is to befuddle him. I bite down to steady my jaw and extend a hand, as if inviting him to shake it. He looks at me then at the hand and for a second I detect his confusion. Taking advantage of the moment, I make a rapid sidestep and lunge through the bead curtain and race towards the door. Suddenly I'm out on the pavement and spinning on my heels. When I look back the pit bull is standing outside with one arm clutching the lamp post and the other beckoning me back, shouting, '*Zezak! Zezak!*'

At the station, I stop running. It's dark now. A lone woman in her forties sits in the shelter. Further down the platform, a group of kids smoke weed on the benches. One of the girls is clutching a bottle of vodka. A bunch of kids drinking before going on to some club or other. The young are springing back from the riots, routing around the damage, putting forth new growth.

The announcement board flashes up the next arrival. Shortly afterwards, two yellow eyes appear in the pink gloom of the suburban night and the train begins to crawl along the platform. The lone woman disappears into a carriage further along.

At Surrey Quays, Gloria calls. She's angry. 'You go back? Without telling me? Act of a crazy bitch. Next time, they say they come for me. You want that?' She sucks her teeth. 'Now I don't know, how can I trust you?'

'I'm sorry, Gloria, but I had no choice.'

The train ticks on through tidy south-eastern suburbs before diving into a tunnel. In the darkness, I say simply, 'Is there anything you wouldn't do to get your Elmira back?'

Silence. And the phone signal fades.

* * *

I get out of the train at Rotherhithe and run along the south bank of the river, hoping the exercise might clear my head. At London Bridge, I stop for a moment. A dazzling view pours out on either side, the blaze of lights an urban PET scan, buzzing and illuminated, each part of the city interconnected in a million seen and unseen ways to every other, the whole joined at the midpoint by the river. I pull out my phone and punch in my sister's number. A voice heavy with sleep asks me if I have any idea what the time is.

'Is Freya with you?'

'I told you it would take a couple of days to sort out with work.' The lush sound of yawning. 'Everything's fine. I'm picking her up tomorrow afternoon.'

'Has she said anything to her father?'

'About seeing you at the hospital? Or about Ruby?'

'Both. Either.'

'No, I don't think so. You asked her not to, remember?'

* * *

I reach the hotel just before one. The foyer is deserted, the only sound a whine from the vending machine at the back. A lamp flickers as I pass, the fluorescence coming to the end of its natural life. I climb the stairs. In my room, I shrug off my clothes, take a shower and throw on the robe I was wearing when I escaped from Dunster Road. My backpack has chafed where the straps cut in along the shoulder. The clumsy getaway from the cafe. I'm hungry too. Moments later my reflection is dancing disconcertingly among the packets of crisps and bars of chocolate in the vending machine at the end of the corridor. I make my selection. The machine whirs and the cable cars of crisps in row C move forward. A thought stirs and forces a bitter laugh. What if human needs could be met this way? You could plug in the code, there would be a small wait, and the fulfilment would drop into a slot at the base. Of course it would never happen, because human needs are so complex and unpredictable. What need is Ruby serving in terrorising Freya? What starts Joshua's requirement to flush kittens down toilets or set fire to handbags? What leads kids to stab other children they barely know? What hole is being filled in the moment between the clench of Christopher Barrons' fist and its impact on his wife's face?

My therapist had this theory that all human violence, whether internal or external, is an attempt to restore self-esteem. But if that's true then are we nothing more than complex devices designed for the management of our own wayward egos? I wrestle with those kinds of questions daily in my work but in all the years of my research I've hardly come closer to any answers. Because, for all the advances we've made in understanding the human brain, there is still no scan for the human soul.

Sleep doesn't come till after dawn and I wake not long afterwards, unsettled by the wisp of a dream. I am on a camping trip with Tom and Freya. We used to do that some weekends, Tom and Freya and I, when she was very small. Just get in the car on a Friday night with a tent and pitch it where we felt like it. I think we were at our happiest then. But in the dream Tom has pegged out the tent on a clifftop and I am terribly afraid that our daughter might take one step too far and fall to her death. I'm fussing and complaining but still Tom is insisting the tent stay where it is. 'Look at the wonderful view,' he says. 'If we move, we'll lose it.' And I'm looking around but I'm not seeing any view. Because in the dream the tent only looks out across a fearful charcoal-coloured void.

CHAPTER TWENTY-THREE

People find different ways to unhook themselves from their pain. I of all people know that. Some get drunk, either to forget or give them whatever it is they need to hit out at the first unwitting passer-by; others take drugs, hurt themselves or have sex with strangers. People like me, quieter souls, tend to avoid these things. Our demons are the slow-burn, vengeful kind. We don't make scenes or shout or behave badly. People like me wait until all is quiet and still and then we rise from our beds and creep like cats out into the darkness.

A fool might think this makes us less dangerous.

Back in the quiet of my room, I punch in Tom's number on the hotel phone.

This isn't without risk. The terms of the DVPN forbid any contact. If Tom chooses, he could inform the police and get me arrested. But if I know my husband at all, I'm willing to bet he'll at least be intrigued by my call. I can't shake the feeling that Tom's protecting Ruby for all the wrong reasons. And to find out what they are, I need to get him back on side.

Two rings, then before I've had a chance to speak, Tom's voice. 'Cat! This *is* a surprise.'

'How did you know it was me?'

'It's pretty obvious, isn't it?' I let this pass. *This is a game and Tom is very good at games.*

'Listen, I've had time to think. I know I shouldn't be calling but I feel so ashamed of what I did to Ruby. It was so wrong. With all that was happening, I wasn't well, I wasn't coping. I see that now.'

'Hmm,' says Tom.

'I don't expect you to believe me but I wish I could take it all back. The jealousy, the nasty accusations, the attack on a little girl.'

'You were completely out of line.'

'I know, I know. But the thing is, I'm seeing a psychiatrist now and I'm feeling so much better about everything. Clearer. And I want to make it up to you all. I just think, whatever happens to us, for Ruby and Freya's sakes, we need to meet and talk things through.'

Another sceptical hum. 'The thing is, Cat, there's a DV notice. You're not supposed to be coming anywhere near me or the girls.'

'You can have the house, Tom.'

His voice brightens. 'I can?'

'Yes, yes, I don't care about any of that. So long as I can see Freya every now and then.'

'Well, I'm not sure.'

'Let's just talk it through.'

People speak about the epiphany, the moment the scales fall from the eyes, but more often than not what we call the moment of truth is actually the moment the lie finally breaks. Because we all hold on to lies. Sometimes lies are the only thing holding us together. We hang on to them even as we're peering over the precipice. And even when the truth holds out a hand still we cling to the lies, as the world we thought we knew slips slowly from our grasp.

Hoopoes Chicken Shop. Tom is sitting at our usual table, amusing himself with a game, a single curl over his forehead dancing in time with his fingers, a reminder of something else I once loved and maybe still do: Tom's coolness, his cheerful confidence, an inbuilt sense he has that everything will turn out OK. He looks up, sees me and stands up from the table. Those manners.

'Cat, you look great.' His hand against my arm, the old erotic charge.

He waits for me to take my seat and only afterwards resumes his own.

I sit down. There's an opened bottle of San Miguel on the table. 'Beer OK?' I swing my legs in under the table, notice him watching. While his attention is diverted my eyes cut to his phone. I feel an overwhelming desire to let him know how close I am to smashing him at his own game. But I don't.

I say, 'Thanks but I've given up.'

'Oh?'

'The medication.' I'm scanning Tom's face for signs of scepticism, but he's listening, open-eyed, chin on his fists, strangely intimate, like nothing ever happened. Lies. I'm getting better at them. Not in Tom's league, but still.

A waitress approaches and Tom orders himself a chicken burger, sparkling water and a coffee for me. I'm not hungry. Heaving a sigh – always one for the grand gesture – he says, 'God, Cat, how the hell did this whole thing get started?'

It started with a one-night stand, Tom. It began when you decided to sleep with Lilly Winter.

'Oh, I don't know. Maybe we just overreacted a little.'

He straightens himself up and runs his left palm up and down his thigh. 'You put on quite a show.'

I laugh and let this pass.

'How are the girls? How's Freya?'

'Good, both really good. Freya's gone to your sister's for a bit, maybe till after the hearing, just until things calm down.' Tom's left leg begins to jig. Nerves? Remorse? I can no longer tell. I am on new ground now. Or perhaps I'm on old ground and I've just forgotten what that feels like.

'I'm not looking forward to the hearing.'

'No, I don't suppose you are. If only there was a way to stop it, but there really isn't.' A rueful smile. 'The dead hand of bureaucracy.'

I allow my left arm to hang beside my pocket. As he picks up his beer and takes a swig, my fingers are checking the settings on my phone. All good. Keeping it in the left pocket is a stroke of genius. I'm right-handed so Tom will never suspect.

'You mentioned, on the phone…' He tails off awkwardly.

'The house? Yes, well, I've been thinking too, you know?'

Tom takes a sip of his beer and looks at me carefully. 'That's why I'm glad you got in touch. There must be better ways of settling this than getting all lawyered up.'

'So what you're saying is, no lawyers?'

'Let's just keep this low-key. Do what we have to, minimise the fuss and get it over with. I'd hate it for Freya not to see her mother.'

I glance at his face but his expression is giving nothing away. 'You're suggesting some kind of arrangement?'

'Maybe, now the house is in the mix.'

The burger and drinks arrive. Tom waits until the waitress has gone.

'We'd need to sort out the details, of course.'

I smile. 'Of course.'

Tom looks at his food then at me and makes to stand. 'Gents. Old habit. But then you know that.' As he skirts around the table, his eyes cut momentarily to his phone.

'Oh, don't worry, take your time. I need to make a call anyway,' I say.

He eyes me beadily for a second then, against his better judgement, nods and turns away. At the steps down to the basement toilets he thinks better of it, turns and comes back, hand-miming a phone call.

'Forgot it.' He smiles as he's reaching out, his hand at an odd angle, unable to pick up the phone without first moving both his burger and the beer bottle. Then his eyes blade to me, trying to decide if this is a trap. He stops, eases off, rocking his weight into his heels, and, finally laughing, he flaps at the air and says, 'What a bloody idiot phone addict!' Leaving the phone on the table he spins on his heels and hurries back towards the toilets.

In an instant the phone is in my hands. This is better than I'd hoped. I press in the key lock number, the one I've seen Tom enter a zillion times – 0580, the first release date of Pacman – and I'm in and scanning down the list of his most recent calls. Sal's number, mine, Michael's, one or two old friends, nothing unusual. Then to the message folder and I'm scrolling back to the weeks before Lilly's death, speed-reading with one eye on the staircase to the basement toilets. Tom's been gone two minutes now. I've probably got another four. My husband likes to wash his hands. He's a meticulous hand-washer. Still nothing obvious. *Damn it!* Whatever game Tom is playing he's keeping the rule book close to his chest.

I'm placing the phone back on the table beside the beer when an app icon on the home screen catches my attention. A single eye. Checking for any sign of Tom's return and seeing none, I peck it open. A list of numbers scrolls up, followed by a series of URLs. Puzzling. None of this data means anything. And then, an instant later, clarity. My brain connects and it's as if someone has thrown a seed into a freezing pond and the shapes and patterns of crystallising ice are blossoming before me. It suddenly feels very hot. The blood is a torrent in my ears. These are *my* calls, the websites *I've* visited. Every phone call I've made, each text, all the websites. My husband has been spying on me. Until the day I left home, every minute detail of my communication, every GPS location, every message I'd sent, every call received was downloaded to this app. This is not the secret I expected to uncover. But it's a secret I can use.

There's movement in my peripheral vision. Quick as a flash I've let go of the phone. My fingers are trembling now, the blood bubbling inside them. A man walks by but it isn't him. Fingers trembling, I pluck my own phone out of my left-hand pocket, cut the recorder, take a few screen shots, then, spotting the top of Tom's head on the stairs, switch my own phone back to record and return it to my pocket. A second to replace Tom's device on the table before I am in his line of vision. Tom strolls over. As he edges back into his seat and draws up the chair there's nothing on his face to suggest alarm. Our eyes meet across the space, the only sound between us the thin tick of my shoe on the linoleum. His gaze falls on his device, wondering whether to pick it up and then, at the last minute, he decides against it and turns to his burger instead. One misstep now and it's over. I will have revealed my hand. I am struggling to remember how we left things. There are worry lines on Tom's forehead. As he lifts the bun to his mouth I say, 'Good burger?' My voice sounds oddly strained.

'Did you make your call?'

'Yes. Had a work thing but it went to Claire's voicemail.'

'Oh.' The evenness in Tom's expression suggests he doesn't know I've been put out to grass. He puts down his food and wipes his fingers on a paper napkin.

'Look, I've been thinking about what you said. You're right, no lawyers. Let's just keep the hearing low-key.'

He hums through a full mouth, swallows and says, 'It's for the best.'

'So at the hearing, you'll say it was all a misunderstanding? You don't think you saw the things you thought you saw?'

He's nodding. 'In exchange for the house? Absolutely. One hundred per cent.'

This is the time to leave, while he still believes he's won. I rise from my chair. He puts down his burger and reaches for my hand. He's surprised I'm leaving but the ripples on his face soon melt into a cool blank lagoon.

'It was good to see you, Tom. I'm glad we had this talk.'

'Oh, me too, Cat, very glad indeed.' His lips pull into a tight, unfamiliar smile.

Out on the street a piece of advice I read all those years ago in Tom's copy of *How to Win Friends and Influence People* pops into my mind. *Rule number one: make friends of your enemies.*

CHAPTER TWENTY-FOUR

The next morning when I wake it takes me an instant to remember where I am. I moved out of the Travel Inn last night and into the Travel Express a little further down the road. I also deleted my email and social media history and removed the SIM card from my phone, in case Tom has bugged Sal and registered the new number as mine.

I swing my legs out from under the sheets, pad over to the desk and push a capsule into the coffee machine. While it's brewing, I hop into the shower, flipping the temperature dial from cold to hot and back again until my skin feels as tightly sprung as a new mattress.

After coffee, I fling on some clothes and then make my way down to reception. I go to the public phone beside the lifts and punch in Sally's number. My sister answers in a low voice.

'She's fine, she's sleeping a lot.'

'Will you tell her I love her and I'll see her very soon?'

Outside the streets are busy. The traffic is high but not yet irritable and the shops are opening up for business. The slice of sky visible between skyscrapers is an aching, southern blue, as if flown in overnight from the Med. Women and men slide by, lattes and bagged croissants in hand, tapping on their phones. London is healing today, a delicate rim of gliosis forming around necrotised cells, corralling them off from the healthy tissue, the neurons looking for pathways around the dead zone.

At PC Planet I pick up a cheap laptop, a USB hard drive and a pre-pay smartphone. The next couple of hours are spent in my room at the hotel with the 'do not disturb' sign on the door, downloading all my data onto the drive then wiping my old laptop and cloud space, unlinking my old phone, which I'll keep in case Freya calls me, closing all my email accounts and setting up several new ones. Tom will figure out pretty quickly that I've moved on but at least I've bought myself some time.

I call Dominic Harding with my new phone and set up a lunch meeting, then key in Claire's number.

'Emma Barrons has been trying to reach you. Shall I tell her you'll be in touch? She sounds pretty desperate.'

I ask Claire not to give my number out to anyone, and to call Emma and tell her I'll be round at about nine tonight.

At lunchtime, I make my way to The Complete Pig in the shadow of St Paul's. Dominic Harding is tucked away in a secluded booth in the corner, his fingers scurrying across his phone. The place specialises in what it calls 'top to tail' eating. We used to meet here for lunch sometimes in the old days. We'd order brains and cross-examine each other while we ate. *Given the size of the occipital lobe in exhibit A, on your plate, is it your contention, Dr Lupo, that the defendant is a sheep or a wolf in sheep's clothing?* Maybe you had to be there, but it made us howl like madmen. Those were the days, before Kylie Drinkwater, when almost everything amused us.

Today, as Dominic watches me approach, his face is set in its habitual attitude of professional breeziness, but the giveaway is in the eyes. He's worried. Standing, he presses me to him in an affectionate hug.

'Caitlin, so pleased to see you, but, tell me, are you looking after yourself?' This is Dominic's very English way of telling me I look like shit.

'I've had things to think about.'

He colours, mutters, 'Of course,' and leaves the subject.

We settle ourselves and when the waiter appears I order sparkling water. We've not spoken since my meeting with Tom.

We quickly get down to business. The hearing will decide whether the Domestic Violence Protection Notice will be formalised into a court order. If it is, the court has the right to put conditions on my access to Freya. If I lose, I might forfeit the right to live with my daughter.

'Notice has been served with a date for the hearing. Two o'clock on Wednesday at Camberwell Green Magistrates' Court. The courts are always quick with DVPO hearings. We could apply for a stay, but there's no guarantee they'd grant it unless there are extraordinary circumstances, even now, in the aftermath of the riots.' His eyes narrow. 'Are you about to tell me that we need a stay?'

I tell him about the conversation with Tom and, as I'm speaking, he's leaning on the table, one hand on his forehead, shaking his head in exasperation.

'You do know, I suppose, that going to meet him was about the dumbest thing you could have done? You're in breach right there.'

'If I hadn't gone, I wouldn't have found out about the spying. That's got to help our case, hasn't it?'

Dominic considers this a moment then, raising his eyebrows, says, 'If we can prove he's been systematically spying on you, we might be able to get him under the new cyberstalking laws. It won't necessarily help with the DVPN, but it might. What evidence have you got?'

I take out my new phone and show him the screen shots I've transferred from the old one. His eyes widen.

'What's his game plan?'

'Hard to say. Maybe he's preparing his attack at the hearing; maybe he's about to file divorce papers and claim custody of Freya; maybe he thinks I know something incriminating.'

'About what?'

'How Lilly Winter died.'

Dominic's eyes narrow. 'And do you?'

As I detail my suspicions, Dominic's eyes widen again and a look of scepticism shades his face. 'Look, unless and until you've got some hard evidence, what you've just told me is going to sound vindictive, vengeful and a bit nuts, frankly. If you've got proof that Tom was in any way implicated in the death of that woman, you need to go and make a statement to the police.'

'Really? And what's the likelihood they'd believe me, do you think? A woman they consider to be mentally unstable who has a DVPN out on her?'

'All the more reason to leave it. Focus on the hearing and getting your daughter back. You've admitted to pushing Ruby and pulling her hair. Our best strategy is to show you had solid grounds for believing Ruby was a danger to Freya and were taking reasonable steps to protect your daughter. Am I right in thinking that the only evidence the other side has to go on is Ruby's version of that moment in the bathroom? Or did you manage to root out whatever it was you were talking about last time we met?'

'No one saw me hit Ruby because I didn't hit Ruby.'

The waiter bustles up with the drinks, waits for the food order then offers to return in a few minutes. He's picked up the tension in the atmosphere and assumes we're lovers in the middle of a row. When he returns, we order our usual.

Dominic pushes the menu to one side and steeples his hands on the table. 'I've been doing a bit of spying myself and I'm pretty sure the other side are going to produce physical evidence of bruising.'

'But I didn't hit her!'

'I'm just telling you what I know. Is there any other way Ruby could have come by those bruises?'

I think about this for a while and am reminded, suddenly, of the incident with the paper clip.

'She could have done it herself. She has form.'

Dominic sighs. 'No one's going to believe that in court. We need to think laterally, Cat, and focus on your strengths, establish your credentials.'

The food arrives. The brains are soft and sweet and ever

so slightly bitter. For a moment or two it's five years ago and Dominic and I are sliding into something dangerous and thrilling.

Then Dominic puts down his fork. 'Your expertise is your trump card. You need to use it. Supposing there were a way to *prove* Ruby can't be taken at her word. What's the saying? *Genes are destiny.*'

'This is about the scans.' Over the last few days, since Dominic and I first spoke, I've been thinking a lot about the scans, weighing up the consequences of using them.

'I know how you feel but they're all we've really got to go on that isn't just he said/she said.'

'But they're unreliable witnesses. If behavioural genomics tells us anything, it's that there's no gene for lying. People don't lie or do terrible things because their genes make them; they lie and kill because they choose to. Scans are wonderful, they've revolutionised brain science, but they're lousy predictors of human behaviour.'

Dominic rubs a hand through his hair and does his best not to sound irritated. He's frustrated. At some level he thinks I'm being bloody-minded and pernickety.

'Look, Cat, you know as well as I do that people need certainties. We demand them even when we know they don't really exist. Guilty or not guilty? Blameless or culpable? I'm not asking you to lie outright. I'm just asking you to use the scans to say something simple, something certain.' Dominic fixes me with a steady look. 'Think about what's at stake here.'

'I can't lie about Ruby. I thought I could but I just can't.' I push my plate away, disgusted suddenly by the creamy wobble on the plate. Dominic's jaw tightens as if bracing himself for what might come next. He's afraid for me, for the case.

'Then it'll all come down to your word against Tom's.'

I pause. 'If I *did* use the scans, the other side would be bound to bring up the Spelling case. They'll say I have demonstrated poor judgement. It could so easily backfire. Plus, I'd be laying a terrible and unfair burden on Ruby. I'd be sticking a label on her that will stay with her for the rest of her life.'

'But isn't that exactly what you did in the Rees Spelling case – presented the science to spare him the full sentence?'

'They're not the same, Dominic. Rees Spelling was – is – a psychopath and I failed to spot it because I let my principles interfere with the science. I didn't want Spelling to end up in a youth offenders' unit so I convinced myself the science was stronger than it is. I was wrong to give Spelling a second chance but I'd be equally wrong to deny it to Ruby. I've looked at Ruby's scans.' This was true. I had loaded them onto my laptop at the hotel. 'Her profile is almost normal.'

'Almost?'

'There are some connectivity issues and the amygdala is on the small side, but with the kind of childhood Ruby's had, there's nothing I wouldn't expect.'

'But that's not the same as saying she's normal.'

'It's not the same as saying she's psychopathic either. And there's something else. I forged the permissions documents.'

'You did *what*?'

'I forged Tom's signature on the documents giving me permission to take the scans.'

'Jesus, Cat.'

'I had this idea that maybe I could learn something about her from the scans, that maybe I could use that somehow. I don't know, I guess I wasn't thinking straight. It had got to the point where I was desperate.'

I press my fingers to my eyes. Orange patterns dance in the space behind my eyelids. 'There's another thing I need to tell you.'

Dominic can feel the weight of what's coming while it's still a bundle of ideas collecting words and forming sentences in my mind.

'I don't like the sound of that.'

'Years ago – I mean, *years* – I did something terrible. I didn't mean to do it, but I can't say it didn't happen.'

Dominic's knuckles are pressing hard on the table, leaving little pools of bleached, pressured skin.

'You know what a prodrome is?'

He shakes his head.

'It's the first stages of a psychosis. Subtle changes in behaviour that foretell a psychotic episode. Like an aura. They started happening to me about a month before my breakdown. Odd intrusive thoughts, dropouts in my memory, that sort of thing. At first I just put them down to pregnancy hormones. Which was right, as it turned out, but the point is, I ignored them. And then, one morning, about thirty weeks into the pregnancy, I wake up to this *smell*, like the most disgusting stench of dead flesh coming off a vase of lilies. So I go over and, I don't really know how to explain it, I just get this feeling that those lilies have stolen my baby and that they're somehow eating her flesh, like the smell is so bad because she's dissolving inside the vase. It sounds mad because it was. And so I pick up the vase and I can hear myself cry out and my cry must have woken Tom because the next thing I know his arms are around me, trying to hold me back, and I'm thinking he's trying to stop me from saving my baby, so I wheel about and I punch him, hard.'

Time slows and for a moment I am back in that dream lift, rising through a tall building and heading shakily out towards the atmosphere, out beyond the air.

'Does anyone else know about this?' Dominic says.

'Tom called 999. The police arrived along with an emergency psych team. They put me under observation for a few hours then discharged me, said it was probably just a hormone spike.

'I came home and for a while I was OK and everything seemed to be fine between us. Until, about a month later, I woke up to the smell again. Things just spiralled downwards very quickly from there. It was like an earthquake went off in my head.'

'It would have been helpful if you'd told me this before,' Dominic said coolly. He is trying to understand, but he doesn't, he can't.

'The stuff I did, the stuff I said, I know it shouldn't be shaming but it is. I didn't want to live in the shadow of mental illness all my life; I didn't want to have to think about it. A month ago,

I had a good life, a daughter I'd die for, a wonderful career and a serviceable marriage. And now what? I've got nothing left.'

'You have a chance. All you have to do is stretch the truth and you have a chance to be with your daughter.'

'And lie in the process? Condemn Ruby Winter? If I did that, Dominic, would I even be fit to *be* with Freya?'

CHAPTER TWENTY-FIVE

In a cab. It's eight forty-five in the evening and the night has already closed in. Commuters have hustled back to the 'burbs and the streets are quiet. As we bowl over London Bridge heading south towards Brixton there's no sign of rain but a tanginess in the air is suggestive of autumn. The yellow boards that were everywhere only a couple of weeks ago have disappeared. Shops have been repaired, burnt-out buildings boarded up. No one has mentioned LeShaun Toley in days. All the city's tumult is behind us. Only the taut, metallic aftermath of violence remains, casting its shadow over the capital.

The cab rumbles along past the smart Georgian terraces of Kennington towards more troubled parts of town.

The driver pipes up: 'Springfield Road, that's the one by the park, isn't it?'

'Yes.' *The one ten minutes from my old life.*

* * *

Emma Barrons answers the door in a silk kimono looking like all manner of shit. Something in me can't let go of the Barrons family. I'm guessing I'm still trying to manage the fallout from Spelling, to make up for my monumental failure. Emma gives me a smile and leads me through a bright tiled hallway into a vast, expensively furnished kitchen. She waves me to a seat at the immaculately distressed table and flops down opposite.

'Where's Joshua?'

'Out, with the nanny. He doesn't sleep – well, not much anyway. She takes him to Brixton Tube. He likes to ride the escalators. He'll go up and down for hours.'

'I remember him telling me he wanted to be a Tube train driver in one of our sessions.'

'Yes, he's into dark tunnels, secret places no one else gets to go. And he likes to be in control, too, of course. He's not his father's son for nothing.'

'Where is your husband?'

Emma Barrons lets out the air from her mouth in a long sigh. 'In New York. He's not coming back.'

'I'm sorry.'

She presses her puffy eyes with her fingers then releases them. 'Don't be. He's been looking for an excuse to leave for years. I really don't mind, except that now I'm left to cope with Joshua on my own.' She takes a breath, remembering her manners. 'You'll have a drink?'

'Coffee would be great.'

Emma nods, gets up and goes to the kettle. She lets out a peal of brittle, bitter laughter and, turning back to me with her eyes shining, she says, 'You'll never guess. Joshua has taken to keeping creepy-crawlies in tanks. Did I tell you? They're upstairs. *Ghastly!*' Her smile fades and she's fidgeting with the rock on her finger now to stop her hands from trembling.

'What will you have? Vodka?'

She brings over the bottle, some ice and two glasses, pours herself a double and knocks it back in one. The coffee is forgotten.

'I read somewhere that violence is an attempt to restore self-esteem. Is that true, do you think?'

'Yes, I had a therapist who said that.'

Emma pours herself a second vodka. Emma Barrons is drinking herself stupid. There's another laugh, this one indistinguishable from the yelp of a kicked dog. 'It's funny, when you think about it. We've built society around the assumption that human beings want to be socialised. What are we supposed to do with ones like Joshua who don't?'

Emma pulls out her chair and swings her legs over as though any moment she'll be making a bid for freedom. 'They told me you'd left for disciplinary reasons.'

'It's complicated.'

Another drink is poured. 'Did you speak to Anja De Whytte?'

'Yes.'

Her face registers mine and falls.

'I'm sorry.'

'Do you read the Bible ever, Caitlin?'

'My dad read it to me sometimes, when I was a kid, but no.'

'You know the parable of Abraham and Isaac, though, I suppose?'

'Of course.'

'Don't you think it's odd that God wanted Abraham to sacrifice his son? How could anyone seriously love a god who could even suggest such a thing?'

I say nothing. Thoughts about Ruby and Tom dance through my mind.

The silence is finally broken by the plink of ice cubes in Emma's glass.

'You're in a lot of trouble, aren't you?'

Ignoring this, I say, 'There might be a way to help Joshua, but it would mean blowing a few whistles. There'd be press, and I wouldn't be able to guarantee to be able to keep yours or Joshua's name out of the papers.'

Emma Barrons blinks and with a croak in her voice she says, 'Anything's better than this awful fear, the unbearable daily dread that my son is going to end up doing something terrible.'

* * *

Back outside it has begun to rain and the air is damp and cool. Walking down Springfield Road around the corner of the Grissold Park, I am overtaken by a tremendous hollowing thump in the gut. No one ever speaks of the awful animal loss, the pang in the chest, the constant tug of blood and genes that makes a battle of your body when you can't see your child or know they are safe. But if I feel this way, how much worse it must be *not* to miss your kid, to wonder why you ever had him, to look at his face and not see anything to love there without hating it a little too.

CHAPTER TWENTY-SIX

The hum of traffic over London Bridge not far off midnight, inky water on the high tide slapping on the stanchions, and the shadow of Rees Spelling casting across the river to Joshua Barrons on the other side. I'm tapping numbers into my phone.

A wary voice answers. 'Who is this? Have you seen the time?'

'It's Caitlin Lupo. I've got a story for you, White. You already know we were treating Joshua Barrons at the clinic. As I remember, it was about the only piece of information you've had on me that you haven't used to screw me over.'

'You might not believe it but I do have some scruples. A few anyway.'

'It was Anja, wasn't it, who leaked that particular nugget of information? She was hoping you'd print it and I'd get the blame.'

'I can't reveal my sources.'

'Did Anja also tell you that she discharged Joshua Barrons from the clinic and deleted all his files? The institute's line is that he was never officially a patient.'

'Why would she do that?'

'Christopher Barrons is a principal trustee of the Halperin

Trust. They support a lot of the institute's research. He was terrified word would get out that his son was in treatment and what for. He threatened to cut off the Halperin money and the institute went along with it and, just to be on the safe side, erased Joshua's records. I can't prove who gave the directive to delete the files but I know it was done to protect the Halperin funds. I can email you the deleted records. Every last one of them.'

'You got anyone who can corroborate this?'

I've already thought of this and made the necessary calls.

'Claire Turnbull and Lucas Stavlinski, respectively my administrative assistant and my research associate. They were both present when Joshua Barrons was either discussed or in treatment and they're willing to go on the record.'

White lets out the air with a hum.

'This kid is going to do something bad, probably to his mother or his nanny or someone close to him, but maybe to some random child he meets on the street. He's not going to get treatment till someone rolls over the stone and deep cleans all the shit lying under it.'

'Sounds like someone wants her job back.'

'I took the job to help kids like Joshua.'

'How noble. There was me thinking it was because you'd screwed up the Spelling case and were trying to redeem your-self.'

'Look, White, I don't give a shit what you think my motives are. I'm offering you a scoop. You don't want it, there are a dozen hacks out there who will.'

'So why pick me?'

'Because I have so much respect for you. Why do you think I picked you? Because you'll publish, that's why.'

A grunt on the other end. 'Email me those documents. I'll think about it.'

I finish up the call, take a whisky from the minibar and email over Joshua Barrons' records. I've done all I can for Joshua now. It's time to try to get some sleep.

* * *

Some hours later, I'm woken by the sound of a slamming door. It's not yet light and the air in the room is rank with the empty, plastic smell of recycled corporate hospitality. I'm nauseous and my head is a ball someone has been kicking around the pitch. A groan passes my lips and, as I raise myself onto my pillow, my eye catches sight of two empty mini-bottles of whisky and one of vodka sitting on the bedside table. *Craazy Cat has been at the booze. Shit.* I stumble into the bathroom, grab the mouthwash and gargle. The eyes in the mirror stare back reproachfully.

I am in the shower when my right hand begins to tremble and from there everything goes rapidly downhill – my chest tightens, my whole body is shaking and a gasping sound is coming from my mouth. I just manage to stumble out of the shower on hollow legs before I am throwing up weak brown fluid into the toilet bowl. After that the panic subsides a little. Then it's back to the shower to clean up and take some deep breaths to try to quell the fear.

Three capsule coffees later I'm feeling more myself. I've showered and ironed my navy skirt and white blouse, oiled my hair and I'm anxious but in control. A quick fix in the mirror. The woman who looks back means business.

The facts are… The facts are that I did not hit Ruby Winter or cause the bruising on her body. The facts are that Ruby Winter is a disturbed child and a danger to my daughter. The fact is that Freya is afraid of her half-sister because, among other things, she held her under water until she nearly passed out and then threatened her so she would keep it a secret. The fact is also that Tom Walsh is protecting Ruby Winter or perhaps Ruby Winter is looking out for her father. Or both these things. The fact is that Ruby Winter and Tom Walsh have lied and lied and covered for each other. The fact is Tom and Ruby have a secret.

Human behaviour cannot be predicted from a scan. That's a fact.

A fact is not a fact unless it can be proven. And what about the truth? Isn't that more than whatever fits the facts?

* * *

The *Herald* slides under my door around six thirty. No mention of Halperin or Christopher Barrons or the institute. Nothing on the website either. At eight thirty I leave the hotel and make my way towards the bus stop to meet my fate. Someone has fixed a sign to the railings reading *Hackney is hurting*, with details of a meeting for the citizens of the borough to discuss the riots. The irony of that notice strikes me. We need a brain to read the sentence but the brain is itself incapable of feeling pain. It has no means of hurting. Brain tissue, actual grey and white matter, lacks the necessary nociceptors. The only pain receptors are in the dura and the pia, the brain's protective shields. Thinking is a very different matter. Thinking can leave you chafed and blistered and with painful, suppurating wounds. Thinking should come with a health warning.

* * *

The leaves on the plane trees around St Paul's are beginning to curl, the sky is marbled with clouds and it won't be long now before the city changes out of its summer livery into its grey winter uniform. A young homeless man sitting on a bench outside with his dog asks for money. I'm early for my meeting with Dominic at the Hunt, Baylor, Strachan offices. I find a table in a nearby cafe, stop the waitress and order a double espresso and an omelette. By the time it arrives my appetite has gone, so I ask to have it boxed up with the intention of taking it out to the man and his dog. I'm heading over to them when the pressure of a hand on my elbow brings on a reflexive flinch and, as I turn, I see Dominic standing beside me, dressed in a dark suit, white shirt and conservative tie. Always cool under pressure is Dominic.

'I spotted you on my way to the office.' We're beside the young homeless man now. Dominic bends to pat the dog. 'Hey, Steve.'

'Hello, mate,' the homeless man says. 'A fiver wouldn't go amiss.'

I watch a sparrow hop along the bench then take flight and follow it to its perch on a thin branch high in the plane tree where it bows and flutters to stay upright in the breeze.

Dominic produces the money. 'Get the dog some breakfast.'

Steve rises from the bench and pulls on the dog's lead. 'Nah, you're all right. I've got to be going in a minute, mate. Busy day.'

We watch him leave then, laying a steadying hand on my shoulder, Dominic says, 'Let's go to the office. We can talk in private.'

Walking down the path past the plane trees in St Paul's churchyard and across the street to Dominic's building, neither of us speaks because there is too much to say. The receptionist fills out a visitor badge and Dominic ushers me through the security gate. In the lift, he squeezes my elbow.

'How are you, Cat?'

'Nervous.'

The doors open at the eighteenth floor. Dominic waves me out first then sees me through the glass doors and exchanges a greeting with the floor receptionist. We move into the quiet thrum of the corridor and through a panelled door into his office.

'Coffee?'

I shake my head.

'I had my PA check with the clerk at Camberwell Green Magistrates' Court. Antoinette Spiro's on rota. She's tough but she's a listener and she doesn't like separating kids from their mothers unless there's absolutely no alternative. Plus, she's under pressure to get through a mountain of riot cases. You have court experience, Cat, which will be useful, but you need to be prepared for Tom putting up a good fight. He loses this and you'll have the right to get up from the court and move straight back into Dunster Road.'

'And if I lose?'

Dominic leaves the armchair where he has perched and comes over to sit beside me. 'This isn't a run-of-the-mill case where the wife, husband, partner – usually a bloke with a bit of a history; drunk, high, whatever – hits out. The other side will do their best to convince Spiro that you threatened Tom. They'll call on your history. Even so, my gut tells me they'll fail to impress Spiro. There's no hard evidence that you ever threatened Tom. It's Ruby I'm more worried about, the physical evidence of bruising on her body and the fact that you haven't got any real evidence to suggest she might be a danger to Freya. If there's any question mark over either child's safety…'

'Which there is.'

Dominic absent-mindedly brushes some non-existent lint from his trousers. 'Spiro has the right to issue a temporary custody order. Both girls will go to a relative or into temporary foster care.' He lifts a reassuring hand. 'I'm sure it's not going to come to that but it's only right I warn you that it *could*.'

From somewhere outside comes the soft burr of a wood pigeon. Dominic lays a hand on my shoulder.

'It wasn't always like this with Tom, you know?' I begin. 'Even after Ruby arrived. I'm sure he felt attacked and defensive but he did seem to want to fix things. But then something changed and he began acting as though it was my reaction to events rather than the events themselves that had created the problem.'

'Can you pinpoint the shift?'

'I have to think...' I'm spooling back through the days and weeks. 'Yes! I'd come back from Lilly Winter's flat and I was asking Ruby if she knew anything about the guy who'd come to fix the boiler. Tom overheard me and went mad. I've never seen him so agitated.'

'What caused that reaction?'

My eyes spring open with the suddenness of the idea. It's so simple and so plausible. I twist around until I'm looking directly at Dominic. 'I think he was afraid I would find out exactly what happened in that flat.'

We sit for a moment taking this in, our brains working so hard you can feel the static.

'How would you feel about filing a suit against Tom under a Section Two for harassment, maybe even cyberstalking if we can make that stick? I could send a letter of intent to his lawyers right now. It'll rattle the other side. We can use it at the hearing to damage Tom's credibility and give you a better crack at getting a favourable arrangement order for Freya at some later date.'

'I'd feel pretty good about it.'

* * *

A few hours later, I am sitting alone at a table in the cafe at Camberwell Green Magistrates' Court when my husband walks in. It takes Tom a few seconds to spot me and, when he does, he stops in his tracks, a blank expression on his face. How funny! This man looks just like the man I married – same dark curly hair, same boyish good looks, same air of casual insouciance – but I no longer know him at all. This new guy stands unmoved while anxious-looking youths flow by with their bewildered, beleaguered parents. He always did have a good poker face. I used to put it down to his excruciatingly polite, uptight, English public-school upbringing, but now it seems there is some darker purpose. Since our lunch at Hoopoes I have learned a great deal about my husband, things which, only a few weeks ago, I would hardly have allowed myself to imagine. I know myself to be a good observer so why was it that with Tom there was so much I just chose to ignore?

Is that the hint of a smile playing on his lips? Yes, it is! He thinks I've kept my side of the deal and come on my own. I'm in his little mousetrap and he's about to release the snapper. A defining twenty-first-century couple. *Snap snap snap!*

And then he's gone.

It's a small turnout in court three for the first hearing after lunch. Just me and Dominic, a handful of clerks, ushers, police, Tom and Tom's lawyer. Despite all the talk about keeping this low-key, he's brought one. Of course! But then, so have I. And if he's surprised by this fact, if it catches him the least bit off guard, then he's not showing it. In fact, my husband looks wonderfully cool sitting there, legs crossed, his arms slung around his chair. Perhaps he was as aware as I was that the meeting in Hoopoes was a charade.

Magistrate Spiro arrives. She's a small, tidy-looking woman

with wiry hair, darting eyes and an expectant air. The clerk reads the introductory remarks. These hearings are new, so no one has quite got their feet under the table yet – except Spiro. The clerks, police, the lawyers are all slightly uncertain of themselves. Spiro presides over the unease like a raptor, clear-eyed and sharp-beaked. There are a few introductory remarks then Spiro continues:

'I am being asked to adjudicate on a Domestic Violence Protection Notice which has already been breached at least three times. The only reason the defendant hasn't been arrested is that the police are currently stretched to the limit. In such circumstances, it would be unusual not to grant a protection order. Nonetheless, it must be established that violence has occurred and that an order is necessary to protect the victim from further violence or threats of violence.'

She checks her notes before going on.

'This case has other unusual features in that it involves a threat of violence against an adult and an alleged assault on a minor. On account of her age, the court will hear transcripts of an interview with the minor only.

'As you know, the courts are currently working extended hours and to more than full capacity but the court is sensitive to the fact that, while the protection notice is in force, the defendant has been unable to see her daughter, at least officially, and we wish to conclude the matter in as timely a fashion as possible.'

As she goes on, the air con blasts from the back and the room grows colder. Spiro explains that this is a civil measure, not a criminal one, though the law allows for a fine of up to £5,000 and a custodial sentence of two months' imprisonment for a breach of terms.

Tom and I sit on opposite sides and avoid eye contact. Our lawyers shuffle their papers. Every so often one of the court clerks changes the cross of her legs.

'I am also empowered to make recommendations as to the living arrangements of the various minors involved and shall not hesitate to do so if I feel it to be necessary.'

Ruby's statement is read. It is not very believable if you were there, but if you weren't, it sounds convincing: the pulled hair, the pushing, blows that led to bruising. Tom backs it up and adds more, my history of mental instability and craziness, my previous assault on him, my threat to kill, how, from the moment Ruby arrived on the doorstep in the middle of the night, I resented her and did my best to persuade Tom to 'give her away' to her grandmother and, when Tom insisted on looking after his own child, how vindictive and rageful I became. How I threatened him. And then, finally, how I became so unstable he feared for my sanity. He moves on to my breach, how I came round to the house after the DV Protection Notice had been served and called him, demanding a meeting. Somehow he or his lawyer has found out about my suspension from the institute on a disciplinary matter so he throws that in for good measure. Unlike Ruby, Tom is charming and plausible to the core. Spiro takes it all in without much comment, looking up from her notes from time to time to scour the room.

At cross-examination Dominic rises and asks Tom, 'Do you love your wife?'

Tom blinks and swallows. 'This isn't about love,' he says.

And he's right. This is about revenge.

* * *

At three thirty Spiro orders a fifteen-minute break, after which it will be the turn of the defence to present their case.

We move out to the foyer.

Dominic says, 'I have to tell you, Cat, that it's not looking good. We should call Sally. At least she could back you up on the conversation you had with Freya about Ruby Winter.'

'No. It's too risky. If we lose, Sal's the only person on my side who'll have access to Freya. She'll be the only protection my daughter's got. If Sal speaks out against Tom, I'm afraid he'll stop her seeing Freya.'

Dominic gives me a careful look, the meaning of which is unmistakable. The scans.

'We've already talked about this.'

'Is it worth losing your daughter over a principle?'

'This isn't just a fight about me pushing my stepdaughter. It's not even a fight about who gets to look after Freya. I've been thinking that Ruby was wrapped up in her mother's death but I'm beginning to feel that something happened at Lilly Winter's flat to incriminate Tom. Ruby Winter is being asked to side with her father against her mother. Do you have any idea what that does to a kid, Dominic?'

Dominic pats the air in a calming gesture.

'I'm not saying you're wrong, but please, keep your theories out of the courtroom. At least for now. You start meeting Tom's accusations here with any kind of counter-accusation, particularly one as – forgive my frankness –outlandish as this, it's going to backfire.'

'Men kill women who get in their way all the time.'

'But you can't prove it, Cat, and even if you could, it's a matter for the police. Right now all we've got is the cyberspying thing. And yeah, it's creepy and maybe it undermines Tom's credibility, but it's all after the fact. It doesn't go anywhere towards explaining why Ruby is a threat to Freya or why you lashed out at her for that matter. The scans are something we can bring to play here right now. Given the way the morning session's gone I'd say they're your – *our* – best hope.'

I rest a hand on Dominic's arm. 'Over all the years we've known one another, how often have I told you that you're wrong?'

'That's because I've never *been* wrong.'

'Well, you're wrong now.'

Dominic places his hand on mine and gives it a pat. 'I'll go easy on you in there, but I can't account for the other side.'

* * *

Dominic starts his questioning by taking me back to Ruby Winter's arrival in the middle of the night. Did I find it difficult to accept my husband's 'love child'? Yes, of course, what wife wouldn't? I take responsibility for failing to bond with my stepdaughter. It hasn't been easy.

'When did you begin to have suspicions about Ruby Winter's behaviour towards your daughter?'

I talk about Ruby's arrival, the discovery of the dead hamster, the iPad with its morbid threat, the crude graffiti on the gravestone, the marks on my daughter's arms. I speak about Ruby Winter's persistent fascination with death and my husband's refusal to get Ruby into any therapy and, most worrying of all, the incident at the lido.

'You're not denying that you got into a tussle with Ruby Winter?'

'No, I am not. I pushed her and grabbed her hair. I bitterly regret that but I did not hit her or cause the bruising on her arms.'

Tom's lawyer steps in. A broad-shouldered woman with a neat bob by the name of Rebecca Tranter. With a cool but casually insistent manner.

'We've heard about your mental health, Dr Lupo, in particular a prenatal psychosis which led, among other things, to you assaulting your husband. Is it at all possible that when you pushed Ruby Winter something like this former psychosis was in play?'

'No, it's not possible.'

'How can you be so sure?'

'I'm a neuro-psychiatrist. Don't you think I'd have noticed?'

'You were a neuro-psychiatrist when you assaulted your husband.'

'I was also under the delusion that my baby was being stolen by a bunch of lilies. I think you'd find it hard to claim that I'm deluded now.' From the corner of my eye I spot Spiro swallowing back a smile so I move in. 'I have never once slapped or hit my daughter or any other child. Not once.'

From his place at the table beside his lawyer Tom shakes his head, as if more in sorrow than in anger. It's all a performance in the end, a game in which one side will outsmart the other. Tom knows how to play and he has the better hand. But Spiro doesn't see his move. Her eyes are on me.

'Let's get on to your persistent breaches of the Domestic Violence Protection Notice, Dr Lupo,' says Tranter.

This is my weakest position and the other side knows it.

'The first time I needed to fetch my things. Because my husband locked me in his study and I was obliged to leave my own house in the middle of the night through a window.'

'So you say. But you could have gone to your sister's flat, could you not?' asks Tranter.

At this Spiro looks up and raises her eyebrows.

'You chose not to, Dr Lupo. Why was that?'

I've seen this coming and have my answer to it. 'Because Tom had done his best to convince my sister I was going out of my mind.'

'Why, I wonder, would your sister have considered this a possibility?'

'My husband can be very persuasive.'

Tranter takes this with an 'um' and steers us back to the issue of breach. A tricky one. Whatever my reasons, the law leaves Spiro little leeway. This may be the other side's trump card because it is undeniable. I broke the law. The only defence can be that I had no choice. In the first instance, because I needed my things; in the second, and more importantly, because my daughter was ill.

Tranter consults her notes. 'A panic attack, I believe. Brought on, I would suggest, by her mother's inconsistent and unstable behaviour.'

'By weeks of psychological bullying at the hands of her half-sister.'

'Which oddly Freya neglected to mention at the time,' Tranter says.

'My daughter is loyal to a fault.'

'And you, Dr Lupo, are an expert in psychological disorders of children, are you not? But apparently you allowed your daughter to be bullied, as you put it, without intervening. Why was that?'

'I brought up the subject with my husband on many, many occasions. I was clear that I wanted Ruby to get some psychological help.'

Tranter turns on her heels then spins back around to face me. 'Would you agree that, for the last four years at least, your husband has been your daughter's primary carer?'

'Yes.'

'Would you say he has been a good father?'

'Yes.'

'But you seem to be implying that, on this occasion, your husband turned a blind eye to his daughter being bullied, as you put it.'

'Yes.'

'So he was willing to sacrifice the well-being of the daughter he has cared for for years in order to keep his other daughter, the one he has only really known a few weeks, out of trouble.'

'It would seem so.'

'In your opinion, Dr Lupo, would that be the act of a loving father, a man you yourself describe as a "good father"?'

'No, it would not. It *was* not.'

'Then how would you explain it, I wonder?'

Beside me, Dominic shifts in his chair, the rhythm of his breath quickening, and in a cautionary gesture invisible to anyone else, gently presses his knee against my leg. If there is a moment to voice my suspicions about the death of Lilly Winter, then this is it. Finally, to get out there in public the secret I have been holding on to. If only there were no shadow over me, I would do this, I would tell the court what I think I know. But Tom has me trapped. Anything I say now is only going to condemn me as the unstable woman he's set me up to seem. Craazy Cat. *Outplayed again. Clever Tom.*

I scan the room. The court is still now, poised for my answer. From the corner of my eye, I can see Dominic's lips tighten; his eyes flash a warning, a tiny almost imperceptible shake of the head.

'Dr Lupo?' Tranter stares intently.

'I'm a neuro-psychiatrist, Ms Tranter, not a mind reader.'

Spiro regards first me then Tom with a steady eye and takes further notes.

Dominic stands. Time to put the knife in. 'We have evidence that my client's husband has been spying on her.'

We've got Spiro's attention. Tom's too. The knife is in and now it must be turned. Hard. Out comes a blown-up screen grab I took of Tom's phone. Tom splutters. His lawyer is frowning. Even Spiro is taken aback.

'We believe this amounts to coercive and controlling behaviour, which, as Madam knows' – he tips a nod to Spiro – 'now constitutes a criminal offence.'

Spiro readjusts her face and calls a ten-minute recess in order to discuss this with the lawyers. I use the time to take a stroll outside and clear my head. I am not out of the woods. On the contrary, I am still deep in the forest with the sun starting its descent. If I don't find my way out soon, the light will fail and all will be lost.

Court begins again. Spiro takes her time shuffling through her papers, calls both lawyers to the bench.

This seems to go on for hours.

Eventually, Dominic returns to the table, winks at me on his way. It's looking good then.

Spiro clears her throat, calls for quiet and begins giving her judgement. 'Whilst the original Domestic Violence Protection Notice was undoubtedly given in good faith, I am not convinced that either of the alleged victims were aggressed by the defendant in quite the way they claimed in their statements to police. It appears there has been a degree of malice on the part of Mr Walsh in the reporting of the incident. I am confident that neither of the alleged victims is in any danger of violence from the defendant. Given the nature of the allegations against

Mr Walsh, the police may well consider it opportune to open an investigation, though that is, of course, a matter for them.'

Peering at me over her glasses now, Spiro says, 'By your own admission, Dr Lupo, at the very least you pushed your stepdaughter and grabbed her hair and there remains a question mark over your mental health. And the court cannot take any breach of the terms of the notice lightly, let alone three such breaches. I am therefore going to grant the DVPO for fourteen days, pending further reports. During this period, you shall have no further contact with your immediate family and will not go within five hundred metres of the family home. You will also undergo a psychiatric assessment and further evaluation as to your mental state. Your allegations concerning the behaviour of your stepdaughter towards your daughter are worrying, though I note they are also completely unproven. In my opinion it is best for Freya Walsh to remain with her father for now, pending an urgent report from social services. Until such time as we are able to substantiate or dismiss your allegations, Ruby will continue to live with her father and her half-sister at the family home.'

Spiro goes on to say that the matter of Tom's electronic spying is beyond the remit of the court but will be passed on to the police. Then she snaps her file closed and pushes back her chair.

I've fought and it has made no difference. I've lost. I have kept to my principles but I have failed to keep my daughter out of danger. I have required Freya to pay the price for my integrity. I have failed.

Moments later, Tom and I rise and leave without meeting one

another's eye. It's odd to think that if our brains were scanned now there would be no battle scars or marks of victory, no love or hate, only billions and billions of neurons transmitting electrical impulses through synapses to other neurons and out to the farther reaches of our bodies. It is amazing, even to me sometimes, how little the science can really tell us about *who* we are.

James White is waiting on the pavement outside the court with a photographer. Dominic sees him before I do and edges him off the pavement into the road, then bundles me into a cab and tells the driver to drive in any direction, so long as it's away.

We're almost at London Bridge when Dominic takes my hand and squeezes hard. 'You really think Tom had something to do with Lilly Winter's death? Find the evidence and bring it to me.'

CHAPTER TWENTY-SEVEN

Three times in my life I've come so close to giving up that I could feel the breath of defeat on the back of my neck. Once was just before I left the Pemberton. I was eighteen, living with an out-of-control drunk for a mother and a sister who showed signs of heading the same way. The second time was when a dog walker whose name I never knew stumbled upon the decomposing body of Kylie Drinkwater. And there is now. Each time, a young and vulnerable girl has needed my help and I have failed to help her. My sister, a baby I never knew and now my daughter, Freya. Three girls. Quite a pattern, isn't it?

And so I've failed. For now, at least. But – and I'll say this in my favour – I haven't given up. I'm glad to have Dominic remind me of that.

Back at the hotel, I call Gloria again. She's wary and a little angry with me still.

'I miss my daughter, so I know how you are feel terrible, but you did a bad thing and it have make everything more difficult for me,' she says.

'I know, I'm sorry.'

'I have informations, but this time I want something in return.'

'You've found Ani?'

'Kind of. But your lawyer friend must help me find my daughter. You must say this.'

Gloria has not found Ani. But Ani has spoken to Gloria's contact.

'He doesn't want to meet. He say the problem with the boiler was very simple and he fix it. He say he switch the batteries in the CO detector, test it, everything. All running fine.'

I feel a quickening. Hadn't the police said there were no batteries in the detector? And hadn't I come across batteries in Ruby's room in the flat?

'Anything else?'

'Ani says the girl and the man in the flat watch him fixing boiler so they know was a good job.'

'A girl? Or a woman? Did he describe either of them?'

'Girl with red hair.' I am trying to quell feelings of queasiness. Ruby Winter told me she'd never seen a boiler repair man. Why would she lie if she had nothing to hide?

'And the man?'

'Dark curly hair.'

A lurch followed by a letting go. 'That could have been anyone, Gloria.' All the same, my voice is wobbly and I am having trouble steadying my breathing.

'Ani say the girl is calling the man "Dad".'

CHAPTER TWENTY-EIGHT

What if Tom is keeping Ruby's secret and Ruby is keeping Tom's? Wouldn't that account for Tom's refusal to allow Ruby to go into counselling? All those opportunities to tell. Didn't Sal and I keep Heather's alcoholism secret all those years? Don't children keep secrets for their parents all the time? What if Tom has terrorised Ruby into keeping quiet about his role in Lilly Winter's death?

Ani remains the key, though perhaps not for the reasons I originally supposed. But Ani won't talk or meet with Gloria and he certainly won't meet with me or the police or lawyers. The morning after the hearing I'm back in my room at the Travel Express going through what I know in my mind and trying to figure out how to get to Ani. What if he was telling the truth and the boiler at Lilly Winter's flat was broken and he fixed it? What if he really did check the carbon monoxide detector and change the batteries? And what if Ruby and Tom both saw him do it? Could Tom have somehow sabotaged the boiler in a way that would make it seem like an accident or, if not that, then the fault of Ani's repairs? An opportunistic move. Would that have been possible? And what if, on the appointed day, Tom had shown Ruby Winter how to remove the batteries from the detector?

Think back to the night Ruby Winter arrived on our doorstep. The doorbell ringing, Tom hunched over the bathroom toilet, the look of dread on his face as he went to answer the door. What if Tom knew what was about to happen that night? And the knowledge made him sick? What if Ruby somehow helped? Is it possible that what happened to Lilly Winter was planned by Tom and executed in part by his daughter? Was she bleeding him dry? Didn't his bank accounts, the loan on the house, prove that? Hadn't he felt cornered by her? A single, miserable one-night stand that he had been paying for ever since? Maybe Lilly got greedy, increased her demands. Or maybe, after all these years, Tom had just had enough.

What if, on that day when Ani came to fix the boiler, it set off an idea in Tom's mind? And what if Tom had taught Ruby how to blow out the pilot light and obstruct the flue then remove the batteries from the carbon monoxide detector and stuff the gap under her door with damp towels, the towels that were still strewn around her bedroom when I arrived to pick up her things? Ruby hated Lilly. And the way she'd been brought up, Ruby barely understood the idea that actions have consequences. Wouldn't it have been easy to persuade her to do whatever was necessary to kill her mother and in such a way that nobody would suspect anything other than a terrible accident? The spotlight would be unlikely to ever land on Ruby. Who would suspect an eleven-year-old child? And if Ruby did tell, who would believe a disturbed kid who had proved herself to be obsessed with death? Killing by proxy. Wouldn't that be one way to pull off the perfect murder?

Because he knew. I'm sure of that. Tom knew it was going to happen that night and the thought of it made him queasy and that was why I found him in the bathroom throwing up.

Everything comes back down to the boiler guy. To get my daughter back I need to find the evidence against Tom. And to do that I must first talk to Ani and then I must find a way to get Ruby to tell me what she knows.

I reach for my mobile, tap in Sal's number and am shocked to hear a deranged-sounding voice.

'Oh, Cat, I didn't have your number, thank *God* you called.'

A mental alarm starts up. 'What's happened?'

A rising fall followed by a sob. 'You've gone too far. Tom is going mad. The police are here.'

My throat is a car in first gear with someone pressing on the accelerator. Inside my chest the breath stops. From a blizzard of thoughts, a single point of clarity crystallises. When I go to speak only one word emerges: *Freya.*

'I'm outside Brixton police station. Tom is inside. Shelly is at the house with Ruby. The police want me to go back to Fulham just in case you decide to come to my flat.'

'Where is Freya?' Something in my tone stops Sal short. There's a pause. An interminable two or three seconds in which my mind becomes eerily calm. 'My daughter. Where is she?'

Sal begins to whimper and the whimper becomes a whisper. *Oh my God, oh my God.* And then she is speaking but her words are vanishing. There's a twisting as the blood begins to rush around my limbs. Every cell is rising up like some great army. Still Sal burbles on and I am wanting to speak but cannot. A fearful voice is calling me, 'Cat? Cat? Are you there?'

It is 11.56, nearly two hours since my daughter disappeared from Grissold Park. In broken sentences Sal tells me what she knows. Freya and Ruby were at the swings with Tom. They went off to play in the trees. Fifteen minutes later, Ruby came back alone. I force myself to picture the scene, the enclosed playground surrounded by benches, the utility area and railings, the gravel path snaking off into the woods, the exact configuration of tree trunks, the shape of their branches.

'I would have called you but I didn't even have your number. I thought of calling Claire but it took me a while to get her mobile number then she wasn't picking up. The police are looking at the CCTV but the camera only covers the playground itself.' Sal is flaming but she's managing to pull herself out of the dive. 'They've been to the school, checked your neighbour's house, called Michael, all the obvious stuff.'

From the terrorising jumble of mental noise, a memory surfaces.

'There was a boy. Freya told me. She and Ruby have been playing with a boy.'

'Yes, Tom says he's about the same age as the girls, maybe a little older, thinks his name is George maybe? He comes regularly with a woman, presumably his mother. Ruby doesn't seem to know anything more about him. But it doesn't matter, Cat, because they're looking for *you*.'

'I have nothing to do with this.'

'They know you went to the hospital in breach of the notice. They've got CCTV footage of you. Tom is saying you went to try to persuade Freya to run away.'

'Sal, that's insane. You were there. Tell them that's insane.'

More slowly now, as if Sal doesn't quite get it, she says, 'Is it, though? Ruby says she saw you in the park this morning.'

Somewhere far in the distance Sal's voice is jangling away but I can't make out the words for the blood screaming in my head.

'I didn't go anywhere near the park.'

'The cops say they've got CCTV of you beside the park from the night before the hearing. They say you were probably staking it out.'

Panic rising. Mine. Sal's.

'No, Sal, I was going to see the mother of one of my patients in Springfield Road. This is ridiculous. Let me speak to Tom.'

'I'll have to go and get him and call you back.'

The wait is endless, a thousand seconds, each one elongated into a year. An age passes: 12.03. 12.05. Then the phone rings and my husband's voice is on the other end of the line and I feel far, far away.

'Tom, please, listen to me, I swear, I *swear* I haven't got Freya. Please, please believe me. We need to keep looking. The police need to search. That boy, maybe she went off with that boy and his mother?'

'Ruby *saw* you. The police have you staking the place out the night before. Caitlin, before this gets out of hand, for

Chrissakes, just drop Freya off at a police station and that will be the end of it.'

'No, Tom, no, please, *please* believe me, the police have to keep looking for her. The boy...'

Footsteps. The background echo from the speakerphone clicks off. Tom is speaking so quickly now that the words are sliding about like surface water on an ice rink. 'Listen, you cannot do this, Caitlin, you fucking mental *bitch*. You have absolutely nowhere to go. They've got all the ports and the airports covered. Don't you even realise you could go to prison for this? You bring my daughter back now, or I swear, I will find you and fucking *kill* you.'

I cut the call and punch in Dominic's number.

'Caitlin, thank God. Claire called me. She tried to get back to Sally and to you but your phones were busy. Have they found Freya yet?'

'No, and they won't. Because they're not looking for Freya. They're looking for me. They think I've taken her because I lost the hearing.'

'I'll call them. I'm not sure what good it'll do but it might at least buy you some time.'

I give him my new phone number and tell him to call me when he's spoken to the police. 'Only please, don't give them this number.'

'Of course not. Client privilege. But, Caitlin, what *are* you going to do?'

'What any mother in this situation would do. I'm going to find my daughter.'

But how? My first impulse is to search the area, comb the streets, knock on all the doors. Where to begin? And what if I run into the police? Another course of action comes to mind. Go to the police and convince them you don't have Freya. But then I run the risk of taking up police resources and time. While they're grilling me about where Freya might be they're not out there looking for Freya and nor am I. If this were a piece of research, a neuroscientific problem to be solved, how would I go about it? OK, then. What I would do is set the terms of the investigation, design the methodology, amass the data and analyse the shit out of it.

This morning, shortly after 9.15 a.m., my daughter and her half-sister were playing in the tiny strip of woodland in the south-eastern corner of Grissold Park. Ruby emerged from the woodland at around 9.30 a.m. and reported Freya gone. At some point in the intervening fifteen minutes, Freya either left the park of her own free will or was taken. At around the same time someone – a dog walker, a parks attendant, a gardener, a jogger, a kid, a commuter – will have been in the park taking a picture. Most likely they'll have uploaded the pictures onto the net. There will be images. They may be helpful.

I pull out my phone, key Grissold and the date into the search engine and wait for it to load. Up comes a selfie of a woman and her baby, someone's lurcher, an array of roses. Nothing useful. Removing the date parameter results in thousands of images. That's no good either. It will take too much time.

Think again, Caitlin. Think harder, think smarter.

A thought arrives with a hunch attached. Or maybe not a hunch so much as a faint hint of possibility. When Sally told me the news my first thoughts went to the boy. Call it a feeling or an intuition. A murky sense of the direction of travel. Who is the boy and his mother? It's hardly strange to me that Tom seems to know so little about him. Whenever Tom takes Freya out to the park or to swimming he absorbs himself in a computer game. But isn't it odd that having played with him all these weeks, Ruby suddenly claims she knows nothing about this boy? What if this is just one more secret Ruby is keeping from the world?

I have pictures, I remember now. That first week after Ruby arrived and Tom took the girls to the park, he emailed me some pictures. They may confirm my suspicions or take me down a different road. Either way, I need to look at them. Or rather, at one of them, an image of the two girls by the swings, with, I remember now, a blurry figure in the background.

The picture won't be hard to find. I'm organised with my data. I like to keep it filed and logged and tagged. The new laptop takes a moment to boot up. Since the discovery that Tom has been spying on me I've been turning it off rather than leaving it on standby. I push in the memory stick, go into the picture folder and enter some search criteria and it comes up almost immediately – a photo of Freya and Ruby in Grissold Park. Ruby is swinging too high and Freya is watching with that awe which was a permanent fixture in the early, happier days. And there it is, in the background, the real object of my interest. Standing beside the swing, a dark-haired boy, about the same age as the girls or maybe a little older. There's a stick in his hand, more like a small branch actually, which he's digging into the gravel. His face is out of focus as if he's been caught mid-movement turning to something on the outer edges of the image. Or not to something, but to *someone*. And at the very periphery of the picture there's a woman making her way towards the boy, her arms outstretched and her mouth open to call him or perhaps shout some instruction. The woman's face has been captured in motion and, like the boy's, it's blurry and out of focus, but it's what she's wearing on her feet that draws my eye. Big feet in distinctive shoes, tomato-red sequined trainers, a swoosh on the side and a sparkle at the toe. Shoes that once tramped through the drab corridors of the institute and right into my office.

In an instant I'm pecking out Emma Barrons' number.

'Emma, it's Caitlin Lupo. I need you to tell me where Joshua is.'

'I imagine he's with his nanny. Is there something wrong?'

'Are you at the house?'

'In London? No, no, I went to the country this morning.'

'I need you to give me the nanny's number.'

But no, Emma says, better if she calls the nanny, because it's a condition of her contract that Erika always picks up if it's her boss calling. So she gives me the London landline instead. Whatever.

The number clicks to voicemail. I'm telling the recorder this is an emergency so please answer but no one does. Moments later, Emma calls me back.

'There's a message to say the number has been disconnected. So now I'm worried. Is Joshua in trouble?'

'I think that's possible.'

There's a pause and in a very quiet voice, Emma says, 'Oh God, my son's done something really terrible, hasn't he?'

CHAPTER TWENTY-NINE

When you become a parent you have to trick your mind into believing that nothing will go wrong in your child's life that is beyond your capacity to make right. You have to live this way or you wouldn't be able to live at all. But we all know the trick is fragile, under-rehearsed and unsound. We know every time we switch on the news or read the stories on the web, stories about kids going missing, abducted by strangers or members of their own family, kids catching rare and fatal diseases, kids crushed under cars, kids going down in splintered planes. Tricking the brain isn't easy. Tricking the brain is hard. It's why, in the dead of night, after some confused dream, you've woken quaking and, springing from the bed and with your heart thumping, you've sprinted across the hallway to your child's room. It's why, at the sound of the phone in your child's absence, you've trembled at the thought of who might be calling.

You live this way because you cannot live in any other. And so what happens if the disease sets in, the car fails to stop, the riptide pulls or your child goes missing from the park? What then? There are no how-to guides or manuals, there is no saving formula, no set of rules. And now your back is to the wall. And your mind has run out of tricks.

What happens is you run. You see the abyss opening up before you and as fast as you can you run towards it. Because if she's nowhere else, this is where your child might be, and so this is where you belong. In the heart of darkness, the midst of the horror.

Now is the time to ask myself, *What do I know?*

What do I know about Joshua Barrons? I know he's a smart judge of what the people around him are thinking and feeling. I know he is driven by dark impulses. I know he's a thrill-seeker, forever in search of the next high in order to be able to feel at all. I know that right now his brain is only capable of shallow and fleeting emotions. I know he likes burying animals and setting things on fire. I know that he is driven by vengeful, narcissistic, destructive impulses heightened by the violence he's witnessed on the street and at home. I know he is an explosion being steadily detonated. And I know he is with my daughter.

* * *

I take an Uber across town, sitting low in the seat this time, afraid of being spotted, to the grand Victorian villa in Springfield Road where the Barrons' family drama has unspooled. Hurrying up the black and white tiles to the porch, I find the front door slightly ajar. Leaving it as it is, I slip inside. A child's footprints muddy the black and white hallway tiles but even as I'm calling

Joshua's name I know he's not here. No one is here. The house is empty. There is no Joshua and no nanny.

Gone.

I make my way through to the kitchen where only yesterday I sat with Emma Barrons as she wept over her son. A carton of milk sits on its side beside the fridge, its contents pooled onto the tiles and already smelling sour. There are bowls on the table containing half-eaten mounds of cereals. Broken biscuits lie scattered across the floor. Nothing direct, nothing definite, only clues.

The living room is as torn up as the kitchen. Several cushions are lying on the floor partly emptied and there are feathers everywhere. Beside the fireplace most of a box of matches lie scattered, burnt, but there's no fuel in the grate, only the remnants of family photographs. A single photo sits on the mantelpiece, or rather half of one – the right side has been almost completely burnt away, leaving only the nanny's shiny red shoes. The remnant shows Joshua, looking very pleased with himself. In his hand is a tarantula. A trip to the zoo.

The basement access to the nanny's quarters is unlocked. There are two main rooms, a living/dining area and a bedroom with a cupboard-sized bathroom leading from it. The impression is of a place left in a hurry. The soap in the bathroom sink is still damp and there is bread on the counter in the kitchenette. In the bedroom there is an old pack of cards, some cotton wool balls and a single blue-striped sock. Erika has left the building.

In the seconds during which my mind is processing the scene, I am becoming aware of a strong acrid odour. The smell grows up the steps from the basement to the ground floor. From the hallway by the stairs it is clear that something strange is happening on the upper landing. The patterned stair carpet appears to be moving. My heart ticks. What the hell is that? A shadow?

'*Joshua?*'

The shriek of adrenaline coursing around my body. Otherwise, silence.

Upstairs the carpet seethes. Contradictory thoughts crisscross my brain, trains on tracks with broken signalling. Then, suddenly, something pricks at my left ankle, a small and random neural event or some tiny outpost of a rising panic. I shake my leg to bring it back into my body. Above me the carpet continues to crawl slowly closer. Something begins to fall. Rain? No, tiny black grains, like sand. The line of shadow has progressed almost to the edge of the stairs. Another nervous prickle. I am conscious of some signal flashing in my mind. Ideas shunting into sidings until only one remains.

Those are not black grains. This is not sand. It is not raining. The movement is no trick of the light.

The carpet is alive.

A great tide is washing up against the walls, cresting and falling, the swell advancing inexorably towards the stairs, filling the house with the musty nose-burning stench of formic acid.

Ants.

Insect battalions, seething up the walls and dropping from the ceiling. Ants now in my hair and the insides of my ears.

'What the hell is going on up there?' My voice is loud and met only with the soft burr of the ant army on the march. Steeling myself, I climb the stairs and step onto the upstairs landing. Here the whole carpet is swaying and pulsing now and I am moving across it, leaving ragged prints of crushed ant bodies, shaking insects from my feet. No matter how fast I brush them off, more come on, a relentless, marauding wall of insect life. *Bite. Bite. Bite.*

Please don't let my daughter be here. Not Freya. Anyone, anything but not her. Not Freya. Not Freya. Not Freya.

Three doors lead off the landing. The ants appear to be coming from the one most distant so that's my target. I use my boot to push open the door. The smell inside is almost unbearable. I have to force myself to look around. A boy's bedroom. There's a bed pushed up against the left-hand wall, beside it a small table with a lamp. Three of the walls are covered in shelving, but where most boys might store footballs and model cars, computer games and skateboards, the shelves are stacked almost to the ceiling with rows of formicaria, busy ant farms, their lids removed, tossed to the floor and already half obscured under the carpet of insects. The bed, the curtains, the little nightstand are seething sculptures.

Creepy-crawlies, his mother said. *Joshua likes to bury things.*

In a flash I am hurtling back down the stairs, pulling at my clothes and shoes, palming the insects from my skin, and out through the back door into the garden. Hard landscaping slopes up to flower beds, a summerhouse and a shed. The summerhouse is empty. The door to the shed is padlocked. I press my face against the window. A mower takes up much of the floor space. Neatly stacked garden tools emerge from the gloom. Wherever they are, they're not here. I straighten up, pressing a thumb into the opposite palm to help me focus a moment, and in that pause the rich, soft, horrifying and unmistakable smell of putrescine. My eyes shoot around and alight on a compost heap behind the shed and, before I'm really aware of it, I'm scooping frantically at the pile of lawn clippings, leaves and food waste until my hand alights on some weighty object. A dead rat. I step back, shaken, stamping the compost from my trainers.

Stay calm, Caitlin. Freya is alive. Somewhere in the city, Freya is alive.

Back through the door into the kitchen, I am met by the sound of the front door swinging open. I step back into the pantry, hastily pull the door to and freeze. A child's steps make their way up the tiled hallway and into the kitchen and Joshua Barrons appears, humming a tune I don't recognise. I know that if I confront him, he'll do everything in his power to divert and waylay me. Better to stay hidden and let him lead me to my daughter. The kettle whistles and clicks off. Through the gap in the door, I watch the steam rise as Joshua pours the boiling contents onto the stream of insects. A moment or two later, he disappears, then he's back with a box of matches, singing still. There's a thin fizzle as the tiny flames land on watered tiles, followed by a smell of cordite. The singing stops and is followed by the sound of footsteps leading out of the kitchen and into the hallway. There's a pause then the front door opens and swings shut and, in an instant, I'm out of the cupboard and scooting through the kitchen and out into the hallway past the smouldering stair carpet and through a soup of dead and dying insects.

CHAPTER THIRTY

Along Springfield Road Joshua Barrons marches, hands deep in the pockets of his cargos, a boy on a mission. Whatever he's up to, he's probably been thinking about it for a while, playing it over in his mind, working out the finer points, waiting for the right moment. The street is already busy with commuters. Somewhere sirens are blaring. For a day or two after the riots people would look up in alarm, but no one bothers now. The pavement is sticky and the sky is the boiled, greasy white of restaurant steam. A week is a long time in the capital, two weeks is an eternity, and it's the end of the working week and people are looking forward to getting home to their families. A twelve-year-old boy on his own who seems neither distressed nor lost is unlikely to attract attention. Passers-by look right through him.

At the back entrance to the park Joshua hesitates long enough for a sudden sunburst to light up the crown of his head. A halo for a dark boy. If Joshua were any other child, I would catch up with him now and confront him, cajole, wheedle, threaten if I had to. But Joshua Barrons is not to be persuaded or pressured. The second the kid senses a crack opening up, a tiny tear in the fabric of my defences, he'll dive in. At the clinic I was invulnerable to his manipulation, but things have changed. Now I'm afraid of what I might agree to for the promise of finding my daughter.

While he bowls along the periphery of the park I hang back to avoid being seen. At the north corner of the park he stops again at a yellow crime board, a remnant of the riots, pulls out a single flower from a memorial bunch, stuffs the bloom into his pocket and is off again, doglegging past The King's Arms and into a side street. I am closing in on him, though still keeping back. If I called him now, he would turn but I'm afraid he'll run and then I'll lose him. I know Joshua Barrons, but I can only guess what is going on in his head. A woman sitting on the table outside the pub smoking looks up momentarily from her mobile phone and watches him pass, but he does not appear to notice her.

The woman watches me narrow-eyed then looks away, embarrassed. My guess is she has seen something desperate in my expression and is wondering what I'm doing. I've had the same thought myself. What if I'm wrong and all of this is wasting precious time?

Up ahead Joshua turns into Terrance Grove, a quiet residential street of nondescript Victorian terraces that leads at the far end to the Ravenscourt Estate. At the end of the Grove he dives into the narrow walkway leading through to the blocks of flats. What business could a boy like Joshua Barrons possibly have in the Ravenscourt?

I curl around the edge of Wellesley House and from that

vantage follow the boy's path as he heads north towards Taylor House. Here the path makes a crossroads, the north and east leading deeper into the estate, while the western track snakes towards the periphery at Holland Hill. The boy stops and looks about, then he's off again, bowling along the western path around Enderby House which gives out through a car park onto Holland Hill. At the entrance to the estate he stops and checks up and down as if he knows someone might be out looking for him, then, satisfied that no one is, crosses the road onto the eastern side of Holland Hill.

It's mid-afternoon now and the pavement is busy with commuters flowing up from Brixton Tube; the weekend exodus. Joshua crosses the road at the zebra then shoulders his way into the flow of people and starts off down the hill. Moments later, he doubles back past the bus stop and Jamal's shop, past the makeshift memorial to LeShaun Toley, stopping momentarily to eye a ghost bike chained to the lamp post. A lump of dread materialises in my belly. I have a feeling I know where this boy is going. And whom he is hoping to see.

Outside number forty-two Dunster Road, Joshua stops, brushes himself down and draws a smoothing hand over his head before reaching for the front gate and stepping down the path. He's out of sight for a moment before reappearing and darting out of the gate as though anxious not to be seen. I watch him slink around to the Fricks' house and dive behind the hedge. Moments later, Shelly Frick appears at the gate, scopes about and, with a shrug, retreats back inside. For what seems like an age nothing happens. Then the gate at number forty-two opens and Ruby Winter creeps out onto the pavement. In an instant, Joshua has darted out from the hedge and the two children are hurrying in silence, as if on urgent business. At the top of the road, they turn right towards Holland Hill. I follow on, keeping my head down to avoid the police and staying far enough back that if one of them were to turn, my face would be only one among dozens. Down the hill they go, hand in hand, weaving in and out of the flow of commuters, oddly silent, their shoulders set determinedly forward, two kids engaged in a terrible *folie à deux*. I stay back, keeping their heads in view, determined not to lose them, pulse racing, heart a fist jammed in my throat.

At the junction with Brixton town hall, the duo stop at the traffic lights as if weighing up their options, then, when the lights change, they cross the road and at the corner stop a second before diving into McDonald's. On the other side of the road, two policemen stand watching the crowd, their fingers tucked inside their stab vests. I could go over and explain that the two children in McDonald's have abducted my daughter but they would radio in and know immediately that the police are actively searching for a woman who looks very much like me. They'd be informed that I'm mentally unstable and, having lost a domestic violence case in which my daughter's custody was at stake, I have followed my husband and his children to the park and abducted Freya. They might well go into McDonald's and question Joshua and Ruby and most likely return them to their homes. The only way to deal with me would be at the police station. Even if I were able to convince them about Joshua and

Ruby, precious moments, maybe hours would be lost. *Caitlin Lupo, probably mentally ill, certainly in breach of her DVPO, currently a person of interest in the possible abduction of her daughter. Can you step this way, please, madam?*

Who knows where Freya is and what kind of danger she might be in? Even – paralysing thought – whether she is still alive? Waiting is the worst kind of torture but there's no choice except to hang back at the corner of Acre Lane and hope that no one sees me.

It's not long, though it feels like an eternity, before Ruby and Joshua reappear, each sucking on a domed slush. They seem distracted now – their initial energy has dissipated – but with purpose in mind. Checking for traffic, they dart in between a refrigerated lorry and a bus. The bus heaves forward a few feet. I look on, waiting for them to emerge from the line of vehicles into the central reservation. A minute passes, then another. Commuters sashay between the vehicles. On the other side of the street the two coppers are quizzing a tramp. At the Tube station a busker starts up. The lights change to green and the traffic begins to heave clear of the lights. There's a sudden blast of diesel fumes as the driver of the lorry hits the accelerator and the line of vehicles fans out as it crosses over the lights and up the hill. A gap opens up. The bus dives into the opening then swings over to the side of the road to pick up passengers. I rush across. Up ahead, Joshua's head becomes visible for an instant before he disappears into the early rush-hour crowd sweeping inexorably towards the station.

CHAPTER THIRTY-ONE

Question: in a city of eight million souls, where do you find a single hidden child?

Answer: you look in the heart of the person who hid her.

What would you like to be, Joshua?

A Tube driver.

And why's that?'

Because when people jump in front of the train their heads explode and it's cool.

The station is a human cascade. For weeks an escalator has been out and there has been chaos at both ends of the working day. I hover on the periphery, checking out the cameras and waiting for the police to turn their backs, then I'm inside, pressing against the flow towards the station concourse. In the background, mostly drowned out in the roar of human traffic, a Beethoven piano sonata is playing. A consultant's version of traffic calming. No sign of Ruby or Joshua but I'm convinced, now, that they have Freya trapped somewhere here in the Tube. Psychiatrists have another term for a *folie à deux*. We call it Shared Psychotic Disorder. Not as pretty, but more accurate. In the plan Joshua has concocted with Ruby he *is* the Tube driver. What that makes Freya doesn't bear thinking about.

Approaching the guard at the ticket barrier, a young man, his mouth cracking, distracted by the crowds, I shout over, 'Hey, you see two kids, a boy and a girl? The girl with red hair?'

The youth cups a hand around his ear. 'Sorry?'

Through the ordered chaos of people pressing towards the barriers, an idea springs to mind. Ask the guards to check the CCTV. Jostling my way through the crowd, I reach the control room. Two men are sitting inside on high stools. Both of them ignore the first knock. Only at the second more frantic follow-up does one – a spry-looking man in his late fifties with a reliable face – approach the window.

'Can I help?'

'I've lost my kids.'

'Have you reported it to the police?' The guard chins over the crowd on the concourse towards the entrance where the two officers are now standing.

'We only just got separated, so I'm sure they'll be here some-where. Could I come in and check the CCTV?'

The guard looks unsure. 'Our usual procedure is to put out a call on the PA system.'

'It's so noisy out there, I'm not sure they'll hear. If I could just have a look at the security screens?'

The door peels open. The reliable-looking guard waves me inside. His companion, who is flipping through some kind of technical manual, gets up from his chair, motions me to a seat before a bank of blinking monitors, then returns to his reading.

'Not easy to spot a couple of kids in this crowd. What age did you say they were?' the reliable man remarks, peering at the screens.

'Eleven and twelve. The girl is smallish, just under five foot, skinny with a lot of red hair; the boy's bigger, black hair, a bit chubbier.'

'White?' He raises his eyebrows at me.

'My stepdaughter.'

'Ah.'

In the public areas the cameras catch heads, arms; body parts sail by on their way to and from the platforms. The images from the service areas are eerie, displaying empty tunnels and looped cables. One or two are a mist of static.

What would you like to be, Joshua?

A Tube driver.

My eyes scan the public area screens. For an instant I think I see them, but it turns out to be another child with his mother.

'The blank screens?'

'Vandals,' the guard says. 'Taggers, you know, people coming in to see if they can nick some copper wire, whatever. But they're in the service areas.'

'Are there ways into those areas?'

'Not without a code. We do get a few nuisance homeless living in the tunnels. They get through the access routes. We're always trying to plug the gaps because they leave a mess and they're a security risk, but they still find a way in.'

'Can you get access to the tracks from there?'

'From some of them. Other day, driver on the first Tube of

the morning ran over a body deep inside the line between here and Stockwell. Geezer was dead already. Drink, I dunno.' He points to the row of public area monitors. 'Your lot are much more likely have got themselves lost somewhere between the platforms, I should think.'

For a while we peer, goggle-eyed, at the tops of heads, odd disembodied hands, bit of faces, ponytails, hats. And then, all of a sudden, a flash of red hair and a momentary glimpse of Joshua's face.

'That's them!' My throat tightens. I'm pointing, then standing.

The guard pushes himself from his chair. 'Lower concourse, right-hand side. Here, I'll come with you if you like.'

But as he's saying this I'm already halfway out the door, sharply elbowing my way through the crowd and pushing behind a commuter at the barrier to dart in before it shuts, then I'm tripping down the escalator two steps at a time. A tall man steps out from the right-hand side and begins to descend in front of me and by the time I reach the lower concourse, the children are no longer visible.

Since Brixton is a terminus there's only one direction to go: north. Noting the first departure on the board, I head towards platform two where a train is filling up with passengers but in the cram it's impossible to know if the kids have already boarded. If they're not on this train, they will be on platform one, where another is just pulling in. I duck around the crowd and make my way across to platform one just as the train doors are opening. No kids. Then it's back to the lower concourse, standing on tiptoes, looking about. The indicator board ticks down to one minute and I'm elbowing my way past the hurrying commuters and back onto the platform and then I'm on the train itself, inching around the passengers and calling Ruby's name. But it's hopeless. In the next thirty seconds I'm going to have to decide whether to leave the train or not.

Mind the closing doors.

Two seconds later, the train is hauling away and I am standing alone on the platform, seized by a feeling of panic.

Back on the lower concourse, a few stragglers from the train on platform one are still making their way out. The indicator board announces that the next train north will depart from platform two. In a few moments, a train will appear and disgorge another few hundred passengers and the lower concourse will once more fill with people queuing to get on the escalator heading up and out onto the upper concourse. Still Joshua and Ruby are nowhere to be seen. If they weren't on the departing train, they must have gone back to the upper concourse or maybe they disappeared into the stairwell or a fire exit or access shaft.

When people jump in front of the train their heads explode and it's cool.

On either side there are only service tunnels and maintenance tracks, ghost platforms and evacuation points, deep-level shelters, leftovers from the war, ventilation shafts, odd access routes, a labyrinth no passenger ever gets to see, places only the staff and taggers and vagrants know.

When people jump in front of the train their heads explode...

The door to the escalator shaft is locked but there's another, just inside one of the platform access tunnels, which has been chinked open just wide enough for a child to squeeze through. I shuffle inside. I can stand but only just. The light from my mobile phone blues the walls on either side, picks out swags of cabling up ahead. A train passing beneath shivers the brickwork and crimps the air. There is a smell of burning dust and static. What drives one child to harm another? The question is so complex it's almost unanswerable. But if you put the question another way, it becomes almost frighteningly simple.

Why would a kid like Joshua harm a child like Freya?

Because he wants to.

When people jump in front of the train...

'Freya!' My voice is a hollow howl, an animal yell.

The shout is met by a distant echo and the shuffles of fleeing mice or maybe rats. I edge forward by the light of the phone. Time is slipping away. My daughter needs me to find her. My daughter needs me. Ahead the light from a square grate illuminates a fork in the tunnelling and I stumble towards it. I'm at the fork now, wondering which way to turn. A dim red arrow points left but gives no other clue. Which way would a twelve-year-old psychopath lead an anxious girl? My heart is a bird trapped in a chimney, full of a terrible, fluttering energy. I turn down the right, unsigned fork and into darkness. Partway along the tunnel my foot makes contact with a single adult shoe. A little way further I find myself standing on a piece of cardboard. The walls around are littered with graffiti and there's a faint smell of urine.

'*Freya!*'

Moving through the tunnel in blue light, limbs heavy as a bear's, stumbling a little now, thoughts a magic lantern, nothing sticking. All around the roar and shake of passing trains. A damp stink of impacted earth. Suddenly there's movement up ahead, a shadow of an indistinct presence where the tunnel narrows and takes another turn. The faint shuffle of footsteps and the sudden fast-moving wash of a shadow along the wall.

'Joshua!'

In a split second he's gone and I'm hurrying after him along the tunnel and into the turn and complete darkness.

'Joshua, please come back!'

A scuffling sound, then nothing. The illuminated screen on my mobile casts a triangle of light only three or four feet ahead. The path in front of me is marked by a giant tangle of cable, the entrance to what looks like an access well and a ladder. No sign of the boy. I'm moving forward now, but slowly, one hand directing the light, the other edging along the wall, still calling, hands cupped to my mouth to carry the sound, heart ablaze with terror. The echo hits me like a punch, a deep bellowing sound, followed, dimly, by a tinny echo. Then nothing.

It's cold here; not cool, but cold, a damp, subterranean chill. A cold, black, underground sea and in it somewhere my daughter, drowning.

I move forward down the tunnel, following it through another turn until the dim sodium light begins to dazzle my night vision. I've no idea where I am now, though I can hear the ticking of the live rail which means I must be near the tracks. I

335

call again, once only, holding my breath for a response. 'Freya?' Silence followed by a single, strangled sob.

'Oh God, Freya! Are you hurt? I'm coming, it's OK.'

There's a terrible rattling in my chest now, a mixture of terror and relief. I call again and hold my breath, waiting for a reply that doesn't arrive.

'Freya, where are you?'

Ahead of me, a set of narrow metal steps leading down into a well. Was this where the sob was coming from? It's so hard to tell.

Descent. One foot gingerly tapping on the next rail down, phone in my mouth. A few steps down a low tremble in the metal followed by the *tick, tick* of electricity on a live line. I freeze, take the phone with one hand, shine it downwards and see nothing more than two steps and some cabling running through the brickwork. *Tick, tick, tick.* The rumble of an as-yet distant but approaching train.

A sob-squall. A child trying and failing to catch her breath.

'It's OK, I'm coming. Breathe deep.' *Breathe.*

Stepping further down into the darkness.

'Freya?'

Only panting in response.

I look down and see a faint glow. A lamp? No, the sway suggests something moving. Train lights. Yes. Somewhere heading towards us a train, the passengers on their way home from work, tired, preoccupied. A driver at the front, unaware that not far ahead an eleven-year-old girl is in harm's way. Approaching, drawing closer, the light growing stronger, gradually illuminating the scene below. An access well giving out onto the track. A small figure crouched, back to the wall. The track running close by. *Tick, tick, tick.* Carefully.

'Don't move, just tell me, are you on a track?'

If there is a reply, the fierce echo of the train carries it off.

'Look to your left. Can you see the ladder?'

I'm clambering down now, hands slick against the metal, willing myself to go carefully, not to trip.

The blank white light of the train.

Tick, tick, tick.

When people jump in front of the train…

In that moment the phone clatters down, ricocheting off the wall, bouncing at a wild trajectory as it hits the floor and landing right onto the track. A hand reaching into the light towards it.

'Let it go.'

I can see movement but her face remains in darkness.

'Take hold of the ladder, Freya, climb up the ladder.'

The rumble now a mechanical roar.

My feet tramping down, down. The light flaring, my eyelids snapping shells, my ankle turning over on the step, and then the sensation of the foot stamping air. My hands are clinging to the ladder and I'm shouting something now but I do not know what it is. And the light is a terrible apocalyptic glare. A whipping, electric sound. *Tick, tick, tick.*

'Climb the ladder, Freya.'

'Mum, I can't.' A terrible alarm is sounding in my daughter's voice.

Another louder tick, my pulse drumming in my temple. I can

see the top of Freya's head now, but her body is angled mostly away from my line of vision.

'Are you hurt?'

The sound of sobbing.

A sallow wind as the train approaches and the light whumpf of the air surge.

'Is anyone down there with you, Freya? Talk to me!'

'Please come, *please*, Mum.'

'Stay there.' I'm holding on with one arm and reaching down with the other and gripping only air. Something is badly wrong with my ankle. I've found the step again but my foot is like a rotten apple hanging lifeless on its branch. By using the strength in my arms to cling on to the side rails, I can hop one strut of the ladder at a time. It's clumsy and slow but the train is moments away now, the air beginning to suck back into the partial vacuum of the tunnel. Freya reaches out with one arm and grabs for my feet and I'm lowering myself to the floor oblivious to the pain. At its base, the well gives out onto a section of track from where a thin beam blades through and, in that dim light, I see my daughter scrabbling vainly at a mess of cables around her legs. I'm rushing towards her, calling, but she's flailing, grasping at the air, and I have to fling my arms around her to contain the panic. Immediately, she stills, her whole body shaking now. We're beside the track, the air around us electric and trembling. *Kertum-kertum-kertum.*

Then I'm bent over the cables, freeing my daughter's legs, and in a second I'm pulling her back inside the service well.

And we are safe from the approaching train at least, my hands on my daughter's shoulders, my face in her eyeline.

'Darling, darling, listen to me. Is Ruby here?'

Freya takes a huge shattering breath and, through chest-wracking sobs, shakes her head. An arm comes up and flutters in the direction of the track.

'Don't move!'

In an instant, I'm glaring into the darkness as the track disappears further into a tunnel and makes an arc left and, in the flare of the tunnel lights, there is someone moving.

I scream, 'Get off the tracks!' but the figure takes no notice. The brickwork at the curve of the tunnel is illuminated now with the lights from the approaching train. I take a step out. My eyes are on the figure backlit from the lamps of the approaching train. I'm yelling at the top of my voice for whoever it is to clear the track. Part of me is tempted to run forward but I know I risk my own life if I do so I hang back, one arm slung across Freya in the well, the blood screaming in my head. The train has rounded the curve and is slowing for the approach to the station. The lights are blinding. For a brief moment the figure on the track turns as the train bears down. Instinctively, I turn my head away before the whumpf and a sucking, depressurising feeling of the *kertum-kertum-kertum* as the final carriage thunders by and then away towards the platform.

CHAPTER THIRTY-TWO

Time floats about, melts, then gathers in great pressure ridges, but whenever I try to summon my daughter's face all I see is snowdrift. At some point in the night a fragment of myself crumbles off and floats into distant, unrecognisable waters. I am afraid to stay awake and afraid to sleep and not sure which state I am in. Freya flickers at the edges of the picture and sometimes in the middle. Is this me dreaming or me in the realm of the mad? Slowly my eyes crack open and I am relieved to find that I am still here, on this thin mattress in this blank rectangular room. From under the sheet my plastered ankle throbs. What do I remember? I remember the hospital, I remember a woman with black-rimmed glasses.

I'm sitting up now and a face is coming into focus.

'Cat? It's me.'

I'm blinking away the painkillers. An IV swings from my arm to a saline rack by the side of the bed. In the corner of the room is a wheelchair and a pair of crutches. From somewhere beyond the curtains a monitor bleeps.

'Where's Freya?'

'She's fine, she's with Sally.'

'I want to see my daughter.'

Dominic stills me with his hand. 'It's the middle of the night, Cat. You're in St Thomas's. They had to put you under to pin your ankle. You came out of the OT a couple of hours ago. '

I slump back onto the hospital bed. A smell of stale food rises in my nostrils. Behind the cubicle curtains two shadows play.

'The police are here. They're going to need to talk to you, but only when you're up to it.'

An image flashes across my inner field of vision. The boy on the rails, his face in the moment before… Dominic's hand is on mine and there's a painful tightening in my throat and the thin burn of tears.

'Try not to think about that right now.'

There will be a lifetime of thinking about what happened in that tunnel. 'Can you bring me some coffee?'

'On it.' Dominic reaches across to the bedside table. 'Not sure it's coffee but it's brown and hot and may contain caffeine.' Dominic looks at me for a moment. 'How the hell did you know Freya would be in the Tube?'

'I didn't. I knew Joshua would lead me to her.'

Dominic says that after I'd lost the guard at the barrier, he had returned to the control room and seen me on the CCTV screen. It was he who had alerted the transport police.

'Freya told me it was supposed to be a game. That's what Joshua and Ruby told her.'

'Did she… ?' Dominic doesn't need to finish.

'No, I shielded her from it. There was no sound, even. It was like he just vanished.'

'The police spoke to the guard and I've had a chat with them too. They've accepted that you weren't trying to take Freya, but they'll want to interview her later today or tomorrow, once she's had some rest.'

'And Ruby?'

'She's with her father. They'll want to talk to her, too.' He pats my hand. 'The Barrons family has obviously been told. The father's on his way back from New York.'

My hands move to my face. 'There was no time, the train was right there. I couldn't save him.' Another dead child.

'It wasn't your fault, Cat. You know that. Something very odd must have been going on in Joshua Barrons' mind. I wonder what, though?'

'He was a very disturbed boy. Perhaps he wanted someone to bear witness to his dreams. I should have seen the psychosis coming. He was my patient.' My hands are in my lap now and I'm stroking my thumb along the opposing index finger as if to soothe it. I look at Dominic and feel curiously detached. 'Did I ever tell you why we picked the name Freya, goddess of love and war?'

Dominic's eyes soften. 'No, you never did.' He raises a hand and rubs his eye. He's tired, it's nearly dawn and only part of him wants to hear this story.

'Our daughter had to fight *so* hard to come into this world. But love is worth fighting for, isn't it?'

No answer. None needed.

'I should tell you, James White called. He asked for a comment.'

'*Seriously?* If he'd done what I asked him and broken the story about the files, Joshua might just be alive today.'

'That's what I told him.'

* * *

DS Lisa Crane and DC Mark Williams take up chairs beside the bed to explain that while I'm no longer under suspicion of kidnapping my daughter, they want to hear my story to set the record straight. They're pleasant, efficient and – though perhaps I am imagining this – sympathetic, even as they're explaining that the DVPO against me still stands. They have already spoken to Tom and to Emma Barrons and will be taking statements from Ruby and Freya in due course. There will be an inquest into the death of Joshua Barrons. Though Ruby has not retracted her insistence on seeing me in the park yesterday morning, the police now have reason to doubt her testimony. She has admitted to planning to help Joshua trick Freya into the Tube station but it seems that Ruby, too, was duped by Joshua's plausibility. Both she and Freya had believed him when he said he would let them ride up front as he drove a Tube train, but when the boy had led them through the tunnels Ruby had spooked and run away.

Once the police have gone, social services arrive. Given the circumstances, they've granted Sal temporary custody of Freya until a more long-term solution can be found. In the meantime,

I can call my daughter once every other day, so long as I do not discuss the DVPO. The final call of the day, nurses aside, is a psychiatrist with a clipboard who pokes his head around the curtains and asks if it's OK to do an assessment. I find myself repeating the story, or at least the finished part of it, and he seems to go away satisfied that I am not mad, but maybe that's because I have not told him the final chapter, the big reveal, the common element that ties this all together, the one and only thing I know and cannot as yet prove.

* * *

In the late afternoon, I am discharged a day early, mostly because I insist on it. I cannot put any weight on my ankle but I can hobble around on crutches and the analgesics they've given me are managing the pain. Sally has been to visit and brought a get-well card with a letter from Freya inside. Following the hearing and the incident in the Tube, and while various reports are still pending, I am not yet formally allowed a face-to-face meeting with my daughter. Sally's card wishes me well, Freya's letter reassures me that I am loved. They are the only possessions I take with me. They are all I need.

Dominic picks me up in a cab. He wants me to stay at his flat near Spitalfields until more permanent living arrangements can be found. It's in one of those new blocks thrown up on brown-field sites across London. There's a lift and a concierge and a gym too, not that I'll be using that. Or not for a while, anyway. For now, Tom and Ruby are still living at Dunster Road and I can't go back there.

Dominic's place is large and calm with clean lines and light open spaces. There's something wildly relieving about the lack of clutter, the level of orderliness. It's a place in which to think.

'I've got to go back to work. I've made up the bed in the spare room. Help yourself to whatever you need. We'll talk when I get back.' Dominic picks up his rucksack and moves towards the door. At the entrance, he turns and, lifting a finger, says, 'Oh, and I forgot. A woman called Gloria called. You gave her my number apparently. She said she couldn't get through on your mobile.' My phone had fallen out of my hands in the Tube station. The police told me it had been found crushed on the track beside the live rail.

'Will you be OK?'

'So long as you have plenty of chocolate and Pinot Grigio lying around, sure.'

Dominic's eyes narrow. 'What are you up to? I can tell you're up to something.'

'I'll tell you once it's done.'

CHAPTER THIRTY-THREE

'You don't call. Is very annoying,' Gloria says.

'I've been tied up. It's a long story. But I'm calling now.'

'You still keep our deal, lawyer to help me with Elmira?'

'Yes.' I haven't yet discussed this with Dominic because he thinks I should be going to the police with my suspicions about Tom. But I'm pretty confident that Dominic will find someone in the office who can advise Gloria and if he can't, I'll fund a lawyer myself.

So here is Gloria's news: in return for access to a lawyer who can help him with his immigration papers and immunity from prosecution, Ani is willing to say what he knows about the day he went to repair the boiler at Lilly Winter's flat. We agree to meet with him at 3 p.m. Gloria lists an address in Honor Oak.

'Ani will only talk if lawyer comes.'

'I'll make sure he does.'

* * *

Though it's only been an hour or so since he left the flat Dominic doesn't seem at all surprised to hear from me.

'Thanks for calling back.'

It's then I spot the blinking light on Dominic's phone. I must have been in the bathroom when he called.

'You wanted to tell me something?' I ask.

'Yes. Tom's been picked up by the police for questioning over the cyberstalking. He's at Brixton station. No arrest as yet. They've got a forensic computer guy looking at the evidence. He's also being questioned by social services about the incident with Ruby.'

'The bruising?'

'Freya told Sally she saw Tom hitting Ruby. The day you left. They got into some kind of a fight apparently.'

'Where is Ruby now?'

'Her grandmother refused to have her so they put her in temporary foster care.'

'She'll be safe there.'

'*Safe?* You think Tom might hurt Ruby?'

'He's *already* hurt Ruby. He might well go a lot further. I think he was hoping the problem of Ruby would just go away. He probably figured that Ruby would never tell because she'd be too afraid she'd get the blame.'

'Is this about revenge?'

'It's about all kinds of things, Dominic. Since you ask, among them is justice, and a desire to protect Freya and Ruby, and yeah, because I screwed up with Rees Spelling and Joshua Barrons and I can't go through that again. I can't let Ruby down as well. Revenge is in there somewhere. But don't ask me where.'

When I tell him what I need from him he points out that

he's not an immigration lawyer and doesn't do international child abduction cases.

'But there'll be someone in your building who does.'

'Of course.'

'Right now all they're asking for is a face, Dominic. A friendly face.'

'You know I don't approve of you doing this.'

'But you'll come?'

'You know that too.'

* * *

A nondescript suburban south-east London street, 3 p.m. Gloria, Dominic and I are moving along a Victorian terrace. Beat-up cars squat on cracked paving where once sat pretty front gardens. It's quiet, though by no means emptied out. This part of London saw a night or two of mild disturbances but missed out on the worst of it. Judging from the curtains, the few houses that remain intact are occupied by pensioners, the rest given over to fast turnover, multi-occupancy private rental. Eastern Europeans and, if the flags in the windows are anything to go by, a smattering of Somalis.

Ani – he gives his last name as Njeri, which Gloria says means 'human' so it's probably made up – is waiting for us in the front garden of number twenty-seven. He told Gloria on the phone that he shares a bunk in the shed at the bottom of the garden with a man from Romania. In the summer it's liveable, but Ani has been there long enough to know that in winter it will be hell. Besides, he says, the Romanian is a terrible snorer. As we follow him through the house and into the back across a badly paved yard area to the shed, he outlines his plans. A few more years in the UK saving as much money as he can then back to Albania to be with his wife and three kids. But he desperately needs those few more years.

At the moment the bunkmate is out working. He has the top bed, Ani the bottom. Ani waves us through the door. There is hardly space for all four of us. Ani fills the kettle for tea. Gloria and I find a spot on Ani's bunk. Dominic is in a chair. Ani distributes sweet black tea in small glasses then props himself up against a small, shaky-looking table. The incident with the woman and the boiler has made him think. He struggles to explain himself in English then gives up and reverts to his own language.

'What did he say?' Dominic asks Gloria.

'He must turn his life around before his bollocks freeze to his bunk. In summer, this is not way to live, this only way to survive. In winter, this is way to die.'

Ani wants to talk to Dominic about his immigration problems. Then he'll decide whether or not he wants to tell us what happened on the day he came to fix Lilly Winter's boiler. Gloria will translate where necessary. After the right assurances, he begins.

It happened like this. A friend of Ani's had done some odd jobs on the Pemberton and recommended Ani to a neighbour, who must have passed the recommendation on to Lilly Winter. When she called, Lilly told him she was behind on her rent and the council was trying to evict her and wouldn't come and fix the boiler. She said she knew someone who'd give her the rent and the money for the boiler repair in a couple of days. Ani didn't ask too much about it, or about Lilly. He told her to call him when she could pay for the work. For the next few days he got on with other jobs and thought no more of it.

When Lilly Winter rang again to say she had the money, Ani went right over. He was met by Lilly, a girl who looked just like her and a man who didn't introduce himself. Ani got the impression this was the money guy. The atmosphere was tense, he was pretty sure there had been a row, so he was keen to fix the boiler and leave. The fault was a small electrical problem, nothing that could have made the boiler dangerous. Fiddly, but an easy fix. While he was working, Ani could hear Lilly and the man arguing over money in the living room and he became anxious about not getting paid. He struggled to understand all the English, but it was his impression that Lilly was threatening to tell the man's wife about something unspecified. The man started shouting. At one point it got so bad that Ani thought he should intervene, if only to keep the police away. To his relief, not long afterwards Ani heard footsteps in the hallway then the slam of the front door and the man's voice calling Lilly back. She didn't return and Ani didn't blame her.

Dominic, who has been listening to all this, leans forward in his chair and in a careful voice says, 'Did this man tell you his name? Anything at all about himself? Can you describe him?'

All Ani can recall is a man of medium height with dark curly hair, a description so generic it could apply to more or less any male between the ages of eighteen and sixty. Plus, there is the possibility that Ani too might be lying. There's no way to know. Gloria says something to him in Albanian. He lets out a sour laugh and goes on.

The man stayed in the living room for a while. When he finally came into the kitchen he seemed eerily calm. He didn't mention the fight but seemed very curious about the operation of the boiler. Ani played along. There was something about the man that frightened Ani a little, a kind of unpredictability. And he was now seriously worried about getting paid. Ani recalls the man asking specifically whether the boiler would become dangerous if the pilot light blew out. Ani said not really, at least, not unless the flue was blocked. In any case, Ani pointed out, there was a carbon monoxide alarm that would warn anyone in the flat if the levels were getting too high. He told the man that he'd check the alarm to make sure it was functioning before he left.

A few minutes later, Ani realised he'd left a screwdriver he needed in the van he'd borrowed from his friend. He told the man he'd decided to have a break and eat the sandwich he'd brought while he was gone, but the truth was he wanted to call his friend and ask him whether he should just leave in the middle of the job. Something about the situation spooked him and he was becoming convinced that he wasn't going to get paid. In any case, he left, telling the man he'd be back in an hour. As he was emerging from the flat, Gloria appeared and offered him a cold drink. He thanked her and said there was something he needed to fetch from his van but after that he'd love a drink. He got to the van and called his friend but there was no answer. He decided he needed the money too much to walk away from the job. When he returned about fifteen minutes later, Gloria had left a glass of iced Coke and some biscuits out on the walkway, so he stood there and ate his lunch and the biscuits and had a smoke. He didn't know at that point whether the woman had returned but he could definitely hear the voices of the man and the girl inside the flat.

Something strange happened then. The window of the bedroom at the front began to open and shut and it went on like this for several minutes. The sun was glaring on the glass and he couldn't see who was behind the window. The opening and shutting began noisily then became progressively quieter until you could barely hear it. Ani decided this was just one more weirdness about the job and the smartest thing to do was to finish up and go. He swallowed the last of the biscuits and the drink, had another quick smoke and went back inside.

The moment he entered the hallway, he sensed something conspiratorial going on. The man and the red-haired girl were hunched over the carbon monoxide detector. They both straightened up the instant they saw him and the man told Ani he was showing his daughter how to replace the batteries, but there was something off-key and edgy about the whole scene which left Ani with the sense that he'd come in on a secret. Shortly afterwards, the man left and not long after that the woman returned with the money for the job. Whatever had been said between the man and the woman had evidently upset her. She looked like she'd been crying and she smelled of alcohol. Ani finished up the job, cleared away and took the money, though the woman didn't give him nearly as much as they'd agreed. He felt sorry for the little girl trapped between two warring parents but he was glad to be gone. Even if the woman had ripped him off, Ani sensed it was a bad situation and he wanted to be shot of it. Of them.

It wasn't until his friend told him what had happened at the flat a week later that Ani became convinced the man had set him up. Here he was, an immigrant without papers or good English, working illegally fixing up boilers: the perfect stool pigeon.

'In my country I am engineer, working big projects. I make boiler good, impossible kill anyone. But now I am afraid this man, afraid police, afraid everything.'

'Do you think you would recognise the man if you saw him again?'

Ani exchanges a few words with Gloria then says he would.

'Well, that's something,' Dominic says.

'But not all,' adds Gloria. 'Ani has something you will want to see.'

CHAPTER THIRTY-FOUR

When he left Lilly Winter's flat that day Ani had taken a pair of sunglasses. He'd spotted them on the table in the hallway. He hadn't intended to take them from the beginning but when the woman only gave him half the money she owed him, he figured he would help himself to payment in kind. They were clearly expensive and Ani reckoned he might be able to sell them on.

'I not thief. This world make me thief.'

In any case, God punished him for thieving. When he got home he discovered the glasses had prescription lenses. He could barely see out of them. He reaches into a box under the bed and pulls out a pair of thick-rimmed boxy tortoiseshells.

'Do you recognise them?' Dominic asks me.

'Of course, I bought them as a birthday present for Tom last year.'

Dominic wants us to go directly to the police but Ani won't agree to come. In any case, what does this prove? Only that Tom was in Lilly Winter's flat that day. We have no physical or forensic evidence linking Tom to Lilly Winter's death and unless we can guarantee Ani's co-operation we have no circumstantial evidence either. I've been in court enough to know that we wouldn't get anywhere without more.

'Would you be prepared to give evidence in court?'

'Maybe you fix my papers I come.'

'Gloria?'

'My daughter, Elmira.'

Dominic looks momentarily defeated.

'It's worth a try, isn't it?' I say.

We agree that Dominic will get started on Ani's papers and look into Gloria's case with her daughter. We'll meet later. In the meantime, there is something I need to do.

* * *

It's still light by the time I reach Dunster Road. Rush hour is mostly over and the sky is dreary with the first hints of twilight. If there were anyone home, there would be lights on. But the house is dark and silent. The police have twenty-four hours to hold and charge Tom. Fortunately, they're taking their time. I open up with the set of keys that was in my bag. Tom has not got round to changing the locks.

Inside, the house is a small oasis of familiarity in a life turned upside down. The umbrella Sal gave me one Christmas still sits in its stand, my mackintosh hangs on the hook in the hallway besides Freya's winter coat, there's the old crack in the plaster by the kitchen door that we've been meaning to fill for years. Some things have changed. The warm aroma of family life has gone and in its place there is something sharper and sadder.

In the kitchen is Freya's favourite *Pippi Longstocking* DVD. One blink and it is the start of the school holidays and we have the long summer ahead of us. Charlie Frick's birthday party is looming and there are plans for family trips and barbecues and weekend summer blockbusters followed by plates of grilled chicken at Hoopoes. The reminders of us in happier times. All that is gone now. Already the leaves on the shrubs in the garden are darkening and the branches of the ideas tree hang thick in the last of the summer heat. Autumn and winter are imminent and those summer days are already etching themselves into our memories. I don't want to linger here. And I won't have to. What I am about to do is the work of ten or fifteen minutes.

I walk over to the dresser. The receipt for the sunglasses is clipped to a bunch of others in the left-hand drawer. The glasses were expensive, an extravagance for a man I no longer know and perhaps never did. I slip the receipt into my jacket pocket then turn my attention to the other part of the plan, the one that will take down Tom and finish the game. So far as it can be, I have it all mapped out. The only really unknown quantities are Tom himself, the stranger in my bed, and the woman inside me, the other stranger I am about to get to know.

The door to Tom's study cracks open. Inside everything is as it always was: the large wooden desk with its matching ergonomic chair and tasteful mid-century lamp. Behind it the L-shaped shelves of games and developers' magazines, the Marvel comics Tom loves, the precious CDs he couldn't bear to part with when MP3s came in and, at the end of the shelving against the side wall, the love seat where we first talked about starting a family.

I'm waking the screen on Tom's laptop and thinking how different it all could have been. If the Rees Spelling case hadn't happened, if Kylie Drinkwater had survived, if I'd had an easier time getting pregnant, if Tom hadn't had a drunken fling, if Lilly Winter hadn't become pregnant, and Tom had come clean, if Adrenalyze hadn't let Tom go, and Lilly Winter hadn't demanded money from a man who increasingly had no means of providing it. And yet none of that explains it. Who hasn't found their heart suddenly overwhelmed by a dark rage? Or woken up one day to discover that someone they don't know has taken up residence inside them? Who hasn't watched their moral compass fail and found themselves tempted to take desperate measures, then come to their senses and been shocked by what they had, only moments before, been contemplating? Tom Walsh made a choice to do what he did because he thought he would get away with it. Because men like Tom are raised to think they can.

The screen lights up then fades to the password page. I tap in Ruby Winter's birthday and it fades again. Recent history leads me to several multiplayer games sites: *League of Legends, Counterstrike, Diablo.* The passwords to these are lodged in Tom's keychain. I check the accounts. Turns out my husband has been gaming for money. Small bets at first, by the look of it, little sprinklings of spice to heighten the play. A few larger sums on his own game at first, a few more, some wins, mostly losses, then expanding out to bets on games played by strangers, tournament betting, bet and counter-bet. No wonder he was broke.

I key *Labyrinth* into the search box. Dozens of files appear, named *Labyrinth 1, 2* and *3* all the way up to – let's see – *268*. I check the date last modified – about four years ago – click open file one and see... absolutely nothing. A blank. File two is the same. Three, four, eight, one hundred and ninety-six, all the same, all blanks. Is this it? The culmination of late nights and early mornings, of money spent and time gone by? Was *Labyrinth* never more than a few blank files and an ever-evolving fantasy in Tom's head?

'I've always hated snoopers.'

He's standing in the doorway, his hands in the pockets of his old jeans.

'That's funny coming from you.' At some deep, survival level my brain is conjuring Tom's hands around my neck. He would like that, if he knew. The power he has over me.

'You're not supposed to be here.' I am fit but Tom is stronger. My eye falls on the door. Would I be able to slip by him and into the corridor? I watch Tom following my gaze. A thin smile appears on his face. There was a time that smile would have melted me but not now.

'In all our years together you've never been afraid of me. Until now. I rather like it.'

'I'm not afraid.'

'Maybe you should be.' He laughs. 'I always thought you were hopelessly deluded, Cat. The very first time we met at that games conference, remember? When you gave me that spiel about games helping kids with empathy issues. What you never understood was that games aren't about teaching some fucked-up kid who doesn't give a shit to be able to pretend to. Games are about winning. They're pure. That's why I like them.' One more step towards me. 'You want to know how this game ends? Is that why you're here?'

Stay cool.

'You know why I'm here.'

A look. The look, which in recent years I've seen only in flashes, the gaze I once mistook for passion. He's beside me now, that raw, dazzling, predatory intelligence, the long, soft voice whispering in my ear. 'You're wondering what I'm capable of.' He lurches back. 'Jesus, Caitlin, you're even crazier than I thought.'

You are not afraid. You cannot afford to be afraid.

'You can win this, Tom, only not in the way you imagined.'

He rocks back on his heels and crosses his arms. 'Shall I tell you what I planned to do this morning? I planned to take an axe to the "ideas" tree.' He air quotes the word 'ideas'. 'Because you know what? I've never had a single fucking idea under that tree. Not one. But then the police came so I had to postpone my little piece of forestry management. The police. You send the fucking *cops. To my home.*'

I've risen from the chair now but I know better than to retreat. The instant I show fear I've lost.

'You know, I suppose, that if anything happens to me, the police will be all over you.'

'What *is* going to happen to you, Caitlin?'

For an instant his eyes meet mine but they're not seeing me, they're seeing the game.

'Eventually, Ruby will stop being loyal to you. You know that, don't you? That's why you didn't want her to get into therapy. You thought she might blab. And you're right. One day she will. She will tell someone what you tricked her into doing to her mother. You're banking on people not believing her. Maybe they won't. But they'll believe me. And what are you going to do then, Tom? Kill Ruby? Kill me too?'

Tom stiffens and takes a step back, a sudden reckoning on his face. His mouth opens but the tongue seems stuck in his palate.

'I don't think what you did was anything most of us haven't thought about. Killing someone, I mean. I thought about it once or twice, when Heather was on her Slow Stoli Suicide Slide and terrorising Sal. I thought, well, maybe this is the best way out of the situation, for all of us. I could put a pillow over her head and in minutes it would be over.'

Tom closes his eyes and screws up his face. 'The bitch was milking me dry. Endless demands and none of it spent on Ruby so far as I could see. Always more, more and more. I couldn't see an end to it.'

'Why didn't you tell me?'

'We were Couple Number One. Don't you remember how that felt?'

'But it wasn't real, was it?'

Tom laughed. 'It felt pretty bloody real to me.' His head is turned away from me and cocked a little. He's considering his options.

I take a step towards him. 'Walk away, Tom. Wind up this game. There's one on every corner if you know where to look. And *you* know where to look. You can start again, set up somewhere else with a new set of people.'

'You'll call the police.'

'You're the father of my daughter. And besides, I'm not supposed to be here, remember?'

His eyes find mine. He smiles and for just a moment, as his face relaxes, Thomas Walsh might almost be the man I thought I married. Then, turning away from me, he walks from the room. There's the sound of footsteps on the stairs followed by the sweep of cupboards and drawers being thrown open. His tread on the stairs again and the sight of his legs and the leather weekend bag I bought him for his thirtieth birthday.

And I'm there in the hallway, waiting for him, his daypack dangling from my hand.

'Don't forget this.'

He shoulders the bag. A pause at the door, then the mortise lock clicking open, footsteps along the front path, the gate swinging open and the shapeshifter who was my husband steps into the street and away.

For what seems like a long time after he has gone I am fixed to the spot, my mind a sea of white horses crashing on a distant shore. Then the nausea rolls in and I am mobile once more but with only a few moments to lock the mortise and fit the chain in the door before I'm throwing up.

I do what I need to then call Dominic. He sounds upset.

'It's nine o'clock. Where the hell have you been?'

'At Dunster Road. Tom left the house five minutes ago. He's about to jump bail and disappear.'

'Call the police.'

'No, I want to do this one in person. Will you meet me outside Brixton police station? And bring Ani and Gloria.'

A few minutes later, I am running down Holland Hill, past the shrine to LeShaun Toley and Jamal's shop, past McDonald's and the Tube, past the yellow boards appealing for witnesses to the riots, past what used to be the covered market and is now gourmet food shops. Every so often a bus rumbles by. It's plenty dark now. And there's an autumnal zip in the air. But for the uneasy quiet and the presence of boards over the darkened shop windows, this could be any other night in this corner of south London.

I stop for a moment under Brixton railway bridge and there in the sickly glow of a luminescent tube I see my mother, Heather Lupo, standing beside Lilly Winter, LeShaun Toley, Kylie Drinkwater and Joshua Barrons. The dead lined up like warriors about to go into battle. And as I'm standing there, the crumbled growl of a train taking me from my thoughts, some kind of growing happens, some kind of awakening, a consciousness of being on the threshold of something. Turning my back to McDonald's and the Tube, I set off in the only direction I can.

On the pavement beside the station, Dominic is waiting with Gloria and Ani.

'Let's go.'

At the desk the custody sergeant raises a weary and familiar head. *Oh, it's you, the DVPO woman.* He scans the four of us warily, checks the wall clock, and draws a blank. Dominic turns and, with an encouraging look as if to say, *This is yours now*, nods me on. I close my eyes for a moment and I think to myself, *Remember this moment, Caitlin, remember it for you and Freya and Ruby, but most of all, remember it for Lilly Winter.* I take a single step towards the desk. The custody sergeant leans forward.

'So what can I do for you this time?'

For a second or two the words are hard knots in the brain then there's a sudden softening and as they tumble out I hear myself say, 'We've come to report a murder.'

EPILOGUE

It's cold now, and dark; the streets are heavy and wet with winter. From every shop and office door warm, electric air billows. London is bracing itself for Christmas. At the institute, the cucumber-green corridors are rimmed with shabby tinsel and a dusty fir tree strewn with lights squats forlornly in reception. Festive cheer, institution-style.

It is Tuesday morning. On any other Tuesday morning it would be my job as head of the CU clinic to sit down with a set of anxious parents and explain why their child has been diagnosed as having callous and unemotional personality disorder. But not today, not so close to Christmas. There are limits. Today we are having a Christmas party at the clinic. Adam is coming, and Ayesha is returning with her mother to say hello to old friends.

Otherwise, life at the institute is pretty much back to normal. The article exposing the Master of the Neuroverse appeared in the *Herald* eventually and created a predictable shitstorm both within the institute and beyond, but what was more surprising was how quickly everything settled down. Once MacIntyre and Anja and the accounts department employee who assisted them were dismissed, the waters quickly closed over the episode and everyone got back to doing what they do best: research and clinical work. The institute's governing board sensibly decided that the best kind of damage limitation was the kind that dealt swiftly with the chief offenders then shut the hell up. And that was what happened. Within a day of White's piece, both MacIntyre and De Whytte were suspended, and within a month they had both been let go. The incident swiftly became a non-story and the media moved on.

Claire and Lucas celebrated by getting engaged. They'd kept that one very quiet. There was a party where you had to come dressed as a brain scan. Cute. More recently Claire has taken to salsa-ing in with my morning coffee. She's practising in order to be able to shimmy down the aisle to Celia Cruz next spring.

'It's not as easy as I'm making it look,' she says today at our daily diary check-in. 'You should come to the club one evening, check it out.'

'Sweet of you, but a world-beatingly bad idea. I am the anti-stereotype, a brown girl who can't dance.'

'Oh phooey,' Claire says.

'Well, OK, let me get this grant proposal in first then I might feel like dancing.' I'm hopeful. The first research results from the CU clinic are looking promising enough to suggest trialling the programme through Child and Adolescent Mental Health Services. There's a unit in Manchester who are interested and we're hoping to hook up with a clinic in Ohio to pool our expertise. Five years ago the kids on our programme would almost certainly have been heavily medicated, and some of the most challenging cases – like Joshua Barrons – would have ended up in secure facilities. But who deserves a second chance more than our children? Kids *are* our second chance, in a way. When we get the grant we need we'll set up a unit named after Joshua Barrons so that we never forget what can happen if we fail.

Claire brings up my patient list and reminds me that I'll need to look at the scans for my ten o'clock. After that we go through the diary. 'And don't forget you have a lunchtime budget meeting with the acting head.' When MacIntyre left his deputy took over until a permanent new head could be appointed. This one's sensible, northern, nice. Bit of a movie buff. For a while after the scandal of the missing files broke, there was talk of me taking up the post, but that was never going to happen. I like my patients too much.

At the door Claire turns. 'Oh, and your sister called, but she says it's not urgent.'

The evidence against Tom stacked up. The glasses put him at the flat and Ani's statement condemned him further. Then there are the batteries and the towels. When the police came to search the house at Dunster Road they found no evidence of cyberstalking. Tom must have come straight back home and deleted all the spyware on his devices. What the police did find, though, were the batteries and towels stashed in Tom's locked cupboard, which I had moved from Ruby Winter's room and put there. Ani was able to confirm that the batteries were the same make as those he'd placed in the carbon monoxide detector at Lilly's flat. And forensics turned up carbon smuts trapped inside the towel fibres. Gloria can give evidence about the window. And finally, there's me. I can testify that, after putting our daughter to bed the night before Lilly Winter's arrival, I went for an hour-long run, time during which my husband could easily have driven over to sixty-seven Ash Building and sabotaged the boiler. Naturally, I don't think he did. He is too smart for that. What I think is that he showed Ruby how to do it and remove the evidence. But I won't be giving voice to my theory. After all, it's just a theory, isn't it?

And who, honestly, would believe an eleven-year-old daughter actually committed the crime. Where's the evidence? Only three of us know what really happened: me, Tom and Ruby. I won't tell and I don't think Ruby will, at least not for a very long time. As for Tom, well, who knows where Tom Walsh is? The chameleon will have long since shed his skin. Perhaps the police will find him one day. And if they do? He might try to pin the death of Lilly Winter on her daughter, but he will have no means to prove it. The secret will be kept so long as Ruby wishes to keep it.

I hope, one day, she will share it with someone who will help her to bury it. Perhaps that someone will be me. It's been four months since Ruby Winter went into emergency foster care. Freya and I have visited her regularly. In that time she hasn't asked after her father. Which is perhaps just as well since none of us would know what to say. It's a good family she's with. Solid, loving, reliable people.

After the hearing, Freya stayed with Sal until my psych

assessment came through then returned to live with me at Dunster Road. She's still going to the therapist Spiro mandated. From time to time, I tag along but I always stick strictly to the therapist's rules. If Freya brings up the subject of her father, we talk about him, but she doesn't very much. She misses him, I think. I trust her to talk about it all eventually. Between times I try to give her space to think and feel.

At some point I'll have to decide whether to keep some of the details of the story from her forever. So much has been revealed which neither of us could have guessed at. Most of it shows Tom in rather a poor light. But it doesn't leave me untarnished either.

I still keep Lilly Winter's picture on the table in the living room. Sometime after the hearing it dawned on me that I have a lot to be grateful to her for. In life she gave my daughter a sister. In death she exposed Tom for what he is and enabled me to find my freedom. I think she probably understood Tom's nature before I did. She had him down as a predator and tried to play him at his own game and lost. Tom refused to remain trapped for long. Though he was once one half of a defining twenty-first-century couple, his greatest skill was to remain slippery and impossible to pin down. Maybe, in the end, the only way to explain what he did was that it was a game. And the one thing that really mattered for Tom about playing a game was winning.

For the most part, Tom was a good father. To Freya at least. My daughter loves him. I never wanted her to grow up in the kind of household I grew up in, fragmented, split, and catastrophically unhomely. And for eleven years we managed that. He loved Freya too, as much as Tom could love anyone. Perhaps in her he saw a reflection of his genes, the pool into which he could gaze and have a version of himself reflected back.

Right now is not the time for thinking, at least not about this. For now, there are scans to check and research papers to write and budget meetings to endure and Sal to call back. And hope to hold close. There is always hope.

And so the morning passes. At lunchtime I throw on my scarf and my good winter coat and head out to meet my sister. It's still cold and some early snow has painted out the worst of the urban grime. London looks luminously beautiful, at least in this normally murky south-east corner. You forget sometimes how quickly the city can be made new. A sunny day, some spring leaves, the first whitening of winter.

Through the fug of superheated air at the Wise Owl Cafe I spot my sister waiting for me at the table at the back where not so long ago Anja and I talked about the future over tuna salad. It's soup weather now. Sal's been shopping; a large bag sits at her feet. We greet each other and she waits for me to settle, then she pulls out her iPhone and flashes me a calendar set to 7 January. She waits for me to make the link. It takes a while. My head is still full of scans and experiments and grant applications.

'The fostering panel!' Of course. How could I have forgotten?

'The social worker says I'll sail through.'

For the first time in her life, Sal has a plan. It's a big thing she's doing, not just for Sal but for Ruby Winter. If she gets through the panel, she could be fostering Ruby by the end of January.

Pulling a small green coat from her bag, she says, 'Look, I got her this for Christmas. It'll go so brilliantly with her hair. That's not too creepy, is it? What do you think?'

'I think it's great.'

A waitress comes over and takes our orders.

'It's not going to be easy, you know that, don't you? Ruby's not going to be easy, she may never be.'

Memories move across my sister's face. 'Do you remember the day you came for me?'

'How could I forget?' It was a drab, early winter day, the sky a bleary drape behind which the sun sat sulking. I was eighteen years old, newly installed in a grimy room in a house share, and very pleased with myself. Sal was four years younger, with sharp eyes and a blistering tongue. No one's fool, even then.

'You had one of those Chinese laundry bags with the blue and red checks,' Sal goes on.

I can see it now. 'And you went on about there not being enough space for all your stuff, and I said, "*What stuff?*"'

'In my head I had wardrobes and wardrobes full of lovely glittering outfits.'

'What you actually had was a pair of shoes, a pair of trainers, a couple of pairs of jeans, and three tops we got in Brixton Oxfam.'

Sal lets out a dry laugh. 'God, is it any wonder I've got a shopping habit?'

I can see Heather now, wrecked and slumped at the table,

watching her two daughters leaving for a new life, so pissed she could hardly string two words together but still managing to mutter darkly.

I questioned myself constantly in those days and so did Sal. Hours spent combing the streets after I'd come home from one shit job after another to find my sister gone. Our mother refusing to speak to me.

'She said, "So you're abandoning me just like everyone else." I don't want to think what would have happened if you hadn't rescued me. You did that for me, now I want to do it for Ruby. We'll get help. Social services, the fostering people. More help than you ever got.'

'You're my sister.'

'And Ruby's my niece.'

* * *

The run home later that afternoon is through darkened, patched-up streets. The snow has mostly melted, leaving only nuggets of ice where the wind has swept it. The yellow boards are gone now but LeShaun Toley lives on in the shrine beside Jamal's store. I head in for lasagne pasta and popping candy. Jamal won't be closing for Christmas; he needs to stay open to make up the money he lost in the riots. Besides, he's Muslim and Christmas isn't his thing. On Holland Hill, though, the atmosphere is loose and anticipatory. For now, the capital is held together with Christmas lights and the promise of the holidays.

In January a public inquiry into the riots will begin its

investigations. We have been warned that it will probably go on for months, maybe years, before reporting. Most likely nothing will be laid to rest, least of all the ghost of LeShaun Toley. But things will be quiet for a while as the old, restless energy of the city gathers itself and looks to the future.

The 'For Sale' sign still sits in next door's garden but someone from the estate agency has slapped an 'Under Offer' banner on it. It didn't take long to go. Shortly after Tom's arrest the Fricks decided they didn't like the new basement and moved away. Well, that's what they said. I don't know anything about the new owners except that they will be people who like dug-out basements.

At number forty-two the recycling bag has been collected from inside the front gate and the porch light is on. Inside everything is warm and orderly. Gloria and Freya have been tidying up. The new arrangement is working well. Gloria prefers coming here to cleaning the school. Freya has fallen madly in love and calls her '*Teto*', which means aunt in Albanian.

Speaking of which, here she is, thundering down the stairs to greet me. She's holding out an open book.

'Mum, look what I found.'

I set my backpack on the floor and move over to her so I can see what she's trying to show me. It's the copy of *The Adventures of Pippi Longstocking* I'd taken from Freya's bedside all those months ago. Freya doesn't read Pippi anymore, or even speak about her. She's moved on to Agatha Christie now. But she wants me to see a drawing of Pippi skipping hand in hand with another girl. Someone has scribbled a halo of orange hair in crayon around the other girl's head. They look happy.

'Ruby must have done it.' Despite it all, Freya remains loyal to her sister. 'What are we going to get her for Christmas?'

'I don't know. What do you think?'

'Definitely something purple.'

Gloria appears from the kitchen door. Today she's dressed in leopard-skin leggings, a pink frilled sweater and a pair of yellow Marigolds. She eyes the plastic bag in my hand and checks her watch.

'Got time for a cup of tea, Gloria, or do you have to get off?'

'Maybe.' Gloria likes to keep the household guessing.

'I bought the wafer biscuits you like.'

'OK, so I stay just this long.' She makes a pinching motion with her fingers.

Over tea she announces that she's decided to come for Christmas lunch after all. I've been petitioning her for weeks.

'But only one thing,' she says now, playing with the biscuits. 'I cook, you and Freya and Dominic slice vegetable. We have proper Kosovar feast.'

Gloria and Dominic have been seeing more of one another. They've begun legal proceedings to try to locate Gloria's daughter. Dominic seems to think it's unlikely she'll be found, but what can you do? There is a rip in Gloria's heart that can only be mended one way.

'Come as a guest, Gloria. You don't really want to cook.'

'No way. Your cooking so bad. We must not poison lawyer. If he dies, he doesn't find Elmira.'

Freya takes my hand. 'You want to see what we did today?'

'You bet.'

'Close your eyes.' She helps me up, walks me to the French doors, turns me to face the garden and flips on a switch. Everything close to the house lies in darkness but at the back of the garden the ideas tree is a luminous miracle, lit up in swags of blinking Christmas lights.

'We gave the ideas tree a brain. Look! All that electricity going to and fro. The ideas tree is having ideas!'

Christmas falls over a weekend this year. On Christmas Eve I will drive to the cemetery where Kylie Drinkwater's body is buried and I will say the only kind of prayer I know then leave. Her parents don't know I visit. I'm not sure they'd like it if they did. But for tonight I will light the fire and cook bad lasagne and Freya and I will curl up together on the sofa in the living room opposite the table of family pictures, Tom's and Lilly's and Ruby's, and maybe we'll watch a film. Later, as I pass by the darkened study on my way upstairs, I won't think about Tom's Christmas. I won't think about Tom at all.

ACKNOWLEDGEMENTS

I am indebted to two inspiring women, Dr Fiona Norwood and Dr Lade Smith who introduced me to the complexities of neuroscience and gave me an insight into the differences between mental illness and mental disorder. Thanks to Brian Spiro who was so generous with his expertise on the law surrounding domestic violence. It goes without saying that any scientific, legal or other inaccuracies or failings in this book are entirely mine.

I'm grateful to Lisa Milton for championing the book early on. I'm very lucky to be in the hands of the terrific team at HQ. Thank you to all, and most particularly to my editor Clio Cornish, who whipped the text (and, when it was required, and in the nicest possible way, me) into shape. Peter Robinson is the kind of agent every writer should have. He's been on my side from start to finish. Thank you too to Marina Benjamin, Dr Tai Bridgeman, Simon Humphreys, Ian Jackman, Lynn Keane, Olivia Lichtenstein, Jane Spencer and Al Upton. Simon Booker deserves a medal for putting up with no small quantity of late night whingeing and still, somehow, managing to be supportive, patient and tirelessly loving. The title is all Simon's doing too.

A huge fistbump to my 'crime wife' and Killer Women co-founder Louise Millar and to all the talented women crime writers I've had the privilege to get to know better through Killer Women and otherwise. Last, but definitely not least, thanks to the men, writers, friends and partners, who have cheered us on. You all rock.

READING GROUP QUESTIONS

1) Cat allows her husband's daughter in – despite not knowing anything about her, or where she came from. Would you have made the same decision? What would have gone through your mind?

2) Are some secrets a natural part of any healthy relationship?

3) Do you think there was ever a point where Tom could have behaved differently and saved his marriage – and, in so doing, got away with what he'd done?

4) Who should take responsibility for rioting teenagers? Their parents? The state? The teenagers themselves? At what age should young people be held accountable for their actions?

5) Is it fair to ask children to keep adults' secrets?

6) *'You really think if it comes to me versus you, you'll win?'* asks Tom. How does Tom use Cat's perceived 'flaws' in the first part of the novel to retain control?

7) If a child commits a crime, like the stabbings and intimidation we see in this book, should they be punished? How?

8) Both Tom and Cat have had moments of flirtation with people outside the marriage – Tom with Lilly, and Cat with Dominic. Clearly Tom went further than Cat. But is flirtation adultery? At what point does it become something which compromises a marriage?

9) How does the stigma around mental health affect different characters in Give Me the Child?

10) When faced with the option of 'stretch[ing] the truth' in order to get her daughter back, Cat says: 'And lie in the process? Condemn Ruby Winter? If I did that, Dominic, would I even be fit to be with Freya?' Would she?

11) Who is to blame for the death of Lilly Winter?

12) Should Cat tell Ruby the truth about her mother's death? If so, when? What should she tell Ruby about Tom?

13) What does a 'bad mother' look like? What about a 'bad father'?

You can find out more about Give Me the Child and future books by Mel McGrath by following **@mcgrathmj** and **@HQStories** on Twitter.

Join the conversation with **#GiveMetheChild**